THE BRIDE WORE PEARLS

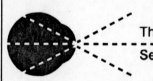

This Large Print Book carries the
Seal of Approval of N.A.V.H.

THE BRIDE WORE PEARLS

LIZ CARLYLE

THORNDIKE PRESS
A part of Gale, Cengage Learning

GALE
CENGAGE Learning·

Detroit • New York • San Francisco • New Haven, Conn • Waterville, Maine • London

LIBRARY OF CONGRESS CATALOGING-IN-PUBLICATION DATA

Carlyle, Liz.
    The bride wore pearls / by Liz Carlyle. — Large print ed.
      p. cm. — (Thorndike Press large print core)
    ISBN-13: 978-1-4104-5280-1 (hardcover)
    ISBN-10: 1-4104-5280-8 (hardcover)
    1. Secret societies—England—Fiction. 2. England—Social life and customs—19th century. 3. Large type books. I. Title.
PS3553.A739B74 2012
813'.54—dc23   2012028713

Published in 2012 by arrangement with Avon, an imprint of HarperCollins Publishers.

Printed in Mexico
3 4 5 6 7 16 15 14 13 12

THE BRIDE WORE PEARLS

PROLOGUE

If it were done when 'tis done, then 'twere
well It were done quickly.
William Shakespeare, *Macbeth*

Newgate Prison, 1834
It was a fine day for a hanging. In the City
of London, the spring air held a promise of
the bucolic summer to come, and high
above the gallows, the spires of St.
Sepulchre-without-Newgate melted like
warm cream into the clouds of an azure sky.

The beautiful weather had, of course,
brought out a larger-than-usual mob of
gawkers and hawkers, all of whom were now
wedged cheek-by-jowl together, enjoying a
capital lark. This, even before the condemned had been dragged out to pray and
to plead and — if the crowd was lucky —
perhaps even to piss himself.

Above the rumble of the crowd came the
cries of the pie-men and the orange girls,

7

along with the perky toots of a hornpipe wielded by a swarthy sailor who roamed the crowd, a miniature monkey perched upon one shoulder. Lastly came the newsboys, waving their papers and shouting out headlines as grisly as they were salacious, for today was the day to recount every detail of Lord Percy Peveril's brutal murder and all its overwrought aftermath.

After all, what more could one wish for in such a cautionary tale of angst and woe? A duke's son cut coldly down by a notorious and dashing card sharp, leaving his noble father to vow revenge. This followed by a suicide, a trial, and a beautiful fiancée twice collapsed with grief. Truly, for the pressmen of Fleet Street, did opportunity knock any louder?

Just then, the door onto the platform high above flew open and the thickset hangman trundled out. The aforesaid fiancée shrieked, then collapsed — yet a third time — against her sister's shoulder on a wretched sob. For months now, Miss Elinor Colburne had been bravely proclaiming her intention to stand stalwart to the end — though this was not, in point of fact, *her* end. And never mind the fact that prior to this drawn-out melodrama, the lady had never stood stalwart in the face of anything more catastrophic than a badly knotted hair ribbon.

Around her, however, the crowd had surged on a collective gasp, and the condemned — the man whose end this was truly meant to be — lifted his chin and stepped unhesitatingly onto the platform, coatless and hatless, his thick, dark curls ruffling lightly in the breeze. His hands were bound tightly behind him, so tight that his fine brocade waistcoat was drawn taut across a broad width of chest, displaying an expanse of costly linen that had once been starched and snowy white but had long ago gone gray with the filth of Newgate.

A black-garbed clergyman by the name of Sutherland was introduced. A grim-faced Scot, the fellow stepped to the edge of the platform, a Bible already open across his palm, to rattle off a few perfunctory passages about death and forgiveness, followed by a fiery invective on the inherent evils of gaming.

Then, as was the custom, the condemned was invited to speak his last words.

The broad-chested young man gave a succinct nod and stepped forward, dropping a steady, crystal-blue gaze directly upon Elinor Colburne. It was as if he knew to an inch precisely where the lady stood in the silent, suspenseful throng.

"Miss Colburne." His powerful, upper-class voice held a hint of northern broadness. "I did your Percy no harm, save fairly relieve him of a few hundred pounds. And eventually, I'll prove it. To you, by God, and to every man-jack standing in this mob of inhumanity."

At that, the hangman uttered an irritated oath. The bound man was yanked impatiently back from the platform's edge. In an instant, the black bag was thrown over his head, and the noose jerked taut. The entire crowd drew one great, collective breath. Then, with a mighty yank, the lever was thrown and the platform dropped, dangling the body like a marionette.

The crowd exhaled, then broke into a mélange of jeers, tears, and raucous applause.

Elinor Colburne released her sister's arm, then fell to her knees, collapsing on a bone-wracking sob into the filth of the street.

The time to stand stalwart was, apparently, at an end.

"There, there now, Ellie." Her sister knelt to embrace her, murmuring softly into her hair. "Papa and Lord Percy are avenged, just as Mr. Napier promised. Come, dear, 'tis over. This terrible thing is done."

But it was not over.

And — did any of them but know it — the terrible thing was far, far from done.

CHAPTER 1

Against the envy of less happier lands,
This blessed plot, this earth, this realm,
this England.
William Shakespeare, *Richard II*

The Docklands, 1848
The English aristocracy held sacred two
tenets; firstly, that they were born to rule by
right of blood, and secondly, that a man's
home was his castle. The Scots, however,
being a more pragmatic race, believed only
that blood was thicker than water and that
a man's castle was his home only until some
avaricious Englishman laid siege in an attempt to steal it. In which case the castle
was more apt to become someone's tomb
— the Englishman's, it was to be hoped.

But those who ventured from that
scepter'd isle, that precious stone set in the
silver sea, quickly learned that once one was
far enough beyond it, blood mattered less

than sheer survival, and home became something one had to haul round in a traveling trunk. This was particularly so for the adventurers of the East India Company, who, try as they might to forge a Britannia-in-the-East, never quite succeeded, for the Hindustan would not be tamed into home. And sometimes *she* tamed *them.*

The Scots, however, accustomed as they were to the vagaries of fate, struggled less with the harsh new reality that was India and succeeded admirably, for a Scot either went home rich or, like a Spartan fallen in battle, went home on his shield. In the early years, some assimilated quite thoroughly; forging treaties, heeding the customs, and occasionally taking to wife native women who in turn bore them fine, sturdy children. And a few simply never went home again, choosing instead to simply stay in India and die there.

And die damned inconveniently, too.

That, at least, was the considered opinion of Lady Anisha Stafford, who laid aside her thoughts and her needlework one hot Calcutta afternoon to snap open the thick fold of letter-paper a passing servant had thrust into her hand, only to discover her own harsh new reality. Not only was her rich Scottish father now in his grave but her impecunious English husband had followed him, and rather more swiftly than one might have wished. The fog and the sand of Sobraon's bloody battlefield had swallowed up the arrogant man, and Anisha had become, in short, that most pitiable of creatures — a woman alone.

A woman alone in a land that did not really quite claim her — and with two fatherless children to raise, along with a young scapegrace of a brother who had become almost dangerously charming. And over the coming weeks that turned to long months, as her husband's body was borne home and his affairs slowly settled, it came clear to Anisha that there was little left for them in India. That this time it fell to her to pack up her traveling trunk and forge a new and better life for her family's sake.

But Britain, too, was a land that mightn't claim her, for like so many of her kind who came out of India, Lady Anisha was neither fish nor fowl. Her elder brother, though, had found London to his liking. He had begun his life anew. And when he wrote insisting she bring the boys to England, Lady Anisha allowed herself a good, long cry, then began the process of swaddling her family's home in holland cloth and pensioning off most of the servants.

Still, a nagging uncertainty followed her over what felt like half the seven seas, and it was still threading through her uneasy dreams one miserably cold dawn when she was roused from a restless slumber by a harsh, scrubbing sound that vibrated through the walls of her cabin.

Startled fully awake, she lashed out blindly with one hand, seizing hold of her wooden berth as her eyes blinked, adjusting to the low light of the lantern that swung from its hook, casting wild shadows up the cabin walls.

Land?

Clambering down in agitation, Anisha made her way to the small aft window and threw back the muslin curtain. Through the haze of salt rime, a seemingly endless row of oily yellow lights winked tauntingly back at her.

A shoreline. No, a *riverbank.*

And beyond it, in a dusky gray sky, one could just make out a hint of the pink, wintry sunrise to come. Lady Anisha cursed beneath her breath.

Just then, the door flew open. Janet burst in, wild red hair sprouting from beneath her nightcap. "Lud, ma'am!" said the servant. "Reckon this'll be London?"

"Having never seen it, I could not say,"

Anisha grumbled, already hastening about the postage stamp of a cabin, yanking on her wrapper as she went. "But it assuredly isn't Calcutta. Janet, you were to wake me at — what was it? Gravesend?"

"Aye, and how, pray, was I to do it, ma'am, when no one knocked me up?" she squawked, seizing Anisha's portmanteau and throwing it open on the mattress. "And me telling that fool of a cabin boy, plain as day *three times* last night, that I was to be woke soon as we entered the river!"

The servant began to hurl stockings and undergarments from the drawer beneath the berth. "And February's wicked cold here, my lady," she added, "so mind you put on your warmest drawers. For my part, I'll be so happy to get off this infernal boat, I believe I shall dance a jig."

"And I believe I shall partner you." Anisha tossed out her comb and hairpins from her dressing case. "Go, Janet. I can fend for myself. Hurry and dress. Oh — wait! Where's Chatterjee? Did he wake Lord Lucan? The boys?"

Alarm sketched across Janet's face. "Best check, hadn't I?" As quickly as she'd come, the servant was gone, very nearly catching her hems in the cabin door as she flew out again.

It took Lady Anisha less then ten minutes to wash, dress, and twist up her hair. A military wife knew how to travel light and move fast. And haste was surely needed, for already Anisha could hear more scraping and thudding, the sound of cargo being hauled up from the hold. Moreover, while her elder brother had many qualities — both good *and* bad — neither tardiness nor patience was amongst them.

Oddly, though, the thought of seeing her brother Raju again after so many years apart left her a trifle unsettled. Suddenly, it seemed as if their frequent letters had not been enough. The nagging uncertainty turned to a sick, awful knot in the pit of her stomach.

What would he think of her now? Did she look too foreign? Did he look too English? Would he grow to resent her coming here? Had he changed at all during his years of grief and wanderlust? Had *she?*

Tom and Teddy assuredly had, for they had been infants. And Lucan — Luc had been but a gangling lad.

Well. Perhaps they were all going to have to grow up now.

A little ruthlessly, she stabbed the last hairpin into place, then, after an instant's hesitation, unscrewed the tiny nose-pin from her left nostril. Though her father had disapproved, Anisha had worn it through her first confinement to ward off sickness and labor pain. After his death, she'd worn it always. To please herself. To make a statement, she supposed.

Ah, but Calcutta was far behind her now.

On a sigh, she dropped it into her traveling jewelry box with her grandmother's pearls and her mother's priceless kundan choker. But she felt suddenly . . . wrong. Out of place. Which she was, in a manner of speaking. She had learned long ago that removing her *phul* would not remove the Rajputra in her, nor did she wish it to.

But she did wish, for the boys' sake, to fit in. And she wished, honestly, to ease her own transition into this frigid, water-bound empire. Yet at the same time, Anisha had grown a little weary over the years of having one foot planted here and another there; caught forever in that shifting dance between who she was and who someone else thought she ought to be.

For an instant, John's disapproving scowl flitted across her mind. Anisha swiftly shut it out, stepped to the mirror, and let her eyes run down the bodice of her ordinary English gown, then back up again to her not-especially English face.

"And when I was a child," Anisha whispered to herself, *"I spake as a child, I understood as a child, I thought as a child."*

But now came the time — the grievous, heartrending time — to put away childish things. Or to put away, at the very least, childhood's comforts. For the truth was, like her elder brother, Anisha had never really been a child. And now she was, she supposed, as prepared for her first appearance in England — for her new *life* — as one could hope.

With another sigh, she began the last of her packing but on the next breath was struck with an urge to check on the boys. Together they made for a cheeky pair of monkeys and, in all fairness to Janet, not a task the girl had signed on for. But this journey had been trying for all of them. The boys had become more mischievous than usual and, by Cape Town, had already parted ways with their put-upon tutor, Teddy having laid the last straw upon the camel's back by running the poor man's drawers out the bowsprit.

In six short steps, Anisha reached her cabin door. Throwing it heedlessly open, she hurled herself at once against a tall, broad-shouldered slab of masculine imperviousness.

"Ho!" said the slab, who smelled of warm leather and smoky sandalwood. He steadied her with a pair of broad, ungloved hands. "Lady Anisha Stafford, I presume?"

"Oh, I beg your pardon!" Anisha blinked up at a pair of merry blue eyes, her thoughts skittering across the deck like aimless birdshot. "I'm sorry. I didn't mean — that is to say —" She drew herself up and stepped back. "I'm sorry. Do I know you?"

It was a witless remark, of course. Beyond Raju, she knew not a soul in this cold, gray place.

With a smile as wide as his shoulders, the man dipped his head and somehow followed her from the shadows into the light of the minuscule cabin. "No, I haven't the pleasure," he said, his voice a low rumble in his chest, "which I now see was a tragic oversight on my part."

"I'm afraid I don't quite follow," she said, backing further, only to hitch up against the end of her berth.

Half inside the narrow space, the man set a shoulder to the doorframe, looking utterly relaxed. "I mean that I should have come all the way to India myself had Ruthveyn troubled to tell me how breathtaking his little sister was," he said, the grin deepening. "On the other hand, I had been until rather recently . . . well, let us call it a *guest* of the Crown, so my travel has been curtailed." He thrust out a powerful, lightly callused hand. "Rance Welham at your service, ma'am."

"Oh." Anisha's eyes dropped to the ornate gold pin nestled in the folds of his cravat. "*Oh.* Sergeant Welham!" Relief and recognition came as one, and she shook his hand. "A pleasure, I'm sure. But my brother — ?"

"Detained with *Fraternitas* business." At her questioning look, he continued. "Just the usual trouble in Paris. Guizot's about to be thrown out, and the Gallic confederation cannot decide if we are friend or foe. Regrettably, Lord Ruthveyn's our only diplomat."

"Ah." Anisha wondered if those clear blue eyes ever stopped twinkling. Or was it more of a dangerous glitter? It really was hard to tell.

"Which is to say, *Ruthveyn* regrets it," the man went on. "I, however, do not. And since I'm the brawn rather than the brain of the organization, he's sent me, a brace of footmen, and three fine coaches to bid you welcome and fetch you home to Mayfair."

Home. To Mayfair.

Wherever that was.

"And so quickly," she murmured.

"Oh, we've had a rider on watch down at Dartford for a se'night, ma'am," he said, coming away from the door. "I do believe Ruthveyn is anxious to see his little sister."

Sergeant Welham was still smiling and twinkling and looking almost dangerously handsome. Anisha knew a little of the man from her brother's letters, but nothing to prepare her for such an onslaught of male charm.

His elegant hat tucked into the crook of his arm, Welham displayed a tousled pile of dark curls and a pair of deep dimples to either side of a mouth so full it clearly belonged on a sybarite. Worse, the height and width of him literally filled the cabin.

"Now, my girl," he said, stepping into the tiny space and somehow sketching her an elegant bow, "have you a lady's maid hereabouts?"

"N-no, it's been a rather trying journey," Anisha uttered. "I lost her in Lisbon."

At last some of the flirtatious glitter faded from his eyes. "Fever, eh? Tragic shipboard hazard."

"Oh, no." Anisha shook her head. "I fear the tedium unsettled her brain, and she eloped with Lord Lucan's valet."

His grin returned. "Ho, marriage! A true tragedy, then."

"I fear you cannot know the half of it," said Anisha dryly, "for you've not seen Luc's valet."

"What, bad-tempered? Drunken?" He winked at her. "I've been both, from time to time."

"No, bald and pocked," said Anisha. "And *prosy*."

Welham laughed richly. "Well, no accounting for taste, is there? Good luck to 'em. Now, have you something I might carry up? This small trunk, perhaps?"

The trunk in question was not small, and in fact took up the entire rear corner of the cabin. "Thank you, but are there not porters here?"

The smile deepened. "I believe, ma'am, that I can manage a trifling piece of baggage."

"You must suit yourself, then." Anisha had already turned to shove the last of her things into the portmanteau. "Just let me finish —"

"Ah!" His gaze having dropped to the floor, Welham bent down to grab something, his head so near it brushed the fringe of her shawl. Then he came back up at once, his lean, hard-boned cheeks faintly pink. "I fear, ma'am, that you have dropped an . . . er, a garment of a personal nature. I shall restrain the temptation to retrieve it."

Anisha looked down to see her *zari* peignoir in a puddle of green silk beneath the berth. Faintly mortified, she snatched it up and stuffed it into the portmanteau. Welham swallowed a little oddly, as if his mouth had just gone dry.

"Thank you," she managed and latched the portmanteau shut. "Well, then, let us make haste. Though I should first look in on —"

But somehow, they had managed to leap into action at once; she toward the door, and Welham toward the trunk, awkwardly wedging themselves between the berth and one of the massive wooden spars that ran down the wall.

For an instant, they froze, so close the swell of her belly was pressed to his groin. So close, Anisha could see the stubble of blue-black beard beneath his skin and the tiny white scar just below his left eye.

"Oh." Anisha let the portmanteau fall from her grip. "How frightfully —"

"— awkward?" he supplied. But Welham was no longer grinning, and his gaze had shifted to something far more than mere warmth.

"I believe, sir —" Anisha tried to slip to her right and heard a stitch rip. "Drat!

Please, if you would just turn —"

But again, they twisted in unison. And suddenly, as was apparently his habit, Welham smiled down into her eyes; smiled in a way that warmed straight through to the pit of Anisha's belly. She cut her gaze away.

"Well, look at it this way," he managed. "Someday we'll be old friends and have a good laugh about this."

But Anisha, her breasts pressed nearly flat to the solid wall of his chest, was not feeling especially amused. She felt as if she was melting; as if her good sense had been drowned in the rich, masculine scent of him. Inside her head, her pulse was so loud that she was certain he must surely hear it.

Sensing her discomfort, Sergeant Welham grasped her shoulders and, with a little grunt, somehow managed to maneuver his way through. The sharp oaken edge of the berth slipped past her spine. But his hands did not release her, and she could feel the heat of his gaze burning into her.

Left with little choice, Anisha lifted her eyes to his and was shocked at the sudden tenderness she saw there.

"I beg your pardon," he said softly. "I forget that you are unaccustomed to our wicked Town ways. I am an incorrigible flirt, I know, but I ought not flirt with you.

Indeed, Ruthveyn will have my head for it."

But Anisha's mouth had gone dry. "Were you flirting?" she managed.

He winked. "Oh, a little, perhaps."

When her gaze dropped in embarrassment, Anisha could read the very inscription upon his solid gold cravat pin.

F.A.C.

He was a member of the *Fraternitas Aureae Crucis.* The Brotherhood of the Golden Cross. Even in childhood, she had been taught to turn to them in time of trouble. And Welham had come — in keeping with his vows — to help her, even in this small way. Incorrigible he might have been, but the man meant only kindness.

The knowledge comforted her and brought her somehow back to herself. Pulling away from his grip, Anisha threw on her heavy cloak, then snatched up her portmanteau in one hand and her dressing case in the other. The moment of unease had passed.

"Now I have these two, my lord," she said, smiling. "If you can indeed fetch the trunk?"

A few moments later, they were emerging topside to a bitter-cold sunrise, the heavy, brass-banded box balanced effortlessly upon

Welham's shoulder, to a land surrounded by towering brick walls and the unmistakable sweep of the river, which was not remotely straight, as she had somehow assumed it would be.

Had she imagined it would run stick-straight, like the Hooghly as it drifted past her house? Assumptions — about anything — were clearly misplaced here.

Anisha glanced anxiously around to see the boys half-hanging over the gunwale and pointing downriver as Lucan looked on. His cage sitting on the deck beside the three of them, their parakeet, Milo, swung from his perch, bobbing back and forth as he watched the hubbub unfold.

"Pawwwk!" he complained, eyeing her approach. *"British prisoner! Let me out! Let me out!"*

Dropping her bags, Anisha hugged the boys in turn, then knelt by the cage. "Teddy, where is Milo's blanket?" she chided. "The poor dear cannot bear this frightful cold."

"He wanted to look around," said Teddy defensively.

"Mamma! Mamma!" said six-year-old Tom. "We saw a dead man!"

Anisha took the bell-shaped blanket from him and knelt to swaddle Milo's cage. "A dead man?" she said, flicking a quick, anxious glance up at her younger brother.

Lord Lucan Forsythe came languidly away from the rail. "There did indeed appear to be a corpse," he said breezily. "Come portside if you like, and I'll show you."

"Heavens, no." Anisha secured the last frog on Milo's blanket as Welham reached down to help her to her feet. "But really, a dead man? In the water?"

"No, he's been hung," Tom piped, rather too cheerfully.

"Hanged, you dolt," his brother corrected, pointing downriver. "He's swinging from a jib back there. And he's in a *cage.*"

"Teddy, that is quite enough." Mildly horrified, Anisha made the introductions in haste. Lord Lucan shook Welham's hand warmly, but the boys could not get past the grisly excitement of the dead body.

"And he hadn't any eyes, Mamma!" said Tom, his face twisting grotesquely.

" 'Cause the birds pecked 'em out, you *boka chele,*" said his brother.

"Boys, that will do!" Anisha lifted one eyebrow warningly. "Teddy, we will discuss later where you learnt that phrase."

"It's what Chatterjee calls the *punkah wallah,*" said Teddy. "It just means —"

"I know what it means," she interjected. "And gentlemen do not insult one another

29

in a lady's presence. Nor do they speak of dead bodies. I am delicate. I might faint."

"Oh, Mamma!" Teddy rolled his eyes. "You never faint."

Welham bent to ruffle Teddy's hair. "She looks pretty hardy to me, too, lad," he murmured. "But it isn't really a dead body, just an old prank."

"A prank, sir?" Teddy looked up at him, puzzled.

"Aye, they call him Dashing Davie the Pirate Prince." Welham grinned at the boys. "Occasionally some of the stevedores drink too deep and run him up just for fun. But old Davie's naught but cotton wool and canvas. Something to frighten the tourists."

"Oh," said Tom, obviously crestfallen.

Welham seemed to relent and knelt to look the lad in the eyes. "But the gibbet and cage are real," he said almost consolingly. "Look, do you see that marshy spot across the river's crook? That's Blackwall Point. That's where they hang the real pirates and leave their bodies to rot as a warning."

Tom's eyes widened. "Do they?"

"Well, it's been awhile." Welham winked. "But one never knows."

At this hopeful news, both boys brightened considerably. Really, did the man turn his winking, sparkly charm on everyone he met?

30

Just then, however, their only remaining manservant strode across the deck, Janet on his heels. "All the baggage has been off-loaded, ma'am," said Chatterjee with an elegant bow.

"Excellent. Thank you." She turned back to the boys. "Now let's have no more talk of gibbets, please," she added, including Welham in her sweeping glower. "From *any* of you."

Welham laughed. "Sounds like fair warning, lads!" he said. "Off we go, then. London and all her fine adventures await."

But the boys allowed as how it was more likely a new tutor awaited, sounding as if they were going to the gallows along with Dashing Davie. Soon they had taken up the related subjects of beheadings and Traitor's Gate, speculating about whether or not they would be able to see the Tower along the way.

"I will ask the coachman to drive by it," Welham assured them as they stepped onto terra firma.

"I am not certain, Sergeant," she muttered beneath her breath, "that you are being helpful here."

Nonetheless, Welham's promise seemed to appease the boys, so Anisha spent the next several minutes looking about her new home, or what she could see of it. Though the twinkling lights of the docks and shoreline had melted with the dawn, the vastness of London — or at least her warehouses — was still apparent.

Never in her life had Anisha seen so much activity as at the East India Docks at daybreak. Already lighters and barges were skimming to and fro in the water, and a dozen ships appeared ready to offload, while many more bobbed, bare-masted, up and down the Thames. Workers swarmed like ants about crates and barrels, dark warehouses looming up behind them in every direction.

At first the port smelled much like that of Calcutta's; heavy with the scent of rot and effluent. However, when at last she moved beyond the shadow of the Blackwall frigate and nearer the warehouses, Anisha was struck by the more pleasant scents of pepper and ginger and a hundred other things she could not identify — the smell of money, her late father would have termed it.

With a gait that was long and lean-hipped, Welham cut a smooth swath through the morass, the throng falling respectfully from his path as he escorted Anisha and her company safely out into a wide lane that ran behind a row of warehouses. In short order, they were being bundled into the carriages, with Chatterjee and Lucan taking the first, the former having been pressed into her brother's valet service. Janet shooed the boys into another, and after surveying that all was in order, Welham threw open the door of the third — a fine, fully enclosed landau with a gold coat of arms painted on the door.

"After you, ma'am."

She was oddly a little wary of being alone again in close quarters with Welham, but pride stiffening her spine, she swept her skirts up perhaps a little more regally than she might otherwise have done and climbed inside.

He followed her in gracefully, shutting the door himself and tossing his tall hat onto the seat beside him. Almost at once, Anisha heard the lead carriage begin to rumble forward, harnesses jingling. She and Welham were utterly alone again, the gloom and close confines of the carriage surrounding them with that same sense of intimacy she'd felt inside her cabin.

Drawing her cloak a little tighter against the cold and damp, Anisha broke the heavy silence. "Sergeant Welham, perhaps I ought to apologize."

"Should you?" he murmured. "For what, pray?"

"Tom and Teddy," she answered. "All that talk. About . . . well, *hanging*. To you, of all people. They meant nothing by it, and you were sporting enough. But still . . ."

The merry twinkle returned to his eyes. "I'm afraid I lost my delicate sensibilities on the battlefields of the Maghreb, ma'am," he said. "Those boys look a handful, by the way. How old are they?"

"Tom just turned six," she said, "and Teddy eight. And Luc, at all of eighteen, fancies himself quite the man grown."

Something in Welham's gaze suddenly sobered. "Then let us pray Lord Lucan soon learns better — for London has a tendency to teach young men harsh lessons in a hard school."

He spoke, Anisha knew, from experience.

Just then, they made a sharp turn. Through the wavy glass window, her gaze followed the sweeping vista of masts and warehouses. In an instant they were rolling beneath the arched entrance of a clock-towered gatehouse set into the brick wall that surrounded the dockyard, the carriage lurching a little sideways as it turned right. A few yards further along, and the carriage slowed again, this time to enter a main thoroughfare.

Barking Road, the signpost read.

What strange names this place had. The carriage swung away from it, toward the west. And then, just as they swept out of the turn, Anisha saw him. A somber young man in a long coat standing by a lamppost, his gaze following hers as if locked to it.

Unable to stop herself, Anisha twisted around to look out the rear. Just before vanishing from sight, the man lifted his hat as if in silent salute, revealing a shock of rich, red hair and a quizzical, almost insolent smile.

She turned back, her gaze going at once to Welham, who cursed softly beneath his breath. He, too, was watching, looking past her shoulder with eyes that no longer laughed but instead now glittered with menace.

"That young man," she murmured, "do you know him?"

A dark look sketched over his once-amiable countenance, and Anisha was struck with a chilling certainty that Welham would make for a brutal enemy.

"I do not," he gritted. "But it now appears I shall have to."

"I don't understand."

Welham's every muscle seemed suddenly

taut, like those of a great cat ready to pounce. "I'm told the man works for a newspaper," he answered. "Until this moment, however, I imagined his name did not much matter."

"But my brother wrote that the Lord Chancellor overturned your conviction." Anisha glanced uneasily over her shoulder, but the man, of course, had long vanished. "What could the papers want of you now?"

"In my experience, most of the world's evils have to do with money." Welham's jaw twitched. "Specifically, the gaining of it. And usually at someone else's expense."

"True," she acknowledged, "but . . . ?"

He shrugged. "A great many people believe my father bought my justice for me," he said. "More than a few would be pleased to see me fall from grace. And that, I daresay, would sell a vast number of newspapers."

For a moment, Anisha considered it. "It's an ugly thought," she said softly. "How horrible for you."

"Horrible?" he echoed, his voice dangerously soft. "No, ma'am. Horrible is being left to rot in prison for a crime you didn't commit. Horrible is having a noose drawn round your neck and not knowing for certain you'll breathe your next. Horrible is watching good soldiers left to die in the blood and mud of Africa because they have no better way to earn a living. And if you can survive that, then you generally don't give a bloody damn what people think. But that fellow has begun to ask questions about my father. And your brother. Twice he's been seen skulking round the St. James Society, trying to worm his way inside."

"The St. James Society?" Anisha's eyes flared with alarm. "That is your new name for the *Fraternitas* here in England, is it not?"

"More of a camouflage." Welham's jaw was set tight, his eyes still hard. "A safe house of sorts, and a way to explain away the scientific research Dr. von Althausen is conducting. Your brother's former diplomatic standing helps justify some of the odd traffic in and out."

Anisha hesitated, unsure how to ask her next question. "And so this reporter," she said. "Have you met him? Touched him?"

His smile was strained. "I am afraid, Lady Anisha, that I am rather ordinary," he said. "I have nothing like your brother's strange talents."

"So I understand," she said. "And I am happy for you."

He shrugged. "Perhaps, were I to spend

some time in the reporter's company, I might glean something of his true nature," he acknowledged. "Or perhaps not. Some days I'm not persuaded I have any special skill in that regard."

"And I'm not persuaded I believe that."

"Believe what you wish, ma'am, but many people are inscrutable to me." His hard gaze was fixed watchfully out the window now. "Yourself, for example, I should wager. But I believe, too, that there are a rare few to whom evil is so natural and so connate, so much a part of what they are, there is nothing more to perceive. And that reporter — he's watching the *Fraternitas*'s every move, our every breath."

"Good Lord."

"And now, it would appear, he means to watch *you*. Your children and young Lucan, too, perhaps. And there are a few things, by God, which even I will not tolerate — as he is perilously close to discovering. So it's time I settled this business." His voice fell, as if he spoke only to himself. "It is time — past time — for me to do what I swore I would."

Every trace of humor had vanished from the man's countenance. And however much charm he might feign, Anisha was no longer fooled. *Incorrigible* was not the word for this man. Even had she known nothing of his dark past, she could see that Rance Welham carried himself with the barely leashed strength of a soldier.

His gaze was quick — unnervingly so — and she was now convinced he could turn lethal in an instant. There was a veiled anger in him, Anisha sensed, that had burned through to his very core; a bitterness eating like a cancer behind that amiable façade and those laughing eyes. It unnerved her, yet she found it oddly humanizing.

Anisha knew from her brother's letters that in his youth, Welham had been convicted of murder and twice put in prison. The first time he had cleverly cheated the gallows. The second time, a witness's deathbed recantation had saved him. In between, he'd fled England, landed in Paris, then shipped off to Africa in the French Foreign Legion — an organization made up of criminals, thugs, and mercenaries, and only a little less deadly than the gallows.

They continued on in silence for a time, but the mood inside the carriage had oddly shifted. There was an unsettled emotion in the air that even she, in her limited abilities, could discern.

Not knowing what to say, Anisha instead watched through the window as their little caravan wound its way through streets that alternated from dark and narrow to wide and elegant. Never in her life had she seen so many church spires, and as they progressed, the streets were increasingly choked with traffic and people. At every turn, one could observe wagons and carts being offloaded and doorsteps being swept as the banks and storefronts of London opened to embrace the day's commerce.

Inexplicably, however, Anisha's new home could not hold her attention, and her gaze drifted back to her companion. Dressed more for a ride in the country than a drive, Welham was a large, long-legged man with few pretensions to sartorial splendor. He wore a snugly cut coat of black superfine — but not so snug as to have required the assistance of a valet. His high boots and breeches showed his muscular legs to quite good effect, though Anisha suspected trousers might have been the more fashionable choice.

In fact, the only hint of elegance about Welham was a charcoal silk waistcoat with tortoise shell buttons, a blindingly white cravat, and the tall black hat lying beside him. And when he twitched back his coat to extract his pocket watch, Anisha could see the lean turn of his waist and almost sense the strength that lay beneath his sleeve.

Rance Welham was, Anisha concluded, a man's man — which regrettably made him all the more intriguing.

After checking the time and tucking the watch away, he relaxed against the seat, one arm draped across the back of the banquette, his booted legs set wide such that he seemed to own every inch of space around him. He dipped his head to the window, one lock of dark hair falling over his forehead as his quick gaze swept the streets beyond his carriage window. The whole of Welham's demeanor left Anisha with the vague sense that the man missed little and was intimidated by less than that.

She searched her mind for what else her brother had said of him. Welham descended from a wealthy family in the north of England, but his mother had been a Border Scot. Raju and Welham had met perhaps four or five years earlier in Morocco — or was it Algiers? — but doing what, precisely, her brother had declined to say. Something not fit for a lady's ears, Anisha gathered, for at some point in their checkered history together, Raju had come to realize that both he and Welham bore the mark of the Guardian.

And thus had their inseparability begun.

The mark was most commonly etched high on the left hip, to indicate that a man had been chosen by his family — by dint of temperament, tradition, and the alignment of the heavens — as a Guardian of the Old and Noble Order of the *Fraternitas Aureae Crucis*. Part religious order and part secret society, the *Fraternitas* was ostensibly devoted to the study of natural philosophy and its connection to the great Greek and Druidic mysteries.

Guardians served as the protective arm of the society, like Christian soldiers sworn to the sword. The mark itself was simply a Latin cross positioned above a crossed quill and sword. Sometimes, if the family descended through the Scottish line, their mark would be enclosed in a thistle cartouche. The symbol in both forms was common, hidden in plain sight on pediments, crests, and gravestones all across Europe, much like the fleur-de-lis.

The *Fraternitas* had roots, it was whispered, in the ancient Celtic world and the Christian Templar tradition, perhaps even a vague connection to Masonry. Vague seemed to be the operative word when it came to the organization. Nonetheless, Anisha's father had belonged, as had generations of Forsythes before him.

But none of this mattered, really, to Anisha. Her children had not been born in the Sign of Fire and War. They could be initiated into the *F.A.C.* in some intellectual, legal, or religious capacity should they wish — a Savant, an Advocati, or a Preost — but her sons would never be Guardians.

Never would they be cursed with the Gift, thank God.

No, her sons would never have need of a Guardian. It was a small blessing for which Anisha was deeply thankful.

She must have sighed, for she realized that Sergeant Welham was staring at her across the depths of the carriage, his once-sparkling eyes now sharply focused, as if he had been ruminating over something and did not much care for the conclusion he had drawn.

"That fellow on the corner," he said, his voice a low rumble. "This whole business, really — it doubtless makes you wonder why your brother sent me, of all people, to fetch you. Indeed, I advised him to send someone else, but —"

Almost without thinking, Anisha reached through the shadows to set a gloved finger to his lips, her expression lightly chiding. "But it is you whom he most trusts," she said quietly. "And so it is you whom *I* most trust."

His answering smile was muted. "I believe, though, that Ruthveyn hopes you will take here in Town, Lady Anisha," he said. "I rather doubt your being seen in my company will serve that cause — and I told him so."

"I beg your pardon? Take what?"

He smiled again, but this time it did not reach his eyes. "Ruthveyn desires you to make the proper social connections," he clarified, "and forge a new and happy life for yourself here in London. He is determined, I collect, that you will marry again, so my company is not ideally —"

Anisha went perfectly rigid. "I beg your pardon?"

Welham's expression stiffened. "Sorry, I put that boorishly — I'm too plainspoken, you'll find — but I daresay you'll hear the same hope from his lips within the week."

Anisha drew a deep, steadying breath. "Shall I?" she said stiffly. "And tell me, sir — has my brother chosen this new husband as yet?"

At that, Welham's eyes widened. Then, as he apparently recognized her pique for what it was, his smile returned, the tiny lines about his brilliant blue eyes crinkling once

44

again. "I believe, ma'am, that he does in fact have one or two candidates in mind," he murmured. "And I can already see that you will be perfectly content to leave the matter in his capable hands."

"Oh, perfectly," she said sweetly. "And I, in turn, shall be equally happy to assist *him.* Indeed, having scarcely laid eyes on the man in the last five years — and knowing absolutely nothing of his life here, nor of his wishes nor of his hopes or his dreams — I am utterly certain that his widowhood cannot suit him."

"Lady Anisha, forgive me." His gaze sobered. "I ought not suggest —"

"No, no, suggest away," she cut in, her voice shrill. "I mean to do precisely that. Why, there must be at least two dozen simpering English roses willing to hang on every pearl of my brother's wisdom, and tell him what a charming devil he is, all in exchange for a countess's coronet and his fat fortune. And trust me, Sergeant Welham, I shall manage to ingratiate myself with each and every one of them should my brother dare fling me out into his so-called English society."

"Shall you, indeed?" he said.

"Never doubt it," she returned. "And then I shall bring them home in turn to dinner until hell freezes over. But whilst waiting for that happy occasion, I shall turn my attention to his bad habits. His womanizing. His drunkenness. His habitual use of opiates. No, Sergeant Welham, Ruthveyn's secrets do not escape me. Indeed, I shall be perfectly relentless in *my* pursuit of *his* self-improvement. What do you think of that? Will it make his life happier, do you imagine?"

But Sergeant Welham no longer looked quite so relaxed or sanguine upon his banquette. "Good Lord!" he murmured.

"And what of yourself?" she asked, cocking her head to one side. "Perhaps you, too, could benefit by my help?"

"Oh, I think not," he demurred. "Though I thank you, ma'am, for offering."

"Quite sure, are you?"

"Quite, yes," he answered. "And now, ma'am, if you will look to your left, you can see the Tower of London."

"Thank you," she said tartly. "But I have no interest whatever in tourist attractions."

"Hmm."

Then Welham simply set his hat back on his head and tipped it forward over his eyes.

Anisha forced her gaze to the window and watched the grim gray walls go flying past. They rumbled on in silence for some time, through the seemingly endless quagmire of streets, until Welham actually began to snore quietly.

She glanced across the carriage in exasperation. His chin had fallen to his chest, and his fingers were interlaced over his waistcoat. Really, how *could* he sleep? And how irritatingly large London was! Were they never to arrive at wherever it was they meant to go? Impatience bit like a horsefly at the back of her neck.

Then she realized, suddenly, the obvious. That she had just shot the messenger and now burned to sink her claws into the arrogant ass that had sent him.

"Sergeant Welham," she said a little loudly.

"*Umph* — ?" His head jerked up, his elegant hat tumbling onto his lap. "We there?"

"No, I merely wish to beg your pardon," she said. "I spoke wrongly. I'm angry with my brother. And you have been all kindness. I am sorry."

"Hmm," he said again, slapping the hat back on.

"Now this lovely old church we are passing," she said, "what is it called?"

"Oh, overdone, my dear," he said darkly. "You have no interest in tourist attractions, I seem to recall."

She blinked her eyes twice, slowly. "I see you do not mean to let me out of this graciously," she said. "I deserve it, I daresay."

"St. Clement, then." His voice was gruff. "It is called St. Clement Danes."

"And would it be your church?" she asked conversationally.

"Lord, no." He lifted both his dark, slashing eyebrows. "Besides, London has a thousand, and I haven't darkened a church door in . . . aye, well, I don't know how long." Suddenly, his shoulders fell, and he scrubbed a hand almost pensively around his jaw. "I will do, though, before long, I fear. And far too soon, at that."

Anisha realized at once what he was speaking of. Welham's father, Raju had written, was dying.

"I was sorry to hear about your father," she murmured. "My brother's last letter reached me in Lisbon. He said the Earl of Lazonby's health had collapsed."

"Aye, broken down by his years of suffering," said Welham grimly, "and his unrelenting efforts to get my conviction overturned."

"I am so very sorry," she said again. "Raju says the title will go to you. I'm sure you take no pleasure in it."

"Aye, but I shall have a few more months,

if God is kind," he said, his eyes no longer smiling. "And no, I take no pleasure whatever from it. He is scarcely sixty, and now we're both to be cheated of his last years — and someone, eventually, is going to pay for it."

Anisha had no answer to that. Moreover, she had no doubt he meant it. Welham looked like a man who made promises, not idle threats.

Welham turned his gaze to the window, staring out almost blindly. With the wintery light casting a shadow beneath his cleanly chiseled cheekbone, his profile held such a stark, hard beauty she scarcely recognized the laughing man who had stepped into her cabin this morning. And that mouth — oh, that lush, lovely mouth! It was the only thing that softened him; saved him, perhaps.

Ruthlessly, Anisha forced her gaze away, heat rushing over her. Good Lord, she was not some grass-green goose of a girl to be swayed by a man, no matter his rugged good looks — and she sensed enough of human nature to recognize torment and trouble when she saw it in the flesh.

She turned to the opposite window and tried to think of what was to come. It was spitting an icy rain now, the promise of the pink sunrise having turned to leaden skies with a wind that thrashed the bare tree branches and whistled through the carriage door. Suddenly her vague longing for India turned into a bone-deep ache, and she was terrified she had made an irrevocable mistake.

The dread had not lifted when, just a few minutes later, the vehicle slowed to a halt, drawing between a pair of massive, lamped gateposts and round the semicircular drive of a grand, porticoed mansion set a little back from the street. Reluctantly, she picked up her reticule, then drew her cloak a little tighter, as if doing so might ward off the inevitable.

Carrying somber black umbrellas, a trio of liveried servants came in lockstep down the sweeping staircase, putting Anisha a little in mind of a firing squad. Her trepidation must have sketched across her face, for at once Rance Welham caught her hand and carried it to his lips.

"Courage, my dear," he said softly. "Your brother awaits. Your new life awaits. And you have all of two months before the London Season begins."

She felt her eyes widen. "The London Season?"

"At which time you will set society on its ear with your beauty," he went on, his smile firmly back in place.

For an instant, she hesitated. "Sergeant Welham," she finally said, drawing her hand from his, "let us be realistic, even if my brother cannot. London society will tolerate me, yes. But they will have about as much real interest in a mixed-blood army widow as *I* shall have in *them*."

"I would not have thought you such a coward, Lady Anisha," he said, his smile muted.

"I am not —" She exhaled sharply, crushing her reticule to her lap with both hands. "I am *not* a coward, Sergeant," she finally said. "I am just . . . different. That is all."

"Just *different?*" he softly echoed. "Oh, aye, my dear. Now *that* you surely are."

But Welham's brilliant blue eyes were once again smiling, his true nature once again hidden.

CHAPTER 2

From year to year, the battles, sieges,
fortunes, That I have passed . . .
William Shakespeare, *Othello*

As so often happens with most of life's
dreaded changes, what felt at first to Lady
Anisha like an almost intolerable upheaval
became quickly drowned out by a bucket
brigade of small, day-to-day disasters. There
were tutors and maids and music masters
to hire. Tom and Teddy required cloaks,
coats, and all manner of woolens to ward
off the frightful English chill. The crate
containing the boys' pressed leaf collection
and *Encyclopedia Britannica* had vanished
into thin air. The bird did not like Raju's
cats.

The cats, on the other hand, liked the bird
very well indeed.

And then there were Raju's bullheaded
notions of society and marriage to be

dispensed with — a notion that Anisha did not, perhaps, crush as thoroughly or as ruthlessly as she ought to have done. . . .

Still, for good or ill, London blew over her like a Bengali cyclone, beginning the moment Rance Welham handed her down from his carriage, leaving Anisha little time to fret, or even to mourn her beloved home, and she soon became, if not inured to her new life, then at least accustomed to it — all while scarcely realizing the change was occurring.

And in this way, winter turned to spring and summer to autumn, until one day Lady Anisha awoke to realize her first year in London had long since passed, and with it, much of the storm. The boys had fallen into something like a routine. Lucan had fallen in with a cadre of dashing young blades — and their raffish ways. After despairing of Lucan and throwing up his hands, Raju had shocked everyone by falling in love with the boys' governess.

And Anisha — well, fool that she was, *she* had fallen just a little bit in lust with Rance Welham, the newly invested Earl of Lazonby.

But it was so very hard not to when his eyes were so teasing, his smile so enigmatic, and his hidden depths so intriguingly beyond her reach. And he was — just as he'd professed — an incorrigible flirt, at least outwardly. A dozen times Anisha had entertained the notion of something more than mere flirtation, but each time womanly instinct had warned her away.

And then had come that day, some months past, when she'd come upon him unawares and realized with a stark and sudden clarity that perhaps her instincts had warned her away for a very good reason. That perhaps his flirtations really were meaningless; his depths farther beyond her reach than even she had imagined.

Lazonby was thirty-five years old, and there was no woman in his life — nor had there ever been, so far as she knew. And Anisha had begun to wonder if she now understood why; if perhaps his passions drove him in an altogether different direction.

But it almost didn't matter, for he was her brother's dearest friend — and her friend, too. More than friendship, however? No. Lord Lazonby was too closed off inside; too obsessed with his mad, furious notions of truth and revenge. And Anisha was wise enough to know a façade when she saw one; wise enough to know that on some level, she really didn't know him at all, and likely never would.

So Anisha had looked about for something to distract her from those dancing, devilish eyes. And as a result, she had proceeded to do what she now feared was a very foolish thing. She had listened to her brother.

She had done precisely what she'd told Lazonby she *would not* do.

Irritated by the recollection, Anisha plopped a huge pat of butter in the middle of her kedgeree. The fact that she did not particularly like the dish — and certainly never added extra butter — seemed this morning to have escaped her. She stabbed into it with a vicious relish.

At the opposite side of the breakfast table, Lucan lowered his head and eyed her warily across his eggs. After cutting him a decidedly irritated glance — perhaps the third or fourth of the morning — Anisha began to chew. A small part of her was angry; not with him but with Raju.

She had come here in large part for Lucan's sake, so that their elder might give the young man a bit of gentlemanly direction — or at least a hard boot in the arse. Now here she was in London, still staring at Luc over breakfast, and Raju was off on a months-long wedding trip.

So today was decidedly *not* the day for

Lucan to ask for money.

Again.

But he had.

Men, she had begun to believe, were nothing but a plague.

But Lucan was still looking at her across the breakfast table from beneath his sweep of long, almost feminine eyelashes. Lady Anisha slammed down her fork with an ominous clatter.

"Stop it, Luc," she warned. "Do not dare look at me with those great, pitiful eyes. I shan't do it, I tell you. Just because Raju has gone abroad does not mean I have suddenly lost my spine, for I quite assure you I did not need him to shore it up. I am quite put out with you all on my own."

Lucan hung his head another notch lower. "Just a loan, Nish, until Midsummer's Day?" he pleaded. "Just enough to —"

"To what?" she snapped. "To pay off your bookmaker? Your haberdasher? Your mistress? Let me remind you that in the last year or better, you have frittered away every penny of your allowance and once even landed yourself in a sponging house. And but for my mercy, there you would still likely be."

"No, I'd have graduated to debtor's prison as Raju intended," he said glumly.

"As I'm painfully aware." Anisha shoved away her tea with the back of her hand. "So I got you out. And at extortionate terms, too. *And* I suffered Raju's wrath for my efforts. So yes, pray do not let it come to that again. Well, go on. What is it this time?"

"Baccarat," he muttered into his plate. "At the Quartermaine Club. And now there's nothing else for it. I must behave as a gentleman ought, and you know it as well as I. The nabob stench is still near enough to draw flies." His voice turned grim. "And I will *not* have it said, Anisha. Not of me, and certainly not of *you.*"

It was Anisha's turn to look away — not that she was ashamed of what she was. She was inordinately proud of it. And yet she was weary of thinking about it.

Absently, she picked at the pleated silk of her gold and turquoise skirts, her thin gold bracelets faintly tinkling as she did so. It was true some might have called their father a nabob, for like so many of his ilk, he'd gone off to India merely comfortable and come back shockingly rich. Half diplomat and all business, Anisha's father had left his children very well provided for indeed. But that did not give Lucan cause to live like a wastrel.

Unlike Anisha and Raju, Lucan was the

product of her father's second marriage; a marriage made out of love, not politics, as his first had been. Pamela had been as pure as an English rose. She had been kind, too, and doting. Too much so, perhaps, for she had spoiled Lucan beyond reason. And yet Anisha loved Lucan; loved him as much as, and in some ways more than, she loved Raju, for Pamela had died too young, leaving Lucan to need his sister in a way that her elder never had.

Just as he needed her now.

And she would help him, of course. But she was not about to make it easy on him. Anisha bit her lip, trying to think what was best done.

"Nish," Lucan's wary tone cut into her thoughts. "Nish, you're chewing your lip again. Now *promise* me you aren't thinking of speaking to Ned Quartermaine. I should simply die of embarrassment."

Her mind suddenly made up, Anisha pushed back her chair with a harsh scrape. "I cannot loan you money again, Luc," she said firmly. "I cannot, for you never learn anything from it. Nor will I speak with Mr. Quartermaine on your behalf. I can, however, be persuaded to bargain — and bargain like a good Scot, be warned."

"Aye, hard and relentless, you mean." Lucan sighed and dragged a hand through a shock of what had been, until that moment, flawlessly pomaded gold curls. "But please, Nish, I beg you. Don't make me play nanny again! Tom and Teddy — they are — good God! They are beyond me! If they aren't jumping half-naked into the Serpentine or darting through traffic in Piccadilly Circus, then the day holds no challenge for them."

"Oh no, I don't want you buying yourself out of indentured servitude again." Anisha eyed him assessingly across the mahogany table, then slid her bracelets pensively back up her arm. "So I think neither a loan nor a bargain will do this time."

Lucan exhaled and fell back against his chair.

"No, this time," she said, ignoring his sigh of relief, "we shall have a clean, outright transaction."

"A transaction?" Lucan jerked upright again, eyes narrowing warily. "Of what sort?"

Anisha's wide, amiable mouth curled slowly into a smile. "Your new curricle," she murmured. "The high-perch phaeton, I mean, with the pretty red wheels? I confess, it does catch one's eye."

"My *phaeton?*" His eyes widened in horror. "Surely you cannot mean it! Whatever would you do with —"

"And the horses," Anisha continued, undeterred. "Those lovely, prancing blacks? Yes, I think I should like to have them, too."

But Lucan had begun to sputter. "My matched blacks? You must be mad. Why, I spent two days straight at hazard to win those off Frankie Fitzwater! Besides, no lady of fashion would dare drive such a team."

"Do you suggest I cannot?" Anisha arched one eyebrow.

"Well, no, you're a fine whip — for a woman — but . . ."

"And do you suddenly take me for a lady of fashion?"

"I — well, what I meant was —"

"Come now, Lucan." Anisha stood, drawing herself up to her full height — which was something less than five feet. "I think we both know that London's fashionable set scarcely spares me a second glance."

Lucan's eyes glittered. "But Lord Bessett's mother does," he warned.

But Anisha would not be cowed. "Lady Madeleine is neither here nor there," she replied, tossing down her napkin. "She's a good friend to me, no more."

"Ha!" Lucan threw his arms over his chest. "So you are not in love with him?"

"Good Lord, Luc! Do not be ridiculous."

60

"But you *are* going to marry him." Lucan lifted his chin almost challengingly.

"I might," she said coolly. "Or I might not. I have not yet consulted the stars."

Lucan gave a dismissive grunt. "Stars or no, Raju told Aunt Pernicia you were, just before he left on his wedding trip — specifically, that as soon as Lord Bessett returned from his *Fraternitas* business in Brussels, our family would have 'a happy event' to announce."

Inwardly, Anisha cursed her own stupidity, as well as Raju's big mouth. Lucan's Aunt Pernicia was Pamela's much-elder sister, a venerated member of the *ton,* and a gossiping old tabby. And Bessett was one of London's most eligible bachelors.

But Anisha maintained her cool posture. "Well, Raju isn't here now, is he?" she said, setting both hands on the table and leaning into him. "So the only happy event you'd better be anticipating is the payment of your gaming debts — *before* either Claytor writes Raju or Aunt Pernicia catches wind of it."

Lucan's cheeks flushed bright crimson.

Anisha forced a sugary smile. "Now what is it to be, my dear? Social ruin? A fraternal flogging? Or that shiny new phaeton?"

Lucan threw up his hands, but any comment he might have made was forestalled by the entrance of their butler.

Higgenthorpe gave a tight bow at the neck. "I beg your pardon, my lady," he said, "but Claytor is in his lordship's study with some papers which require your signature."

Claytor, her brother's secretary, handled all the family's business affairs. Lady Anisha sighed and glanced down at her attire. As no guests had been expected, she was dressed for the privacy of her home, and in the comfort of the traditional clothing she often favored.

Today Anisha had thrown on an old *lehenga cholis,* a diaphanous skirt and short tunic that had been her mother's, both heavily embroidered with fine gold thread. To ward off the English chill, however, she'd tossed over it a plain cashmere shawl such as any English lady might have worn. Like her odd collection of jewelry, the combination was a metaphor, she supposed, for the whole of her life.

She folded her hands serenely in front of her. "I should go up to change," she replied. "Kindly ask him to wait."

The butler bowed again and turned as if to go.

At the last instant, however, Anisha frowned. "Higgenthorpe, you've dark smudges under your eyes," she said. "You are struggling to sleep again?"

The butler's smile was wan. "I fear so, ma'am."

"Your *vata dosha*," she murmured. "You have an imbalance again. I will make a mustard oil for your feet, but you must rub it on each night before bed. Will you?"

"Of course," he said swiftly. "And the powder, ma'am? For my milk?"

"You have run out?" she said. "Higgenthorpe, you must speak up."

"One hates to be a bother," he said quietly.

Anisha shook her finger at him. "You are no bother," she said. "Have Cook set out fresh gingerroot in the stillroom, then fetch some cardamom pods from that odd little fellow in Shepherd's Market — and mind he doesn't sell you the green, for it isn't at all the same. I will make it tonight after dinner."

Higgenthorpe looked relieved. "I would be most grateful, ma'am."

"And you will remember to spend a few moments focusing on your breath?" she suggested. "Do you wish me to show you how again?"

"Oh, no, my lady," he said. "I do it every night without fail."

"Excellent," said Anisha. "Oh, by the way — I mean to go down to the St. James

Society at two o'clock. Will you please have the red-and-black phaeton brought round?"

"The phaeton?" Alarm sketched over the butler's face but was quickly veiled. "Yes, my lady."

Anisha moved to follow him out, but Lucan caught her arm as she passed. "A word of warning, Nish?"

Higgenthorpe forgotten, she stiffened. "Warning?" she said, turning to face him. "Of what sort?"

But for once, Lucan looked serious. "Do you think it entirely wise to go down to St. James again?" he murmured. "Bessett may be none too pleased to return from Belgium and find his chosen bride is haring about London with Lord Lazonby — not to mention the fact that the fellow still drops by at least once a week."

"Oh, for God's sake," she gritted. "Rance is like family, and you know it. Besides, I am not betrothed, and I am certainly not *haring about.*" It was guilt, perhaps, which drove her to speak so sharply. "I took Lazonby to the theater at Bessett's mother's request — not that it's any of your business. And I went to Whitehall with him to see Assistant Commissioner Napier at *his* request. Moreover, the man calls here because Raju told him to keep an eye on us whilst he was away. Now I am going to St. James to pay a call on Miss Belkadi. Have you a problem with that?"

Lucan flashed a skeptical smile, one corner of his mouth turning up. "Dear little Saffy, hmm?" he said. "I didn't know she had a social life."

"Have you a problem with that?" she repeated, more harshly.

But Lucan just gazed at her through his somnolent, knowing eyes.

Anisha stalked out, stewing in her own guilt.

Samir Belkadi was a striking young man of little patience. Possessed of hard, dark eyes which had seen much and gave nothing back, Monsieur Belkadi was also blessed with innate good taste, courtesy of his French father. From his mother, however, he had inherited talents far more useful: the ability to adapt and to change and to overcome incalculable odds; in short, the ability to survive. He was also secretive, cynical, and, if circumstance required it, utterly without conscience.

Belkadi was employed, nominally speaking, as club manager of the St. James Society, a position for which these diverse talents made him uniquely suited. The society itself was an island of elegance in an ocean of sophistication — which was to say that, in its rarefied little corner of London, the house scarcely stood out.

This was precisely as its founders had intended, for the true purpose of the St. James Society was not one which wanted advertising. The purpose was, however, marked on its pediment if one knew what to look for: a Latin cross above a crossed quill and sword. To those who understood the significance of this symbol, the house provided safe harbor and solidarity to any member of the *Fraternitas* who might find himself traveling through — or fleeing to — Britain.

The house sat in a dead-end street near the Carlton Club, just a stone's throw from those bastions of clubland, White's and Brooks's. Indeed, at first glance, there was no appreciable difference between any of them; all large buildings with impressive entrances manned by impeccably attired doormen who spent their days bowing before a constant stream of England's most affluent and most noble.

But none was quite like the St. James Society. And none was managed by anyone half so Machiavellian as Belkadi. Moreover, in this particular establishment, everyone involved in its direction was also a member, which left Belkadi in the unenviable position of having no one to complain to when things went wrong.

Today, things were going wrong.

This was partly due to the fact that two of the house's three founders, Lord Ruthveyn and Lord Bessett, had gone abroad; the former for love, the latter to defuse a dangerous situation in Brussels. This, alas, left only the offhanded Lord Lazonby in residence.

Quite literally *in residence.*

And it would not do.

"Again, Lazonby, we've only the two suites," Belkadi repeated, setting away his tea. "Herr Dr. Schwartz is a handsome enough fellow, but unless I misinterpret his inclinations, I doubt he will wish to *sleep* with Mr. Oakdale."

At that, Lazonby tried to smile, but it came out as more of a wince, one hand going to shade his eyes. "Could you just draw the damned drapes?" he grumbled.

"Drink more coffee," Belkadi suggested. "Or, better yet, stop drinking altogether, and we won't have this nonsense to deal with."

Lazonby eyed him a little nastily across the coffee room table. "Ever the upstart,

67

aren't you, Sam?"

Belkadi ignored the remark. "Do you want to know what I think about all this?" he continued, waving a languid hand to indicate the whole of the house.

"No, but you are bloody well going to tell me," Lazonby grumbled.

"Oui," said Belkadi, "for you are the man who had me hauled over here and given the management of it. And what I think is that *this* is not your home — nor was it ever intended to be."

"I bought a house," said the earl darkly. "Don't start ragging on again."

"You bought a house," Belkadi agreed. "In Ebury Street. A fine new house with every modern convenience. You even hired a servant or two. Yet you never stay there. But from now on, you must. You will."

"You sound very sure of yourself."

"Very sure." Belkadi flipped open the ledger he'd been carrying when he'd run Lazonby to ground. "Safiyah has the footmen upstairs packing you even as we speak."

Lazonby looked wounded. "Really? After all I've done for you, Samir? This is like a knife to my heart, you know."

"Save your breath to cool your porridge," said Belkadi almost absently. "Isn't that a Scottish expression?"

"For a chap who once spoke not a word of the King's English, you've managed to get the sayings down in a hurry," Lazonby said dryly. "The more mean-spirited ones, at any rate."

"I find malice has its uses, *oui*." But Belkadi was consulting his baize ledger with total equanimity, ticking off a row of numbers. "Now — do you wish me to resign my position here, *Sergent-Chef-Major?*"

The use of his former rank was done with a purpose, Lazonby knew. "Of course not," he grumbled. "How can you even ask it?"

"Then pray let me do my job," Belkadi returned. "I've got Ruthveyn out at last, and you need to follow his good example. Your things will be carted back to Belgravia by dinnertime. Now, I'm to update you on matters in Saxony."

Lazonby yawned hugely.

Belkadi pinned him with his dark, cold eyes. *"Saxony,"* he said again. "It's *serious.* The King has allowed Prussian troops into Dresden. There's been a bloodbath, and the court has withdrawn to Königstein."

At this, Lazonby bestirred himself, and sat more upright. "Damned quarrelsome Continentals," he muttered. "Did Curran get out?"

"Three days ago," said Belkadi. "He's taking Frau Meyer and her children to van de Velde in Rotterdam. He means to leave her there for the time being."

Lazonby relaxed. "Then in all *seriousness*," he said pointedly, "there's nothing for me to do about *Saxony*, is there?"

Belkadi shrugged. "With everyone else away, it falls to you to be aware of our goings-on in the greater world," he said. "And to deal with the annoying day-to-day minutiae as well. So, back to the claret. The '44 Quinsac can be had more cheaply than —"

"Ask Sir Greville," Lazonby interjected.

Samir lifted his hard eyes from the ledger. "That's your answer? Ask someone else?"

"No, ask *Sir Greville*," Lazonby repeated. "If you wish to send me to Saxony to beat back the Prussians, I'll give it a go and draw their blood doing it. But if you want to know about wine, ask a barrister. To chaps like me there's just the red kind, the yellow kind, and that watery pinkish swill. Every good field officer must know, however, how to delegate. If I've taught you nothing else these many years, Samir, I hope I've taught you that."

"It sounds like evasion to me." Belkadi slapped the ledger shut. "*Très bien*. I'll just get the '42 and hang the money. Ruthveyn has the good taste to prefer it, and with any luck he'll be back before it empties out again."

At that, the clock struck half past two. Abruptly, Lazonby jerked from his chair. "Your pardon," he said. "I just remembered I'm wanted across the street at Ned Quartermaine's."

He was out and down the elegant marble staircase before Belkadi could form a sufficiently scathing reply.

Lazonby was bloody tired of decisions. He knew how to *act,* damn it. Thinking had never been his strong suit — which was, admittedly, the source of much of his trouble in life. And just now, he needed air, he decided, his hand seizing the massive brass doorknob. He needed Westmorland. The damned North African desert. Anyplace with some bloody space. London was going to choke him. He wanted only one thing from this godforsaken place.

He wanted his life — and his honor — back.

Yes, he believed in the *Fraternitas* — believed in everything they stood for, and had very nearly given his life for it on a couple of occasions. He understood, too, that the house — the St. James Society — was a critical front for the organization. He knew that some with the true Gift needed protection, especially the women and children, and particularly so when revolution was rife across Europe. But he hadn't much use for ceremony or science. And he certainly didn't give a damn about politics.

A man more at ease sleeping in a tent and living in a pair of filthy riding boots, he found the constraints of London trying, and the prying eyes of society an interminable pain in his arse. But on this particular afternoon the pain had relocated to his head after a night of drunken revelry in the card room. He'd not wanted for company, either — for while the *Fraternitas* might be sworn to God's service, not a man amongst them was bound for sainthood.

Admittedly, however, Belkadi's strong coffee had cleared the cobwebs. And now it was time to get back to the business of vengeance. It was time to call on Quartermaine. He wondered he'd never thought of doing so before now. The keeper of their local gaming establishment was a right royal sharper, but he was wise to the game — in every manner of speaking. A man like that, even young as he was, might well know where some of the old bodies were buried. Certainly he knew people who could uncover a few of them. . . .

That thought served to cheer him considerably, and Lazonby was already whistling his way down the club's front steps when a black phaeton with ruby red wheels came tooling briskly round the corner into St. James's Place. It splashed through what was left of the morning's puddles, then drew up on the cobbles but a few feet away.

The fine-boned, perfectly matched blacks stamped and shook their heads with impatience, but the driver held them easily. "Good afternoon, Rance," Lady Anisha Stafford called down. "What a pleasant surprise."

He watched in mild stupefaction as the lady descended, all compact grace and vibrant energy, to toss her reins to the club's footman, who had come dashing down the stairs to bow and scrape before her.

Lazonby was taken aback to see her, though he shouldn't have been. While it was true females were not permitted to join the *Fraternitas* — though an especially determined young lady had recently tried and been shipped off to Brussels with Bessett for her trouble — scientific-minded members of the public were often allowed to use the St. James Society's reading rooms and libraries.

But more importantly, Lady Anisha's

brother was a founding member of the Society. So, yes, she had every right to be here — no matter how uncomfortable it might make him. No matter how his breath might catch when he looked at her. They were friends, and dear ones at that.

He forced his usual broad, good-humored smile. "Well, well, Nish!" he said, leaning on his brass-knobbed stick. "Fending for yourself now, eh?"

"It's a hard life." Lady Anisha smiled, stripping off her driving gloves as she came down the pavement. "Do you like it?"

She meant the carriage, of course. "It's . . . dashing," said Lazonby, struggling to keep his jaw from hanging. "I'm just not sure it's you."

"Well, perhaps it should be?" the lady murmured cryptically.

Lazonby's critical eye swept over the conveyance, finding much to admire. It was high, but not perilously so. It was perfectly slung, with front wheels reaching to Lady Anisha's shoulder and paint that glistened like onyx set with rubies. It was a carriage no young man of fashion would willingly have given up — and one very few ladies would have driven.

"In any case," Lady Anisha continued, "I'm merely holding on to it, shall we say,

74

for my brother Lucan."

"Ah," said the earl knowingly. "Pup's under the hatches again, eh?"

Lady Anisha's smile tightened. "Quite so," she said. "Baccarat this time. But he's learnt the hard way that if he wishes my help, there's a price paid. And this time the price is his phaeton. I confess, I've come to quite like it. I'm not at all sure he'll be getting it back."

Lazonby turned his attention from the phaeton back to the exquisitely beautiful woman. "Have you come to visit the Reverend Mr. Sutherland again?" he asked, curious. "Because he's still off in the wilds of Essex."

"Well, he could hardly go all the way to Colchester and not visit his sister, could he?" said Anisha. "But I've actually come to fetch Safiyah. I'm going to make her drive in the park with me."

Lazonby drew back a pace. Safiyah Belkadi, Samir's sister who helped look after the house, rarely left it. "Well, good luck with that," he murmured.

"I know." Anisha screwed up her face. "She'll likely refuse. What about you? Dare you trust your life to my hands?"

"I can think of few I would trust so readily," said Lazonby truthfully. "But no, I was just headed across the way to the Quartermaine Club."

"Rance!" she said chidingly. "You are not gaming again."

He grinned down at her. "Not at Ned's, that much is certain," he said. "He won't let anyone from the St. James Society sit at his tables."

"Heavens, I wonder why!" she murmured. "Look, at least ask me up to the bookroom for a moment. I have something I ought to tell you, and I don't want to stand in the street."

With a sudden and grave reluctance, Lazonby inclined his head and offered his arm, realizing yet again how exquisite she was. Diminutive and fine-boned, Lady Anisha did not quite reach his shoulder. Her hair was as dark and sleek as a raven's wing, and a pair of sharply angled eyebrows merely served to accent her delicate features and warm, flawless skin. Onyx eyes seemed to fire with diamonds when she was in a temper, which she often was. In short, Anisha was the most beautiful, most exotic thing he'd ever laid his eyes on.

But he gave voice to none of this. He never did. Instead, he escorted her up the stairs, rattling glibly on as he always did, and about nothing more significant than the weather.

Two minutes later, they were seated on the long leather sofas in the club's private library, looking at one another a little uncomfortably across the tea table. Lazonby very much hoped Lady Anisha had forgotten the last time she had come upon him in this room.

He had been in a terrible state then, roiling with thwarted rage and something else he would as soon not think about. He had been caught by Nish's brother in what had been a most compromising position; caught with Jack Coldwater, the hot-headed, red-haired newspaper reporter who had seemingly made it his life's ambition to ruin Lazonby.

Well, Coldwater, the cheeky little bastard, had turned up rather too late for that. Lazonby had ruined himself long ago.

But regrettably, Nish had been with Ruthveyn that day. He only hoped she had not quite seen . . . well, whatever it was that had been going on. Her brother most certainly had seen — and had given him a fierce dressing-down for it. Not because Ruthveyn was a judgmental sort of man; he wasn't. No, the scold had been on account of Nish.

He watched her now; her dark eyes flashing, her small, perfect breasts so snugly

77

encased in her black silk carriage dress, her neck long and elegant as a swan's, and he wished a little forlornly that he had not passed her on so swiftly to Lord Bessett.

Not that Nish was anyone's to pass on. She was not. But it little mattered. They might have been closer than brothers, linked together for all eternity, but Ruthveyn had made it plain that Lazonby would never be good enough for his sister. And God knew he owed Ruthveyn — owed him his life, practically.

Moreover, he knew in his heart that Ruthveyn was right.

He might worship the ground her tiny, bejeweled slippers trod upon, but Lazonby had lived a life of wickedness and debauchery that at times could shock even him. And having survived that, he had gone on to make revenge his life's obsession. No, if ever he'd had a chance with Lady Anisha Stafford, he had lost it long ago.

As if to break the awkward moment, Lady Anisha reached up to pull the long pin from her jaunty hat, then set them down beside her. "There," she said on a sigh. "It was poking me. Now, Rance — you were very bad to abandon me in Whitehall the other day. Whatever were you thinking?"

He jerked to his feet. "I did not abandon

you," he said testily. "I left you my carriage, my coachman, and my footmen — with instructions to convey you safely back to Upper Grosvenor Street. I thought it best I walk home, for I was in a temper and not fit company for a lady."

Anisha watched as some inscrutable emotion passed over Rance's ruggedly handsome face. So, she had made him angry. She wasn't sure she cared. They were still friends, yes, but she had grown tired of letting him off so easily.

She had gone with him to Whitehall — practically to Scotland Yard, a place most ladies would sooner die than visit. But she had gone at Rance's request, and against her better judgment, to request a personal favor of the Assistant Commissioner, a man who seemed to hate Rance with his every fiber but who, rather unhappily, owed Anisha's elder brother a large favor.

And so she had gone. But Rance — in his usual bullheaded pursuit of a justice he would likely never see — had pressed the man until Napier's temper had snapped. Little wonder, when Rance had so arrogantly demanded the man reopen his late father's old investigation into Lord Percy Peveril's murder. Napier, of course, had refused, maintaining that Rance had been fairly convicted. At which point Rance had stomped out in a furor, cursing the entire Napier family.

"You left me," she said, following him to the window. "Honestly, Rance, I can't think what's got into you these past few months. You are behaving most strangely."

Lazonby was staring down at the entrance to the Quartermaine Club, watching as Pinkie Ringgold, one of the club's bully-boys, came out to open the door of a waiting carriage. But eventually, he turned around to face her.

"I'm sorry," he rasped. His eyes, suddenly bleak, seemed to search her face. "What was it, Nish, you wished to say to me?"

She ignored the little rush of heat that ran down her center and shifted her gaze. "Two things," she said. "Firstly, what do you know of Royden Napier's background?"

Lazonby lifted both shoulders. "Not a damned thing, save he's old Hanging Nick Napier's get."

"Lud, Rance, your language!" Anisha rolled her eyes.

But Rance, at heart, would always be a Legionnaire, where only the most hardened of the hard survived. And Hanging Nick Napier had been one of the men who had driven him to it, by sending him to the gallows for a murder he had not committed. Now Napier's son held not just his father's old position, but the key to Rance's revenge — *perhaps.*

"In any case," she went on, "Lady Madeleine told me something interesting over dinner last night."

Lazonby grinned. "Getting awfully cozy with your new mamma-in-law, aren't you?"

Anisha felt her anger spike. "Just hush, and listen," she demanded. "A few months ago, when Napier rushed to his uncle's deathbed —"

"Aye, to Birmingham, someone said," Lazonby interjected. "Probably some jackleg silversmith. What of it?"

"Well, it wasn't Birmingham." Anisha dropped her voice. "Belkadi misunderstood. It was *Burlingame* — as in Burlingame Court."

For a moment, Lazonby stared at her in bewilderment. "To Lord Hepplewood's?"

"Well, Hepplewood is dead, is he not? Or so Lady Madeleine says." Anisha tossed her hand dismissively. "I confess, I know nothing of these people. But I think it odd that Napier is nephew to a peer so well connected."

"Connected, then, on Lady Hepplewood's side," Lazonby murmured.

"Lady Madeleine says not," Anisha countered. "I was wondering if perhaps Napier was illegitimate."

"No, but old Nick might have been." Then Lazonby shrugged again. "But I don't give two shillings for Napier's family. I just want him to get off his arse and do his job."

He wanted Napier to clear his name — but to do so, Napier would have to discredit his father's last, most prominent, case. So they were going to see, Anisha thought, just what Royden Napier was made of . . .

She drew a deep breath. "Which brings me to my second point," she continued.

"What?"

For an instant, Anisha snared her bottom lip between her teeth. "I've convinced Napier to let me look at the files in the Peveril case," she finally said.

"You what?" He looked at her incredulously.

"He's going to let me see the files," she repeated. "I can't take them from his office, of course. But they are a matter of public record — well, sort of — so he's going to let me see them. His father's notes. The witness statements. That sort of thing. So . . . what do you want to know?"

Rance could not take his eyes off her. "I . . . good Lord . . . *everything,*" he managed. "Everything you can learn. But how . . . ?"

Anisha cut her gaze away. "Vinegar and honey, Rance," she murmured. "You know the old saying. I think you'd best let me deal with Napier from here out — especially since you can't keep a civil tongue in your head."

Rance closed his eyes and swallowed hard. "Thank you, Nish," he whispered. "I don't know what you did, but . . . *thank you.*"

She waited for a heartbeat — and yet it was a moment that seemed to stretch into eternity. Beyond the open window, Anisha could hear the carriages rattling over the cobbles and the doves cooing on the eaves. And when Rance opened his eyes, she could only stare at him; at his world-weary gaze that so often seemed to drill down into the heart and soul of her, stealing her breath away.

"You are welcome," she somehow managed.

And in that one surreal moment by the open window, he set his warm, long-fingered hands on her shoulders and drew her slowly, inexorably, to his chest. She came against him on a breathless gasp, and their lips met.

He kissed her gently at first, slanting his mouth over hers as his nostrils flared wide.

And she responded; responded as she so often fantasized, by kissing him back, then opening beneath him. Inviting him. Tempting him. And in answer, Rance deepened the kiss, sliding his tongue into her mouth, and the thread of lust that ran through her turned to a raging, twisting river of need, threatening to wash away Anisha's restraint.

This — oh, yes, *this* was her fantasy . . .

Then abruptly, almost ruthlessly, the fantasy ended.

Rance tore his mouth from hers and set her away. His breathing was rough, his eyes wild, and beneath the fine worsted of his trousers she could see the hard outline of his arousal. A rather impressive arousal, to be blunt.

"I'm sorry," he rasped, letting his hands fall. "Good Lord, Nish. Forgive me."

She let her hands drop and stepped away, suddenly infuriated with herself. But in that instant, she caught a hint of motion from one corner of her eye. She glanced at the door, alarmed.

Nothing.

Relief surged — along with a flash of guilt.

Suddenly Rance reached for her. "Wait," he rasped.

"No," said Anisha quietly, stepping back another pace. Strangely, a calm certainty was settling over her. "I'm not waiting. This thing between us . . . it won't ever be, will it, Rance?"

He shook his head. "No," he agreed. "I could make love to you, Nish. I could. I . . . I want to. But Ruthveyn would kill me. And Bessett — *good God,* what am I thinking?"

At last she lifted her eyes to his, her face flaming. "A better question might be, what am *I* thinking?"

"You should marry him, Nish," said Lazonby. "He's a good man. He'll give you an old, honorable, untarnished name — something I could never do. And he'll be an extraordinary father to your boys. You should marry him."

"Yes," she said, her hands fisting at her sides. "I should."

"And will you?" he rasped. "Will you do it? I hope you will."

She could not hold his gaze. "Perhaps," she finally said. "If he asks me — and he has not — then yes, for the boys' sake, perhaps I shall."

Rance heaved a sigh of obvious relief. "Good," he said. "You will never regret it."

She pinned him with her stare, determined, finally, to get an answer to at least one of her questions. "And you will never regret it, either," she said, "will you?"

He thinned his lips and looked away. "You do not love me, Nish," he said quietly.

A long, expectant moment hung over them. Then, "No, I do not," she finally said, her voice surprisingly strong. "I occasionally desire you, Rance. You are . . . well, the sort of man who brings out the worst in a woman, I suppose. Or perhaps it's the best. But no, I do not love you."

The arrogant devil looked at her as if taken aback.

"Is there anything else, then?" she asked coolly. "Before I go back to Whitehall? I don't know how many trips I can make before Napier's patience gives out."

Rance's face seemed to flame with heat. But he was, as ever, perfectly shameless.

"Yes," he finally said. "There is one particular thing." He went to the small desk near the door and extracted a piece of the club's stationery. Impatiently, he scratched a name on it and handed it to her.

"John Coldwater." She flicked an irritated glance up at him.

"Or Jack," Rance rasped. "Jack Coldwater."

In an instant, her heart was in her throat. The scene from that awful day came hurtling back. "I know who he is."

"Or any name in the file that might be

loosely connected to a person named Coldwater."

"And how am I to know that?" she snapped.

"That's why I was headed over to Ned Quartermaine's," Rance replied. "I'm going to hire one of his informant thugs to dig the chap out. Find out where he came from, and who his family is."

"Why?" Anisha felt her lips thin with disapproval. "I should have thought you'd learnt your lesson on that score."

Somehow, she resisted the urge to hurl the slip of paper back in his face. She wondered yet again just what he and Coldwater had been doing that fateful day when she and Raju had stumbled upon them together. It had looked very . . . *physical.* And very angry, as if thwarted rage and frustration and yes, even something akin to lust, perhaps, had driven Rance to the edge of madness.

But anger was a complex emotion, and men — well, Anisha could not claim to understand what drove them. And really, Rance's emotions were his own problem. She had begun to grow weary of worrying about him.

Rance cleared his throat a little awkwardly. "Coldwater is dogging me for a reason,

Nish," he answered. "This is more than the *Chronicle* looking for a story, because I'm old news now. No, this is personal."

"Personal." Anisha crammed the piece of paper into her pocket. "I'll tell you what I think, Rance. I think your obsession with Jack Coldwater is *personal.*"

"Do you?" he asked a little snidely.

"Yes," she snapped. "And very, very unwise."

For an instant, he hesitated, his jaw hardening ruthlessly. And for a moment Anisha was perfectly certain he meant to kiss her again — and that this time he would not be so gentle. That this time, he would not stop until she begged, and perhaps not even then . . .

The thought sent lust twisting through her again, hot and liquid.

In the end, however, he did not kiss her at all.

"You will pardon me," he finally managed, his voice tight. "I am wanted elsewhere."

Then Rance turned on one heel and stalked out the door, leaving her alone in the bookroom.

Slamming the door shut behind him, Lazonby strode out, blinded by anger and a churning, thwarted lust he'd too long suppressed. By God, he wanted, suddenly, to kiss Anisha Stafford until she shut the hell up and surrendered to him — surrendered what she must surely know by now he wanted.

What he had always wanted.

So blindsided was he by this notion that he bumped squarely into Lord Bessett, who stood just a few paces down the corridor, one shoulder set to the passageway wall, his fingers pinching hard at the bridge of his nose, as if he was holding back some powerful emotion.

"Christ Jesus!" Lazonby uttered, throwing up his arms. "Where did you — ?"

Too late he realized Bessett had laid a finger to his lips. "For pity's sake, Rance," he managed, his voice choked with either rage or laughter, "get the hinges on that damned door sanded if you mean to keep kissing people you oughtn't behind it."

"You!" said Lazonby again, hands fisting at his sides. "What the hell are *you* doing here?"

"It appears I might ask you the same thing, old chap," he managed. "But me — well, I've just come by to pull an iron out of the fire. Higgenthorpe said I might catch Nish here."

"An *iron* out of the fire?"

"Aye," said Bessett, eyes dancing with mirth, "though frankly, old chap, it looked rather as if you were doing the job for me."

Lazonby was struck by a wave of pure nausea.

God. Oh, dear God.

He opened his mouth. Unfortunately, the abject apology the situation demanded seemed stuck in his throat and came out as a sort of guttural, choking sound.

But Bessett's mirth was shifting slowly to exasperation. "You had only to claim your interest in the lady, Rance," he said, his voice low but chiding. "I asked you, you know, before I left for Brussels. I gave you every opportunity."

"But I haven't — I don't —"

Lazonby paused to swallow hard, clawing through his mind for the right words. The words to undo a thousand small regrets. To salvage his friendship with Bessett and give Anisha the happy life she deserved — with a decent man who possessed the wealth, polish, and character she deserved.

"It was a moment of madness," he finally snapped. "Just lost my head and forced her to kiss me. I *am not* interested."

But this, oddly, did not seem to be what Bessett wished to hear.

"Oh, you'd bloody well better be interested, old boy." Bessett's countenance was darkening. "There is a word for a gentleman who toys with a lady's affections, and the word . . . well, it is not *gentleman.* It is *cad.* And I ought to slap a glove in your face for it, by God."

Lazonby drew back as if Bessett had, in fact, done so. "I beg your pardon," he said softly. "Aye, you have every right. After all, Nish is . . . why, she is all but your affianced wife."

But now the color seemed to be draining from Lord Bessett's face. The groom-to-be cleared his throat yet said nothing. The painful vision of Nish and Bessett standing before a padre stopped worming around in Lazonby's head, and a cold sense of dread began to steel over him.

"Geoff . . . ?" He dragged the word out, giving Bessett every chance to interrupt. "That kiss was entirely my fault. Call me out. Pink me good and proper; I won't so much as flinch. But Anisha is practically your *affianced wife.* She deserves . . . well, someone like *you.*"

The muscles of Bessett's throat worked up and down. "I did ask Ruthveyn if I might court her, it's true," he finally murmured.

"Oh, you did better than that!" Lazonby glowered. "Your mamma's been squiring her all over town, Geoff, puffed out like a mother hen and laying hints like eggs. People are talking."

But Bessett just stood there, turning his hat round and round by its brim.

"So — ?" Lazonby finally prompted.

The hat stilled. The air, in fact, seemed to still. "So things have changed," Bessett said after a long moment had passed.

Lazonby's senses leapt to full alert. "What sort of *things — ?"*

"Things." Bessett's voice was low but strained. "My affections. They are — they have become — otherwise engaged." Bessett moved as if to push past Lazonby. "Look, just get out of my way, Rance. I came to talk to Lady Anisha. You can go to hell."

"Otherwise engaged?"

Lazonby seized Bessett's lapel and yanked him back, an incomprehensible mix of rage and relief exploding inside his head. "What the devil does that — oh, wait! — I see how the wind blows! You practically pledged your troth to Anisha, then went ripping off to Brussels with that black-haired Tuscan wench, and suddenly your head is turned? And *you* have the bollocks to call *me* cad?"

"Miss de Rohan." Jerking from his grasp, Bessett flung the hat aside. "Her name is Miss de Rohan, which you should well

92

know, having sponsored her here in one of your mad, drunken whims. And she is not a wench. Nor is she Tuscan, precisely. But she *is* a lady — one whom you, Rance, insult at your peril."

"Peril? I'll give you peril, you mewling whelp." Lazonby rolled onto the balls of his feet. "You *dare* to throw God's gift over as if she's *nothing?* As if she has no feelings? And for what — ? For *Anaïs de Rohan?* That ax-wielding Amazon will never be a fraction of the woman Nish is. Why, I ought to slap a glove in *your* face, you faithless bastard. But since I am not much of a gentleman, perhaps I'll just knock your teeth down your throat!"

Bessett shoved up one coat sleeve to come at him, but suddenly the air was punctuated by the sound of slow, solitary applause.

On a low curse, Lazonby turned to see Lady Anisha step from the shadows deep in the passageway.

"Oh, bravo!" she said, strolling languidly toward them, still clapping. "*That,* gentlemen, was a most worthy performance."

"Lady Anisha." Flushing profusely, Bessett bowed. "I do beg your pardon."

Lazonby could only wonder, speechless, if there was any way this dreadful day might worsen. But when Anisha finally reached them, her black eyes shooting even blacker fire, and looking so like her demon of a brother it made him shudder, Lazonby began to wonder instead just how fast he could run.

Anisha's gaze swiveled from Bessett to flick almost disdainfully up and down Lazonby's length. "I cannot say which one of you pays me the greater insult," she said musingly. "You, Geoffrey, for assuming I wished to court you and then trying desperately to foist me off on someone else. Or you, Rance, for trying to force Geoff's hand merely to spare yourself . . . well, whatever it is you wished to spare."

"But Nish —" they said as one.

"Oh, do hush, the both of you!" Anisha's temper fairly crackled in the passageway. "Lord Bessett, I am eight-and-twenty years of age, long widowed, financially comfortable, and — if I do say so myself — reasonably lovely. Though my blood isn't quite what some might wish, I have no doubt that I can find myself a husband *somewhere* — if and when I wish one."

Bessett had lost the rest of his color. "Why, without a dou—"

"*If* and *when*," she repeated, cutting him off. "But it occurs to me now, sir, that only a coward approaches a widow's brother behind her back. Had you any real affection for me, you would have sought me out, declared your intent, and kissed me passionately. Perhaps even invited me to your bed so that you might, shall we say, *demonstrate* precisely what you had to offer?"

Bessett had gone rigid as a beanpole. "Really, *Anisha* — !"

"Good Lord," Lazonby murmured.

"But you did none of that, did you?" Anisha pressed on. "You let your friendship with my brother override any passion you might have felt for me. And that, sir, is no sort of passion at all."

"She's right," said Lazonby aside. "It *was* badly done."

"And you!" Anisha whirled on him, eyes rekindling with fury. "You are a bigger coward, even, than Bessett. Bessett is merely passionless — at least where I am concerned. But you, sir — you are gutless."

"The devil!" Lazonby felt oddly wounded. "I — why, I would walk over hot coals for you, Nish! You know I would."

"That, sir, is not where I wished you to walk." Her arms were crossed now, one toe tapping impatiently upon the carpet. "Do you know, Rance, I used to fantasize about inviting *you* to *my* bed. I yearned for it, in fact, fool that I was — even knowing as I do what a single-minded scoundrel you are. But I am now exceedingly glad I never gave in to that idiotic inclination. I daresay you would do nothing but disappoint — just as you have done today."

Rance could only stare at her, gape-mouthed.

Bessett, however, cleared his throat and stepped boldly forward. "You are right, Anisha," he said quietly. "I esteem you greatly — *adore* you, actually. And you are quite likely the loveliest woman I've ever known. But I've never felt much more than a passing interest in you — or, quite honestly — in any other woman."

"Flatterer," said Lazonby snidely.

Anisha ignored the aside. "And now — ?" she asked, waving one hand expansively.

"And now . . . it's different," said Bessett, looking perplexed. "I met the woman for me, and I did not hesitate an instant. I did not ask anyone's permission. Not even hers. Not even, sadly, her father's — a circumstance I now mean to rectify, with your blessing."

Anisha's toe stopped tapping. "Good, Geoffrey," she said softly. "That's very, very good. And may she lead you a merry dance. She will, I daresay. You look utterly besotted."

"Well." Bessett, always a little high in the instep, cleared his throat and snatched up his hat. "Well, I daresay she will. But first, ma'am, with your permission — ?"

"Oh, for pity's sake, go!" Irritation sketched over Anisha's face. "You need beg no permission from me, Bessett. I am exceedingly glad to be shed of you. And as I said, you never asked me to court you, and I certainly never meant to ask you. So yes, go make your proposal to this mysterious lady — this Miss de Rohan. I hope she says yes — but not, I trust, until she has made you get down on one knee to blubber and beg like a fool."

With that, Geoff declared his undying admiration for Anisha, seized her hand to kiss it, then hastened off down the stairs.

Lazonby watched him go from one corner of his eye. "Good Lord," he said again when the front door thumped shut in the hall below. "That was a bit of a shock."

"To you, perhaps," she retorted.

Trying to bestir his charm, Lazonby flashed his most beguiling smile. "Well," he said softly. "Where does that leave us, old thing?"

"Well, *old thing,*" Anisha echoed, teeth gritting a little, "I daresay it leaves us just where we've always been. Absolutely no-where."

CHAPTER 3

Why, sir, for my part I say the gentleman
had drunk himself out of his five
sentences.
William Shakespeare,
Merry Wives of Windsor

Late that afternoon, Lord Lazonby went
home; home to his town house in Belgravia,
Samir having left him little choice. Once
sequestered in his upstairs suite, he stripped
naked, tossed on a worn silk dressing gown,
and, after uncorking a fresh bottle, made
love to *La Fée Verte* for the rest of the night.

It was a bad habit; one of many that had
followed him home from the French army.
It was also a dreadful error, given his state
of mind. Rage, frustration, and, yes, even
lust were always magnified by absinthe. And
as he sat alone opposite the cold hearth
watching, almost rapt, as the water trickled
through the sugar and silver, down into the

green void below, he thought of Anisha, and wondered.

Was he a coward?

Well, he was afraid — which was the very definition of a coward, he supposed.

He thought again of how she'd looked this afternoon, so elegant and so beautiful and so angry. Nish, whose eyes often held a hint that her favors might be his would he but ask. And her kiss — *good Lord.* It had been the smallest thing. And yet it had been something else entirely.

He could not let himself think of what that *something else* might be.

And it would be such folly! Not to mention an utter breach of the promise he'd sworn her brother. Yet he considered her again and wondered what sort of red-blooded man would not want her to the exclusion of anything else in life, even honor. His duty to Ruthveyn, his hatred of Coldwater, the revenge he so desperately sought — all of it should have paled by comparison to that one simple kiss.

It almost did.

It *would,* if he let it.

And that, perhaps, was the most frightening thing of all.

Always, always there had been that ethereal something between him and Anisha.

And he had known enough lovers to recognize that sidelong, simmering look a woman gave a man when she was sizing him up, so to speak. A few ladies of the *ton* had even found Lazonby's rough edges and bad name intriguing enough to invite him to their beds — but never, of course, to their dinner parties.

Anisha, however, genuinely liked him — or had until today. But he was not free to love her, were he even capable of it.

Oh, he wasn't imprisoned, precisely, nor likely to be. The reach of the *Fraternitas* in Britain had once again grown too strong — and, under Ruthveyn's deft hand, too useful to the Crown. Until Lazonby actually *did* murder someone — today Bessett sprang to mind — and got caught in the act with blood on his hands, then Royden Napier dared not touch him.

Odd how little satisfaction that brought him tonight.

He would never be truly free until his name was cleared and honor restored to his family. *To his father.* And Coldwater somehow held the key. Yet after better than a year of dogged pursuit, Lazonby was no closer to that goal than the day he'd walked out of Newgate. He was frozen in time. Shackled by his own hatred. He could move neither forward nor backward with his life.

He reclined now like some indolent pasha upon a tufted chaise by the window — an almost feminine piece of furniture his estate agent had acquired along with everything else in the house — and felt the lethargy melting deep into his bones.

He could go, he supposed, to Mrs. Farndale's for the evening, to watch her girls prance and laugh and feign an interest they did not have. But it was hard to take much pleasure in it when a man could sense with his every fiber that the desire was just a bought-and-paid charade. That in truth, such women were as jaded and mired in *ennui* as he was. It required a lot of alcohol — or a lot of *something* — to deaden his intuition and take from them a physical pleasure that was hardly pleasure at all.

He rarely ever bothered anymore. He did not bother tonight. Instead, he watched as the sun slanted low across the roofline opposite. Leaning into the glass, he savored the coolness that radiated from it. Up and down in the street below, he could see the bankers and the barristers alighting from their carriages and going up the steps to kiss their children or take a glass of wine with their wives.

Soon, however, the doors and carriages

would fall silent. Then, in another hour, the Commons would recess for dinner and a second wave would begin. It was upper-middle-class Britain at its most industrious — which was to say, not very — and Lazonby had no more part in it than he did in his own so-called class.

He had lived too long in a different world, forgotten the comforts and petty follies of an ordinary life, and become more comfortable there than here. He belonged with people more like himself; the self he had become after long years spent, both emotionally and literally, in the desert. He'd been twice imprisoned, and in between those years, he'd steeped himself in blood and debauchery. He did not belong with someone like Anisha — or her two impressionable young children.

So it was easier, then, to simply not think of what might have been and live only with what *was*. What had to be done. And as he swirled about what was left of the cloudy green liquid in his glass, he forced his attention to the fact that he never had made it to Quartermaine's.

For a moment he considered dressing and heading back across Westminster for the evening. Though he was no longer the infamous gamester he'd once been — Hanging Nick Napier had cured that habit — Lazonby still felt drawn to the hells. To the elegant atmosphere. The hope and desperation. The faces feverish with excitement, or deathly pale with dread. And then there were the women, so beautifully befeathered and beribboned, and trained to urge a chap on; to encourage him to part with just another sou — for this one, *this one,* would surely be the charm.

But he did not go. *L'heure verte,* along with its inevitable languor, was upon him now, and Lazonby could think of nothing save Lady Anisha Stafford. Of the hopelessness of it all.

He drained the glass, his fourth, perhaps, then plucked another lump of sugar from the silver bowl and perched it delicately atop the pierced spoon to begin the process again. He watched the liquid emeralds drip through it to pool like sweet poison in the bell of his glass. Then came the water, and the swirling nebulousness that reminded him of life itself; so sharp and clear one moment, so utterly obscure the next, all its many truths hidden in a milky, celadon haze.

He drank it down, knowing, of course, that the absinthe had already affected him, and that what seemed a brilliant insight was little more than the ramblings of a mad-man's mind. But he scarcely cared. In time, the bottle became half empty, his carafe of water the same, and Lazonby had no memory of the glass which followed — or the one after that.

When he did not go down to dinner, a servant brought up a tray, which sat forgotten. Vaguely he recalled hearing a clock strike midnight. He must have gone to bed thereafter, for at some point he began to reemerge into pitch darkness, caught in the tentacles of an all-too-familiar dream.

He was on the gallows again, the noose growing tighter and tighter. And this time there was no brace beneath his collar. No trick knot to slow it. He realized in a panic that Sutherland was not there. That the priest wore instead a hooded cloak, eyes burning like the coals of hell. He fought to force his lungs to work and failed. He felt death slip nigh.

And then the noose softened, relented, and became something else altogether, and he was floating above, looking down at himself. He lay naked across a bed, caught in a tangle of sheets as he stroked himself. The rough rope had become a silken cord. Coldwater lay naked beside him, his hand slowly drawing down the knot, watching Lazonby's face almost lovingly as he choked the breath of life from his body. And yet there was no pain, but only the sense of an extreme, blinding pleasure. A pleasure not unlike sexual release, and yet it shimmered all about him as his vision began to darken.

It was le petite mort *at its most literal.*

At its most exquisite.

And then he could not breathe, and true death was upon him, and Lazonby knew that he had been tricked. Enticed. That Jack had finally seduced him and taken his revenge . . .

On a guttural cry, Lazonby came bolt up in bed, clawing desperately at his throat.

His cock was so rigid and the room so black that for an instant Lazonby *believed* himself dead; that this time Jack had finally found what he'd so long sought. But when his hand came away from his throat, Lazonby clutched only the silk tie to his dressing gown. The death-erection was just an ordinary cockstand, and the rest of the garment was entangled about his knees.

Strangled whilst frigging himself.

And by his own robe, no less. An ignominious death indeed.

But he was not dead. The hollow sound of his breath sawing in and out of his chest reaffirmed it. Flinging off the robe and linens, Lazonby rolled up onto his elbows, eyes darting about in the gloom. The windows.

The shadows. All were just as they should have been.

Aye, he'd cheated the hangman for yet another night.

Still, he worried about himself. He truly did. In a thousand lifetimes, he would never have guessed that a life of hard living and licentiousness could leave a man so jaded. To dream such things. Sometimes night after night . . .

And why was Jack Coldwater always mixed up in his nightmares of execution and eroticism? Good God, he was sick to death of thinking of him. What was it about the man that obsessed him so? He could feel the malice radiating from the man's every pore — that much Lazonby did *not* mistake — and yet when he was near the man, he felt a sick, twisted, almost sensual awareness.

And he feared others saw it. That *Anisha* saw it. That it had given her a disgust of him.

Suddenly hinges squalled and a bright, wavering light cut across his face.

"My lord?" The whisper belonged to his new valet. "My lord, are you quite all right?"

Yanking up the sheets to cover his waning erection, Lazonby lifted one arm to block the light.

Good God, he must look like a madman, sitting thus in the dark.

"Yes," he finally managed. "Thank you . . . Horsham, is it? Quite all right. Just a bad dream."

Horsham cleared his throat sharply. "It's the absinthe, sir, if you'll pardon my saying," said the valet. "The devil's in that green bottle."

"Aye." Lazonby's breath was calming now. "Aye, I think I met him tonight."

The servant still held his lamp aloft.

"Thank you, Horsham," Lazonby rasped. "You may go."

There was a moment of hesitation. "Sir?"

"Yes?" Lazonby said a little impatiently.

To his dismay, the fellow came fully into the room and set the lamp down on the night table. In the flickering shadows, consternation was writ plain on the man's face. He reached out as if to touch Lazonby.

Lazonby drew away. "Damn it, Horsham, don't mollycoddle," he said gruffly. "I'm a man of bad habits. Said as much when I took you on. Go the hell back to your bed."

Horsham shocked him then by seizing his wrist and lifting his hand from the tangle of sheets. "But sir, your hand is bleeding."

"The devil!"

Then Lazonby looked down. Horsham

had forced his hand over to reveal a gash from the base of his ring finger straight down his palm. Lazonby turned to see his bolster slip streaked with blood already going brownish-red against the freshly starched linen.

"Well, I'll be damned," he muttered.

"Probably, sir." Horsham let his hand drop. "And all the sooner if you bleed to death."

"Hmm," said Lazonby. "An honest man. I like you better and better, Horsham."

But the valet had vanished below the edge of the bed. Lazonby leaned over to see the man on his knees, picking glass out of the Turkey carpet. "You crushed it, sir," he said, the thick wool muffling his voice a little. "You must have gone to sleep holding it, and suffered a nightmare."

"The devil," Lazonby said again.

But Horsham was right. The empty bottle lay on its side by his night table. The silver sugar bowl was upside down, the lid and spoon nowhere to be seen. Only the stem of his glass lay intact.

Horsham picked it up, and the lamplight caught it, sending shards of light through the room. It was antique Venetian *cristallo* — another of his estate agent's luxuries — and he had crushed it. Ruined it, just as he had every beautiful thing in his life.

I daresay you would do nothing but disappoint . . .

Thank God, he thought. Thank God she had sense enough to know it.

But the terror of the dream was fading now, and the memory of Anisha's hot black gaze was stealing over him as the lethargy seeped back in.

He remembered no more until he woke to a shaft of morning sun edging through the draperies and the chatter of an annoyingly cheerful bird somewhere beyond his window. Lying flat on his belly, he dragged a hand down his face, only to realize it had been bandaged with muslin.

Horsham.

On a muffled curse, he rolled over, dragging his arm over his eyes to block the blade of light that threatened to slice into his absinthe-pickled brain.

Just then, someone in the depths of the room cleared his throat.

Lazonby rolled up on one elbow, his bandaged hand coming up to shield his eyes. A man sat in the shadows by the window, a saucer in one hand and a teacup pinched delicately between two fingers.

"Ah, good morning, Rance!" The teacup clicked softly onto the saucer and was set hastily aside. "Back amongst the living, I see."

Forcing his eyes to focus, Lazonby dropped his hand. The contrast between the black wool and white cleric's collar told him at once the identity of his uninvited caller.

"A dangerous lady, this." The Reverend Mr. Sutherland pinched the empty bottle by its neck as if it were a snake that might strike — which perhaps it was. "The Green Fairy, they are calling her in Paris. 'Tis said she causes madness."

"Balderdash," Lazonby managed, dragging himself half upright, the sheets pooling round his waist. "Keeps the malaria away."

"Hmm." Sutherland set the bottle away with a hollow *clunk*. "But absinthe isn't just spirits, my boy. Dr. von Althausen theorizes the wormwood makes it chemically similar to cannabis. It's hallucinogenic."

Lazonby scratched his chest absently and said nothing. But after last night's dreams, he was beginning to wonder if perhaps he and *Madame la Fée* weren't done for.

"By the way, we missed you last night." Sutherland had gone to the draperies and was throwing them back on rings that shrieked with appalling volume. "Von Althausen was demonstrating his latest experi-

111

ment in galvanization and its effect on the senses."

Lazonby grunted. "I have no appetite for watching Dieter and his twitching amphibians," he said in a thick morning voice. "Who let you in, anyway?"

"The new chap. Horsham." With that, Sutherland threw up one of the sashes and leaned out into the street, breathing deeply. "I believe he feared you dead — and who better to deal with that sort of unpleasantness than a clergyman? They're forever sending us round, you know, after it's far too late."

Somehow, Lazonby sat fully upright and waited for the room to stop spinning. Cold spring air was flooding into the room now. He dragged both hands through his unruly hair, resisting the urge to toss his visitor out on his ear.

Sutherland was an old friend of his father's and had long been an important Preost — a high priest — within the old *Fraternitas*. He had played an important role in resurrecting and reorganizing the brotherhood, and had taken on the duty of reconstructing the old genealogies so that they could ensure no one who might possess the Gift was lost or left unprotected.

Sutherland, perhaps better than any of

them, understood the organization's long and murky history. Moreover, Lazonby respected him. Loved him, actually.

"Have you another cup there, Padre?" he said more amiably. "If so, take pity and fetch it here."

The Preost did one better and carried the entire tea tray to Lazonby's night table. "I've had a letter from Ruthveyn," he said, tipping the pot over the empty cup.

Lazonby blinked. "Aye? From whereabouts?"

"Majorca," said Sutherland.

"Making slow progress, isn't he?" Lazonby took the proffered tea, the cup chattering a little dangerously upon its saucer. "Should have thought he'd be halfway to Gibraltar by now."

"I believe they were detained in Paris," said Sutherland, pulling his chair nearer. "Lady Ruthveyn wished her new husband to meet her uncle, Commandant Gauthier's brother."

Henri Gauthier had been Lazonby's superior officer in the Maghreb, and one of the finest men he'd ever known. Gauthier's only child, Grace, was one of Lazonby's few true friends outside the *Fraternitas*. But now, through a strange twist of fate, she had married Ruthveyn.

113

"So you've come to tell me what was in his letter," Lazonby muttered.

Sutherland chuckled. "You're very astute, Rance, even when scarcely sober."

"It's a simple enough deduction," said Lazonby. "Ruthveyn isn't one for writing. And you never turn up unless you wish to chide me or send me off on some mission. So what was in the letter?"

The Preost seemed to sag a little in his chair. "I fear Lord Ruthveyn has caught wind of Bessett's adventures in Brussels."

"But he sat at the table whilst we devised the entire thing," Lazonby argued. "Half of it was his idea."

The man lifted a weary gaze. "I meant the part about de Vendenheim's daughter."

"But he knew that, too. He agreed Miss de Rohan might go along."

Sutherland merely stroked his graying beard with his thumb and forefinger. "But something happened between them in Brussels," he said vaguely.

"Ah, *that* something." Lazonby threw up both hands. "Yes, Bessett fancies himself in love with the girl. I've had the whole story already."

"So have I." Sutherland picked up his teacup almost absently. "I met them in Harwich, you know, as they returned. And to be

114

honest, they are quite perfect for one another. But what of Lady Anisha? It troubles me, Rance."

"Oh, she knows." Lazonby snorted with disgust. "Ever the perfect gentleman, Bessett told her at once. And frankly, I think she was relieved."

Sutherland lifted his gaze a little incredulously, then he, too, sighed. "Well, Lady Anisha may be relieved, but I rather doubt her brother will be. Already, he grows suspicious. He senses something, or has seen something — you know Ruthveyn; the Gift is strong in him — and he won't be well pleased with this turn of events. Bessett pressed his luck by merely asking to court the lady. To now throw her off . . ."

"Aye, Ruthveyn might tap old Bessett's claret when he gets back," Lazonby admitted.

Sutherland seemed to consider it. "No, I think not. Ruthveyn is not as rash as you, my boy. He seeks to maintain this new façade — the St. James Society — at all cost."

"At the cost of his sister's happiness?"

"Perhaps. Perhaps the happiness of one person is trumped by the importance of the good we do. Indeed, have we not all of us made sacrifices?"

Lazonby gave a sharp bark of laughter. "I've made damned few," he admitted. "This St. James business, the formal reorganization of the *Fraternitas* across Europe — all of it was Ruthveyn and Bessett's idea, concocted whilst I was behind bars waiting for the rope."

"Again," said Sutherland dryly.

Lazonby's smile was bitter. "Aye, and if they'd got me on the gallows a second time, no trickery on earth would have saved me," he said. "From the moment those gendarmes seized me in Morocco, I fully expected to die." He stopped and dragged a hand over his face. "I thank you, Sutherland — you and Father — for persuading Henry East to recant on his deathbed. For had you not . . ."

"The *Fraternitas* looks after its own, my boy," the Preost advised. "Stop thinking of it. 'Tis over. And by the way, you do sacrifice — sometimes more than any of us. Do I not recall it was you who volunteered to lead Jack Coldwater off our trail the night we were planning that mission to Brussels? And led him a dangerous chase through the rookeries, I might add, merely to keep him from our business."

"But I *am* Coldwater's business," Lazonby protested. "Though his reasons are beyond me. Still, there's no denying that my story has brought the full light of the *Chronicle*'s lantern shining down upon the St. James Society. That's my fault — so it falls to me to fix it. To lead him off our scent."

At that, Sutherland reached out and laid his hand over Lazonby's. "Oh, young Coldwater is nothing but a meddling young radical, I expect. Some of them hate the aristocracy. This has less to do with you, perhaps, than the *Chronicle*'s politics."

Lazonby's hand fisted. "A part of me thinks if I could just unmask Peveril's killer — if I could clear my family's name — all this would end," he said. "Yet I'm thwarted at every turn. No one knows anything. Most won't even receive me. Scotland Yard refuses to open their files. I'm free — and deeply grateful — and yet I'm still convicted."

"As to that, my boy, I pray the truth will out. You'll settle it in time."

"I wish, honestly, I believed that," Lazonby grumbled. "In any case, what are you going to tell Ruthveyn about this little romance?"

"Nothing, I think." Sutherland relaxed into his chair again. "It's not my place to do so, is it? It is Bessett's. And he is, as you say, ever the gentleman. Most likely he has already penned the letter."

Lazonby grunted, took a long sip of his

tea, then set the cup away and turned to sit on the edge of the bed, drawing the sheet along for modesty. "In all the great hurrah yesterday," he said, bracing his elbows on his knees, "I forgot to ask if Bessett and Miss de Rohan got the Gift safely out of Brussels."

"Indeed, the child has gone to her grandfather near Colchester. I've appointed a new Guardian."

"Aye? Who?"

"Mr. Henfield."

"Ah." Lazonby had met Henfield once, when he had come to London to be studied in Dr. von Althausen's basement laboratory. Von Althausen had confirmed the man hadn't a hint of the Gift himself, but he was from an old *Fraternitas* family, and a stalwart country squire of even temperament and common sense. Henfield would watch over the family and ensure that the child's special gifts remained hidden — for her own safety.

Sutherland rose and drifted to the window by Lazonby's wardrobe, where Horsham, ever the optimist, had laid out fresh clothes on a chair. "You have not been entirely given up on," Sutherland said, glancing down at them, "unless this was what Horsham meant to bury you in."

"And lo, here is the gentle lark, weary of

rest!" Lazonby quoted, grinning. "Best roll out before he sends down to the Strand for the undertaker." He stood, dragging the sheet about him as he went. "Yank the bell there, won't you? I require a bath rather desperately."

Sutherland did as he asked, then said, "I'm off to the Traveler's Club for luncheon. I'll wait if you care to join me?"

"Thank you, no," Lazonby said. "I've plans for the afternoon."

"Oh? Of what sort?"

"I've a call to pay in Upper Grosvenor Street."

"Lady Anisha?"

"Aye, I'm in her black books again."

Sutherland's expression turned solemn. "There was a time, Rance, when I hoped you and she might make a match of it," he said. "Are my hopes entirely dashed in that regard?"

Lazonby felt something inside him still. His heart, perhaps. "Entirely, sir," he finally replied. "I'm sorry. I beg you won't bring it up again."

"But Lady Anisha is such a fine young woman," said the Preost, pensively stroking his beard. "And I know you are deeply fond of her."

"Deeply fond, yes," said Lazonby tightly.

"Too fond, sir, to burden her and her children with my reputation. You know that I am right in what I say."

Sutherland looked sad. "Aye, Rance, but she's fond of you, too. And you'll settle this business. I have faith. Perhaps . . . perhaps the lady will wait?"

"I cannot ask it," said Lazonby, heading for the bathroom. "I won't. But I do find myself owing her yet another apology for being boorish. After that I'm down to the Quartermaine Club."

"Rance, I do hope you know better than to gamble." The Preost's chiding voice echoed through the open door. "Quartermaine's is hardly the sort of place for a man of your — well, let us call it ill fortune."

Lazonby was already shaking out tooth-powder. "Ah, you are a master of the under-statement, Padre!"

As Sutherland launched into the inevitable lecture, Lazonby carried on, scrubbing up the powder and brushing his teeth, scarcely able to hear any of it. But he said nothing. Sutherland was entitled to his rant. The poor fellow had worried much on his ac-count.

The scold was cut short, however, when Horsham entered with three footmen toting massive brass cans of hot water in either hand. The new valet seemed to have the gift of prescience himself — either that, or just bloody good timing.

Lazonby watched them pour it out, then dropped his sheet to the floor and climbed into the tub, savoring for a moment the warmth of the water as it surged round him.

But it could not last. Peace never did.

"You may as well come in," he called to the Preost through the door. "I wouldn't cheat you of the joy you take in thoroughly raking me."

Sutherland appeared on the threshold. "Be serious, laddie," he said, setting one shoulder to the doorframe, watching as Lazonby unwrapped his bandaged hand. "You are more than a Guardian. You have the Gift. And you must be ever so careful with it. The *Fraternitas* can ill afford to hide you away in Africa again when you might be needed here."

Lazonby delayed what would have been a snappish response by scooping up great handfuls of water and sluicing it over his head. "The greatest gift I have," he finally said, "is the gift of good friends who care about me. And I thank you. But we've had this discussion a thousand times, and by God, I don't mean to have it again."

"Rance —" the Preost began.

121

Lazonby scooped more water, then regarded the Preost grimly through strands of wet hair. "I'm not my mother, Sutherland," he interjected. "Not remotely. And I'm not mad — well, not yet, at any rate."

"You are not mad," said Sutherland calmly. "You never will be. And poor Moria was not mad, either. She just . . . wore out with it."

"The Gift," said Lazonby flatly. "Admit it. It slowly drained her, and I finished her off. And all of it blighted my father's life."

Sutherland did not answer for a time. Then he puffed air through his cheeks and said, "Aye, in some ways. But your father was a Guardian, Rance, as you are. He knew his duty to Moria. But he *chose* to marry her. Not just to keep her safe but because he loved her."

Lazonby, however, was not about to discuss the tragedy of his parents' marriage. "And I do not gamble." He seized the soap and began to scrub with rather more vigor than the job required. "I do not even play at hazard, a game of pure and utter chance. I do not so much as bet on whether the sun will rise. Not because I know anything but because I do not care to be called a cheat again."

"It is not cheating to know what is in a

man's heart, Rance," said Sutherland softly. "To be able to sense what a man feels or fears in the black pit of his soul. But it does give you an edge at the table, my boy."

"An unfair advantage, you mean."

"There is no other kind." The Preost's voice was firm but gentle. "And had you not spent half your life denying the Gift was yours — even in this small, subtle way — then years upon years of tragedy might have been spared."

It was an argument they had had so often that Lazonby had lost count. Hell, it wasn't even an argument. He let the soap fall with a loud plop and slid into the depths of the hot water until it surged round his ears.

Sutherland was right — or partly so. Now, at the seemingly ancient age of five-and-thirty, Lazonby understood. He might have dismissed it to Anisha in the carriage all those months ago, but in his heart, he knew. He was not like other men — not most of them, anyway.

Did he have the Gift? Not a Gift such as that which Ruthveyn and Geoff possessed. Not remotely like that hellish thing which had gripped his mother — and thank God for small mercies.

But like a dozen generations of his mother's Scottish ancestors, he carried it strong in his blood. And like most all Welham men born in the Sign of Fire and War, he had sworn to guard it, and all who possessed it. At the age of fifteen, he had been marked for it and his duty laid out before him.

The duty he could have refused. But the Gift — *if* he had it — that, no man could refuse. It came from God. Or the devil.

Did he have it?

A million times he had asked that question. And a million times he'd reassured himself that he merely possessed good instincts. That he could smell anger and fear and duplicity on a man's skin. Or that he could see those same emotions in the small flicker of a man's eyes, or the way he twisted his mouth or twitched his cheek.

Did he have it?

He had something. Though he possessed nothing in the way of prescience, he could read some people, some of the time. A rare few spewed emotion like blood from a gaping wound. Others merely seeped or gave up nothing at all.

As a young man he'd believed that everyone knew this. But they did not. And this difference had been enough to make him a damned fine card player — the finest, perhaps, that the hells of London had ever seen. And he was an even better soldier, especially in close combat. Gauthier had often remarked that he had the reflexes of a cat and the strike of a cobra, for he'd known instinctively what his enemy's next move would be. Known it not in a calculated way but in a way that had found him reacting to it even before he'd known what he'd been reacting *to.*

Le serpent de la mort.

Or so Henri Gauthier had often called him. And that skill had kept Lazonby alive, sometimes even when he'd sooner have died. But the will to fight and survive and even to thrive surged so strong inside him that even Lazonby himself could not quell it. It was the Sign of Fire and War. It was why he *was* what he *was* — and just as it was with Lazonby's reactive instincts, no thought or choice was given to it. It was primal.

He sat up in the tub with a loud *slosh!* and let his shoulders sag.

"Well," said Sutherland, coming away at last from the doorframe. "I should leave you now. Will I see you in St. James later tonight? Safiyah's got the chef roasting a joint."

"Can't say." Lazonby fished the soap from the water, then lifted his gaze to his old friend's. "I'm sorry, Sutherland. I've a frightful morning head."

Sutherland's smile was rueful. "No apology needed."

"Aye, it is," Lazonby returned. "But don't fret, for there's no gaming at Ned's this time of day, and I wouldn't play even if he'd let me — which he won't, for he's suspicious of the whole lot of us now."

"Then why go? Not neighborly concern, I'm confident."

Lazonby managed to laugh. "No, it just occurs to me that Ned might know something about Peveril's death, or the game at Leeton's that long-ago night. He might have heard something over the years. Something he discounted, perhaps, or did not grasp the significance of."

"Quartermaine is well connected, 'tis true." The Preost cast his gaze up, as if musing upon something. "But he cannot be any older than you."

"Considerably younger," Lazonby agreed. "But I also mean to ask him about Coldwater. I see him sometimes, loitering at the club's entrance with that scurvy dog of a doorman."

"Pinkie Ringgold?"

"Aye, Pinkie-Ring." Lazonby snorted. "And we know he can be bought. So perhaps I should buy him? Or at the very least, bribe him to tell me whatever he knows about Coldwater and the *Chronicle?*"

Sutherland mulled it over, toying absently with his watch fob. "What about Leeton himself?" he suggested tentatively. "Would he see you, do you think?"

"I daresay he would, but what's left that wasn't said all those years ago?" said Lazonby. "He gave his testimony, and it was of little value to me — or to the Crown. Besides, he's an honest businessman now. I rather doubt he'll wish to revisit his inglorious past as a secret hell owner."

"But *is* he honest?" asked Sutherland.

"Lord, no," said Lazonby. "Deceitful as the day is long. How could he be otherwise, in that sort of work? But I never actually sensed much emotion from the man."

"Aye, so you've said."

"In any case, it was a private game between Peveril and me, and pure chance we were playing at Leeton's at all. Moreover, it was Leeton who warned me the police had come round. No, he's done all he can, I expect."

"Aye, you're right." Sutherland smiled absently and turned as if to go. "Well, good luck with Quartermaine, my boy. I'll hope to see you at dinner."

"We'll see," Lazonby said from the tub.

Eyes closed against the soap, he listened

as Sutherland's heavy tread sounded toward the door, then reversed and came back again.

"Oh, and Rance?" Sutherland said from the threshold.

Lazonby's hackles went up at once. He had known there had been something besides Ruthveyn's letter setting the Preost on edge. "What is it?"

"I've instituted a bit of a change down at the St. James Society," said the Preost. "One with which I shall require your help."

Lazonby sluiced off the soap and opened his eyes. "Help?" he asked suspiciously. "In what way?"

Sutherland's smile was tight. "I've initiated Miss de Rohan."

Lazonby looked at him blankly. *"What — ?"*

"Yesterday at the train station in Colchester," the Preost said. "I finished our ceremony. The initiation. She's one of us now."

For a moment, Lazonby could only stare. "The hell you say," he finally managed.

But Sutherland's countenance had taken on a mulish look. "Aye, I do say," he replied. "As of — oh, twenty-nine hours ago — Miss Anaïs de Rohan is now a Guardian, and a fully fledged brother in the *Fraternitas Aureae Crucis* — like generations of her people

128

before her."

Lazonby shot him a warning look. "Oh, Sutherland . . . ," he said slowly. "Oh, this will not go over well."

The Preost shrugged. "Can't say as I care," he replied. "I know the girl's work, and I know God's will when I see it. Aye, the lads will kick up a bit, to be sure. But you are a founder, so it falls to you to ram it through and make them grow accustomed to it."

"Me? Why me?"

"Because *you* sponsored her," said Sutherland flatly. "And rightly so, as it happens. But you thought it a lark, didn't you? Now it has backfired, my boy. She was trained and sent by our best blade in Tuscany. She brought us his documentation and she said all the right words. Now she has passed a trial by fire in Belgium. Only a Preost can initiate a new member, and I've done it."

"Yes, but Sutherland, they will —"

"No, she's in, and she's to stay in," Sutherland interjected, "or the lot of you will answer to me — and, I daresay, to Bessett."

"The devil!" said Lazonby again, for it seemed the only response.

"Not the devil, laddie," said the Preost grimly, "but the good Lord. May His will ever be done."

Lazonby was still sitting in the water, eyes wide, when his bedchamber door thumped shut. Almost immediately, however, it opened again to admit the efficient Horsham, who swept the untouched dinner tray away, then returned to lay out the shaving things.

Well. Anaïs de Rohan had got what she wanted. She was a Guardian. A *brother,* as it were.

Inwardly, Lazonby shrugged. What was it to him, after all? Indeed, he had great admiration for the lady's mettle, despite his snide comments to Bessett. It was mere chance that her file had come to him for approval, and sheer perversity that had made him approve it and pass her on for initiation.

The initiation ceremony, however, had not got far. Not, apparently, until yesterday. But Sutherland was right — she was indisputably qualified.

Still, a *female* . . .

But that thought merely served to return him to his more pressing problem.

"Horsham?" Lazonby called through the door. "What do you know about flowers?"

The valet lifted his head from his work. "A bit, sir."

"What sort of flowers does a fellow send

130

to a friend?" he asked. "A lady friend whom he has — well, inadvertently insulted?"

Horsham drifted to the door. "Yellow roses should suffice, sir. For both friendship and regret."

Friendship and regret.

That seemed to sum the whole bloody mess up pretty thoroughly. . . .

Moreover, he liked roses. And ladies liked roses. He put himself in Horsham's hands. "Excellent," he said. "Fetch me some, won't you?"

Horsham gave a little bow. "Certainly, sir," he said. "Shall you require rather a lot of them?"

"Oh, aye, a rude plenty." Lazonby snatched his towel and rose, streaming, from the water. "How did you know?"

The faintest hint of humor flicked over the valet's face and was quickly veiled again. "Oh, just a guess, sir."

CHAPTER 4

I pray you, do not fall in love with me, For
I am falser than vows made in wine.
William Shakespeare, *As You Like It*

The afternoon had turned quite warm by
the time Lazonby dressed, penned his note
of apology, and called for his cabriolet.
Despite the faint dread simmering inside
him, he drove up to Mayfair at a brisk clip,
savoring the feel of the spring breeze against
his face, having long ago learned in prison
never to take such small pleasures for
granted.

As he turned up Park Lane, however, he
began to reconsider his strategy with regard
to Lady Anisha. It would have been better,
perhaps, to have sent one of the footmen.
He had told himself that Ruthveyn's house
was practically on the way to St. James —
which it was, he supposed, if one preferred
the long way round. And just as his new-

found dread blossomed into grave reluctance, Lazonby had the good fortune to spy Higgenthorpe, Ruthveyn's butler, striding some distance up the pavement carrying a shallow basket filled with what looked like small, misshapen parsnips.

Ah, there was his out!

Drawing at once to the curb, Lazonby leapt down, his groom following suit at the rear, the wrapped cone of flowers cradled in the crook of his elbow.

"Drive round to Adams Mews, Jacobs," he said, taking the bundle from the servant. "I'll be but a few moments."

Higgenthorpe had already crossed over Mount Street and made the turn. Hastening up Park Lane after him, Lazonby wove between the oncoming pedestrians — ladies twirling parasols, mostly, chattering arm in arm, and drifting up from Mayfair in the direction of Oxford Street, doubtless for an afternoon's shopping.

It seemed foolish to chase after a butler, but Anisha's sitting room sat just above the front door and she had a bad habit of glancing out to observe who came and went. There was no need to see her; indeed, he did not wish to. What further did they have to say to one another, save for his making an abject apology? Her scorn yesterday had made her position plain. And Higgenthorpe, Lazonby reasoned, obviously meant to go in through the servants' entrance.

Ruthveyn's butler, however, had a block's lead and legs nearly as long as Lazonby's. Higgenthorpe crossed Park Street, then vanished by turning up the alleyway. A few yards further along, Lazonby heard what could only be the back gate clattering shut behind the fellow.

But Ruthveyn's garden, as Lazonby recalled, was deep, the path long. Reaching the gate just as Higgenthorpe started up the steps to the back door, Lazonby opened his mouth to call after him, but just then a flash of motion caught his eye.

Anisha.

Lazonby went perfectly still.

She sat in the small arbor at the easterly edge of Ruthveyn's garden, turned slightly away from him, her head bent to some sort of task. Through the sprays of yellow forsythia that swayed gently round the latticework, he could easily make out her smooth, shining cap of inky hair, for Anisha rarely wore a hat. She hated them, in fact, and thought them a strange English affectation.

It was one of the things he liked best about her, he realized.

Not her contempt for hats but her quiet disdain for conventions she found foolish.

And when she lifted her hand to brush back a loose wisp of hair, he wished, suddenly and acutely, that he were a different sort of man. That his life had turned out differently. Or that he had never left Westmorland as a hotheaded young fool and set out for the excitement of Town.

He had been but eighteen years old and truly had not grasped the fact that a man's misjudgments could follow him the whole of his life. Despite the visions of evil that had haunted his mother and his own rigorous training as a Guardian, he had wanted to escape; to blot out his own secret fears with wretched excess. Young, wealthy, and charming, he'd believed the world his oyster to seize, and had waded out into those dangerous currents after it with a naïveté that now astounded his older, wiser self.

Just then Anisha lifted her chin and laughed. Her laugh was light and always put him in mind of tiny bells. Tiny, *elegant* bells.

He realized then that he was still standing at her gate like a startled stag, simply staring — and further, that Anisha was not alone. Indeed, at that very moment she stood and turned, as if to step back onto the meandering garden path. And when she froze, he knew that he had been seen.

"*Lazonby* — ?" Her voice rang out across the garden, sharp in the spring air.

A pity he had not gone up the front steps and rung the bell like a gentleman ought.

A pity he was such a fool.

But there was nothing to be done now save brazen it through.

"Lady Anisha!" He leaned over the gate. "Pardon the intrusion. I thought I heard your voice round back."

It was an obvious lie, for the house was massive and the wind blowing north, but she seemed not to heed it and came down the steps, leading someone by the hand. "Do lift the latch and come in," she called out. "Look, I have had a visitor. I think perhaps you know her?"

A second lady followed from the arbor — and even at a distance, she was easily recognizable.

Good Lord.

"Lazonby! How fortuitous." Anaïs de Rohan wore one of her dark, vibrant gowns, with her hair tumbled atop her head like an afterthought.

Left with no alternative, Lazonby pushed open the gate and started up the walk, wary now on two fronts. Miss de Rohan swept down the garden path beside Anisha, standing a head taller and wearing her soft, Madonna-like smile. The path was meandering, allowing time for his unease to take a good, firm grip.

An ax-wielding Amazon, he had called her. That had been uncharitable — and untrue.

But when she reached him, Miss de Rohan caught his empty hand almost affectionately, then hesitated. "Oh, dear," she said, brow furrowing. "Am I now to set my palm on your right shoulder and address you in Latin?"

It was the formal *Fraternitas* greeting, but Lazonby had never been much for tradition. "Don't trouble yourself," he said, bowing low over her hand. "You have made a new friend, I see. I commend your good taste."

Miss de Rohan blushed and stepped back. "I took it upon myself to call," she said, catching Anisha's arm in her own. "Forward of me, was it not?"

Lazonby let his gaze slide to Anisha's, gently probing. He had half a mind to turn Miss de Rohan over his knee for a thrashing — and as her *Fraternitas* sponsor, he probably could have done it.

Anisha's countenance, however, was as lovely and as serene as ever. If having her former swain's new love thrust upon her

137

had distressed her in any way, one could not discern it. But then, Anisha was every inch a lady — and possessed a lifetime's experience, Lazonby suspected, in camouflaging her wounds and glossing over social awkwardness.

"I am glad you called, for we have news," said Anisha, glancing up at her caller with what might have been genuine warmth. "You must congratulate her, Lazonby. Miss de Rohan is to be married very soon."

"Congratulations, then," said Lazonby, his voice a little cool. "That's your second triumph in as many days."

"Thank you." Miss de Rohan gave a little curtsey, then cut a shy glance at her hostess. "Well, I had better go," she said. "Cousin Maria says we must have new carpets before the big day, so I'm to meet her in the Strand. I appreciate your kindness, Lady Anisha, more than I can say. Especially the dinner party — if you are indeed sure?"

"Nothing would give us more pleasure," said Anisha.

"A dinner party?" Rance murmured.

"To celebrate the betrothal." Anisha smiled at him. "Lucan and I are giving a dinner party for the happy couple. It will be, I daresay, my only social coup. And yes,

Lord Lazonby, you will be expected to put on your best coat and turn up. Saturday at six."

"Wouldn't miss it for the world," he said smoothly.

Anisha turned to Miss de Rohan. "I'll draw up a guest list," she said, "and we'll finalize it tomorrow over tea."

Miss de Rohan smiled. "You truly are too kind," she said. "And to do it on such short notice. Now I'm afraid I really must run. But thank you again, Lady Anisha, for telling me all about India. And for your . . . well, your good advice."

"Wedding advice, eh?" asked Lazonby.

"Not exactly." Miss de Rohan cast Anisha a sidelong glance, her cheeks warming faintly.

Anisha gave one of her calm smiles. "*Hasta Samudrika,* Lazonby," she said, her hands set serenely together. "I have seen her palm."

Miss de Rohan held up one hand, now gloved. "I believe Lady Anisha has satisfied herself as to the nature of my character, and kindly explained to me how best to manage Geoff," she said, sounding entirely sincere. "It will be a challenge, since we are both born *Mesha,* the Ram. Still, I am to marry him with her blessing. Also, I am healthy, long-lived, and exceedingly fertile. I should warn him straightaway about that last one, don't you imagine, Lazonby?"

Lazonby felt his eyes widen but could not think of an appropriate response. Miss de Rohan, apparently, expected none, and instead set her hands to mirror Anisha's, then bowed to her hostess.

"*Namaste,* Lady Anisha," she said. "This has been a great honor. May I let myself out the back?"

"Yes," said Anisha. "Of course."

But at the last instant, Miss de Rohan turned back to him. "Oh, by the way, Lazonby," she said offhandedly. "My parents are hastening home from the Continent. I collect you do not know my father?"

"I know of him," said Lazonby reluctantly. "But no, I've not the pleasure of an acquaintance."

The young lady smiled a little wanly. "He is hard to get to know," she admitted. "But through his work in Whitehall, he does have contacts — even I, in fact, know some of them — the sorts of people, I mean, who might be of use to you in your . . . well, shall we call it your quest? Now is not the time, of course. But you will remember, I hope, that I have offered?"

Lazonby gave a tight bow and thanked her.

He watched her go, not entirely sure what Miss de Rohan had just suggested. Her father's help, perhaps, in return for his support of her marriage? That was of utterly no value to her, though perhaps she did not know it.

But there was no doubt as to her father's influence; de Vendenheim was a sort of *eminence grise* within the Home Office, and though he had never been officially employed or elected — never officially anything, really — he was a force to be reckoned with when it came to police matters within London and far beyond.

In fact, he probably held Royden Napier's bollocks in the palm of his hand . . .

Well. What *had* she been suggesting?

True, there was a Masonic-like bond within the *Fraternitas.* They were sworn to one another's welfare. It was the reason Sutherland had helped him survive the gallows. The reason Bessett and Ruthveyn had followed him out of Morocco, and why the Gallic brotherhood had sent Geoff to Belgium. Perhaps, like all of them, Miss de Rohan meant merely to do her duty?

For the first time in a long while, Lazonby felt the stirring of hope.

But the young lady had already turned at the gate and waved good-bye, her Madonnasmile still firmly in place.

Lazonby lifted his hat, and Miss de Rohan hastened away. He and Anisha were left standing together on the garden path, less than an arm's length apart. He looked down at her, and suddenly — for reasons that utterly escaped him — he couldn't quite catch his breath.

Her dark eyes were wide, her countenance as open and earnest as ever, and it felt for an instant as if the whole of his world had somehow altered; as if black might be a little more gray than he'd once believed, and everything he'd been so sure of might — just *might* — be wrong.

Damn it to hell.

He had let Sutherland put mad notions in his head.

Then Anisha broke the spell by laughing, her thin, elegant fingers going at once to her mouth. "I *am* sorry," she said on a gurgle of laughter, "but you look like you've just burgled a hothouse."

Lazonby looked down and realized he still held the massive cone of roses in the crook of his arm — about half a bushel, by his reckoning. "These are for you," he said, resisting the urge to thrust them at her. "May I carry them inside?"

"For me?" Her gaze fell to the flowers,

her throat working up and down a little oddly. "Well. How odd."

"Odd?"

She lifted her gaze back to his. "I do not think anyone has ever brought me flowers."

Her husband, thought Lazonby, *had been ten times a fool.*

He wanted, fleetingly, to tell her so. But the moment passed, and Anisha's matter-of-fact tone was returning. "Just set them down, and Chatterjee will put them in water." She turned and pointed to a little stone bench tucked into the shade. "Thank you. They are lovely — and *huge.* Now come sit with me in the arbor. I wish to speak with you."

But he caught her arm, all but forcing her to turn round to face him. "Anisha, I —"

She widened her eyes. "Yes?"

"Tell me, are you all right?"

"All right?" Her delicate eyebrows rose. "In what way?"

She did not mean to make matters easy for him. Well, he did not deserve for her to do so. "Miss de Rohan," he said, jerking his head toward the gate she'd just exited. "It was rather bold of her to come here, wasn't it?"

"She strikes me as a rather bold young lady," said Anisha. "I gather she went all the way to Brussels with Bessett and practically ran some evil Frenchman through with her sword saving that poor child. And Rance, if you mean those flowers to be a gesture of sympathy, you'd best take them away again. I want no one's pity."

She had resumed her walking — and her use of his Christian name, as she so often did in private. Lazonby laid the flowers down and went after her, catching her arm again.

She froze, her gaze dropping to his fingers where they gripped her bare arm. He could feel the warmth in her; could almost feel the coursing blood — and coursing emotions — beneath her skin. She was not angry, he sensed, but there was a message in her eyes. Unsure what it was, Lazonby jerked back his hand and extracted the note from inside his coat.

"Those flowers are an act of contrition," he said. "Along with this abject apology. I behaved abominably yesterday — abominably when I kissed you, and even worse when I —"

"Rance, just *stop!*" Anisha interjected. "I swear, every time you open your mouth nowadays, you dig yourself a deeper hole."

"What — ?" he demanded.

But exasperation had settled over her face.

"I grow so weary of men treating me as if I have no mind of my own," she muttered. "That kiss — I *wanted it,* damn me for a fool. And had I not wanted it, trust me, I would have struck you a cracking good blow across the cheek for your impudence."

He drew back a pace, a little surprised by the vehemence in her eyes.

"Rance, you have —" She stopped, closed her eyes, and balled up her fists as if fighting the urge to strike him. "*You* have what Bessett does not — you have *raw passion.* It is what draws everyone into your sphere. It's what makes you bold on the battlefield, and what makes you burn inside. It is, I daresay, what keeps you up at night. But it isn't something one ought to apologize for."

"Come, Anisha, don't make me out —"

"I don't make you out anything!" she snapped, eyes flying wide. "But you — *you* make yourself out to be nothing but a charming debauchee one moment, and some misanthropic avenging angel the next — neither of which is what you are." She snatched the note from his hand. "Thank you. I accept your apology. You made an ass out of yourself with Bessett, and you made me angry."

He dropped his chin. "I know."

"But do not apologize for the kiss," she

went on, crushing the note, unread, in her fist. "We are bloody idiots, the both of us. But we are adults, and if we wish to be idiots, that is our God-given right."

"All right," he said at last. "I will remember that." Lazonby hung his head, as if ashamed. "I will remember, Anisha, that you are not a child —"

"Thank you," she muttered.

"— but that you are, by your own admission, a *bloody idiot.*"

For an instant, the garden went silent, even the birds, it seemed. He could feel her there, quivering with suppressed emotion, though he dared not look. But when at last he lifted his head and cracked one eye, she was shaking.

They burst at once into peals of laughter.

"You *wretch!*" she cried, swinging wide and striking him once on the chest — *hard.*

"You asked for it, Nish," he declared, catching her arm in his before she could hit him again. "Now, come with me, my girl. We were going to sit in the arbor. And you were going to tell me something."

"I think I was going to tell you not to let the gate hit you in the arse on the way out," she grumbled.

He threw back his head and laughed. "No, I'm pretty certain that wasn't it."

She jerked away, lifted her skirts a little disdainfully, and swept past him, her spine regally stiff.

But she was not angry; not really. And his sick dread had been for naught.

They were, after all, still friends.

He had not realized until just that moment how terrified he had been of losing that.

He could bear a great deal — indeed, he had borne a great deal; the loss of his good name, his friends and his freedom, the family he'd so dearly loved — but he was not at all certain he could have borne the loss of *her*. It would have been, he was suddenly certain, the very last straw laid upon a very tenuous camel's back.

And so they were reconciled.

Something stung and swam in Lazonby's eyes and he blinked it back, unwilling to think what it was. It did not matter. He would simply be more careful in the future; careful to set a little distance between them and to keep things blithe and teasing. He would resume his light flirtation, secure in the knowledge that neither of them needed anything more. His baser needs, those he could slake anywhere. But friendship? Ah, that was rare.

And yet he could not keep himself from

watching the way her silk skirts shifted so temptingly over her slender hips. Not for the first time he felt lust stir deep in his loins; something primitive and raw, and he realized with a grim certainty how easy it would be to tumble over that edge from deep affection into raging desire.

He would not do that to her; would not attach so much as a whisper of rumor to her on his account. God knew she had trouble enough as it was. Ruthveyn's title and wealth might overcome his Anglo-Indian heritage, but Anisha had not his advantage. She did not need her name dragged into the mud, where his already wallowed.

He forced his gaze up to the elegant twist of her hair that was entwined today with silken cords of cerulean blue that matched her vivid blue and white striped frock. The arrangement was elegant in its simplicity, and not especially fashionable. Nonetheless, Anisha had a knack for choosing just the right colors and fabrics to suit her fine bones and dark coloring.

And though she disdained hats, Lazonby had caught sight of her once wearing a diaphanous veil over her hair, one which had hung nearly to her hips, along with one of the brilliantly hued skirts and shawl-like garments which she had brought with her from India.

The attire had looked at once sensual, practical, and elegant; her mother Sarah's things, mostly, Ruthveyn had said, for until her death, the pair had been inseparable. After Sarah's death, however, their father had had little use for a daughter. Anisha had been left to the care of their few Rajasthani servants and a maternal aunt, sent out to Calcutta to care for her.

It was the way of things, Lazonby supposed. But as he watched her now, he wondered if anyone had ever appreciated Anisha Stafford simply for what she was. Her boys, of course, loved her as their mother; Lucan doubtless felt similarly. In other words, they loved her for what she gave to them. Her husband, according to Ruthveyn's intimations, had loved mostly her dowry. Ruthveyn adored her but saw her also as an obligation, and tried to swaddle her in cotton wool.

And Anisha knew all of this. One could see it in the infinite sadness that sometimes softened her eyes.

She drew up by the arbor seat and smoothed her skirts gracefully beneath her as she sat, then motioned for him to join her. "So, I called on Mr. Napier this morning as promised," she said, coming straight to the point. "Unfortunately, he was out again."

"Did you wait?"

"It would have been a long one," said Anisha. "He's off to Burlingame again, and if his clerks know why or how long he means to be, they weren't about to tell me."

Rance cursed softly beneath his breath. "At least a week, don't you reckon?"

"I do," she said a little grimly. "In any case, it seems we'll be busy with a wedding. This dinner party will be only the beginning." She stopped, and sighed. "Oh, I *do* wish Raju and Grace had not gone away."

He laid an arm loosely along the back of the arbor seat, careful not to actually touch her. "I know you miss them, old thing," he said lightly, "but you and young Lucan can throw a dinner party as well as anyone."

She looked up at him and smiled. "I daresay."

"I confess, though, to being surprised." He let his gaze drift over her face, still searching for hurt or unhappiness. "You don't have to do this, Nish. No one expects it of you."

"No, they expect me to be crushed," she said. "Or angry. I'm neither, and I'll have no one thinking I am. Even I have a little pride."

"I don't believe Bessett's intentions were too widely known," Lazonby reassured her. "Though both he and Ruthveyn mentioned it to me."

Anisha lifted both shoulders in a resigned gesture. "I should have liked to have been spared even that," she said. "But in any case, this is what my brother would wish done. He would want us to welcome Miss de Rohan into the *Fraternitas,* and into our family."

Lazonby was not entirely sure of the first. "You understand, then," he said quietly, "that Sutherland has initiated her?"

"And I think better of him for having done it," said Anisha. "But I am exceedingly glad not to be her."

He smiled down at her. "Ah, but I think you are very bold, Nish, in your own quiet way."

Anisha shrugged. "That life is not for me," she said softly. "My boys, Rance, they are my life. And I am glad to have been born when the stars were otherwise aligned — not that my father would ever have agreed to such a thing."

"I'm not sure hers did," said Lazonby dryly, his gaze drifting over a long swath of daffodils. "In any case, you saw her hand today. She claims she does not have the Gift. Do you believe her?"

Anisha lifted her narrow shoulders. "How does one define that word?" she mused. "I have never understood. Do I have the Gift? Do you? Miss de Rohan reads the tarot, she says. Is that a Gift? I do not know."

"You can read palms and the night sky, so what is the diff —"

"Those are *sciences,* Rance," she said in a tone of exasperation. "For many long years I studied, first with my mother, then with my aunt, to gain that knowledge. Do not disparage my hard work by claiming it was *gifted* to me. As to Miss de Rohan, she has . . . good instincts. But nothing haunts her dreams, waking or otherwise."

"Ah," he murmured. "But your skills go a little beyond mere study, Nish. You know they do."

Anisha chose to ignore that. "Miss de Rohan is more like you than Geoffrey," she added. "She senses things — but she does not *see* anything. Moreover, it is a skill she does not yet entirely fathom."

"Saw all that in her hand, did you?" he remarked.

But he did not for a moment doubt that she had done so.

It was their strange mix of Scottish and Rajasthani blood, Ruthveyn had once said. Their father's line had been a part of the *Fraternitas* since the time of the Druid priests, and their mother had been a *rishika* — a sort of mystic, well-read and given to extraordinary visions; visions that had left her princely Rajput father eager to marry her off to anyone who would take her, for such a gift, while highly prized, was still unwelcome in a wife.

Anisha's father, apparently, had not understood quite what he'd been getting in his Anglo-Indian political alliance. Saraswati Singh might have been rechristened Sarah Forsythe, but the truth had told in their children. Anisha's gift was not the same as her mother's, nor even her elder brother's, but like her mother, she had studied the ancient Indian scripts, and she understood things like medicine, palmistry, and the movement of the heavens in a way few Englishmen could have comprehended.

Lazonby understood, too, what Anisha meant about Miss de Rohan not entirely fathoming her abilities. He had been nearly a man grown before he had truly comprehended that he sensed things others did not — and even then, he had denied it.

His father had likened it to the story of

their old smithy, Clackham, who, as an apprentice, had been ordered to fetch some wealthy young lordling's green curricle from the local inn for repairs. But finding nothing wrong with it, Clackham had simply rubbed a little rust off the shaft shackles and returned it to the inn-yard, for as every working man knew, there was no accounting for the folly of the rich.

The young lordling had not been amused; he had been left with a cracked axel and missed the 2000 Guineas Stakes at Newmarket. And afterward, no one had been able to explain to Clackham that he had taken a *red* curricle, not even when his irate customer had parked them side-by-side, forced him underneath, and shoved his face into the broken axel.

Poor Clackham had not understood he was partly color-blind. His arrogant customer had been blind, too, for he'd been unable to grasp that one man could discern what another so plainly could not.

But Lazonby now understood that that sort of ignorance could be lethal.

"A penny for your thoughts," Anisha murmured.

"Oh, nothing worth mentioning." He turned a little on the bench, drawing his arm away. "Listen, Nish, I'm glad you brought up Napier. I've been meaning to talk to you about him."

"About Napier?" she said a little too swiftly. "Why?"

Lazonby set his elbows on his knees, his hands loosely clasped, and studied the moss growing round the cracks in Ruthveyn's flagstone. "Perhaps his going away is for the best," he said, giving voice to a nagging doubt. "Something about Napier's offer troubles me. And I'm not sure I want you mixed up in this."

Her finger, light and cool, touched his cheek, turning his face to hers. "Rance, it's too late," she said, her intelligent brown eyes searching his. "I'm already mixed up in it. And Napier owes my brother. You might as well use me for what I'm worth."

Lazonby really did not like her choice of words — and they struck at the heart of what had begun to trouble him. "No, his going away is for the best," he said more firmly. "There is no good reason for Napier to help you. He owes Ruthveyn, aye. But he mortally hates me. No, I think the fellow is up to something."

For a long, expectant moment, he could sense the hesitation in her. She cut her gaze away and focused it somewhere in the depths of the garden. "Rance, I think Napier has his own reasons for cooperating with me," she said quietly.

"Aye?" He set his head a little to one side and studied her. "What?"

"I think he is . . . well, he is just a little intrigued. By me, I mean."

"Intrigued?" His motions tight and controlled, Lazonby rose from the bench and slowly turned to face her. "What do you mean? In what way?"

"Rance." Hands folded in her lap, Anisha lifted her inky eyebrows.

He set the flat of his hand to the arbor's post and waited. "Aye?" he said.

"Will you make me say it, then?" Her cheeks flushed a pretty shade of pink. "I think we both know there is just one way in which a man is intrigued by a woman. Besides, you suggested as much when you persuaded me to go see him."

"The devil!" he said. "I did no such thing!"

"Yes. You did." Those hot-chocolate eyes were hardening to a glittery black now — and she was definitely looking at him. "You were talking about Napier's watching me at Raju's wedding breakfast."

"What? Oh, that! I just meant —"

"No, no, I recall what you *said*," Anisha cut in. "You said — and I quote — *'The man never took his eyes from you. He fancied you — either that, or he thought you were pinching Ruthveyn's silver.'*"

Lazonby could only stare at her. *Had* he said it? And when was it his world had turned so upside down?

"So which is it?" Anisha pressed, her voice dangerously soft now. "Was Napier imagining me a thief? Or was he imagining me naked in his bed? You cannot have it both ways — and if you'd believed it was the former, you would never have asked me to Whitehall to begin with."

He felt his hands ball into tight fists. *"Anisha —"*

But Anisha had begun to tremble a little — and not from nerves. "Oh, I understand that I am not to some men's taste!" she said sharply. "That has been made abundantly plain. But does it shock you so deeply that there might be at least *one* handsome man who wants me?"

"What? No! Good Lord, of course not." Lazonby looked at her, his stomach almost churning. "And *handsome?* Napier is — good God, Nish, the man has a nose like a hatchet and eyes like a pair of kitchen knives."

"I know," she said quietly. "He is . . . dashing, I think, in a lethal sort of way."

"Dashing? Are you mad? Napier isn't good enough to dust your slippers! He is — he is a *policeman,* for God's sake."

"He certainly is not," said Anisha tartly. "He is a respectable, if middle-class, civil servant, not that social status much matters to me. And as I told my brother at the outset — a claim I should have stuck to — I don't want another husband. Perhaps I am looking for something else."

For a moment, his breath seized. "Something *else* — ?"

"Not that it's any of your business," she went on, speaking over him. "Moreover, if rumor can be believed, Napier is somehow related to Lord Hepplewood. That should be a fine enough connection to suit anyone — again, *not* that it matters to me."

"Perhaps, Anisha, you would be so good as to tell me what *does* matter to you?" Lazonby gritted. "Does it not matter to you that the man has tried to ruin my life?"

"What matters to me is that Napier finds me attractive and interesting," she replied. "And it was his father who tried to ruin your life. The fact that Royden now holds his father's old post and defends his father's reputation does not make malice contagious, or even hereditary."

"Royden — ?" said Lazonby softly. "So

you are now calling him *Royden?*"

She gave a sharp sigh. "Merely to differentiate from Nicholas, his father."

"I do not believe you."

"Oh?" Anisha stood, drawing herself up regally, her skirts swishing over the mossy stones. "Very well, then, believe the worst," she said. "After you stalked out of his office that day, the man tossed up my petticoats, bent me over his desk, and had a nice, quick pump, right in the middle of Whitehall. And I was so good at it, he swore his undying devotion and vowed to grant me anything I desired. So I asked to see your files — by which time he'd quite forgotten who you were anyway — and he begged me to call him *Royden.* So there. Do you like that explanation any better?"

Lazonby felt as if his head might explode. "Damn it, Nish, you are going to force me, aren't you?" he growled. "You are going to force me to write to your brother. To have him order you to — to show some bloody sense!"

"Oh, *order* me?" Anisha trilled with laughter. "And just where will you write to him, Rance? The Indian Ocean? And what, pray, will you tell him? That you dragged me down to Scotland Yard, threw me in Napier's face, and now you wish to drag me out again?"

When she put it that way, it sounded very grim indeed.

Frustration fed the jealousy churning in his heart. "Damn it, Anisha!" he gritted, pounding his fist on the arbor's post so hard the vines above them rattled. "Have you lost your bloody mind?"

"Stop cursing at me," she retorted. "I am *not* one of your soldiers!"

"But you are in my charge, by God," he said, his voice a raw whisper. "And this will not do. I will not have it, do you hear?"

"*You* will not have it?" She sucked in her breath, tremulous. "You had better come to learn, Rance Welham, that you are not omnipotent! And if I am in your charge, I know nothing of it!"

Jealousy exploded, red-hot and infuriating. He slammed his fist into the post again — full on this time — and felt his knuckle split. A handful of dead leaves came swirling down around them. He scarcely realized she'd seized his wrist.

She was shaking, her face oddly stricken. "Rance, stop," she said quietly. "Just *stop.*"

"Anisha, for God's sake . . ." He closed his eyes, uncertain what he'd meant to say.

She forced his hand open — the one that

wasn't already bandaged. "Rance, we are *friends,*" she went on. "This cannot go on. It simply can't. When did we start arguing like fishwives? And saying such vile words to one another?"

He wished he knew the answer to that.

But he did. The truth was, this had been coming on for months now. Ever since she'd stepped off that blasted ship and into his life.

And then Ruthveyn had gone away and left the fox in charge of the henhouse — knowing damned well he'd been doing it, too.

Ruthveyn had believed, Lazonby supposed, that a stern lecture about his sister's virtue would be sufficient. Lazonby had believed it, too. Ruthveyn's warning, and Anisha's likely betrothal, had been enough to put Lazonby off even as it had ratcheted up his frustrations and deepened that aching sense of loss. Even as it had made him question himself — almost hate himself — for what he'd done with his life.

And now this. Anisha was not going to marry Bessett at all. She was free. Free to have an *affaire de coeur.* With Royden Napier. And it was none of his damned business — nor was it her brother's.

"You are right," he said quietly. "When I

pledged to keep you from harm, I made your brother a promise I cannot keep. If you wish to engage in folly, clearly I cannot stop you. And I beg your pardon for my language."

"Rance," she said softly. "Please just don't —"

Don't what? Want her? Fear for her?

He did both, he realized. All the time. Lazonby drew in a deep, unsteady breath.

Anisha had taken a handkerchief from her pocket and was wrapping it round his knuckles. His fist stung — along with his pride and his heart. "Leave it be," he rasped. "It doesn't matter."

She did not look up from the blood she was dabbing away. "Rance," she said very quietly, "everything matters. All the cosmos — all the love and anger, every star and each blade of grass, all that we are and all that we do — the *Vedas* teach us that everything is of a piece. Yes, it matters. We *matter.* But if you wish to have a say in what I do, there is only one way to have it."

A long, heavy silence passed over them. "Oh, Anisha, I cannot —" He stopped and breathed in again. "Oh, love, you honor me, but you know it won't do."

"It might do, if I were really your love," she said, seemingly intent on her work. "But

I am not. I know that."

"And you do not love me, remember?" he whispered, looking past her and into the jungle of green vines beyond. "We just had this discussion."

He felt her tuck the last corner of the handkerchief in and reluctantly looked down. "There," she said, lifting her gaze to his. "And yes, Rance, I remember we had a discussion. But you seem to feel . . . I do not know what you feel. Something more than mere responsibility for me. There is too much anger in you for it to be otherwise."

"Nish."

Lazonby closed his eyes — to pray for strength, he supposed. But against his will, his hands came up to cradle her face, his fingers sliding into the soft, silken hair at her temples. He opened his eyes and kissed her again; this time with exquisite tenderness, his mouth playing over hers, skimming beneath her eye, over her cheek.

He pulled her hard against him, shielded by nothing more than the veil of greenery. She came against him on a breathless sigh, and something inside him wrenched; his heart, he felt sure. Inch for inch, he pressed himself to her.

Yes. Everything mattered. She *mattered.*

He returned his mouth to hers and kissed her deeply, sliding his tongue into her mouth, drowning in the velvety sensation. Her creamy, exotic scent and womanly warmth surrounded him, intoxicating. Her hands stroked round his waist. Against his groin he felt the heat of her and sensed the world slipping away.

As if he moved through water, he followed her back to the bench, still kissing as she drew him down beside her, his hands running over her slight, sweet curves. Urging her back against it, Lazonby planted light kisses down her throat, down and down between her breasts.

Perfect. Exquisite. And so desperately unwise . . .

Anisha shifted, and he slipped one finger beneath the scoop of her neckline. He could hear her breath; the soft pants that betrayed her need. Hooking his finger, he drew the fabric down until one nipple popped free. His mouth found it and he suckled deeply, causing her to arch against him and cry out.

He forced her back, drew his tongue round and round the very tip, then suckled hard again, drawing from her a sweet, enticing innocence. The warmth of her skin filled his nostrils. Her fingers speared into his hair as she held him there, her breath taking on an age-old rhythm that sent a desire so deep and pure twisting through his belly that Lazonby's mind began to betray him and send foolish fantasies spinning through his head.

In Africa he had lived a life sunk so deep in licentiousness that he was ashamed to remember much of it; lain so long and so often in a drug-hazed stupor with God only knew who, he had become more animal than man. But in that moment of perfect innocence beneath the arbor, he felt Anisha's need wash through him like a pure, clean thing. He believed for a moment that he was that different man; forgot for a few fleeting moment the accusations that had ruined him.

Somehow reason reclaimed him, reminded him of where he was. Of *who* he was. He stopped, and she gave a sigh of disappointment.

"Anisha," he whispered, setting his cheek to her breast. "This is madness."

"Is it?" She laid her small, warm hand against his face, holding him to her. "I am asking you to be my lover, Rance. Will you lie and tell me you don't desire me?"

He sat up and she followed, restoring her clothing to order with one well-placed tug.

"I desire you, Anisha," he said, unable to

turn and look her in the eyes. "I . . . I worship you. You know that — but it is madness all the same."

"Then we find ourselves at an impasse again, do we not?" she said quietly. "You wish to tell me what to do. But you do not wish to share my life in that most meaningful of ways."

She was right, he realized. That was the ugly simplicity of it. There was a line between them that would not be crossed. A path already destined. Promises already made. Nothing had changed, save for that dark, yawning chasm of longing, and of opportunities missed, that seemed to deepen every bloody day.

He wasn't sure how long he sat there in the arbor, her hand cupping his face, neither of them making any move.

"I have to go," he finally said.

"Where?" she asked, withdrawing her hand at last. "Where is it you *have* to go?"

"Quartermaine's," he said, straightening. "I was on my way down. I need to talk to him. About Peveril's death."

"You think he knows something?"

Rance just shook his head and stared into the daffodils. "I don't know. I don't know anything anymore."

"Wait," she said, rising to smooth her

skirts. "I will take the flowers in, then go with you."

He made a sound that was half a laugh, and half a sound of dismay. "To the Quartermaine Club?" he said. "That ought to make your brother even happier."

"And I believe we have already established that my brother's happiness is not my problem," she said, turning and starting down the path. "And that my life is none of his business."

He stood and stepped from the canopy of green, unable to do anything but stare after her. Back down the garden path, Anisha scooped up his flowers and turned toward the house. The real world slowly came back to him; the thick, rising warmth of the mews behind, redolent of hay and horse manure. The clatter of traffic coming up Park Street. The sight of Ruthveyn's parlor maid behind the conservatory, beating a small carpet with the flat of her broom.

Anisha wanted to go to Quartermaine's.

And he was tired of fighting with her.

He had believed that Bessett was going to save her from him. But he was not.

A few yards along, she turned, shooting him an impatient glance. "Well?" she said, both arms heaped with his roses. "Are you coming? Or not?"

He shoved her handkerchief into his coat pocket and pushed away from Ruthveyn's arbor.

The Strand at midday was no place for the leisurely shopper. Unlike the fashionably sedate venues catering to Mayfair — Bond Street, Burlington Arcade, and that burgeoning gentleman's paradise, Savile Row — the Strand was all elbows, clamor, and clatter.

Today was especially frenetic, with midday shoppers out in force, pushing past one another amid the hawking cries of newsboys and street vendors. Anaïs de Rohan, however, knew how to use her elbows as well as the next person. She put both to good use now, forcing an especially pushy pieman from her path while simultaneously holding a bandbox and wedging open the shop door for her elderly cousin.

Maria Vittorio stood pat on the pavement, scowling. "Not this one, *cara.*"

Exasperated, Anaïs puffed out her cheeks. "There will be carpets here, Maria," she insisted. "The best ones — and for us, at a good price."

Maria glanced at the shop's only marking, a discreet brass plaque:

M. Jean-Claude Lefèvre
Purveyor of Elegant Oddities and Fine Folderol

"See?" said Anaïs. "Under new management."

Maria rolled her eyes, muttered something in Italian, and pushed past.

Once inside the shop, Anaïs gasped. As always, elegant glass cases lined two walls, catching the early afternoon light to set row upon row of antique stemware and gem-crusted jewelry afire. In a rear corner, a mysterious-looking Egyptian sarcophagus stood on end, open but absent its corpse. An array of chandeliers glittered above hideous, befeathered masks from savage lands and Grecian statues which had survived the vagaries of history, while fine carpets lined the floors and walls — the latter interspersed with rows of Dutch landscapes.

Though she had little understanding of antiquities, Anaïs had occasionally come here as a child with her father, always going away breathless. She was not perfectly sure what had drawn de Vendenheim to this place; something to do with ill-got gains and police business, she supposed, the former proprietor having always danced on the edge of the law.

Still, regardless of the shop's chequered past, it was quite an impressive sight.

It was also quite unoccupied.

She drifted past a table artfully arranged with a dozen blue and white porcelain vases — Yuan Dynasty, the rarest of the rare, and more costly than a small house in East End — all of which Anaïs knew only because the thick, white card propped on the table told her so.

"No one is here," said Maria sourly. "Quick, stick one in your bandbox."

"I heard that!" Suddenly, the jangle of curtain rings cut into the silence.

Anaïs spun around. A lithe, elegantly dressed man wearing a black monocle stood bracketed by the bottle green draperies that still shimmered from the force of having been thrown wide.

Il figlio del diavolo! said Maria under her breath.

"Mr. Kemble!" Anaïs cried. "What are you doing here?"

"Slumming, my dear. And *frightfully.*" George Kemble popped the monocle from his eye and strolled toward them, swinging it lazily from its black silk cord. "How do you do, Miss de Rohan? And look! You've brought Catherine de Medici again!"

170

"Mr. Kemble," said Anaïs chidingly. "I think you know my cousin."

"Indeed," he said, walking a bit of a circle around Maria as he came. "And whilst my Italian is a tad rusty, I gather she just called me *Satan's spawn*."

"No," Anaïs lied, catching his arm and turning him back toward the showcases. "She said you had delightful taste in interior design."

"My dear girl, one knows the evil eye when one sees it." Kemble cut a glance over his shoulder. "Why do I always get the sneaking suspicion that woman is placing some strange Tuscan curse upon me?"

"*Sì,*" said Maria snidely. "On your first-born. When do you think that will be, eh?"

Kemble trilled with laughter. "Oh, you are ever a sly one, Mrs. V," he said.

Defensively, Anaïs seized both the conversation and Kemble's arm. "My, what a lovely spittoon," she interjected, motioning through the glass to distract him. "How much is it?"

Kemble looked at her a little witheringly. "Oh, you really are your father's child. That's a hand-carved jade, Qing Dynasty cachepot mounted on solid silver. And it is priceless."

"Well, *priceless* would be out of my price

171

range." Anaïs steered him further from Maria. "And yes, Papa always found you invaluable. But tell me, why are you here? He said you'd sold the business."

"Apparently, I cannot even *give* this place away!" he sniffed with an airy toss of his hand. "Jean-Claude is off in Provence. Another dying grandmother — the cemeteries of France must be perfectly *clogged up* with them, for it's his fifth or sixth, I'm sure. So I'm stuck here cooling my heels amidst the riffraff of the Strand, whilst the aphids make ready to feast upon my roses."

He did not, however, look especially displeased, Anaïs thought, her gaze running over him. Though he was not as young as he'd once been, George Kemble still looked lean, quick, and faintly predatory, the silver at his temples serving only to lend him gravitas — not that he'd needed it — and the shade perfectly matching the faint gray stripe in his oh-so-fashionable trousers.

Anaïs had no doubt the fabric had been chosen for just that reason. Kemble's particular friend, Maurice Giroux, owned many of London's most exclusive tailors and haberdasheries.

"I'm very sorry about Jean-Claude's grandmother," she said solemnly.

"And my roses?" he asked tartly, pausing

172

to polish the monocle with his silk handkerchief.

"Well," said Anaïs, smiling, "I think I shall feel more sorry for the aphids once you can turn the full force of your wrath on them."

Mr. Kemble sighed, his shoulders sagging a little as he tucked the monocle away. "Well, I suppose the truth is," he said without looking at her, "that life in Buckhurst Hill has been a tad tedious ever since old Dickie Turpin turned up his toes."

Anaïs hesitated. "But . . . wasn't that a hundred years ago?"

"My point precisely," said Kemble with a disdainful sniff. "Dull as ditchwater ever since, the whole village. Were the man still breathing, the boredom would kill him. But the occasional holiday was not enough for Maurice. He wanted a proper garden. A bigger kitchen. A *conservatory,* for God's sake. 'How much money, George,' he often said to me, 'does one require to be happy?' And the answer is *pots.* But we've got buckets. And yet, sometimes it just isn't . . ." His words withered.

"Sometimes it isn't about the money," she finished, catching his arm again.

"Just so! It's about the thrill of the thing. The chase, so to speak." Kemble waved his free hand theatrically as they roamed the shop. "That dark, glittering edge of . . . well, let us call it *intrigue*."

Anaïs knew precisely what he meant. She often felt it, too. And he was not talking, precisely, about the acquisition of rare antiquities. Over the years, George Kemble had had his fingers in a great many pies, some far less wholesome than others. And his business dealings had not been confined to selling pretty pieces of porcelain to the dull dowagers of Mayfair.

His relationship with her father, too, had been complex. Sometimes adversaries, sometime allies, the men had forged a strange, unholy alliance, with her father often looking the other way, since his occasional need for Kemble's specialized knowledge had sometimes superseded the strictest requirements of the law.

"Well," she said consolingly, "at least you have roses now."

Kemble smiled tightly. "And so I do," he said. "Ah, well, my personal travails can be of no interest to you, child. What brought you to Jean-Claude today?"

"Oh, yes!" Anaïs returned her mind to the mission at hand. "Maria thinks I ought to purchase new carpets for the drawing rooms. I thought he would have only the best."

"And he shall," said Kemble confidently, "having been trained by that most discerning arbiter of good taste and fine décor — *moi*."

"Indeed. So will you help me choose something?" asked Anaïs, unfurling her upholstery sample from the bandbox.

He sighed again. "Someone must, I daresay, for both your parents are hopelessly without éclat, verve, panache, or any other fashionable French phrase," he said, snatching the fabric. "Follow me into the back."

Anaïs glanced around. Maria had dozed off in a chair by the door. "But there are a great many nice carpets here," she said, her eyes settling on a gold fringed affair beneath the sarcophagus.

Kemble turned to shake a finger in her face. "No, no, my dear girl," he said. "This is the commonest stuff imaginable. I will show you our private stock."

"Will you?" Anaïs followed him through the green draperies. "I feel honored."

"As well you should." Kemble trailed through the workbenches and cupboards to a higgledy-piggledy stack of Turkey carpets piled twenty or thirty high. "But only the best will do, I think, since I hear *these* carpets are to be for a most special occasion."

"Oh, you heard that, did you?" Anaïs grinned.

Kemble began to throw back the corners of the rugs, as if searching for something in particular. "Indeed, and I hear, too, that you've fallen in with the *Fraternitas*. I always knew the women in your family were fey. Now, morning sun? Or afternoon?"

For an instant, Anaïs froze. "Uh, morning, mostly," she said. "And the . . . *Fraternitas?* I'm not sure I follow."

Kemble cut an incredulous glance up from the pile, then, "No, no, no, no, no," he said, snapping back the next five rugs. "Now, Monsieur Belkadi. *There* is a young man after my own heart. And handsome Lazonby, the infamous card-sharping killer is simply too luscious for — ah! *Here* it is."

"Here is what?"

"A Persian Bidjar," he said, seizing her fabric. "And I have a *pair.*"

"A pair? So you'll discount one, then?"

Kemble looked at her in exasperation. "Have you any notion how rare a matched pair of Bidjars is?" he asked, billowing the upholstery out until it settled across the exposed carpet. "You say it like we're discussing butter and eggs when — *oh, my God!*"

Anaïs looked down, gasping when she saw

176

how perfectly the upholstery contrasted with the rug. Even to her untutored eye, it really was quite splendid. "Now *that*," she said quietly, "is truly amazing."

"Yes, yes, the very thing!" Kemble chortled, clutching the fabric to his breast as he glanced heavenward. "Oh, George! You are *still* the fairest of them all!"

CHAPTER 5

There is no vice so simple but assumes
Some mark of virtue on his outward parts.
William Shakespeare, *Merchant of Venice*

Anisha said little as Rance drove from Mayfair down to St. James. For the first time,
she could sense a deep fissure between
them. Rance sat ramrod stiff upon the
cabriolet's seat, his eyes focused straight
ahead through the afternoon traffic, his jaw
set hard — but no longer twitching from his
temper.

It struck Anisha that she had never seen
him quite so angry — or as tormented — as
he had been in the garden. She saw no point
in pressing him further; she had made her
point. But it did strike her that he was
behaving rather like the proverbial dog in
the manger. Rance did not want her, yet it
seemed he wanted no one else to have her.

Was that it? *Did* he want her?

Inwardly, she sighed. Of course he desired her, but sometimes lust was just lust. More likely he'd merely meant what he'd said. He felt accountable to her brother. And the fact that she might strike up anything remotely like friendship with Napier apparently struck Rance as a pure betrayal.

Still, she found Royden Napier to be a most intriguing man. And she was inordinately curious to see just what his late father had written about Rance all those years ago. No, she would not alter her plans merely to set Rance's mind at ease. She had grown tired of trying to please the men around her and meant now to please herself.

The fact that she was pursuing Napier in order to help Rance, however . . .

Ah, well. *That* she would as soon not think about.

They turned into the environs of St. James Place, and, seeing the familiar carriage approach, a footman dashed down the steps of the St. James Society to take Lazonby's reins. Across the street, Mr. Ringgold, the usual doorman, was nowhere to be seen, and the entrance to the Quartermaine Club was unmanned. It was, Anisha supposed, too early in the day for hardened gamesters, though she'd often seen disheveled, weary gentlemen trailing out of the club at an hour better suited to breakfast than dinner.

The door was answered by a portly servant who looked to have been roused from his luncheon, for he had a bit of cress stuck in his teeth. Anisha's eyes roamed through the elegant entrance hall that looked much like the one across the street, with its broad marble staircase and ceilings vaulting two floors high. Indeed, the house was decorated almost as tastefully as the St. James Society, with silk-hung walls and a collection of fine French landscapes marching up the turn of the stairs.

Despite its beauty, however, the house felt cavernous and entirely empty. *Soulless,* Anisha thought, was the word.

Rance stated his business and, after cutting a curious glance at Anisha, the servant led them downstairs to the ground floor. The air in the stairwell was redolent of cigar smoke and, beneath it, a musky, citrusy scent that was decidedly male. Here, the décor became more subdued, and Anisha saw that the passageway below was lined with doors; the offices in which they counted their ill-got gains, no doubt.

Somewhere down the corridor a door opened on faintly squeaking hinges, then softly closed again, but there was no one to be seen. Anisha felt suddenly ill at ease for reasons she couldn't explain, and was very glad she had come with Rance.

As if sensing her disquiet, he edged nearer to her side and set a hand almost possessively at the small of her back as they walked. She could feel the weight of his palm warming her through the fabric, and she was strangely comforted. It was always thus when she was with him, she realized. Even when they quarreled, she felt . . . safe, somehow. More at peace. And she wished, not for the first time, she understood why.

At the very end of the passageway, they were shown into a private chamber that could have been a gentleman's study. Decorated in shades of dark green and cream, the room was large, high ceilinged, and comfortable without being ostentatious. Three French windows overlooked a small but lush rear garden, while books lined two walls.

A large walnut desk sat before the windows with a matching chest behind; a massive piece of furniture that held wide drawers covered by a pair of large doors. Anisha could see all this because the chest doors were thrown open, and a sort of leather-covered brushing slide was pulled out. A man who looked like a clerk stood there, his back to them as he counted out tall stacks of banknotes atop it.

The portly servant cleared his throat.

The man glanced over his shoulder as he put the last stack of money away. "Good afternoon," he said, closing the slide.

"Peters, these people are here to see Mr. Quartermaine," said the servant.

The clerk looked mildly surprised. "Certainly." He shut both the doors, then locked them with a key that dangled like a fob from a chain at his waist. "I shall just see if he's in."

An odd smile played at one corner of Rance's mouth. "You can tell him it's Lazonby," he said. "But I expect you knew that already."

The man bowed. "Thank you, my lord. Yes, it is my business to know."

With a stiffly polite gesture, he motioned them in the direction of the two tufted leather armchairs positioned opposite the desk, then vanished through a narrow passageway set into the wooden paneling beside the massive chest. Had one not seen it open, Anisha realized, the door would have been nearly invisible.

She cut an uncertain look at Rance. "Is that a secret passageway?" she asked.

"Something like that," he said. "It probably runs between some of the gaming rooms, giving Ned a way to move about, and see without being seen."

"None of this looks quite as I imagined," she said, gazing about the room.

"Expected something more garish, eh?" Rance shot her a wink. "It's just a gaming hell, Nish, not a brothel. And to the sort of clientele Ned attracts, gaming is a deadly serious business. They don't welcome any distractions."

"Ladies do come here, though, don't they?" she said. "The more dashing ones?

Reaching across the distance, Rance laid a hand over hers. "Please, Nish," he said quietly. "Don't even think it. Not just now. I've had about all the change in you I can fathom for one day."

Having utterly no interest in spending an evening in a gaming hell, she cut him a dark glance. "Really, Rance," she muttered. "I sometimes wonder if you know me at —"

The rest of Anisha's retort fell from her lips. The paneled door swung open, and Ned Quartermaine strode in.

A man of perhaps thirty years, he moved with grace and radiated sophistication — as well as something a little more sinister, she thought. Anisha had seen him at a distance, but as he approached she could see that his eyes were green, and very sharp.

His hair was golden brown, and he wore, to Anisha's surprise, a pair of eyeglasses. Oddly, she found herself wondering if they were worn, perhaps, to disarm people.

"Lazonby." He offered his hand but fairly bristled with displeasure.

"Quartermaine." Rance shook it. "I think you've not met Lady Anisha Stafford?"

"No, but I believe I know the lady's brothers." With a tight smile, Quartermaine bowed over her hand. "How do you do, ma'am?"

After a short exchange about the weather, they settled back into their chairs and Quartermaine offered Anisha tea.

"Thank you, no," she said. Despite his spectacles, Anisha could still see a guarded wariness lurking behind the man's eyes as they shifted back and forth between them.

"Doubtless you are wondering what brings us here," Rance added.

"There are surprisingly few things I wonder at anymore," said Quartermaine, steepling his fingers almost pensively. "No, with Ruthveyn abroad and the two of you seated here, one can only conclude this has to do with certain monies owed this establishment by Lord Lucan Forsythe."

"Now *that's* not a bad guess," said Rance almost admiringly. "But no."

Anisha managed a smile. "My brother will be settling his account with you tonight, as it happens."

"Ah." With an almost silky gesture, Quartermaine touched the tips of his index fingers to his lips. "Then you wish me to give my word I'll no longer allow him to sit at my tables?"

"That must be your choice," Anisha replied, "and his, if he is fool enough to play."

Quartermaine dropped his hands and arched one eyebrow. "Then you wish me to arrange for him to lose?" he murmured, his tone vaguely menacing. "Lose, that is to say, deeply enough and badly enough that he never dares venture into a gaming hell again? For I can assure you, ma'am, that is *not* my job. Nor is it in my best interests."

Anisha lifted her chin a notch and refused to be intimidated. "Oh, I think we need not inconvenience you with Lucan's tutelage," she replied. "It has been my experience, sir, that one way or another young men eventually learn life's lessons. He has already spent a stint in the sponging house. It remains to be seen if a turn in debtor's prison will be required."

At that, Quartermaine laughed, and some of the distrust fell from his eyes. "Well, he is not a bad player, if that helps you any."

"Not remotely." Anisha flashed an acidic smile. "In any case, I am here only as Ruthveyn's representative, not Luc's. It is Lazonby's business that brings us."

It was a thin excuse, she realized, but better than none. And Quartermaine did not seem to question it. "Lord Lazonby is not welcome at my tables under any circumstance," he said smoothly. "But I believe he knows that already."

Rance threw up a hand. "Pax, Ned, I no longer play," he said. "I've learnt my lesson."

"As did anyone who ever dared play with you, or so I hear," said Quartermaine. Then he opened his hands expansively. "But there. We are neighbors. Let us be neighborly. How may I be of use to you?"

Rance shifted in his chair uncomfortably. "You came to London, I believe, some years past? From the army, was it?"

"I came from somewhere, yes, at some point in time." Quartermaine's smile was thin. "I cannot think it much matters where or when."

"Not particularly." Rance glanced at Anisha. "I was wondering, though, when you went into business, what you heard round Town about me. About my past."

Quartermaine's gaze shifted uneasily to

Anisha then back again. "I read the news-papers, my lord," he said, dropping his voice. "What more would you have me say?"

"Anything you wish," said Rance. "I have no secrets from Lady Anisha or her elder brother. And what I am asking you is, from a professional standpoint, what do you know about my case? What rumors might you have heard about how and why I came to be convicted of murder?"

Quartermaine pulled off his eyeglasses and tossed them onto his desk. "I can't think that matters, either," he finally said.

Anisha leaned a little forward in her seat. "Sometimes, Mr. Quartermaine, the past is better viewed through more impartial eyes," she said. "I believe Lazonby's point is that perhaps you arrived in London after he was imprisoned, then spent those early years building your business. Surely, given your line of work, you heard rumors from your colleagues? And when he returned from North Africa and was exonerated, surely you were warned?"

Quartermaine laid both hands flat upon the well-polished surface of his desk. "Very well, if you wish to hear it," he finally said. "I was near London, actually, at the time of your trial. It was said you'd come to Town a few months earlier and cut quite a swath, most of it through the hells and the whore-houses — your pardon, ma'am — and that you were nearly impossible to trounce at any card game of strategy, but that your odds were no better than any man's when it came to games of pure chance. Still, a few concluded — even before your trial — that you were some sort of sharper, and quite a good one. So let's just say the Crockfords of this town were glad to see the back of you, and none too happy at your return."

"For the record," said Lazonby coolly, "I never cheated."

"Then you had uncommon good luck," said Quartermaine. "It's possible, but rare. And it is why I will not have you here, Lazonby. That uncommon good luck seems to be a *common* thread across the street, by the way. And I cannot help but wonder why that is."

"I can't think what you're getting at," said Rance tightly.

A little too casually, Quartermaine lifted one shoulder. "I hear, by the way, that your good doctor is working with St. Thomas' Hospital now," he said, dropping his voice, "and that he is conducting some interesting experiments having to do with memory and how electricity affects the brain."

"I'm flattered you take an interest in our

188

little scientific society and Dr. von Althausen's work," said Rance coolly. "As to cards and dice, we play only amongst ourselves nowadays. I think that need be your only concern."

It was time to steer the conversation elsewhere. Anisha leaned forward in her chair. "Please, Mr. Quartermaine, do continue," she said. "You were talking about the rumors?"

As if recalling her presence, he turned toward her. "Of course, where was I?" he said, his hard gaze softening. "Ah, yes. Some of the other young bucks took exception to your uncommon luck — Lord Percy Peveril in particular."

"Peveril took exception to his future fiancée tumbling into my lap at the Haymarket Theatre," said Rance grimly, "and merely waited to exact revenge. He had no cause to call me out and so decided to call me a cheat instead."

"Heavens!" Anisha lightly lifted one eyebrow. "I don't believe I ever heard this part."

Rance twisted uncomfortably in his chair. "Because there's nothing to hear," he said. "Wilfred Leeton invited me to sit in his box one night, and the girl was there with her father. Leeton often entertained his regular customers in such ways, back before he became a respectable theater owner himself."

"In our line of work, one must keep one's best customers happy," murmured Quartermaine.

Rance made a dismissive sound. "More like the old adage to keep your friends close and your enemies closer," he replied. "I did not delude myself. But in either case, I did not know Sir Arthur Colburne was to be there, or I wouldn't have gone. At the time, Arthur was playing deep, and squiring his eldest around in desperate hope of a title. She was a baited trap — we all knew that — and quite a beauty. I tried to keep my distance."

"But she made it impossible?" Quartermaine suggested. "She flirted with you?"

Rance lifted one hand in an impotent, offhand gesture. "I suppose," he said almost wearily. "Peveril thought so, at any rate."

"You suppose — ?" Anisha murmured.

"Aye, then. She flirted with me." Rance's voice was tight. "It was my father's wealth and title, I suppose. Her attentions were so marked it was dashed awkward. Literally, at one point, she tripped and nearly fell into my lap. I had to catch her — giggles, décolletage, and all — whilst half the theater watched."

"And afterward?" Anisha pressed.

"Afterward, I don't know what lies the girl whispered in Peveril's ear, for I had no designs on her," said Rance. "But it brought old Percy to the point and he bristled at me ever after. He was just the second son of a duke, but in the end Sir Arthur was patting his pockets pretty hopefully, for it was said the duke cut some lucrative marriage settlements to get the boy what he wanted. But the truth is, Peveril wasn't a bad sort; merely spoiled and a little hotheaded."

"Most young gentlemen are," said Quartermaine evenly. "Indeed, most days they are my very bread and butter. But you're saying that after the betrothal, the jealousy prompted Peveril to drink too deeply, then challenge you to play?"

"Yes, and I was hotheaded, too, when it came to cards," Rance admitted. "In those days, I took all comers."

"And you were at Leeton's?" Quartermaine murmured. "He ran a rather dangerous — and very discreet — establishment, I believe?"

"Aye, out of his house in Bloomsbury." Rance's smile was bemused. "One had to be invited, and he only invited gentlemen. The play was strictly cards, no dice, and for very high stakes. And Leeton never kept

191

books; it would have seemed vulgar."

"Thus he pretended it wasn't a hell at all." Quartermaine looked equally bemused.

"Oh, it was a hell," said Rance on a harsh laugh. "For a few chaps, it was an outright inferno. But it was ever so politely done. If you owed him money, you dropped it in a glass jar on the pianoforte as you went out, or gave him your vowels. And likewise in the other direction."

"Oh, I rather doubt there was much *likewise*," murmured Quartermaine. "And on this particular occasion? I should like to hear your view of what happened."

Rance lifted one shoulder. "I was on a bit of a streak that night, and it seemed to stir Peveril's ire. He threw down a private challenge, and Leeton acquiesced. He produced a fresh deck at Peveril's insistence, but when I still thrashed him, there was quite a row, with Peveril insisting the cards were marked."

"Were they?" asked Quartermaine pointedly.

"Not by me." Rance's jaw was set stubbornly. "Leeton testified they were not on the witness stand. And he, of all people, had no reason to lie. He made not a ha'penny on the game, and the whole mess threw rather too much light on his affairs. I often think it was part of what drove him to build his theater empire and get out of the game altogether."

Quartermaine's lips twitched. "Oh, I think we need not grieve for old Will," he said a little sourly. "He has managed to scrape by. And in any case, it was Peveril who accused you of cheating. Then, as I understand it, he refused to settle his debt?"

"Well, he finally gave me a note of hand. Leeton insisted. Then Peveril stalked out, and the whispering began."

"And the next morning," Quartermaine went on, "Peveril was found dead in his rooms at the Albany, the knife still in his back — a knife belonging to you, as it happened. Then the porter, Mr. West —"

"East," said Rance tightly. "The fellow's name was Henry East."

"Ah, I stand corrected." Quartermaine lightly lifted his hands from the desktop. "In any case, East swore he had seen you, or someone who claimed to be you, going up to Peveril's rooms round three in the morning."

"And I was charged with murder on little more evidence than that," said Rance. "Even though, as it later turned out, East was nearsighted as an old badger."

Quartermaine smiled. "Not a quality one

ordinarily looks for in an employee," he said. "Particularly one who's been hired to man the entrance of so rarified an establishment as the Albany."

"But Peveril's father was a duke," said Anisha musingly. "I suppose he wanted someone to swing for his son's murder?"

"Aye, he very nearly got it, too." Rance's hand went to his collar, as if it were second nature. "The knife could have been taken from my rooms by any number of people. But East's testimony . . . that nearly drove the nails in my coffin."

"And afterward," said Quartermaine quietly, "matters merely worsened when Sir Arthur Colburne shot himself. Or so I heard."

Anisha's eyes widened. She was slowly coming to realize just how sordid Rance's story was — and how little of it she actually knew.

Rance was staring blindly through the windows now. "Aye, Arthur blew his brains out two days later," he acknowledged, his voice soft.

"But why?" Anisha whispered.

"He was ruined," said Rance. "Had been ruined for some months. That girl — Elinor, I think — my God, her beauty was like money in the bank. But by the time everything fell apart, the Season had ended.

London's eligible bachelors had removed to their country estates, and Arthur's creditors had turned testy. So he took the most expedient way out."

Anisha leaned forward in her chair. "Could it be Sir Arthur killed Peveril?" she suggested. "Then himself out of remorse?"

Rance shook his head. "Kill the fatted calf? Sir Arthur needed the money."

"But what if . . ." Anisha opened her hands plaintively. "Oh, I don't know . . . what if Peveril wished to call it off? Perhaps he changed his mind? And Sir Arthur lost his temper?"

Quartermaine laughed softly. "Oh, I think we all know an English gentleman dares not dishonor a betrothal, ma'am," he said. "Their so-called honor is all some of these chaps have to keep them warm at night — and they hold it dear indeed."

"Aye, he's right," said Rance grimly. "And my knife . . . no, it speaks to cold premeditation. Someone wanted me hanged. Or needed a scapegoat."

"Cui bono?" said Quartermaine softly. "Who owed you money?"

Rance lifted his gaze to meet Quartermaine's. "Everyone," he said, "eventually. I played every club in town. Even Brooks's. But not a vast sum was owed me anywhere.

Nothing worth killing over."

Silence fell across the room for a time, broken only by the *tick-tick-tick* of the ormolu mantel clock. Finally, Quartermaine cleared his throat. "Well, in any case, your father eventually persuaded East to recant his testimony."

"Yes." Rance's eyes were bleak. "Just before his death, East summoned his priest and his magistrate, and confessed to his near blindness."

"And it is said, too, that the Marquess of Ruthveyn — your pardon, Lady Anisha — used his influence with the Government to cast doubt upon the knife," Quartermaine added. "There was quite a nasty piece about it in the *Chronicle* after the Lord Chancellor's decision not to retry you."

"Aye, East claimed he'd been afraid his employers would realize he couldn't see," said Rance, his voice edged in bitterness. "Said he thought he'd lose his post, but he admitted the fellow who claimed to be me could as easily have been his aunt Agatha, and he'd have known little better."

"The loss of employment sounds like a logical fear," Quartermaine murmured. "Yet not, to be sure, an excuse for sending a man to the gallows."

Rance's gaze turned hot. "Aye, but the

funny thing is, after the trial, East never worked another day in his life. How do you think he managed that?"

Quartermaine gave a sharp, bitter laugh. "Perhaps, he, too, had an uncommon gift at the tables?"

Rance snorted. "And perhaps he developed an uncommon gift for blackmail."

"Yes," said Quartermaine quietly, "perhaps that."

"I suppose Mr. East did not wish to die with a guilty conscience," said Anisha quietly. "What a pity, though, that he waited so long to speak out."

"The old duke died a few months before," said Rance. "That may have been the end of East's income stream. Perhaps . . . perhaps he paid East a stipend out of gratitude? It is the most benign motivation I can think of."

For a time, there was no reply. A dark cloud had settled over the room, and they felt it, all three of them. Even Ned Quartermaine, a decidedly hard case, looked dejected. Rance's face had lost much of its color, all of its usual vivacity, and he now sat a little slumped in his chair, staring through the windows into the garden beyond, as if the key to all the incomprehensibility, all the ugliness, might lay hidden amidst Quartermaine's tidy rows of shrubbery.

For the first time, Anisha began to grasp not just the horror of what Rance had suffered but the pall such a thing might cast over a man's life. Two deaths, and a life ruined. And by whom? Why? For assuredly this had been deliberately done.

The reality of it chilled her. Had she somehow convinced herself this had been a mere miscarriage of justice? A spate of bad luck?

It had not been.

It had been evil, pure and simple. Evil directed at Rance. And suddenly, she wanted to take him away from all this. To whisk him back to Mayfair, pour him a stout whisky, and tell him it didn't matter to her what he had been, or what so-called society thought.

But it mattered to Rance.

It was, just as Quartermaine had said, a matter of gentlemanly honor. Not just his, but his father's. His entire family's.

Quartermaine broke the somber mood by clearing his throat and glancing up. Overhead, a great deal of ominous bumping and scraping had commenced; the sound of chairs being moved, she thought. The gaming salons were being swept, or perhaps rearranged.

Quartermaine pushed his chair back from the desk, as if impatient to be gone. "Well, that is what little I know, Lazonby," he said. "The rumors as they have been put to me. But beyond them, I have no specific knowledge, save what I have pieced together from the papers."

"The *Chronicle,* mostly, you mean."

"They do seem to have a marked dislike for you."

"It is just one reporter in particular," said Rance. "That red-haired chap who's so often hanging off Pinkie-Ring's coattails. Do you know who I'm speaking of?"

"I believe so," said Quartermaine. "I had Pinkie have a long chat with the fellow early on — just to be sure it wasn't club business he meant to meddle in."

"Oh? And when he said it was *my* business, you had no problem with it?"

Quartermaine frowned. "He never claimed that," he said. "And I never thought to enquire further."

"Well, Coldwater has been *enquiring,*" Rance snapped. "Not many weeks past I caught him in St. Bride's churchyard *enquiring* of my second footman — not, apparently, for the first time. The whelp's been paying my own servants to spy on me. I

199

sacked the chap on the spot, but there's little to stop Coldwater from doing it again."

"Hmm," said Quartermaine. "Do you wish me to call Pinkie down here? All in the interest of neighborly cooperation, of course."

"Aye," said Rance, coming upright in his chair. "Aye, I would. I've asked him about Coldwater before, but perhaps your presence will loosen the chap's tongue."

Quartermaine's gaze hardened almost warningly. "Now, I won't have him dealt with sharply, mind, for he's a good employee," he said. "But you may ask him whatever you please. Pinkie has no cause to lie."

But Quartermaine already looked as if he regretted his generosity, even as he strode to the bellpull.

The clerk with the key-fob returned and nodded, and, in due course, Mr. Ringgold appeared — apparently bestirred from taking his luncheon with the fellow who'd opened the door, for his waistcoat was dotted with mustard.

A stout man with brown hair that bristled atop his head like a hedgehog, Pinkie looked like a pugilist, for one ear was slightly cauliflowered and his nose had been broken in at least two places. He came into the room looking askance at them, as if sizing the situation up and deciding they were trouble.

Quartermaine did not invite him to sit. "Lazonby here would like to learn, Pinkie, what you know about that reporter from the *Chronicle*," he said. "And I confess I, too, have become curious."

"Wot would I know of 'im?" asked Ringgold defensively. "We ain't exactly bosom beaus. Chap passes through on occasion, going between Fleet Street and Whitehall. 'E's a reporter, awright? Writes about crime and thievery sometimes. And 'e seems obliging enough."

Anisha wondered what distinction, precisely, Ringgold drew between crime and thievery.

But Quartermaine merely relaxed into his chair and opened his hands wide. "And yet we are not quite on the way to Whitehall here, are we, Pinkie?" he said musingly. "Something brings the chap down this practically dead-end street. And if it is not your charm and wit, then it must be . . . well, what?"

Ringgold's bottom lip protruded a fraction. "Well, I'm wot you'd call a connected chap, sir," he said almost defensively. "You knows that. It's why you hired me. Coldwater knows it, too. 'E likes ter arsk me for information from time ter time. About 'oo is 'oo, and 'oo's up ter what — from the penny-thugs ter the fences and madams."

Quartermaine tilted back in his chair and drew a mechanical pen back and forth between his fingers as he regarded Ringgold across the wide, walnut desk. "And what's his interest in Lazonby?" he said quietly. "What has he asked you? And be precise, if you please."

Ringgold's lip drew in again, and his eyes narrowed. But he said nothing.

"Pinkie — ?" This time Quartermaine's tone brooked no opposition.

"Says 'e finks Lazonby 'ere got away wiv murder," Ringgold finally answered, baring a set of yellowing canines. "Says the gents over at the St. James Society 'elped 'im do it, too. A cabal, 'e called them — like the Masons, but wicked. Claims they'd lie and cheat for one another, and that they do just enough of 'er Majesty's bidding to be o' use to 'er, and that's 'ow they stay above the law."

"If I were above the law," Rance growled, "I'd already have strangled that lying little bastard."

"Lazonby, really," murmured Quartermaine, tilting his head in Anisha's direction.

Rance looked at her and blanched. "I beg

your pardon," he said, "again."

"And you, too, Pinkie," Quartermaine added. "Keep a respectful tongue. Now what do you know of the man? Where is he from? Has he a family?"

Ringgold shrugged. "American, someone said," he answered. "Never asked, meself. Got a sister up in Hackney, though."

"How do you know?" Rance shot back.

Ringgold narrowed one eye at him. " 'Cause I makes it me business ter know," he said nastily. "Do I look like a bloomin' idjit? A chap needs ter be sure just 'oo 'e's dealing wiv, so I followed 'im one night as 'e left Fleet Street. But 'e don't really live there. Keeps bachelor rooms off Shoe Lane."

"American, hmm?" Quartermaine seemed to be mulling that one over. "A genuine revolutionary, then. No wonder he works for the *Chronicle*."

"Aye, he might be American," said Rance musingly. "There's something odd about the fellow . . . something I've been unable to put a finger on."

Inwardly, Anisha sighed. How had this conversation turned so completely to Jack Coldwater? Really, why had she come here? Rance did not need her; he was capable of feeding his simmering obsession with Coldwater without anyone's help.

"These rooms near Shoe Lane," said Quartermaine. "Have you been there?"

Ringgold looked uneasy. "Once er twice," he admitted. "Coldwater's been known ter grease a chap's palm when he could provide certain kinds o' information."

Quartermaine cut him a dark glance. "You'd best not provide him any information about anyone in this street," he growled. "And that includes the St. James Society, Pinkie. We've an understanding with the gents across the way — they don't trouble us, and in return, we do not trouble them."

Guilt sketched across Ringgold's face, but he said nothing.

Quartermaine leaned across the desk. "I hope I have made myself clear," he said warningly. Then, without waiting for an answer, he extracted a piece of paper from his desk drawer, slammed it shut, and handed it across to Ringgold. "Now write down the direction of Coldwater's rooms and this sister."

With another dark squint in Rance's direction, Ringgold wrote out the addresses in a surprisingly neat copperplate as Anisha looked on.

"Thank you," said Quartermaine, snatching up the paper to fan it dry. "Now from here out, you're to tell Coldwater to stop loitering. Whatever his quarrel with Lazonby, he needs to take it elsewhere — they *both* need to take it elsewhere. I'm tired of hearing they've come to near fisticuffs on my doorstep. None of us need" — here he cut a warning look at Rance — "*any* undue attention from the authorities down our quiet little lane. Do we, Lord Lazonby?"

Rance stood, Anisha following suit. "No, I daresay not," he said, taking the proffered paper. "Thank you, Quartermaine, for your help. And you, too, Pinkie. I've no quarrel with you. I'm an innocent man, and I'm just tired of Coldwater dogging me."

Ringgold shrugged. "Eh, newspaper chaps," he said off-handedly. "Obsessed wiv getting at the truth, I reckon."

"If he's so obsessed with getting at the truth," Rance retorted, "tell him to figure out who killed Lord Percy Peveril, because by God, it wasn't me."

At that, Ringgold flashed his yellow teeth again. "If yer wants that little mystery solved," he said, "seems to me yer about to put an influential friend in yer pocket."

Rance looked at him blankly. "How so?"

The grin widened. "Wot, din't I 'ere weddin' bells across the way?" he said. "Reckon yer little scientific society is about to snare old Roughshod Roy by 'is —" Here, Ringgold looked at Anisha and blanched. "Well, by 'is nose, let's say. De Vendenheim's chit, now, *that's* a prize."

Rance grunted dismissively. "De Vendenheim's not apt to intercede with Royden Napier on my behalf," he said. "He doesn't know me. Besides, he's coming back to England but briefly. Just for the wedding."

But Ringgold just shrugged. "Pr'aps so, but sometimes it's more 'ow things looks that counts, Lazonby. I'd say Roy won't trouble you further. And de Vendenheim — now there's a chap that knows people. People 'oo knows people, and a lot of 'em dodgy. If yer knows wot I mean."

Anisha understood. Like Calcutta, London had a desperate and furtive underclass — a world where the rule of law meant little and a man's life could mean even less. Pimps, pickpockets, and prostitutes vied with cracksmen and con men to see who could most easily separate the other side of society from their coin — or their morals. But more interesting still was that twice in as many hours, someone was suggesting Geoff's new bride might be worth more than her pretty face.

But there was nothing further to be said

on the subject. Quartermaine meant to get on with his day and was already shaking Rance's hand good-bye.

A few moments later, Anisha found herself going back up the stairs on Rance's arm to the grand, sunlit entrance hall. "Well, that was interesting," he said, pushing open the door for her and again setting his hand almost protectively at her spine.

Outside, Anisha turned on the pavement to look at him, but his hand lingered before falling away. "Well, what were you able to discern from them?" she murmured, setting her head to one side. "Is Quartermaine honest? Is Pinkie?"

Rance shook his head. "Quartermaine's always been a hard one to judge," he confessed. "In that line of work, they always are. Otherwise one cannot survive."

"Do you think he's evil?" asked Anisha.

Rance shrugged. "Define evil," he said, turning to offer his arm. "He is dangerous, yes. But he's also a businessman. Pinkie, on the other hand, is only as honest as he has to be. Nothing he said today was a lie — nor was any of it entirely the truth."

"Do you still have a notion of hiring someone to poke about?"

Rance shook his head, then drew her to his side and laid his hand protectively over hers. "No," he said as they set off. "No, I don't think I trust them."

At least the awkwardness between them had been dispelled, and she was glad they were at peace again. "Oh, well," she said. "For my part, I thought it all rather exciting. After all, it was a gaming hell."

But Rance did not reply. Instead, he was looking down the pavement — looking past her, and in the direction of St. James's Street.

"What?" she said, following his gaze.

Something inside her went perfectly still.

Jack Coldwater was calling an omnibus to the corner by waving his black umbrella, his back turned to them. But his lithe frame and dull-colored mackintosh were unmistakable, even to Anisha.

She stopped abruptly. "He's been poking around again, I suppose."

"Aye, looking for Pinkie, I daresay." Rance's jaw was set implacably. "I ought to follow him. By God, I ought to follow him, corner him, and give him a piece of my mind — or my fist."

Anisha glanced toward the St. James Society. Rance's groom had already walked his horse down to the end of the lane and turned the carriage. And Anisha had had enough.

"Just go, then," she said sharply. "Run after him, act the brute — or whatever game you mean to play — and make a fool of yourself again."

The omnibus driver had clicked to his team, and the van was pulling away. Rance was watching, seemingly transfixed, as Coldwater shuffled sideways toward a thin woman with a large market basket. The wheel struck something, causing the van to lurch, and Coldwater was flung awkwardly into his seat.

Rance cursed softly beneath his breath. His horse had clopped to a halt and now stood at Anisha's elbow, mouthing his bit and snorting impatiently.

Anisha felt much the same. "Look," she said less sharply, "there's a hackney drawing up near the Carlton Club. Go. Take it. I can drive myself back to Mayfair."

She could see that Rance was eager to do just as she'd suggested — fairly aquiver with it, like a foxhound waiting to be unleashed.

"I said *go,* for heaven's sake," she repeated.

Something in her sharp tone got through to him then. Rance turned on the pavement to face her, his back to the street. His hands caught her upper arms harshly, as if he might shake her. "Anisha, please. I —" His words fell away, his eyes drifting over her face, bleak and sad.

She threw him off almost violently and stepped back into the shadow of Quartermaine's door. She was *jealous.* Jealous of his obsession with Jack Coldwater. And the realization sickened her. "What?" she whispered. "Just go, Rance. I am not stopping you. You owe me nothing."

He swallowed hard, his throat working up and down. "Anisha, I sometimes think I owe you — well, more than I can ever repay. And I'm afraid . . . I'm afraid perhaps you will never know."

They were not talking about the fact that he had escorted her down to St. James and was now obligated to escort her home again. No, the conversation had somehow — and suddenly — gone in an entirely different direction.

But Anisha was having none of it. "All I understand is that you are still obsessed with Jack Coldwater," she said, her voice low and tremulous. "You hate him, and yet you think of him constantly. You think . . . my God, Rance, I don't know what you think. But Coldwater cannot help you exonerate yourself. He wants you to *hang,* can't you see?"

"But he knows something," said Rance.

"Doesn't he? I mean — he *must.*"

"He knows how to yank your leash, certainly," she retorted. "Now I am going to take Jacobs and drive myself up to Mayfair. Shall I send your carriage home? Or will you retrieve it?"

"Nish, I can't let you do that," he said.

"Why? I invited myself, did I not?" She turned and climbed into the cabriolet alone, then snapped her fingers for the reins. "Up on the back, Jacobs, if you please."

Without so much as looking at his master, Jacobs leapt to do her bidding.

"Anisha, really," Rance said, but it was a lame protest.

"Oh, for pity's sake, if I can drive Luc's phaeton, I can manage this," she said in a rush. "Now look. You've lost your hackney, and that bus is likely halfway to the Strand. Hurry down to palace corner and hail another."

And with that, Anisha snatched his whip, gave it a neat crack, and set off.

CHAPTER 6

Let us assay our plot; which, if it speed,
Is wicked meaning in a lawful deed.
William Shakespeare,
All's Well That Ends Well

The remainder of the week passed before Anisha made any further effort to call upon Royden Napier. And gloomy, altogether disheartening days they were, filled with cold spring showers and copious self-flagellation. Indeed, still simmering in her anger for much of the first day, she vowed not to go to Napier's at all, reminding herself that Rance scarcely deserved her efforts.

Miss de Rohan returned at midmorning to plan the dinner party. Anisha felt a fraud for even aspiring to be a London hostess, but her new friend seemed not to notice. Indeed, Miss de Rohan seemed undyingly grateful for her help. Anisha decided the poor girl was, indeed, quite desperate.

Still, she found herself liking Miss de Rohan and was grateful to her as well, for she had saved Anisha from a difficult decision: whether to do what was best for Tom and Teddy, always her foremost concern, or do what was best for herself — not that she was especially clear on the latter point. Nonetheless, Bessett would have made an ideal stepfather, of that she'd harbored no doubt. It was the only reason she'd permitted things to go as far as she had.

That evening, Lucan decided to dine at White's before heading out on the town with his perpetual partner in debauchery, Frankie Fitzwater, leaving Anisha alone to ruminate over her quarrels with Rance, like someone bent on picking at a scab. In the end, Anisha decided that it wasn't just that Rance was undeserving of her efforts but that *she* did not deserve the inevitable scars.

But that was not, after all, the end. On the second day she awoke to the sudden realization that her *not* going to visit Napier would give Rance rather too much satisfaction. And that it might even — horror of horrors — leave the overbearing man with the impression he had cowed her. Anisha sent a note round to Number Four at once, enquiring whether Mr. Napier had returned from his travels.

The following day, however, she was forced to stop waffling between indignation and doubt when Tom came back from a romp in Green Park with a sudden, frightful fever, shutting all else from Anisha's mind. She called at once for Chatterjee, who ordered the footmen to move Teddy's bed out.

Once Tom was tucked in, they hovered over the child. "My lady, what would you have me do?" asked the servant.

Anisha set her fingers to Tom's forehead. "Go into the conservatory, to the pots behind Milo's cage," she murmured. "We shall need a great handful of *tulsi*. Take it to the stillroom, and set out my seeds — coriander, cumin, and fennel to start."

And so Anisha spent the next days remembering what she had learned of the ancient *Charaka Samhita Sutra* texts as she chopped and ground and steeped the things required to keep the fever in check, while allowing it enough latitude to burn out Tom's illness.

As always, when the fever became too high, she soaked cloths in salt water and laid them upon his forehead and belly until it subsided. When he became too agitated, they sat on the bed together as she showed him how to perform a simple *kapalabhati pranayama* to help purge the illness with his breath. Every six hours, she stroked his feet, pressing all the right points to release his healing energy.

Tom was a stoic little soldier. And throughout it all, she spared Rance and his vendetta little thought. Still, for nearly two days, the child lay pale and profusely sweating, the English servants looking on curiously as she cared for him. In those rare hours when Anisha slept, Chatterjee and Janet took turns at Tom's bedside, never leaving him alone until, in the wee hours of the third morning, his fever broke, and the over-brightlook left his eyes.

"Heavens," whispered Higgenthorpe, who peeped in an hour later, swathed in a nightcap and wrapper. "The lad looks himself again."

Anisha looked up wearily from her chair. "Higgenthorpe, you should be abed."

"Something woke me," the butler murmured. "I'm glad, for I shall sleep far better now."

"Higgenthorpe," croaked Tom from the bed, "what sort of pudding was there at dinner?"

Anisha managed a soft laugh. "Oh, not yet, my love."

But just then Chatterjee came in, flushing

215

Higgenthorpe out and ordering Anisha to her own bed. She went. And only then did she fully relax, drawing up the bedcovers and collapsing into the deep, undisturbed slumber of a mother reassured.

Shortly after dawn, however, she arose to find Tom's bed empty and, after a moment's panic, found him in the kitchen being dandled like a baby on Janet's knee, his grin stretched from ear to ear, his cheeks stuffed fat as a squirrel's with bits of warm toast dipped in treacle.

"P'rhaps it's not in your *Ayurveda,* my lady," said Janet defensively, "but my mam always said black treacle strengthens the blood. And I don't know a blessed thing about fancy breathing or special energies. But he's weak, the poor, wee mite."

But Tom was no longer ill, not seriously, that much was apparent — and at the grand old age of seven, no longer very wee, much as it pained his mother to admit it. And Janet was right. It was time for the boy to begin eating. So when the front bell rang an hour later, bringing a message from Whitehall to say that the assistant commissioner would be pleased to see Anisha at her convenience, there was no further excuse for ignoring what she had vowed to do — and no more subduing her curiosity, either.

And it was Rance's murder conviction, she reassured herself, that she was curious about. That hot, penetrating emotion in Royden Napier's eyes when they swept over her did not intrigue Anisha in the least.

It was, however, a bit of a balm to her wounded psyche.

So leaving Tom in Janet's capable hands, she put on her favorite amber carriage dress, then wrapped her hair and shoulders with a black and gold paisley shawl, stuffed one of Raju's folios full of blank paper, and ordered the big traveling coach brought round.

The building known colloquially as "Number Four" was unchanged from her first visit, still rank with the smell of over-cooked cabbage, moldering ledgers, and unwashed bodies. This time, at least, the front porter was on duty.

After glancing at her obviously expensive, if slightly untraditional, attire, he apparently judged her worthy and waved her up the creaking, badly lit stairs to the second floor. There she strode to the rear of the building to wait in one of the stiff oak chairs under the sidelong gazes of Napier's clerks, who resembled nothing so much as a brace of black crows perched upon a pair of gate-posts.

The wait seemed interminable but was in

reality less than an hour, for she could hear the clock at St. Martins-in-the-Field striking, the faintly mournful sounds carrying on the sharp spring air.

From time to time, one of the crows sailed down from his tall stool to flit about the office, pecking at this and that before hopping up on his perch again. In the Great Scotland Yard behind Number Four, Anisha could hear through the open windows as the occasional cart rumbled in, bringing criminal suspects, perhaps, to appear before the magistrate, for twice there was a slight hue and cry followed by the rattle of chains in the courtyard below.

After a while, Anisha tuned all of it out, closed her eyes, and focused instead on willing the tension from her body. It was a learned skill; one that helped her maintain balance and order through life's tribulations. And in time, as it always did, the strain left with her breath, and a quiet peace flowed through her.

But mere moments later, Napier's hinges creaked and the peace was lost again.

A dapper, dark-clad gentleman with a black satchel stepped out — a young barrister, perhaps — and, after dropping Anisha a long, passing glance, strode out of the room and down the dark passageway.

Anisha looked round to see Napier glaring at her — at least glare was the word that first sprang to mind — his feet set wide upon the threshold. "Lady Anisha Stafford." His voice, always low, was pitched even lower. "You wished to see me."

Anisha rose, seizing her folio. "Indeed, if you've time."

A bitter smile twisted at his lips. "For Lord Ruthveyn's sister?" he murmured, moving to hold open the door. "Were I to ask our Lady the Queen, she would doubtless assure me I have all the time in the world for such a task."

Anisha felt her temper ratchet up again, but she held her tongue and swished past him. As soon as the door shut, however, she laid the folio on the edge of Napier's desk and turned to face him. "Let us understand one another," she said as sweetly as she could muster. "I am not a task. I did not ask the Queen's favor. I can assure you my brother did not. You promised, all on your own, to allow me to read through Peveril's murder file."

"No, *task* is entirely the wrong word for you, Lady Anisha," he quietly interjected. "On that, I stand corrected. But there. I have interrupted your diatribe, I collect. Pray continue."

219

Napier's hands appeared to be clasped behind his back. His posture was rigid, his eyes dark with what looked like unspoken anger and, if she guessed aright, taking in her every inch.

Pushing the cashmere shawl back from her hair, she swept past him to the open window, suddenly in need of air. "All I am saying," she answered, setting one hand on the sill, "is that if you mean now to renege on what was offered, kindly say so. I do not need another lecture — not from you — on my brother's influence, nor on Lazonby's culpability. By no one's definition has the man been an angel."

Until he set his hand over hers, Anisha hadn't realized Napier had followed her to the window. "I beg your pardon, Lady Anisha," he said quietly, "but it is hard to watch you obsessed by this vile business. Especially when Lazonby, I fear, is not worthy of your regard."

She turned then, eyes blazing. "Indeed, I hold Lazonby in the highest regard," she retorted, "but that does not make me any more blind to his faults than I am blind to yours."

He had withdrawn his hand at once. Now his smile curled almost indolently. "Have I a great many faults, then, my lady?" he asked. "And would you care to enumerate them for me?"

"It would be a short but grave conversation, sir."

"By all means," he murmured, his eyes drifting over her face, "indulge me."

Anisha considered it only a moment. "The Vedas — the Hindu Holy Scriptures — teach us the story of Yajnavalka, who became so wrapped in his own certainty, he dared challenge the knowledge of his *guru*, his teacher, and was driven from the learned fold," she said. "It is the Hindu way of saying, I suppose, that pride goeth before destruction, and a haughty spirit before a fall."

"Ah. And so I am prideful." Napier's voice was soft. "Or is it haughty?"

"Is there a difference?" she asked. "I confess, my English is not always as nuanced as one might wish."

Napier shocked her then by laughing; one deep, loud bark which sounded wholly undignified — this from a man who was, so far as Anisha had seen, the very embodiment of dignity. "Oh, come now, Lady Anisha," he said. "Your English — faintly lilting though it may be — is about as imprecise as a surgeon's blade. But do go on. You were punishing me, I think?"

"And you seemed to be taking a perverse sort of pleasure in it," she replied, her gaze running down him. "There are men who do, I'm told. Though I would not have taken you for one of them."

Napier lifted one slashing, dark eyebrow. "Indeed not, my lady," he said. "I prefer to take my pleasure in quite another way. But like any man who earns his crust in government service, I am hardened to criticism. Fire at will."

Anisha lifted her chin. "Very well, then, yes, you are prideful," she said. "And if you don't have a care, it will be your downfall. Humility, even a little, can bind us together. But pride can only blind us — particularly to our own faults. Like Yajnavalka, you possess great knowledge, but as yet, little wisdom. You cannot see beyond your own assumptions."

This he seemed to ponder seriously, at least for a moment. "And what would you have me do?"

"Open your knowledge to me," she said, tossing one hand in the direction of his desk. "Do what you have promised. That is, after all, the Peveril file open upon your desk, is it not? I saw it, you see, when I laid down my folio."

He fell silent for a moment, his gaze turning inward. "You are quite as clever as your brother Ruthveyn, I think, Lady Anisha," he murmured, "but a good deal more subtle."

When she said nothing, he merely watched her for a time, the mood in the room oddly shifting. "You are in love with him, aren't you?" he finally asked. "With Lord Lazonby."

For an instant, Anisha could not hold Napier's gaze.

He had suggested as much, though less bluntly, when she had come here with Rance that first time. And she had asked him — quite bluntly, once Rance had been tossed out on his ear — why he'd never stopped looking at her.

He had not answered. But it had had nothing to do, she was quite certain, with the security of her brother's silver. Napier wanted her. And at the time, she had wanted to make him say it, for reasons she had not fully understood.

Perhaps she had been searching for a balm to her wounded female pride. Or perhaps she had fleetingly toyed with the notion of an *affaire.* She was not sure now. But she was sure, if he asked, what her answer would be. Her heart had flown — traitorous organ that it was — and trying to imagine herself with anyone save Rance was just an exercise in futility.

She should have been thrilled at Napier's interest. Indeed, she was a fool for not pursuing him. He was a captivating man. And she — well, she had been alone for a very long time, and lonely for longer than that.

She believed Napier misguided and Rance stubborn. But it was also remotely possible that Napier had utterly deceived her; deceived her about all of this — his desire, his honesty, and his true intent in helping her — and done it so cleverly that she had failed to sense it. She thought not. But only a fool would fail to question such a man's motivations.

He broke the silence with a long sigh, his chin down, his hands shoved deep into his trouser pockets, almost as if he had forgotten her presence. The afternoon sun shone upon him through the tall window that overlooked the yard, casting a gloss over his neat, dark hair, and setting his gold watch chain ablaze. His nose did indeed have a decided hook, and his eyes were more piercing than warm. And yet he was not unhandsome.

Anisha cleared her throat, bestirring him from his apparent reverie.

He lifted those hard eyes to hers again,

but this time they had softened a little. "I had heard, after our last meeting, that you were to be married," he said, his voice uncharacteristically quiet.

"Did you?" she said sharply. "To whom?"

But she knew the answer to that.

"To Lord Bessett," he said. "And frankly, of all the gentlemen in the St. James Society — however suspicious I am of the whole lot — in Bessett there is much to be admired. It would have been . . . easier, somehow."

"Easier?" She moved slowly toward him. "Easier in what way?"

She had the satisfaction of seeing his face color faintly. "Will you make me answer that question, Lady Anisha?" he asked softly. "I think you know I hold you in the highest regard — and you also think, no doubt, that I have looked too high in my admirations."

"Why do the English always say 'no doubt' so frequently and so authoritatively?" Anisha murmured. "Especially when there is every doubt? You cannot know what I think."

"Perhaps not," he conceded. "But I daresay you *do* know what I think — and fairly precisely, I fear."

Anisha could only stare at him for a moment, for his supposition was not in the least rhetorical. "Is that what all this honesty is about?" she murmured. "Do you imagine

I . . . well, that I am like Lord Ruthveyn? That I *know* things even when they remain unsaid?"

"I find your brother unnerving," Napier confessed. "He makes my hair stand on end, to be honest."

"Much of the time, my brother is a mystery to me," she said truthfully. "But I am perfectly ordinary, I assure you."

"Oh, hardly that!" he interjected.

"And if I know what you are thinking," she continued, "it is with a woman's intuition, and no more. You say I must think you look too high. I say you pay me a great compliment by looking at all. You say you esteem me. But I would say you scarcely know me."

His smile was muted. "True, but it seems not to matter," he replied. "And you, I daresay, are using that fact to get what you want. Or Lazonby is. But oddly enough, I almost do not mind. It shames me a little to say that I could be so weak."

Anisha could only respond honestly. "Perhaps I am using you," she admitted. "But as arrogant as I find you, I do find your company oddly refreshing. Should you choose to renege on your offer, Mr. Napier, we will part as friends."

"Will we?" he interjected, his smile doubtful.

"We will," she said more firmly. "And no, as you've likely concluded, I am not to be married. But Lord Bessett is. My brother may have longed to see us make a match of it, but that was mere wishful thinking on his part."

"And so we are back to Lord Lazonby," he said quietly.

"I suppose we are," she finally answered.

"Have you . . . any sort of understanding with him?"

"That is really none of your business," said Anisha, "but no, I have not."

"But you still wish to see his case files?"

"I wish to see the files in the murder of Lord Percy Peveril," she corrected, "as we discussed some days past. Now, may I?"

His eyes warmed a little dangerously. "Yes," he said. "For a price."

"What sort of price?"

"An evening of your company," he said.

Anisha narrowed her gaze. "Are you doing this to make Lazonby jealous? It won't work, you know. Most days I wonder he knows I'm alive."

Napier shrugged. "Then both of you are fools," he said. "But no, I am doing it because you intrigue me. I am doing it

227

because I would like to spend an evening in your company."

"An evening?" she asked guardedly. "Or a night? For the latter, I assure you, will not happen."

The warmth in his eyes deepened to near merriment. "A *night* — ?" he murmured. "Well. *That* would be looking high indeed, my lady."

Anisha felt her cheeks flush. "Very well, you ask only for an evening," she acknowledged. "May it be a night of my choosing? With no constraints or preconditions?"

This time, he hesitated. "Yes," he slowly answered.

"Then will you agree to dine with me?" she asked. "In my home, tomorrow night?"

He blinked once before answering. "Very well, yes. There, are you pleased, Lady Anisha? It appears I am at your command."

"Lovely," she said. "Come at six. I think you know the address. Now, may I have two hours with that fat file upon your desk?"

"Pray make yourself at home." Napier waved toward the desk with a flourish. "Sir George is expecting me at the Home Office for a meeting. In the meantime, I shall instruct my clerks to leave you undisturbed."

"Thank you." With that, Anisha went to

the desk and began to unwind the cashmere wrap.

Napier, however, followed her. "And Lady Anisha?" His hand shot out to seize her wrist — gently, but very firmly. "You are welcome to copy anything you like from that file. But if you dare take anything — *anything* — I will know it. And I reserve the right to search your person before you leave."

Anisha could only look at him and nod.

Lazonby leaned back against the rough-hewn tavern bench and quaffed the first inch of a stout porter, sucking down the foam along with it, his gaze focused sharply through the front window. The rumble of noonday conversation around him had been pushed to the far reaches of his mind, for a stone cottage some thirty yards down the lane held the whole of his attention.

The house was large for a cottage, with six windows up and two bow windows down, a front door painted glossy blue, and a wide garden gate arched over with a tangle of climbing rose. Situated directly in the sun as it was, and the season approaching late May, the bramble was already dotted with tight, green buds so small one's eye had to search, very near, in order to see them.

It would be a white rose, he thought, when the blooms burst.

White like the trim round the cottage's windows and the little vine-covered pergola round back. He had seen that, too, several days past when he'd trailed Coldwater up to the village, then crouched by the rose bush until dusk so that he might climb over the high garden wall. There the white paint had been so fresh that even now he could smell the sharp stench of it in his nostrils.

That's how it was with white. It was a deceptive color. The color of priests and purity and that new peculiarity, wedding gowns. And yet it was also the color of burial shrouds, of cumulous clouds heavy with rain, and of quaking, cowardly surrender.

Himself, he'd never waved the white flag. Not in battle. Not in life. And the shroud? That, too, he'd somehow avoided. But he'd sure as hell been rained on, literally and metaphorically.

He'd been rained on, in fact, today — around four in the morning, when he had returned home not from a night of carousing but from cracking the lock on Coldwater's third-floor office. It had been a bit of a trick, that. And yielded him nothing. Cold-water's desk at the *Chronicle* was that of a wraith; absent anything that told of the man's character.

"Bangers and mash!"

This pronouncement was punctuated by the *thunk!* of heavy crockery striking the oak tabletop.

He looked up to see the serving girl staring at him, her plain face fixed in an equally bland expression, a thick cloth held limply in one hand.

"Thank you," he said, flashing a wide grin. "Smells delicious."

Finally a soft smile curled her mouth. "Oh, 'tis good, sir," she confirmed, tilting her head at his nearly full glass. "Fetch you another?"

"Ah, that might make my head swim," he said, giving her a little wink. "Worse, I mean, than your pretty blue eyes."

"Oh, go on with you!" She smacked his shoulder with her folded cloth. "Anything else, then?"

"Not at present," he said. "But perhaps I'll think of something, if it means you'll come back?"

She laughed. And they both knew he wasn't going to think of something. Not that sort of something.

Still, it was a small enough thing to do, to cheer up a plain girl a bit with a little light flirtation. Besides, she had a lovely, if slightly too plump, figure, and eyes that radiated honesty. Indeed, he sensed not a whit of malice in her. And plain, perhaps, was not the word. The truth was, most women of good heart were pretty in one way or another if a man just took the time to look. So he looked. And he flirted. For no reason. For any reason.

And thinking of all that, for reasons he could not explain, made him long for the one woman he *didn't* flirt with.

How perverse. How *pathetic.*

But the girl's smile had become a grin. "Ta, then," she said, her mood and her step lightening as she turned to swish away. "Have a lovely afternoon."

But at the last instant, he thought of something and caught her wrist, more roughly than he'd intended. She must have made a sound of surprise, for a silence fell across the room, mistrust surging, every eye turning.

"Sorry." Lazonby released her. The girl flashed a carefree glance all around. After a moment's hitch, the tavern regulars fell back into conversation.

That was a small thing, too; a village

thing, to watch out for one another. He was just an interloper, unknown to them all, for though Hackney lay on the fringe of greater London, it was a small place still.

The girl was looking at him enquiringly.

"Are you permitted to sit a moment?" he asked.

"Suppose so," she said, already sliding onto the opposite bench. "Yours was the last from the kitchen."

Lazonby fished in his pocket, then snapped a shiny new florin onto the table.

"Coo!" said the girl, picking it up. "What's that?"

"Two shillings," he said. "Newly minted."

The girl turned the reverse to the light. "Ooh," she said.

"Pretty enough to be a necklace, that is."

"Would you like that?" he asked. "To make a necklace of it? I can get it drilled with a hole, and a silk cord to wear it on."

Her smile fell. "What would I have to do for it?"

"Nothing like that," he said gently, sensing her unease. "It's just that I'm not from here, and I require a house."

"A house?" Her eyes widened. "Can't think 'ow I'd help with that."

"I just wanted to know about the village," he said. "It looks pretty. And friendly. And it's close enough to London to go by train or omnibus, isn't it?"

"Nearly so," she said, pointing over her shoulder. " 'Bus comes up Bethnal Green Road. And there's to be two stations open next year. Kingsland and . . . bless me, but I forget."

"Hackney," said the lone occupant of a table some five feet away. " 'Ow could you forget that one, Min?"

The girl laughed. "Right you are, Mr. Fawcett! Hackney Station."

Fawcett leaned nearer. "What sort of house are you looking for, sir?" he asked more conversationally. "Something to let? Or freehold?"

Lazonby shrugged. "Either, if it's the right sort of house," he said, trying to take the man's measure. "It's for my maiden aunt. She fancies village life, but she's of an age where I need to get her out of Shropshire and closer to London — not *too* close, though, if you take my meaning."

"Oh, aye," said the man, waggling his brows. "Got a mother-in-law in Croydon — and that's close enough for me."

Min giggled again. And the man, Fawcett, smiled. He wanted to suggest something, something to his own benefit, Lazonby's instinct told him. So he pressed on, pointing through the window. "I'll tell you what I like," he said. "I like that house. Has it ever been for sale?"

Fawcett's shoulders fell almost imperceptibly. "Funny you ask," he said, pushing away his empty pint and withdrawing a pipe from his coat pocket. "Changed hands per'aps two years ago."

"You . . . had something else in mind?" Lazonby ventured.

Fawcett looked surprised. "Matter of fact, I did," he admitted. "Got a brother with a place to let. But it's a few miles north, and not much of a village."

"Ah," said Lazonby. "Thank you, but I doubt it would suit her."

"Oh, well." Fawcett shrugged. "But that one, with the blue door, 'tis let now."

"Let, eh?" said Lazonby. "Long term, do you reckon?"

"Couldn't say." Fawcett was shaking tobacco from a leather pouch into his bowl. "Just a brother and sister there now. Keep to themselves, for the most part."

"Cook says they're Americans," Min added. "Dunno, meself. They look reg'lar to me."

"Seen them, have you?" said Lazonby, slicing off a bite of sausage.

"Mrs. Ashton goes to church most Sundays," she answered. "Very involved in their good works, she is — schools and orphanages and such — but the brother, now, never seen much o' him."

"Stays in London much of the time, I believe," said Fawcett, mashing his thumb deep into the bowl. "Has work of some sort in the City."

"Name's not Ashton, though," said Min thoughtfully. "Water . . . *something*."

"Waterston?" Lazonby suggested.

"No, *Cold*water," Fawcett interjected, as if it had just sprung to mind.

"Hmm," said Lazonby. "Aunt Aggie won't budge without I offer her a large garden and a house near to the church."

"Not that near one, for 'tis nonconformist," Min warned, dropping her voice. "She'll want St. John's, I daresay. It's but a little ways on."

"Oh," said Lazonby. "But she's spry enough, too. Yes, that house really is quite perfect. I don't suppose this Coldwater could be persuaded to give up the lease?"

But Fawcett no longer radiated interest. He stood, intent on smoking his pipe. "I'd doubt it," he said, dropping some coins onto his table. "Well, I'd best get back to the shop, Min. Good day to you both, and good luck to you, sir."

Min shrugged as he left. "There's folks will do near anything for money," she said a little sadly. "You might offer for the lease?"

"The sister, though," said Lazonby pensively. "She's a widow, it sounds. I'd hate to displace her if she's happy."

"Per'aps she in't?" said Min hopefully.

"I wish I knew," he said musingly. "I'm not in a huge rush. That house, it would be well worth waiting on. Perhaps they mean to go back to America someday? If that's where they're from."

Min leaned over the table and dropped her voice. "I could ask around," she said. "My ma knows the woman who takes in the washing there."

Lazonby chewed another bite of sausage. "Mightn't that tip this Coldwater chap off?" he said after swallowing. "The fellow might run up the price ridiculously high."

Min's eyes widened. "Oh, no, sir, I wouldn't let on!" she said earnestly. "I'll just have a bit of a coze with her next she's by. I'll just find out everything I can about them."

Lazonby smiled. "Well, that would be kind of you," he said. "I'll tell you what, you keep that florin — call it a finder's fee — and I'll bring you another for your necklace."

"Coo!" said Min again.

"In a few days' time, let's say?" he suggested. "But don't put yourself out, or get in trouble. Just take in what gossip comes your way. Promise?"

Shyly, she tucked the coin away. "Oh, don't fret o'er me, sir," she said. "I could talk the ears off a jug and none the wiser."

He let his eyes rest upon her, savoring for a moment the innocence and honesty the girl exuded. It was rare his Gift brought him any pleasure at all; rare that he saw anything beyond the malice or the deceit or the greed inside people. Over the years, he had learned it was best to simply shut it all out; to ignore it as one might a faint ringing in the ears.

A pity more people were not like Min, who wanted simply to help him, and not even for the coin but for the kindness of the thing. The sweet moment, however, was severed when the girl glanced at his glass and sprang up.

"Lord, you've gone dry as a bone, and here's me, running my mouth."

"You were helping me," said Lazonby.

She cut an apprehensive glance at the kitchen door. "Mightn't look that way to everyone."

Lazonby eyed her calmly across the beaten table. "You were helping me, Min," he repeated firmly. "If there's anything said, you point them this way. My name's Smith."

"Thank you, Mr. Smith." Her smile warmed again as she bobbed to him. "But I'd best fetch another pint, all the same."

By the time the clock at St. Martin's tolled half past one, Anisha was closing the file on Napier's desk. She had passed better than two hours undisturbed and yet felt oddly frustrated. The file laid out a case that was just as Rance had explained it, in pristine, methodical order.

It was perfect.

Too perfect.

There was nothing in Peveril's murder — at least nothing that had been documented — to indicate anyone besides Rance had had cause to wish him dead.

On a surge of frustration, Anisha jerked from her chair and went to the window to stare pensively at the courtyard below, or what she could see of it. The midday rush of bureaucrats was apparent from the sea of black top hats bobbing toward greater Westminster. Only one man remained immobile and wholly apart from the crowd — a thin young man tucked into the shadows, leaning back against the brickwork, a dark folio wedged under his arm.

Anisha drew a sharp breath.

Jack Coldwater?

Despite the fact that he'd cast off his usual mackintosh, there was something in the arrogant lift of his chin that made him unmistakable, even from this height. And in that moment of shock, the young man glanced up at the window, his gaze piercing.

As if the sill had scorched her fingers, Anisha jerked back from it.

She returned to Napier's desk and tried to collect her thoughts. It was nonsense, of course. Coldwater was not watching her. She had come in through Number Four, on the street side. Moreover, he could not know which window was Napier's — nor even that she had come to *see* Napier. And Rance's fears aside, Coldwater could have no interest in her. He was a newspaper reporter.

And where better to find something scandalous to write about than Scotland Yard?

That was it, of course. Coldwater was simply lying in wait, hoping to unearth some scrap of nefariousness that would help sell tomorrow morning's paper.

Anisha realized she was chewing her thumbnail again. She jerked it away, plopped back into Napier's chair, and returned her attention to the real crisis by

paging through the documents one more
time.

Every piece of paper in Napier's file —
save two — was carefully logged and numbered. There were pretrial statements from
Sir Arthur Colburne, and even his daughter
Miss Elinor Colburne. Six gentlemen who
had witnessed the quarrel between Rance
and Peveril, as well as three who had lived
adjacent to Peveril in the Albany, had been
interviewed, and most, it appeared, had
testified at the trial.

A man by the name of Wilfred Leeton had
been interviewed three times — he, Anisha
recalled, had operated the hell, though like
most of his ilk, he'd maintained that the
gathering had been a social one, and that
any gaming had been incidental. Still,
Anisha could see from the late Mr. Napier's
copious notes that Leeton had ceased such
entertainments not long after the murder,
having turned to other financial endeavors.

Anisha dutifully copied all their names
and jotted down the gist of their testimony
and statements. In this way, she slowly
reconstructed not just Nicholas Napier's
old case but a sort of time line of events as
well.

There were two documents, however, that
fit none of these categories. Tucked into the

back of the file like an afterthought were two bits of paper, each about seven inches square, which were clearly torn from Leeton's personal stationery. They were gaming vowels — or more precisely, informal notes of hand — one dated the night of Peveril's murder, the other two days prior. The latter one indicated that Mr. Leeton — or more properly, the house — owed Rance Welham £900. This had been refolded many times, much like the bits and pieces of paper Rance was forever shoving in his pockets.

The more recent one had been folded but once, and set forth that Lord Percy Peveril owed Mr. Welham the sum of £1,350. Oddly, on this one, someone had circled the engraving of Leeton's name and house number, and penciled beside it a phrase: *B.H. Syndicate?* It was a hand Anisha now recognized as the late Mr. Napier's, though she had no idea what it meant.

Anisha glanced at the amounts again. Those were quite large sums. And both, of course, legally unenforceable, could it be proven they were gaming debts; even Anisha had been in England long enough to know that. But for the gentlemen of the *ton* — and for Leeton, who aspired to do business with them — such promises were more binding than the laws of England. More sacred than the Ten Commandments. A gentleman might put off his haberdasher or his vintner or even his mistress. But she knew from Lucan's many misfortunes that a gentleman paid his gambling debts within the week — if not sooner — or was forever shamed.

Closing the file, Anisha mulled it over. Rance, according to the Crown's case, had killed a man who'd owed him money. Peveril's IOU had been given under duress, but given nonetheless. Nicholas Napier, however, had made a case that the men had quarreled over money, or perhaps over the insult. Something about it struck Anisha oddly.

An instant later, however, she heard a hard, purposeful tread coming across the old oak floors, and she knew that Napier approached.

On impulse, Anisha flipped the back of the folder open and snatched the notes. Later, she was never certain why she did it, but in the confusion of the moment it seemed somehow to matter. Moreover, the notes were not documented on the file log.

Swiftly, she tucked them up one of her sleeves, sliding them round her wrist so that they cupped inside her cuff. By the time Napier strode through the door, she was up and draping her shawl over her hair.

"Ah, you have written down a great deal, I see."

Anisha smiled. "My hand is so cramped, I believe I may have copied the entire file."

His gaze flitted over hers, then he came round the desk to flip the file open. "You must pardon me, my lady," he said, his eyes going to the log sheet, "if I do not entirely trust you."

"Well, I cannot say you did not warn me."

Feeling only a little guilty, Anisha moved to the other side of the desk and began to tidy her own papers, making a pretense of rearranging them. Napier did not sit — he could not, for she had not — but instead stood and went meticulously through the file, matching each document to the log attached to the file's front.

When at last he reached the back, Anisha held her breath and prayed.

For an instant, he hesitated, a furrow down the middle of his forehead. "Well, that's everything, then." He shut the file with a snap and looked up at her. "Is there anything else, Lady Anisha, that the Metropolitan Police might do for you?"

"Not today." Brightly, she smiled. "But tomorrow, dinner at six. Don't forget."

Napier's meeting at the Home Office must

have been dull, however, for it seemed to have given him time to grow suspicious. "I confess," he said, "you seem altogether too pleased about that dinner for my comfort."

"I am pleased," she said. "I enjoy your company. Besides, I needed another gentleman to make up my numbers. You will do perfectly."

"I beg your pardon?" Something in his face fell, then darkened. "Your . . . *numbers?*"

Lightly, she touched her temple. "Oh, yes, did I not say?" she returned. "I am giving a dinner party."

"A dinner party?" he said, his outrage apparent.

"Indeed, but this is one you will wish to attend," said Anisha in a conspiratorial tone, "for it is in honor of Lord Bessett and Miss Anaïs de Rohan."

"I beg your pardon?" he said again. "In honor of Bessett and . . . *who?*"

"Miss de Rohan," said Anisha cajolingly. "Bessett's fiancée. Surely you must know her? She is, I believe, the eldest daughter of the Vicomte de Vendenheim-Sélestat. I take it you had not heard the happy news?"

"Lord Bessett —" Napier's face darkened like a storm cloud. "Lord *Bessett* is marrying *de Vendenheim's daughter?*"

245

"Marvelous, is it not?"

"Marvelous?" he bellowed. "Tell me, ma'am, is there any conniving thing those people will not do to —"

"*What* people?" she cut in.

"*The St. James Society!*" Napier gritted. "Was having the Queen in his pocket not enough for your brother? He had to marry Bessett off for the cause?"

Anisha drew herself up to every fraction of her fifty-eight inches. "Mr. Napier, my brother earned the Queen's loyalty by risking his life for England," she said tartly. "And at present, he's on a ship bound for Calcutta, completely unaware of this betrothal. Moreover, scarcely two hours ago you thought he'd arranged for *me* to marry Bessett."

Napier hesitated for a moment, his eyes narrowing. "Oh, this cannot be coincidence," he said grimly. "The fact that one of the most powerful men in the Home Office — a man high above *me* — is now going to be a pawn of the St. James Society? It is beyond mortal comprehension, madam. It is unconscionable."

Anisha looked him straight in the eyes. "Well, I am admittedly new to London," she said. "But I had somehow understood this de Vendenheim fellow to be a singularly independent and hard-nosed man. The very personification of good triumphing over evil, et cetera. So the notion of him being anyone's pawn is . . . well, vastly enlightening."

Napier realized then what he'd just said. He fell utterly silent, his face coloring.

Pulling open his top desk drawer with a ferocious yank, he dropped the Peveril file into it and slammed it shut with a *bang!* Clearly, he wished her to go.

Anisha did not go.

"Mr. Napier," she said, gentling her tone. "Admittedly I am not the most fashionable of society's hostesses, but I am inviting you into our home with all goodwill. Moreover, I am offering you an incredible social opportunity."

"Ah, looking high again, am I?" He turned to stare out the window now, refusing to hold her gaze. "You think I'll jump at the chance to hobnob with the *ton?* Well, you may think again, my lady."

"Oh, for pity's sake, who gives a fig for the *ton?*" she said sharply. "No, I am offering you the chance to befriend de Vendenheim's daughter and future son-in-law — a man whom, by your own admission, you are already inclined to like. Indeed, no one else from the Home Office has been invited.

Not even the Home Secretary himself."

He cut her an odd, sidelong glance. "Just me, eh?"

"Just you," she said. "And you are coming as a friend of the hostess."

"I don't give a fig for politics, either," he grumbled.

"I never thought you did," she said. "But I daresay you give a very great fig with regard to de Vendenheim's favor. Indeed, to account him something of an acquaintance — well, that, I should think might come in handy during your investigations."

"Hmph," said Napier. But he was clearly mulling over her argument. "I know de Vendenheim slightly, and his reputation very well. I spoke rashly when I used the word *pawn.* He is more like a battering ram. He is no one's fool."

"Nor, I think, are you," said Anisha quietly.

"*You* tricked me," he said.

"I did not," she returned. "You said an evening — not *a night* — at the time of my choosing, with no preconditions."

"I meant . . . well, something rather more private than a dinner party," he said.

"Alas, you did not stipulate," said Anisha lightly. "So, will you come?"

His eyes narrowed again, and Anisha realized she might have underestimated him.

After a long moment passed, he spoke. "You came here meaning to persuade me to attend this dinner party, didn't you?" he said, his voice low and accusing. "You were very confident of yourself, too. You needed another gentleman, and you thought I'd leap at the chance."

"You seem intent on making this into something nefarious," she said, forcing a calm she did not quite feel, "when I'm merely inviting you to dinner."

"But you've left it rather late," he pointed out. "Too late, really, to graciously invite anyone else should I refuse."

"It would make no sense for you to refuse," Anisha said.

"It would make a great deal of sense if I wished to make a point."

"And that point would be?"

"That I am not a toy to be played with, madam, as it suits you," he said, planting both hands on his desktop and leaning over it almost predatorily. "No, I think that we shall re-strike our bargain in a way that better suits *me.*"

Anisha did not falter. "Very well. I am amenable to compromise."

"Then I shall come to your dinner party," he said tightly. "I will put on my finest suit of clothes, do my best to keep my elbows off Lord Ruthveyn's dinner table, and try not to trip over my tongue —"

"Oh, what nonsense!" Anisha interjected. "You are quite as polished as any gentleman, Mr. Napier. Pray get on with it."

"All in good time," he returned. "I'm thinking."

"No, you are scheming," she returned.

"Well, you ought to know it when you see it," he grumbled. "You, Lady Anisha, are very unassuming. You purposely put people off their guard. Like a pretty jewel, you are dainty and vivid, thus one does not at first notice all those sharp facets."

"If you mean I'm not some sort of doormat, you are quite right," she answered. "I was once; I cannot recommend it. Now, you want something of me. What?"

"I want you to go to the theater with me," he said. "I have the loan of a box."

Anisha lifted both eyebrows in surprise. "The theater?" she murmured. "Why, how very kind."

But it was not entirely kind. He simply meant, like most men, to have his way. Anisha, however, was not stupid. If it came to it, she had Frankie Fitzwater on the hook to make up her dinner numbers. Still, for reasons she could not quite explain, she very much wanted Napier at that party.

Keep your friends close, Rance had said, *and your enemies closer.*

But which was Royden Napier?

She did not know. And since she did not know, there was only one thing, really, to be done.

"If we may go as friends," she finally said, "and if I may bring my brother, Lord Lucan Forsythe —"

"Yes, yes, of course," he interjected.

"Then yes, I should love to. What will we be seeing?"

"Les Huguenots."

"Les Huguenots?" Anisha felt her eyes widen. "I thought it was gone!"

"It is reopening at Covent Garden." His gaze suddenly warmed. "You are a serious fan of the opera?"

Anisha blushed. "Well, we did not see a vast deal of it in Calcutta," she said on a laugh. "But yes, I have become very fond of it indeed. In fact, I just saw Donizetti's *L'Elisir d'Amore* with — ah, but never mind that."

"Yes, I saw you there," he interjected. "With Lazonby and Lord Bessett's mother, Lady Madeleine MacLachlan."

He had seen her there?

A sudden chill seemed to fall over the

room. Was this really about Napier's interest in her?

Less certain now, Anisha soldiered on. "So you saw us," she said lightly, wondering if he'd been there by chance or for some other purpose. "Then doubtless you noticed, too, that Lazonby slept through it."

"As I've said before," Napier murmured, "the man is a Philistine, amongst other, less savory things."

Anisha grew very quiet. "I am very much afraid, Mr. Napier," she finally said, "that you and I shall soon part company if you insist upon insulting a gentleman I account my friend — however unenlightened his tastes may be."

Napier made a curt bow. "I see I must bide my time," he said stiffly, "and permit Lazonby to prove what he is — which, inevitably, he will do."

"Oh, I already know precisely what Lazonby is," she said, her hand already on the doorknob. "And my feelings for him — whatever they are — will not change. Now, do you still wish to dine with me? Do you still wish to go to the theater? As friends? Feel free to say yes or no."

For a long moment he was perfectly silent. "Yes to both, then," he finally answered, but he did not look happy. "And now I'd best say good day to you, ma'am. I shall see you at dinner tomorrow. And at the theater the week after that."

A few moments later, Anisha found herself emerging from the haze of sweat and overcooked vegetables to step out into the still-crisp air of a spring day, drawing her paisley shawl snug about her shoulders as she went. On the distant side of Whitehall Street, she could see the carriage, and Brogden, their burly coachman, lingering almost guardedly on the pavement near the Admiralty.

She hastened up the street, but just as she neared the corner, a figure practically leapt into her path. Anisha jerked her gaze up, straight into the frigid blue-green eyes of Jack Coldwater.

He threw out a hand as if to block her path. "I beg your pardon," he said, "but you cannot help him, you know, by coming here. You cannot change the truth."

Anisha drew herself up to her full height. "I beg your pardon, sir, but we have not been intro —"

"I should hope, ma'am," he interjected, eyes ablaze, "that something so dire as an innocent man's murder would obviate the need for petty formalities."

"Then you would think wrongly." Anisha lifted her skirts to brush past him. "I shan't bandy words in the street with a stranger. Kindly step from my path."

But Coldwater blocked her, snaring her arm near the elbow and almost dragging her back. On the other side of Whitehall Place, two men froze uncertainly. From the corner of her eye, she could see Brogden hastening across the street.

Anger rising, she jerked against Coldwater's grasp. "Unhand me, sir."

But he did not. "I do not know what manner of game you play, Lady Anisha," he growled, tightening his grip, "but I know this: Lazonby is a cold-blooded killer."

"You are stark mad," she said sharply. "How dare you!"

"But you saw him!" Coldwater's words were choked with rage. "By God, you *saw* him attack me in the library that day. *He* was the madman! Not m —"

His words were cut off when Brogden seized his coat collar, flinging Coldwater aside as if he'd been weightless. The young man sailed with a crash onto the railing alongside Number Four, his hat tumbling off to reveal his shock of bright red hair.

The coachman brandished a beefy fist. "Get up, yer little blighter!" he roared. "Get up and I'll give yer a taste o' this to go wiv it."

Coldwater responded with a curse, staggering to his feet. Across the way, the two men had been joined by two more, these in uniform.

"Thank you, Brogden." A little shaken, Anisha leaned across and laid her hand on his arm. "Come, leave him. Let us go."

Turning, Brogden's countenance softened. "Aye, then," he snarled over his shoulder, "and good riddance."

Coldwater, however, was not done. "Yes, go, Lady Anisha!" he shouted, snatching up his hat. "Go back to that devil's coven of your brother's! Do you think I don't know what you people are? You ought to be burned as witches, the lot of you."

"Pay 'im no heed, m'lady," Brogden grimly advised, urging her up the street.

But the young man continued to shout after her. "You've done naught but fall in with Lazonby's lies," he cried. "He's a murderer! And all of you know it!"

On the edge of Whitehall Street Anisha froze, trembling with sudden rage. "Wait here," she commanded, extracting her hand from Brogden's arm.

Then she turned and marched back down the street to face Coldwater, who looked incongruous with his wool jacket twisted awkwardly about him. But he had shut his mouth, and his eyes had widened at her return.

"You are a newspaperman, Mr. Coldwater, I believe," she said tartly.

"So?" His eyes narrowed with suspicion.

"My point being, sir, that you cannot be an utter fool," she went on, "but merely a misguided lunatic. For surely a reporter knows the laws of defamation? The economic risk, if you will, of standing in a public thoroughfare and calling innocent people witches and murderers?"

"Mind your own business," said Coldwater.

Anisha stabbed a finger in his face. "You made this my business," she retorted, "when you seized my arm and bruised it. And when you slandered me in front of that growing crowd. Shall I go back inside Number Four and show the porter these marks upon my arm? Shall I tell him you have just maligned a peer of the realm in the middle of Whitehall?"

"I did no such thing," Coldwater gritted, but he was inching away from her now.

Anisha turned on the street to face the four gentlemen — who now numbered five — and spoke in a calm, carrying voice. "I am Lady Anisha Stafford, widow of Captain John Stafford, late of the Bengal Horse," she said. "This madman has just assaulted and slandered me in front of you. Who amongst you is gentleman enough to go inside and give the porter your name as a witness?"

Scarcely a heartbeat passed before a whiskered man in the red and black of the 11th Hussars jerked off his shako and stepped across the street. "My brother was at Sobraon and Ferozeshah with the Ninth Foot," he said. "I'll gladly go. But first, ma'am, if we might just dispatch this rascal for you —"

Coldwater, however, had already snatched up his folio and was striding down the street in the direction of the river. And in the back of her mind, Anisha was already wondering what on earth she was to tell Rance.

The answer came to her at once. *Nothing.*

Coldwater really was half mad, just as Rance had always maintained. And there was no point in further inciting Rance's anger. No point in writing to Raju. No point, really, in telling anyone at all.

Anisha turned to the officer and smiled. "Why, I believe you have run that fellow off!" she said. "I thank you, sir, and bid you good day."

Back across the main thoroughfare, Anisha waited until Brogden had let down the steps

257

of the carriage. Then, as he straightened, she set a finger to her lips, warning in her eyes.

Brogden's amiable countenance darkened. Then it relented, and he gave her a conspiratorial nod.

"Aye, then, ma'am," he said. "As ye wish."

Anisha climbed inside. "St. James's Place," she ordered, "but not for long."

Across from the St. James Society, just as she'd hoped, Mr. Ringgold was manning the door at the Quartermaine Club, though it was now just midafternoon. Anisha descended, ordering Brogden to turn the coach at the end of the lane.

"Mr. Ringgold," she said, marching across the street, "be so good as to go downstairs and ask Mr. Quartermaine if he might see me. But across the street, if he would be so kind."

"Hmph," Pinkie grunted, casting a disparaging glance at the St. James Society. But he went, Anisha watching through the glass as he descended the stairs. Hastening across the narrow lane, she requested that tea be sent up to the club's private library.

She was still standing by the window, pondering her words, when it arrived. Quartermaine came in on the footman's heels, his hat still in hand. His eyes were distrustful, but his smile was wry.

"Well, Lady Anisha," he said. "To what do I owe the extraordinary pleasure of being summoned across the street in the middle of my workday?"

She felt her cheeks warm. "I beg your pardon for that," she said. "It was badly done of me. But I thought you mightn't wish an unattended lady calling on you."

His gaze swept down her length. "Actually, I can think of nothing more pleasant," he murmured, "than a lady unattended — especially if she's pretty."

Anisha felt her spine stiffen. "Mr. Quartermaine, it is not necessary to flirt with me."

He shrugged almost lazily. "Most ladies of the *ton* seem to expect it of me," he said, the wry smile shifting to something darker. "And one does hate to disappoint. But this, I collect, is pure business?"

"It is a sort of business, yes," she said with asperity. "I wish your opinion of something. Will you sit down and have a cup of tea?"

"With all respect, ma'am, I have plenty of my own business across the street." Quartermaine propped one shoulder on the doorframe, having hardly entered the room. "More than I can manage, most days."

"Yes," she said briskly. "Yes, I do forget

you've young men to fleece."

"Just so," he said blandly, all flirtation gone from his eyes. "But you may ask me whatever you please, so long as it's quickly done. I'll help you if I can."

Resigned, Anisha withdrew the notes she'd stolen from Napier's file. "I wish you to look at these," she said, thrusting them at him.

He did so, his eyes methodically scanning each, then gave a low whistle. "I don't think I want to know where you got them."

"You do not," she agreed. "Just tell what you think of them. Are they real? Would someone do murder over such a sum?"

"I've seen men knifed over two shillings," he said, passing them back to her. "And yes, they look real enough to me. Why don't you ask Lazonby?"

She snared her lip between her teeth. "I shall probably have to," she confessed.

"Ah," said Quartermaine. "Then he did not give them to you?"

Anisha realized he was probing. "Obviously not," she replied, pointing at the circled word. "And what about this notation? '*B.H. Syndicate?*' Have you any idea what it means?"

Quartermaine's eyes flicked over the paper

again, this time obviously catching on the word.

"Well?" she said.

"It looks insignificant to me," he finally replied, picking up his hat.

It was clearly the end of their conversation. "Thank you," she answered, tucking the notes into her reticule. "I'm very sorry to have troubled you, but I didn't know who else to ask."

Quartermaine bestirred himself lazily from the door. "Well, I might venture to suggest," he said, "that perhaps you ought not ask anyone at all."

She paced toward him. "Whatever do you mean?"

He tipped his hat toward the reticule she'd tossed onto one of the leather sofas. "If you wish my honest opinion, ma'am, those notes make me fear you're meddling in things — perhaps dangerous things — that are none of your affair," he said. "Lazonby, however wretched he may think himself, is, at the very least, free — and still breathing. Perhaps there comes a time to let well enough alone."

Anisha felt herself quiver with indignation. "Is that some sort of threat, sir?"

His eyes softened; genuinely, she thought. "Certainly not, ma'am," he said, slapping his hat back on his head as he left. "But it is what we here in the gaming business would call *very sound advice.*"

CHAPTER 7

Of paled pearls and rubies red as blood.
William Shakespeare, "A Lover's Complaint"

"Ooh, my lady, you do look a sight!"

With that, Janet stepped back to admire the reflected glory of the long string of pearls she'd just wrapped round Anisha's neck — wrapped it twice, as a matter of fact, and then a third time.

"Oh, Janet, I don't know." Anisha stared into the dressing mirror, her hand coming up to touch the ruby clasp. "They just seem so . . . *ostentatious.*"

Janet set her head to one side. "Well, they are a show, ma'am, I do admit."

Anisha stood, went to the cheval glass, and turned a little sideways. "How many are there, one wonders?" she murmured.

"Two hundred and ninety-three." Janet spoke with confidence. "I counted 'em once."

The lowest strand hung below Anisha's breasts, which were nearly bared by her low-cut dinner gown. Against the emerald green silk and her honey-colored skin, the pearls seemed pale as milk. Almost stark, really.

The priceless strands had belonged to her Scottish grandmother, a tall, imperious woman who, even bent with age, had reached almost to Raju's shoulder. Not especially happy with her son's choice of bride, the good lady had made but one yearlong sojourn to India to see her grandchildren. Nonetheless, at her death, the elegant pearls had come to Anisha, her only granddaughter.

And Anisha loved them. She'd even been passing fond of her grandmother, for she now understood how hard it was to meld two cultures into one. Doing so had been the single hardest challenge of her life, and it had brought with it more pain than even her marriage, which had been more of a slow drift into disappointment.

But all the struggle aside, Anisha truly valued her Scottish half just as much as her Indian half. The pearls, however, having been strung for a far larger woman, seemed overwhelming on Anisha's small frame.

And they simply weren't her.

However hard she might try, Anisha suddenly realized, she would never appear — or feel — especially British. And tonight, inexplicably, she felt tired of trying. On impulse, she snapped the ruby clasp open and sent the pearls clattering into the porcelain dish on her night table.

"There," she said, lifting her gaze. "That's better."

Janet tilted her head in the other direction. "I don't know, ma'am," the maid finally said. "Now you look . . . well, *starkers.*"

Returning to her dressing stool, Anisha agreed. Absent the pearls, the emerald gown seemed to bare her flesh from shoulder to shoulder, and nearly down to her nipples. The dress was newly made up by one of London's most fashionable modistes, and very much *le dernier cri* — more so than anything Anisha owned.

But no. It would not do.

A mad, impulsive notion seized her. And then, the more she thought on it, the notion began to feel more brilliant than foolish. "Mother's kundan choker," she finally said. "That's what's needed — and fetch me her green and blue sari. The paisley one."

Janet made a wincing expression. "Oh, ma'am, I don't think English ladies wear them sort o' things," she said. "Not to a

265

dinner party."

But Anisha looked again at her bare shoulders and decided. "This one does," she said. "At least after a fashion. Oh, and the brooch and earrings! I'll need them, too. Besides, Janet, it is my party. I believe I shall do as I please."

Janet set her fists on her hips and grinned. "Well, bully for you, ma'am," she said. "I'll find that thing in three shakes."

The maid trotted good-naturedly off to the dressing room. Anisha unlocked the jewel case and lifted out the pieces she wanted. The long, dangling earrings were easily put on. Then, with Janet's help, she fastened the choker. It lay cool and heavy round her neck like a wide golden collar, the finely hammered metal glowing behind the alternating rows of rose-cut diamonds and multihued gemstones. The last row, the short dangles made of alternating emeralds and sapphires, served to draw the eye up from her bodice.

The distraction was further enhanced when Anisha pleated the sari and fastened it near her right hip with the brooch. Then, wrapping it round behind her back, she brought it over her left shoulder and fanned out the pleats a bit, leaving it to hang almost to her knee, rather like a long, elegant shawl.

"Now," said Janet a little triumphantly, "the peacock feathers!"

"Why not?" said Anisha.

In a trice, the feathers were found and pinned into her hair. Not so much a hat as a sort of headpiece, the long and elegant plumes gave Anisha the illusion of height — well, relatively speaking.

Leaving the dressing table, she returned to the cheval glass and let her gaze sweep critically down. The ensemble looked good, if a bit exotic. The sari was not made to be worn in quite that fashion, admittedly. Yet Anisha found it comfortable. Such was her life, now more than ever — a hash of different worlds.

Janet was plucking at one of the pleats to straighten it. "I like this," she said. "It's a bit like what her ladyship called an arisaid, but silk."

Her ladyship, Anisha knew, was a term the servants had used for her grandmother, but rarely, if ever, for Anisha's mother.

"An arisaid?" she echoed. "What is that?"

"A long shawl of a thing," said Janet. "But you'd not remember it, I'm sure. Lud, I barely do. But if the weather was the least snappish, she'd throw it over her shoulder and pin it on with a big, silver brooch. Sometimes she belted it. Odd, it was."

Anisha searched her mind and came up with just the vaguest memory. But it skittered away again when she heard a carriage slow, then come rattling through the gateposts.

"Heavens, Janet." Anisha's hand fluttered to the choker, as if touching it might give her strength. "Has someone come early?"

Together they hastened through to her sitting room. At the window, Anisha drew back the underdrapes with one finger and peered down. The carriage, an elegant black landau, was drawing to a halt in the semicircular drive. It was easily recognized, for it bore the arms of the Earl of Lazonby and was the same carriage that had brought Anisha from the docks that long-ago day. Rarely, however, had she seen it since, for Rance — independent to the bone — preferred to drive himself, or simply to walk.

The first and second footmen were going down the stairs, but Rance, as usual, was ahead of them, and looking altogether too handsome for Anisha's taste.

Having already thrown open the carriage door, he leapt down unaided, his brass-knobbed stick and top hat caught together in one hand, his black evening cloak billowing out behind to reveal a shimmering, pewter-colored lining. Beneath it he wore a black tailcoat and trousers with an elegant white cravat, and save for his unruly, wind-tossed curls, he looked every inch a man of fashion.

Up close, however, Anisha knew it would be different. No amount of tailoring would ever cloak Rance Welham in civility, for a rough-edged mercenary always shone through any veneer fine fashion might provide.

Janet made a low sound of feminine appreciation. "Lord love us, ma'am, if it isn't Lazonby all togged out to the nines," she murmured, "and a fine specimen of manhood he is, too."

"Yes, and he knows it," muttered Anisha, remembering their last parting. "He is also a full forty minutes early."

"Want me to have Higgenthorpe put him in the parlor to cool his heels?"

"No." Anisha let the curtain fall. "No, Janet, I shall go down. How do I look?"

The maid's critical eye ran down her. "Well, not very English," she said.

Lazonby went up the steps feeling oddly out of place for reasons he couldn't explain. Hadn't he entered this house at least a hundred times before? Two hundred, more like. And yet tonight something hung over him, portentous and unspoken — something besides this rare foray into polite society.

Or perhaps it was the overly elaborate cravat Horsham had practically lynched him with. Perhaps it was choking off the air — oxygen, Dr. von Althausen called it — from his brain.

In Ruthveyn's grand entrance hall, all was as usual; the fine paintings marching up and down the walls, the smell of beeswax in the air, and the thick green Turkish carpet rolled out across the marble floor like a strip of lush bottomland.

Higgenthorpe greeted him warmly, carefully draping Lazonby's evening cloak across his arm and taking the hat and stick as they waltzed through their usual routine of enquiring after one another's health and remarking upon the weather.

This time, however, Anisha interrupted from the landing. "Hello, Rance," she said coolly. "You're rather early."

Lazonby turned, his breath catching at the sight. Something deep in his chest seemed to twist as she flowed gracefully down the staircase, drawing his eyes like a compass to north.

But he regained himself and grinned. "I was all out of whisky," he teased. "And I knew you would feel sorry for me."

She flicked him an odd look as he approached. "That once-dependable old saw is losing teeth, my dear, at a prodigious rate," she said.

He dared not ask what she meant but caught both her hands in his and kissed her cheek anyway. "Anisha," he murmured, drawing back to look her up and down. "You look . . . my God — *breathtaking.*"

She drew her hands from his with a chiding glance. "Oh, don't flirt with me, Rance," she said, breezing efficiently past him and toward the parlor. "Seriously, do you want a sherry? Or something stronger?"

"Something stronger," he said. "If you don't mind."

Following on her heels, he watched the trailing paisley thing shimmer like a silken waterfall behind her as she moved. Anisha's hair was twisted up tonight to reveal the swanlike turn of her neck, the arrangement adorned with peacock feathers that matched the dangling strands of emeralds and sapphires she wore in her ears. He caught up with her just inside the room, and although his instincts were admittedly muted when it came to Anisha, he could still sense her discontent.

This, then, was the thing hanging over

271

him. It had to be. Anisha was still angry over his having left her in St. James. But the truth was, *she* had left *him*. No matter how desperately he'd wished to go after Coldwater, he would never have left a lady standing in the street.

An empty glass already in hand, she cut him an odd, sidelong glance, a smile playing at one corner of her mouth. "At least you came tonight," she said, drawing the stopper from Ruthveyn's whisky decanter. "I feared you mightn't, you know."

"Is that your way of saying you weren't sure you could count on me?" he asked, his voice deceptively light. "Because if memory serves, I have never failed you, Anisha. I have never made you a promise I did not keep. And I never will."

At that, she hesitated, the decanter tipped over the glass. "Do you know, I believe you are right," she quietly acknowledged. "So, did you run your quarry to ground last week?"

"Coldwater?" he said, watching her dainty, capable hands upon the crystal. "Oh, aye. Followed him all the way to Hackney. He's got a cottage there — and a sister, just as Pinkie claimed."

She poured herself a sherry, then led him toward the sofa opposite the hearth. Tonight the parlor had been opened onto the more formal withdrawing room by two sets of double doors in anticipation of the crowd.

He wished, suddenly, that it was the small, intimate room he was accustomed to. But he sat, and sipped for a moment at his whisky — even as he fought to keep his eyes from her. And yet he could feel her warm brown gaze upon him, strong and steady. It was a gaze a man could drown in were he not careful.

It struck him, and not for the first time, that he should simply stay away from Anisha. It would be easier, perhaps. Indeed, he should have insisted to Ruthveyn all those weeks ago to order Geoff to keep watch over his family. But Geoff had been slated to go to Belgium; for how long, no one had known. And Ruthveyn — well, Lazonby owed him. Owed him his very life, really. It was the least he could do, to keep young Luc from utter ruin and to bear Anisha company in her brother's absence.

The fact that it was beginning to feel like a knife twisting in his heart every time he saw her . . . well, that was a pain he would simply have to endure. And he could endure it. The long years in prison had steeled him to survive even when hope was lost.

"So," Anisha pressed, drawing him from

his reverie, "what sort of cottage do they have?"

"Oh, a fine, large one," he said casually. "With a deep rear garden. I got a look at the sister, too."

"Did you? How?"

He flashed a grin. "As any common Peeping Tom might," he replied. "I waited till dark, climbed over the garden gate, and watched her through a window."

"Rance!" she chided. "Well, what was she like?"

He shrugged. "Good-looking, with a great pile of chestnut hair," he said. "Something shy of thirty, I'd guess."

"And God knows you're accounted an expert in such matters," said Anisha with only a hint of sarcasm. "Did you see Coldwater?"

"No, but he was upstairs, for one of the lamps was lit," said Lazonby. "The bounder was probably burning the midnight oil, busy running down the reputation of his next victim."

Anisha laughed, and if it sounded a little forced, well, that was best overlooked. So Lazonby spent the next few minutes telling her what little he'd learned in the pubs and shops he'd visited during his forays into Hackney, realizing, as he stepped through it again, how very much he had needed to discuss it with her.

Coldwater and his sister had come from Boston a year or two earlier. The newspaperman was believed a little younger than she, and had never married. Nothing was known of the sister's husband save that he'd left his wife childless and situated comfortably enough that she could keep a gig, a nice cottage, and two servants who lived in.

At the end, Anisha sipped pensively at her sherry. "And that's it?"

"Aye." Lazonby searched his mind, but there seemed nothing more to say.

A quiet mood fell across the room, broken only by the ticking of the mantel clock, and by the clinking of silver and porcelain as the dining table was laid across the passageway. He polished off the last of his whisky and considered pouring himself another — he'd always made himself at home here — but a glance at the clock suggested he ought not.

Instead, he made the mistake of saying what was on his mind.

"Anisha, you're different tonight," he said. "And it's not just the exotic attire. You feel . . . distant."

"Do I?" she murmured, staring at him over her glass. "I thought your legendary intuition was useless with me."

"And my legendary charm," he said, forcing a smile. "You've always been immune to both."

She lowered her glass, and with it her gaze. "I believe that I am," she said quietly. "What I feel for you . . . well, it has nothing to do with charm."

"Nish." He reached out and brushed her cheek with the backs of his fingers. "We are beyond something so trivial as that, you and I. Aren't we?"

She looked away. "We are beyond a lot of things, I suppose," she said. "We have become — just as you once predicted — old friends."

He sobered his expression. "Aye, and I think any man worth his salt can sense when a woman whom he cares about is not perfectly content," he said. "I wish, my dear, that your spirits were half as high as your looks. I have never seen you more lovely."

At that, she set her glass away with a sharp *chink*. "Please, Rance, I am asking again," she said, her gaze drifting to the window. "Don't flirt with me. I'm tired of it."

"Nish, I don't flirt," he said, touching her lightly on the shoulder.

"Rance, really!" She trilled with laughter, but when she turned back, there was no humor in her eyes. "You are the worst womanizer in Christendom. You've admitted as much."

"Not with you," he said, dropping his hand. "Anisha, I do not flirt with you. Not — well, not since that first day."

"Then save your breath now," she said churlishly, picking up her sherry again. "There will be near a dozen ladies here shortly. One of them will surely suit you."

"Anisha," he murmured. "If this is about what happened in the garden —"

"Look, never mind," she said, rising abruptly. "I want to talk to you about something important."

He wanted to tell her that she was important; that on no account did he wish her unhappy. But something was off between them tonight. It was as if they danced a familiar tune together, yet slightly out of step. So he held his tongue and watched as she went to the small secretary by the door, dropped the front, and extracted a folio.

"I went to see Napier yesterday," she said, returning to her chair.

"Against my wishes," he said gruffly.

"Yes, but in keeping with mine," she retorted. "There was no connection to Coldwater that I could find. But I did take copious notes, which I wish you to read. I think it's nothing you don't already know, but see if a name or detail jogs your memory."

He sighed and held out his hand. "Very well. And thanks."

But she opened the folder and took out two small bits of paper. "Now these I simply stole," she said, passing them to him instead.

"You stole them?" His eyes widened. "From Napier's files?"

"Actually, I reappropriated them," she said, "because, unless I greatly misunderstand the laws of England, they are your property, not the Crown's. They should have been returned upon your exoneration."

He looked at both papers, mildly surprised. "I daresay you're right," he said. "These are, at least on their surface, legally enforceable instruments of debt."

"Yes, so long as no one quibbles about the gaming aspect of the thing," she dryly added. "I take comfort in knowing my travails with Luc have at least gained me an education. So, are they significant to the case in any way, do you imagine?"

"No, they were probably taken from my rooms in the police search." He tossed them back onto the file. "All water under the bridge now."

"Still, that's a lot of money," said Anisha in the tone of a good Scot.

"Aye, well, I played deep, Nish, in those days," he said ruefully. "Those debts are nothing to some I collected at the tables — and nothing to some I lost, once or twice."

"Still, your rare losses aside, there must have been a great many people who were glad to see the back of you when you headed off to Newgate."

"Oh, aye," he said quietly.

"And these notes of hand?"

He shrugged. "Worthless, I expect," he said. "As to the rest of my winnings, I spent that and plenty more on barristers and bribery. Just paying off the dashed hangman to turn his head cost me three hundred guineas."

"How did you manage it?" she murmured. "I have often wondered."

He stared long and hard at her over his whisky. "Sutherland did it," he said quietly. "Sutherland and Father. They took care of everything because, as the padre always says, the *Fraternitas* looks after its own."

"They did not do everything," she said with asperity. "They did not suffer through those awful years in the French Foreign Legion, fighting for their lives in North Africa. They did not live through the horror of being twice imprisoned."

She was defending him again; defending

him even though she was angry with him. And perhaps she had cause to be. The heavy silence washed back in.

"Listen, Nish," he finally said, slumping a little in his chair. "I owe you an apology for last week. For what happened between us. And for allowing you to drive off that day in St. James's."

"As if you could have stopped me?" she murmured a little haughtily.

"Oh, I could have stopped you, my girl," he said grimly. "Depend upon it. And next time, I *will*."

A dark, stubborn expression flitted across her face, as if she meant to snap back at him. Then suddenly Anisha bounded from her chair as if nervous energy propelled her, surrounding him in her exotic fragrance as she swept past. It was a scent he could have happily drowned in, he sometimes thought; a sort of Indian magnolia, she'd once said, blended with a touch of sandalwood. The result was a creamy, spicy, almost erotic perfume that was the very epitome of Anisha's personality.

"I don't want to quarrel with you anymore," she said, drifting about the room. "What's done is done."

"Nish." When he moved to follow her, she held up a staying hand.

"Pray keep your seat," she ordered. "I just . . . I'm all on edge. I need to move."

It was then, just as she turned, that her shawl slipped, revealing three faint bruises above her elbow. "Anisha — ?" he murmured, reaching out to touch her.

She slipped beyond his grasp and looked away. "It's nothing," she said. "I was roughhousing with the boys, I suppose."

And it *was* nothing. Still, his rush of sudden tenderness only added to his confusion. He shut it away and glanced at the clock, to see it was nearly six. Forcing himself to relax, he turned his whisky glass round and round, resisting the urge to comfort her. Even he could see that tonight she did not want his consolation. And he knew he should have been glad.

"You hate this, don't you?" he said. "Entertaining. Society. My God, you're even wearing a hat. Well, some feathers, at least."

She shrugged, pausing to pick up a Meissen figurine of an apple-cheeked lady holding a beribboned spaniel in her lap. "I don't precisely hate it," she said pensively, turning it to the light. "But do you know, I sometimes feel a little like this dog. He looks pampered, does he not? His every need is met. He sits, literally, in the lap of luxury."

Lazonby snorted. "Yes, well, luxury is

overrated."

"It can be, even for this little dog," said Anisha. "Sometimes I think you are one of the few people I know who actually understands that. We can see, you and I, that the ribbon round his neck is in fact a leash that flows to her hand. He is bound to her. Bound to his duty."

"And you think hosting this dinner is a duty?"

She looked at him a little wistfully. "I feel bound by English society," she said. "Sometimes."

Abruptly, Lazonby set away his glass and crossed the room, forgetting his vow. Taking her empty hand, he lifted it to his lips and pressed them hard to the back of it. "Nish," he whispered. "You are the best person I know. Just . . . be yourself. Be as you are tonight, in your mother's silks and jewels. Wear that — that thing wrapped —"

"A sari," she prompted.

"Yes, that." Absently, he stroked his thumb down the back of her hand. "Wear it as you please, and if you like, even put that pin back in your nose to —"

She stiffened. "You've never seen that."

"Nish, there's a little hole," he gently chided, "if one knows where to look. I know. I saw it the day I met you."

"Did you?" she murmured. "Oh, well. It's mostly for childbirth, you know. But my father, he hated it — once he noticed it, three months after the fact."

Rance felt his smile twist. "Nish, your father is dead," he said, "and now, the point is, no one who matters gives a —"

"*Don't* curse," she gently interjected. "And you don't understand. This isn't about what matters to me. If it were, I would never have left India. But this is about Tom and Teddy. *This* is their world. A world I chose for them, Rance, the day I married an Englishman. In that, Papa was right to chide me."

He hesitated, seeing her point. The English were a hidebound lot. "Aye, I'll give you that one," he reluctantly agreed. "But save for what you must do to help the lads get on, stop thinking in terms of *should*s and *ought*s. After tonight, just be Anisha. You don't owe the rest of us anything — especially me."

"Some days you act as if I owe you blind obedience," she said, lowering her gaze. "But I do owe you my loyalty and my . . . well, my friendship, Rance. You have ever been a friend to me. To all of us, really."

Anisha's eyes were focused, he realized, on their fingers, now entwined. Until that moment, he'd scarcely realized he had not

283

released her, and that she had made no move to withdraw.

Instead, her small, cool fingers lay curled in his, the soft scent of sandalwood and flowers still swimming all around them. Her head was turned slightly, exposing the warm, ivory length of her throat, and the tiny pulse point below her ear; a soft, creamy spot that all but demanded he set his lips to it and draw her scent deeper.

Lazonby closed his eyes and realized how desperately he yearned to simply pull her into his arms. To tuck her head beneath his chin and just to hold her close. Not in any sensual way — though it might quickly have come to that — but in the way one might hold a precious, treasured thing.

Unable to completely resist, and having forgotten the servants nearby, he cupped his empty hand around her cheek, lifting her face and turning her gaze back to his. But her warm, brown eyes seemed tonight to hold regret.

Oh, he didn't want that. Not for her, this woman whose price was truly above rubies. For her, he wished only joy, and to make smooth her path through life.

"Anisha," he whispered, "I wish —"

Just then, the knocker dropped, echoing through the downstairs. He cut an impatient glance at the door. He had the oddest sense that they were on the verge of something. But Anisha had fallen silent, one hand in his, the other still holding the Meissen.

"Well," he said, stepping back, "I suppose more duty calls you."

Hastily she set the figurine back down. "Rance, there is something — some*one* — I wish to warn you about."

But almost at once, Lord Lucan Forsythe came bounding down the stairs and into the room, his golden curls still damp, his sunny smile firmly in place. "Rance! Well met, old fellow."

"Evening, Luc," he returned. "You're looking in good spirits."

By the time the words were out of his mouth, the longcase clock at the foot of the stairs was striking six, and an instant later the massive front door swung open and Lazonby could hear familiar feminine laughter ringing down the passageway.

"That's Lady Madeleine," he said, urging Anisha toward Luc. "Go. See to your guests. I'll still be here when all of them are gone."

Her gaze flicked over his face one last time. "I am not at all sure of that," she said.

And then she was striding from the room, her silk wrap floating after her, leaving nothing but a cloud of sandalwood behind.

It was too late to ask her what she meant.

Lucan caught Anisha's arm as she came out of the parlor. "Come along, Sis," he said, grinning. "Curtains up!"

In response, she shot him a withering glance. But this was no time for serious regret. It was, however, time to stop gazing into Rance's eyes and acting like a foolish girl. Even now she could feel the comforting warmth of his hand on her face.

But he would likely be angry with her again before the night was out. Suddenly, something like tears welled in Anisha's eyes. How stupid she was! Blinking hard, she kept walking.

In the front hall, Geoff's mother, Lady Madeleine, and her husband, Mr. Merrick MacLachlan, were already divesting their cloaks. Geoff's much younger siblings were not present, his brother being at university in Scotland, and his sister still in the schoolroom.

Mr. MacLachlan was very dark, very tall, and more than a little intimidating, with hard eyes and a horrific scar curling like a scimitar's blade up his cheek. His wife, in contrast, was like pale, clear sunlight, with her pile of blonde hair and her frothy gown of yellow silk.

Before leaving for Belgium — and falling head over heels in love — Geoff had asked his mother to befriend Anisha, and the lady had graciously done that, and much more. Now she kissed Anisha warmly, and Anisha realized once again how grateful she was to have avoided wounding her new friend by refusing Geoff's suit.

Anisha's salvation in that regard, Anaïs de Rohan, was alighting from the next coach with her elderly cousin, Maria Vittorio, her parents having not yet returned from their travels. Miss de Rohan's foster brother, Nate Corcoran, and her twin, Armand, followed them out, and though Anisha had never met either gentleman, it was easy to guess who was who, for Armand closely resembled his dark-haired sister.

Three more carriages rolled in, and the floodgates opened in earnest. Soon people were everywhere, most of them the bride's family from Gloucestershire, all speaking at once, all of them friendly. Anisha was barely retaining their names when a second set of twins arrived, Chip and Lucy Rutledge, as chattering and vivacious as their elder cousin, and accompanied by their mother, Frederica Rutledge.

Soon wraps were flying, hands were waving across the hall, and Higgenthorpe was busy herding those who would leave off their hugging and kissing into the withdrawing room, where wine was being served.

Passing along the corridor, Lady Madeleine stopped and caught both Anisha's hands. "Oh, my dear, you are too kind!" she said, brushing her lips over Anisha's cheeks. "I do hope, though, that you don't mean to throw me off once it's all over?"

Anisha drew away, puzzled. "Whatever can you mean?"

Lady Madeleine squeezed both her hands hard, then released them. "I just hope we are still friends," she said. "I hope when Geoff is settled, you and I can take up where we left off?"

Anisha felt relief surge. "I should like that," she said. "Very much."

Lady Madeleine hooked her arm through Anisha's and resumed her pace. "I have long been a friend, you know, of Miss de Rohan's aunt, Lady Treyhern," she said. "You will like her, Anisha. She has a most remarkable understanding of . . . well, *things*."

Anisha's brow furrowed. "What sort of things?"

"Well, people, I suppose," said Lady Madeleine vaguely. "She was trained to be a special sort of governess. I consulted her when Geoff was young. And she — well, she understands him, I think. Oh, Anisha, this family is going to be a good match for him. Almost as good as . . . well, I am just reassured, that is all."

Anisha understood what Lady Madeleine had not said aloud. Geoff was very much like her elder brother, his connection to the metaphysical barely leashed at times. It was part of the reason, she knew, that he'd asked Raju's permission to marry her. To Anisha, he'd need never explain his terrible gifts and bleak moods.

But understanding, alas, was a narrow foundation on which to build a passionate marriage. A suitable one, perhaps. A mediocre one, certainly. But Anisha had already suffered mediocrity. Next time, she resolved — if there was a next time — she would have passion; the wild, desperate passion of which poets had written, and of which the *Kāmashastra* spoke.

For an instant, Rance's face flashed through her mind, and in the same breath, she closed her eyes, willing it away.

Lady Madeleine was remarking upon Mrs. Rutledge's gown as she strolled past them and into the grand withdrawing room, but Anisha had already lost the thread of the conversation. Rance stood with Mr. Mac-Lachlan by the pianoforte, the blue heat of his gaze unmistakably following her. Turning slightly, Anisha looked at him, and for an instant, their eyes locked. It was as if, for a split second, she glimpsed a pure truth in his eyes. A longing as deep as it was undeniable.

Or was she just a fool?

For if it were that, how could he not acknowledge it?

She knew him.

He knew her.

They were intimate in every way save one. She desired him; desired him above all things. She was tired of this game. Tired of pretending that something else — or someone else — might do.

But Lady Madeleine was still speaking, and gushing on about Anisha's exotic attire. Anisha picked up her pace and tried to attend.

"I had not seen these Gloucestershire girls all grown up," said Lady Madeleine, changing the subject as they joined the others in the withdrawing room. "So pretty, are they not? And exuberant in the bargain."

Pulling her thoughts back to reality, Anisha surveyed the knots of chattering guests and was forced to concur. Although Miss de Rohan had an incomparable vivacity, Geoff had by no means set his sights on the beauty in the family. That prize would go to one of her young cousins.

Anisha had been forewarned that Miss de Rohan's invited guests would be primarily female, the bride having explained that hers was a true country family, and that spring planting took priority over the social Season: Her uncles would come to London only long enough for the wedding.

It was as well for Anisha, since the *Fraternitas* guests tipped the male balance in the other direction. Save for Anisha's elder brother, no one else amongst the brotherhood was married — perhaps with good reason. Mr. Sutherland had brought his widowed sister, and Sir Greville St. Giles was escorting his mother, who knew Lady Madeleine through her many charitable efforts.

Once everyone was ensconced inside the withdrawing room, Anisha saw immediately that Lucan was flirting with Lucy Rutledge. The young lady's mother noticed it, too, however, and moved at once to her side. Thus thwarted, Lucan simply smiled and turned his attention to another cousin, Lady Emelyn Rutledge, who appeared to be of an age with Lucy and was, if anything, prettier still.

Anisha sighed and turned to chat with the

Reverend Mr. Sutherland and his sister, Mrs. Hathaway. The Gloucestershire ladies, she feared, would have to guard their own.

But on her next breath Anisha realized there was one guest yet to arrive. A chill fell over her, and as if timed by fate, Higgenthorpe appeared at the drawing room door.

"Mr. Royden Napier," he intoned.

A complete silence fell over the crowd.

Wedged in across the room as she was, Anisha was unable to hasten toward the door.

Rance, who moments earlier had been teasing one of the bride's aunts, was now glowering, his dark gaze sliding from Napier to sweep the room in search of Anisha. Their eyes met again, this time his accusing.

Napier stood upon the threshold looking supremely uncomfortable.

But at the last instant, Miss de Rohan stepped from the crowd, her hand extended. "Assistant Commissioner!" she said brightly. "How good of you to come. My father sends his warmest regards."

The fact that Miss de Rohan's father could scarcely have known of the dinner party, let alone the guest list, did not matter to Anisha. The rest of the guests — save Rance — returned at once to their conversation. Anisha exhaled. It had been but a split second, yet it had felt like infinity.

By the time she managed to excuse herself and push through the crowd, Miss de Rohan and Napier had fallen into conversation and he was looking perfectly at ease.

Anisha motioned that the footman should bring Napier champagne. Then she greeted him briefly and left them to it so that she might circle the rest of the room and chat a moment with each of her guests. Nonetheless, for the rest of the evening, even while dining, she could feel Rance's eyes burning into her.

Dinner was served promptly at seven and seemed an overwhelming success. Seated at the head of the table, Lucan managed to enchant everyone, especially the younger ladies — and some of the older ones, too, it appeared. By the time dessert was served, Mrs. Hathaway had been reduced to blushes, while Miss de Rohan and Lady Madeleine, who flanked him, had begun to look upon him almost dotingly.

At last, thought Anisha dryly, *the lad's charm has come in handy.*

For her part, Anisha managed well enough. Geoff was seated to her right, and they fell at once into their old, comfortable ways. To her left, Rance turned his attention to the bride's aunt, Frederica Rutledge — another dark, vibrant beauty. Wisely, however, the lady kept one eye on her daughter Lucy, who kept exchanging low, sidelong glances with Lucan.

After dinner, Anisha served coffee to the ladies in the withdrawing room and found herself a little unprepared. Given their country roots, she had expected, she supposed, that the ladies would chat about something benign; the best methods for pickling and preserving, or the outrageous fashions being worn in Town. Instead the conversation turned political — a spirited discussion of the waning war in Spain, and whether or not the Carlists should be granted amnesty.

"Papa says it scarcely matters," Miss de Rohan declared. "He says no matter which of the Bourbons one supports, they are troublemakers, the lot of them."

"And this from a man who lost his father and half his lands to Napoleon," said Frederica Rutledge knowingly.

"Well, you should know, Aunt," said Lady Emelyn. "Your father died in the Peninsula Campaign, didn't he?"

And slowly, as the conversation progressed, Anisha began to realize these ladies were not quite what she'd assumed; that

Mrs. Rutledge was apparently Portuguese, and that Miss de Rohan's parents were not abroad on a lark but in Catalonia to keep her great-grandmother's vineyards from being torched by the Carlists. In time it came out that Lady Treyhern was French, had been educated in Switzerland, and had lived in Vienna for a time.

Moreover, all of the ladies — even the young ones — held well-informed views, not all of them in agreement, and Anisha suddenly realized that it was *she* who had been guilty of making assumptions. Her guests had likely not spared her unusual background a thought.

They had also been, she had noticed, exceedingly warm toward Rance all evening. Beyond the circle of the *Fraternitas,* people often were not, Anisha knew. And it broke her heart for him.

She hadn't long to contemplate it, however, for the gentlemen lingered less than half an hour over their port, with Rance and Mr. Napier as distant from one another as was humanly possible when they trailed in through the withdrawing room.

Anisha suppressed the urge to laugh. It served them right, really, for they were both too arrogant by half.

The latter gentleman settled on one of the

sofas and accepted a cup of coffee. When Mr. MacLachlan engaged him in a conversation about construction pilferage in the Docklands, Anisha excused herself and went to find Lucan. Lucy Rutledge, too, was absent. Suddenly, Anisha felt a moment of unease.

But as she passed from the parlor into the now empty withdrawing room, someone caught her elbow. She whirled around to see Rance glowering down at her.

"Is that your idea of a joke?" he asked, jerking his head toward the parlor sofas.

"Indeed not." Anisha flicked a glance down at his hand. "It is my idea of getting to know Mr. Napier."

"Is it?" Rance growled. "To what end?"

"Who can say?" Lightly, she shrugged. "Perhaps he is, as you seem to believe, the most conniving man in Christendom. Or perhaps he is merely misguided, with strong but misplaced scruples. Or he may be simply a womanizer."

"And my opinion means nothing to you."

"It means a great deal to me," she replied stiffly. "But might I not be permitted to form my own? And would it not be better if at least one of us got on with the man? For your sake?"

He gave a soft, bitter laugh. "So it is for

my sake that you are doing all this," he said. "Ingratiating yourself with a man who is already enamored of you, and allowing him to think you might —"

"Rance, *stop,*" she interjected. "If you wish to insult me and have your face soundly slapped for your trouble, come back tomorrow. I haven't time just now."

He said nothing but stared hard into the parlor, the little muscle in his jaw twitching dangerously. He clearly wished Napier to the devil. And perhaps he was right; perhaps she was naïve. She remembered the cold feeling that had crept over her upon realizing Napier had been watching her at the theater. But pride stiffened her spine.

"What if he is worse than merely conniving, Nish?" Rance finally said. "What if he is dangerous?"

"I'm not a complete idiot," she whispered, praying she spoke the truth. "I'm being careful. But in a few weeks' time, I have accomplished more by getting on with Napier than you have accomplished in better than a year free of prison. Admittedly, it is not much. But I shall leave *you* to decide for whose sake I am doing all this."

With that, she pulled away from his grip.

"Anisha, *wait,*" he said after her.

But she kept walking, suddenly quaking

with anger. Unfortunately, when she turned the next corner, Higgenthorpe met her with a lavender cloak draped over his arm. "It has started to spit rain, my lady," he informed her. "Mrs. Hathaway has called for her carriage, and I gather the Smythes mean to follow."

Anisha turned around and spent the next few minutes saying good-bye to several of her guests. In the front hall, Napier held back, then bowed politely over her hand when the others had gone down the steps into the drizzle.

"Well, Mr. Napier," she said briskly, "I trust this was not too onerous an evening for you?"

But when he lifted his head again, she saw something she could not quite make out glittering in his eyes. "Oh, I shall forever clutch the memory to my bosom," he said. "A lowly government employee, hobnobbing with the *crème de la crème.* Who could have imagined it?"

Anisha withdrew her hand. "I believe, Assistant Commissioner, that you are poking fun at me," she said tartly, "and that you are not nearly so humble as you make out."

He hesitated, then lifted his gaze to look past her, something quizzical tugging at one corner of his mouth. "And I believe," he replied, "that I shall very much enjoy sharing a quieter occasion with you, ma'am. At the theater, in a few days' time."

"Ah, that." Anisha inclined her head regally, but behind her she heard departing footsteps and guessed at once who it was. "Yes, well. I shall look greatly forward to it. Goodnight, Mr. Napier."

"Goodnight, Lady Anisha." He gave a courtly bow. "By the way, you wear the exotic well. I find the sari and peacock feathers a most elegant touch."

And with that, Napier turned and went swiftly down the stairs, his dark evening cloak swirling about his feet, his black umbrella at his side, unopened. No carriage awaited him. Instead, he set off on foot through the rain and melted into the gloom.

When she returned, many of the remaining guests had drifted into the withdrawing room. Lady Emelyn was there, playing a lively tune at the pianoforte, with Mrs. Rutledge whipping back the pages for her niece. A crowd now surrounded them, enraptured.

Upon settling into her seat, Anisha felt Miss de Rohan's gaze fall upon her, intent and questioning. Anisha met her eyes over her coffee cup and gave a little shake of her head. Miss de Rohan returned her attention to her future father-in-law. His gaze distant,

Rance stood alone by the hearth, his heel caught on the brass fender, a glass of Raju's best whisky in hand. When his eyes did focus, they fell upon Anisha, grim and forbidding.

At the pianoforte, Lady Emelyn began another wildly intricate tune, playing it masterfully. When Mr. MacLachlan rose, Miss de Rohan slid very near, her smile knowing.

"I believe, Lady Anisha, that you have a scorned admirer."

Anisha's eyes widened. "I beg your pardon?"

Miss de Rohan nodded in the direction of the mantelpiece. "Lord Lazonby has scarce taken his eyes from you this whole evening."

"Actually, I am in Lazonby's black books," Anisha returned. "He is angry, not enamored. Perhaps I have even provoked it. I beg you will excuse us both."

"Angry?" Miss de Rohan looked at her curiously. "Why?"

"He deeply dislikes Mr. Napier and did not wish me to invite him," said Anisha honestly.

"Truly? He seemed nice enough — though I did make up that bit about Papa."

By this time, Lady Madeleine had leaned into the conversation. Anisha was well aware there was nothing of Rance's history Geoff's mother did not know. And Geoff's chosen bride was a part of the brotherhood now; their lives were literally open books to one another.

"Lazonby blames Napier's father for his arrest all those years ago," Anisha quietly acknowledged, "and believes Napier refuses to reopen the Peveril case in order to protect his father's reputation."

"Both of which may be true," Lady Madeleine added. "Perhaps he's hiding something?"

Miss de Rohan's eyes widened. "But that is unconscionable!" she declared. "I shall speak to my father. Napier must be made to open the files so that a thorough review can be conducted."

Anisha laid a hand over Miss de Rohan's. "I know you mean well," she said, "but the St. James Society mustn't appear to run roughshod over Scotland Yard. Besides, Napier has opened his files. To me."

"To you?"

Anisha exchanged knowing glances with Lady Madeleine, still aware of the heat of Rance's gaze upon her. "Yes, just yesterday," she said. "I have extensive notes."

Then swiftly she explained all she'd learned in Napier's office. At the end, Miss de Rohan's mouth was practically hanging open.

"It is all perfectly true," Lady Madeleine whispered, her gaze darting toward the hearth. "I remember, for after the arrest, Merrick's grandmother, Mrs. MacGregor, came all the way down from Scotland — for the first time in her life."

"Because of Lazonby?" said Anisha. "Why? Did she know the family?"

"Vaguely, but remember that the *Fraternitas* was in great disarray at that time," Lady Madeleine cautioned. "Mr. Sutherland summoned everyone with ties to the old order. Mrs. MacGregor was one of the great Vateis still living — a sort of white witch, I always thought of her." Here, she hesitated, wringing her hands a little. "Of course that's *wrong,* I know. She was nothing of the sort, and one oughtn't use such a term. But how else can one explain the Vateis? Or the Gift?"

The Vateis, Anisha knew, were the descendants of the ancient Celtic prophets of the druidic age who still possessed the Gift in one form or another. And occasionally, if *Mesha* born, one could be both a Vateis *and* a Guardian, sworn to protect the weaker amongst them. Such was the case with Raju and Lord Bessett — Rance and Miss de Rohan, too, Anisha believed, though in them, the Gift was far more subtle.

"I understand," Anisha murmured. "And what did Mrs. MacGregor do?"

Madeleine twisted her hands again. "I don't know," she said. "Gave her opinion? Gave money? Merrick and I weren't privy, for we are outside the *Fraternitas,* and Geoff was still a lad. But the scandal was in all the papers. Sir Arthur Colburne *shot* himself."

"Did you know him?" asked Miss de Rohan.

"Oh, all girls of consequence did," said Madeleine, "for he was a notorious fortune hunter. Eventually he did land an heiress — Lady Mary came out with me. But that sort of money never lasts, does it? Then Mary died, and Sir Arthur fell back on his cards — and, of course, his charm."

"What do you mean, his charm?" asked Anisha.

Lady Madeleine colored faintly. "He — well, he *befriended* wealthy ladies, I believe," she murmured, "and they gave him gifts to express their gratitude for his skills in . . . in —"

"— in being *very* friendly?" Miss de Rohan supplied.

Her future mother-in-law smiled wanly. "Something like that," she agreed. "In any case, Sir Arthur died long before the trial, but several gentlemen of the *ton* were called to testify, and much sordid information came out. Two young men were disinherited by his fathers for gaming. Anyone who testified for Lazonby was blackballed from White's — Peveril's father, the duke, was very influential. And the scandal nearly ruined Sir Wilfred Leeton."

"*Sir Wilfred* Leeton?" asked Anisha.

"The theater magnate," said Miss de Rohan. "He owns half the theaters in England, I'd wager."

"Yes, I saw his name in Napier's files," said Anisha. "But he was not titled."

"He was recently knighted for his many charitable works," said Lady Madeleine. "Though his wife handles much of the oversight. I actually serve as a patroness to their orphanage."

"How kind of you," said Anisha.

Lady Madeleine blushed again. "Not really," she whispered. "Merrick's firm built several of Leeton's theaters. So I . . . well, I acquainted myself with Lady Leeton. Does that sound terribly scheming?"

"Not if you enjoy her company," Anisha assured her.

"Oh, Hannah is lovely," said Lady Madeleine, "though some think her a *parvenu*. But I find her refreshingly honest. Her first husband, you see, was a trader in Mark Lane and left her frightfully wealthy."

"In Mark Lane?" Anisha's brow furrowed.

"A broker on the Corn Exchange," Miss de Rohan explained. At Anisha's curious glance she added, "I live in Wellclose Square. We have all sorts of interesting characters on that side of Town. People who actually work for a living."

"Oh, Hannah is interesting," said Lady Madeleine, "and she'll allow nothing to stand in her way when it comes to serving a good cause. I'm to attend her annual garden party soon, a fund-raising effort for her favorite charity, a girls' school for the impoverished."

Anisha was mulling something over. "I wonder if I might call on Sir Wilfred someday," she murmured. "Would that be inappropriate? I should very much like to show him my notes, you see, and ask if there is anything that strikes him as odd."

"What do you mean?" asked Miss de Rohan.

Anisha gave a weak shrug. "I don't know," she said. "Perhaps one of those old names might jog a memory?"

But Lady Madeleine looked wary. "Sir Wilfred mightn't wish to revisit his past," she cautioned. "The scandal erupted just as he was attempting to finance his theater business." "Ah, I see," said Anisha.

"Oh, but I have a lovely idea!" said Lady Madeleine. "We must both go to the garden party. You could quietly make his acquaintance."

"But how?" Anisha asked. "Lady Leeton does not know me."

Lady Madeleine looked at her dotingly. "I fear the only requirement is to be moderately wealthy and possess at least a pretension of being well-bred," she murmured. "The purpose is to make money by way of subscription. The place will be cheek to jowl with country cousins and aspiring coal merchants. One must only purchase a certain number of tickets."

"The price of admission, quite literally?" said Miss de Rohan, grinning. "And you just loll about in Lady Leeton's garden?"

"Actually, it's more like a village fair," said Madeleine. "There will be stalls with goods for sale — lots of lace and stitchery — things the girls have made. There's a bandstand and a gypsy with a crystal ball, although I think she is just Hannah's kitchen maid. Still, it really is quite delightful."

"I'd love to go," said Anisha. "And if I could befriend Sir Wilfred, he might eventually prove helpful."

"And if not," said Miss de Rohan acidly, "there's always the *Chronicle,* which seems intent on churning up that old case. Perhaps they have a secret cache of information."

"Oh, they are just dredging up old news," said Lady Madeleine, scowling. "I've grown quite tired of that vexing newspaper fellow. Last autumn, our scullery maid caught him going through our rubbish bins, if you can imagine!"

"He's a radical reporter, Sutherland theorizes," said Anisha. "But I begin to think it's more personal than that."

"Personal?" Miss de Rohan looked intrigued. "Who could it be? Wait, wasn't there a beautiful fiancée? Perhaps she has hired the fellow to drive Rance mad?"

Madeleine shook her head. "Elinor Colburne died of a shipboard fever," she said. "So tragic, for she was the very image of Lady Mary. Fragile and lovely, an ice-blonde with a tiny beauty mark just here." Lightly Madeleine touched the corner of her mouth. "Men *swooned* over her."

But Miss de Rohan was not interested in the dead. "Then it was someone else," she said, seizing on the notion. "Perhaps one of the Peverils hired him? No, I have it! A mistress! Had Peveril a mistress, does anyone know?"

Madeleine smiled. "My dear, you must take after your father," she said. "But no, there wasn't a mistress as I ever heard of. Peveril was, however, the duke's favorite. Still, the duke died last year, and his heir — the new duke — did not much mourn his younger brother's passing."

But before Miss de Rohan could press the issue, Lady Emelyn's incredible piece spiraled up and up and up, held for a moment in midair, then came to a heart-stopping end, the keys crashing in thunderous triumph.

Lady Treyhern and Mr. MacLachlan rose at once to their feet, applauding. On the sofa, Anisha and her party followed suit, further gossip now out of the question.

"Encore!" said Geoff, who was now standing by Rance at the hearth.

"Ladies, take a bow," said Mr. Mac-Lachlan. "That was truly extraordinary."

Frederica Rutledge blushed. "I fear I did nothing but turn the pages," she said, coming to join them in the parlor. "My niece is the virtuoso."

Smiling, Mr. MacLachlan strode toward the sofa and leaned across the back. "Maddie, love, perhaps we'd best go?" he said, setting a hand affectionately on her arm. "Lady Anisha is doubtless tired, and —"

But Mrs. Rutledge suddenly spoke over him. "Chip?" she sharply interjected. "Chip, where is Lucy?"

Anisha looked around to see the young man rouse from a stupor in a chair some yards distant. "Couldn't say, Mamma," he said, his lids heavy. " 'Fraid I was enthralled by Emmie's music."

Mrs. Rutledge's eyes were darting through the room. "I beg your pardon," she said, "but has anyone seen my daughter? Or Lord Lucan?"

Suddenly sick, Anisha leapt to her feet. She had been searching for Lucan earlier when . . .

Oh, dear God.

"Charles Rutledge," said his mother sternly, "you were supposed to keep up with Lucy!"

The young man shrugged. "I haven't seen her since just after din —"

"Lucy just left," Miss de Rohan interjected in a bored voice. "I believe Lord Lucan is showing her the picture gallery. One of the footmen went up with them to unlock it."

Anisha's gaze swept the room. Higgenthorpe and both the footmen stood in the depths of the withdrawing room. Her eyes returned to Miss de Rohan's, questioning.

But Miss de Rohan's smile was placid.

"Perhaps, Lady Anisha, you should go up and fetch them?" she continued. "Your footman is likely needed belowstairs, what with all that plate to be washed. Geoff and I mean to stay here and finish the last of this excellent champagne. Come, the rest of you, and give us one last toast for good luck!"

"What a good idea," said Lady Madeleine, settling back onto the sofa.

"Excuse me, then," said Anisha, moving toward the passageway.

Setting away his whisky, Rance pulled away from the hearth, his eyes narrowing. "I need to stretch my legs," he said.

Her lips in a hard, thin line, Mrs. Rutledge went out into the passageway, too.

"Now this picture gallery," Rance murmured suspiciously. "Which way is it?"

Anisha looked back and forth between them. "We haven't one," she confessed. "Remind me never to play cards with Miss de Rohan."

"The devil!" Rance swore. "I thought not."

Mrs. Rutledge turned white. "And the footman?"

"We've only the two behind us," said Anisha tightly. "But trust me, they will be enough to carry my brother's battered corpse down to the coroner's once I've found him. Please, Mrs. Rutledge, for

Lucy's sake, go back into the withdrawing room and pretend you are unconcerned. If anything is amiss, Lord Lucan *will* make amends."

Mrs. Rutledge blushed furiously. "Perhaps you oughtn't blame him," she whispered. "Lucy is . . . dear God, I think she just breaks hearts for sport. And Chip is worse. I'm just grateful he was asleep in your chair, and not your parlor maid's bed. They are loving children, but . . ."

Rance seized Anisha's arm and propelled her toward the stairs. "I swear to God, I will thrash Luc," he muttered as they hastened up the stairs. "I will put that boy over my knee and give him what he deserves."

"Alas, he is not a boy," said Anisha grimly. "He is nineteen — and I daresay he'd much prefer your thrashing to the lifelong sentence he's apt to get."

Anisha threw open the library door. Nothing. Raju's study was the very same. As were the next two rooms. With Rance taking one side of the passageway, and she the other, they searched every room, then went up another floor.

There they opened every door, checking under beds and inside cupboards, and finding nothing save a little dust the housemaids had missed. The last room was Tom and

Teddy's. Inside, both were soundly asleep. Milo's cage had been brought up from the conservatory and covered for the night.

They backed out, and Rance quietly closed the door, casting his gaze to the attics. "Surely not the servants' rooms?"

Anisha shook her head. "It must be the conservatory," she said. "It's so cold this time of night, but . . . yes. Quick, down the servants' stairs."

Once back down, Anisha made her way quietly through the rear of the house, circling away from the parlor. The conservatory jutted out into the back gardens and was generally shut up for the night.

The door, she saw at once, was unlocked. Her heart going still, she pushed through.

At first, the long wicker chaise was just a shadow in the moonlight. Then her eyes adjusted, and she saw unmistakably the back of Luc's head, and a vast expanse of Miss Rutledge's ivory bosom as she lay back against it.

Gasping, she threw up a hand to stop Rance. *"Lucan!"*

"Bloody h— !" In one motion, Luc lifted his head from Lucy's nearly-bare breast and leapt to his feet, shifting to block the view. "Knock, Nish, for God's sake!"

"Knock?" Anisha stalked toward him.

"Knock? *That* is your answer? And Miss Rutledge! Kindly make yourself presentable."

"I'm p-presentable," Miss Rutledge cried, obviously tugging at her gown. "Really, I was never n-not presentable. Not *entirely.*" Her voice ending on a hysterical note, she elbowed Luc hard in the thigh. "Oh, Lord Lucan, do *move!*"

Luc moved. Lucy jerked to her feet, blinking against the lamp Rance carried in from the passageway. "Lord Lazonby!" she murmured, curtseying. "I beg your pardon."

"It is not my pardon you should be begging," said Rance, his voice tight. "It is your hostess. Your parents. And your cousin, Miss de Rohan, whose evening you've nearly ruined. Lucan, you will come with me — and be quick about it."

Lucy Rutledge set a tremulous hand to her mouth and began to sob.

CHAPTER 8

My salad days, When I was green in
judgment.
> William Shakespeare,
> *Antony and Cleopatra*

His temper barely in check, Lazonby
dragged his quarry from the conservatory
and pitched him headlong into the first
room he saw — which was, thank God,
Higgenthorpe's thick-walled service pantry.
Luc hit the counter, rattling the racks of
china.

Resisting the urge to slam the door,
Lazonby shut it and shot the bolt, the sound
cracking like a rifle in the small room. "Now
what," he said, rounding on the boy, "in
God's name did you think you were doing
just now?" he roared.

Luc cringed but stood his ground.
"Just . . . kissing Lucy," he said. "She —
she didn't mind."

"She didn't *mind?*" Lazonby marched across the narrow room. "What has that to do with anything? Lucan Forsythe, have you any idea the hellfire you've just rained down on your own head? Or the shame you've caused your sister?"

"We were just *kissing,*" Lucan repeated, looking mulish. "Kissing, I mean — for a while, but —"

"Christ Jesus, Luc, do you think these people are *nothing?*" Lazonby cut him off. "Do you think they're just simple country folk who'll let you maul one of their daughters like a ha'penny whore, and throw her back at them again?"

"It — it wasn't like that!" Luc cried, backing up against the counter. "We just — she just — I lost my head. Rance, that's all it was. She's so pretty, and we were bored, and I just thought —"

"You didn't think, you grass-green fool!" Lazonby roared. "A cockstand cuts off the blood to your brain — good God, has Ruthveyn explained *nothing* to you?"

Anger sketched across Luc's face. "No, he's been too busy gallivanting around fixing all the world's problems."

"Aye, then, he's a fool, too," Lazonby returned. "And speaking of that brain-draining appendage, I trust I have suf-

315

ficiently withered it by now?"

The rest of Luc's color drained. "S-Sufficient for what?"

"Sufficient for you to go back in that room, get down on one knee, and do the right thing by Miss Rutledge."

Luc's eyes tripled in size. "M-M-Marriage?" he managed. "B-B-But I'm just nineteen."

"I'll take care of that," Lazonby retorted, "legally, and gladly."

"No. No. I shan't do it." Awkwardly, Luc seized the wooden countertop behind him. "You've taken leave of your senses."

Lazonby took a step nearer, clutching his hands behind him lest he give the boy the pummeling he deserved. "Lucan," he said grimly, "my temper has grown increasingly short with you these past months. You've been little more than a trial to your sister. And that, my boy, has just come to an end. Anisha deserves your help, not your hindrance. She has two fatherless children to raise, for God's sake. And if Ruthveyn cannot take you in hand, rest assured that I have no such scruples."

At last, Luc hung his head. "I'm bloody damn tired of everyone criticizing me," he muttered into the floor. "I just wish my mother were alive."

"Aye, so that she could keep telling you the sun rises and sets in the crack of your arse, I do not doubt," said Lazonby sourly. "But in spoiling you, she did you no favors, my boy. You are as ordinary as the rest of us, and you will do right by that poor girl. Your brother left you in my keeping and it's my decision to make."

Lucan's head jerked up, his eyes glittering angrily. "Oh, like you're a candidate for sainthood!" he said. "That's rich, Rance. Truly."

Lazonby bit back his first retort and drew a steadying breath. "Whatever I am, Luc, I have never debauched an innocent."

"And I have never murdered anyone and gone to prison for it," said Lucan nastily. "Besides, Lucy won't have me. She doesn't want to be married. *Ask* her."

"Oh, trust me, my boy, she'll want it when her mamma and cold, hard logic seize hold of her," Lazonby answered. "Do you have any idea who that girl is?"

Lucan shook his head, his golden curls springing out a little wildly now.

"Her uncle is Lord Treyhern, a man you *do not* want to cross," said Lazonby. "And his brother-in-law, Miss de Rohan's father, is one of the most dangerous men in the Home Office. As to Lucy's father, he wrote the book on hellfire. The last two chaps who crossed Bentley Rutledge got bullets for breakfast and didn't live to complain about it."

Luc's throat worked up and down. "I . . . I didn't know," he whispered. He forked all his fingers through his mass of golden hair, as if it might stimulate his brain. "God, you're right. I didn't think. B-But marriage?"

"Aye, by God, marriage," said Lazonby grimly. "And your only hope — and I do mean your *only* hope — is that your sister and I can hush this up and that Lucy's parents will realize you are too damned green to make the chit any sort of husband at all."

Luc was visibly shaking now.

Lazonby closed the distance between them and set a hand on Luc's shoulder. "Now, Lucan, my boy, you must think carefully," he said, his voice hard, but more kind. "You are a little spoiled, yes, but you are a gentleman at heart. In that, I do not doubt you. And this is what a gentleman does when he makes a grave mistake. He owns up to it. He does the right thing. I will stand by you, but it must be done. So go get it over with."

Head hanging, Lucan went.

Lucy Rutledge was still snuffling on Anisha's shoulder when they returned. Without preamble, Luc dropped to one knee — more in front of his sister than Lucy.

"M-Miss Rutledge," he managed, "I fear I let your beauty overwhelm my sense of pr-propriety. Will you do me the honor of becoming Lady Lucan?"

"Oh, I just don't *know* — *!*" she sobbed into Anisha's sari. "Must I? Just for a little kiss? Have I no choice?"

It was on the tip of Lazonby's tongue to say that it had looked like a good deal more than just a kiss. But Anisha urged her gently away. "Whether you must is up to your parents, Miss Rutledge," she said, looking the girl straight in the eyes. "But you are a lovely young woman. We would all of us welcome you into our family."

"Lucy," said Lucan, his voice withering to a whisper. "I'm so sorry."

But Lazonby could not escape the notion that all Lucan was sorry about was the fact that he'd been caught. Still, he cleared his throat and smiled. "Well done, all!" he said, as cheerfully as he could. "Now let's have no more tears, Miss Rutledge. Go back into the drawing room and kiss your cousin's cheek. This is her night. Then, tomorrow morning, Lucan will call upon your mother and settle this business."

At last, Lucy turned to look at Lucan. "Will you?" she asked pitifully.

Lucan opened his mouth, but no sound came out. His hair looked like a wild, golden halo now, and his shirttail was half out of his trousers.

"He will," said Lazonby. "And I suggest, Miss Rutledge, you prepare her."

Anisha returned to the withdrawing room, her heart in her throat. She could feel herself trembling inside. She tried to control her breath, tried to still her mind and take herself to a calmer place, but for once it was no use. She had to fist her hands to keep from flying at Luc with her nails. And, truth be told, she wanted to rail at her elder brother, too.

She had come here in large part for Luc's sake. She had believed Raju could tame the boy and turn his life around. But things had only gone from bad to worse with his incessant gaming and carousing. The extravagant bills. The flagrant flirtations. Luc's behavior toward Grace during her early days as governess had been especially egregious, once even compelling the poor girl to jab him with a fork under the dinner table.

And now this — potential social humiliation for all of them — when Anisha had meant only to do the right thing.

Inside the withdrawing room, however, social humiliation did not seem especially imminent. Everyone had crowded, laughing, all around the sofas, and chaos seemed at hand. Miss de Rohan was leading the guests in a game, of all things, and lumbering about with one hand curled like a snout, and the other twitching behind like a tail while everyone shouted wildly.

"Good God, charades?" Lucan muttered.

"Horse!" Rance shouted, nonchalantly resuming his position by the hearth.

"Elephant!" cried Lady Emelyn. "Lord Lazonby, isn't she an elephant?"

"No, she's an anteater," Geoff declared.

"An *anteater?*" Lady Madeleine turned to look at him incredulously. "After all we spent on your education?"

"I should have guessed aardvark," Chip Rutledge drawled.

Still trundling awkwardly about, Miss de Rohan grunted.

"Pig!" screeched Lady Emelyn.

"Yes, pig! Pig!" someone shouted.

"Oh, foul!" declared Mrs. Rutledge, keeping one eye on Lucy. "You cannot make sounds, Anaïs! That's cheating."

"Cheat! Cheat!" Chip shouted. "Anaïs

always cheats."

Miss de Rohan smacked Chip hard on the back of the head, then fell onto the sofa beside her Aunt Treyhern, laughing hysterically.

"*Ça alors!* We have descended into absurdity!" declared Lady Treyhern, shoving her off. "Get up, you buffoons. We must go home before we humiliate ourselves in front of everyone, especially Lady Anisha and her brother, who have been so very hospitable to us."

The lady's graciousness made Anisha only feel worse. Within ten minutes, however, only Miss de Rohan, Geoff, and Rance remained, Lucan having at last slunk upstairs to lick his wounds, and Higgenthorpe having gone to bed at Anisha's insistence.

As the last of the Gloucestershire guests climbed into their carriages, Anisha closed the front door and fell back against it, exhausted. She yearned for her quiet space and her comfortable clothes; wanted to sit and focus solely on her *pranayama,* purging her mind of these last hours.

In the entrance hall, Geoff cut a sidelong glance at his bride-to-be. "Well," he said quietly, "do the three of you want to let me in on this? Or is it better if I know nothing? And by the way, Nish, if you've a picture gallery in this house, I'd like to know where."

Miss de Rohan rolled her eyes. "You must excuse my cousin Lucy," she said. "She has never had much luck remembering that prayer book bit about 'leading not into temptation.' "

Geoff smiled wanly. "I suspected as much when you began carrying on like a lunatic to distract everyone," he said.

Miss de Rohan blinked. "To distract everyone?" she said innocently. "I beg your pardon, my love. I adore charades. Indeed, I could play it every night of the week."

"And all that berating your kin over their poor skills?" he murmured, staring down at her. "Cheating? Going out of turn? Flailing at one another? Nothing unusual in any of it, eh?"

"Indeed, we are a happy, boisterous family," said Miss de Rohan, stifling a yawn with one hand. "*And* we play to win. Besides, it's too late to buck up about now, Bessett. You proposed too quickly, and you know what they say — marry in haste, repent at leisure."

"Hmm," said Geoff. "We shall see who does the repenting in this marriage."

At that Rance guffawed. "I can place my wager on that one now."

Unperturbed as always, Geoff leaned into Anisha and kissed her cheek. "Thank you so much, Nish, for this evening. It was lovely."

Anisha felt a smile curl her mouth. "I believe I should thank Miss de Rohan," she said. "That was quite a set of countermeasures, my dear. I think almost no one realized my brother was busy attempting to debauch your cousin."

Miss de Rohan patted her on the arm. "Oh, don't fret over Lucy," she said. "She's like a cat, and always lands on her feet."

"Regardless," said Rance, "Lord Lucan will wait upon your aunt tomorrow to grovel deeply. I'll send word to Ruthveyn as soon as the date is fixed."

But Miss de Rohan's eyes turned to saucers. "As soon as the date is fixed?" she echoed. "Oh, no. Lucy would just run off with a traveling circus — *not,* of course, that Lord Lucan isn't a lovely young man."

Anisha felt a stirring of hope amongst the ashes. "You imagine the Rutledges will refuse Lucan's suit?" she asked. "I vow, I do believe they are both too young and too selfish to marry happily."

"Practically speaking, we'll all lay low and see if scandal bubbles up," Miss de Rohan predicted. "If not, Lucy will be put back on a tight leash, or sent off to wait hand and foot on some elderly cousin for a few months, and that will be the end of it. Oh — wait, I almost forgot." Snapping open the beaded reticule that swung from her wrist, she extracted a fold of paper and pressed it into Rance's hand.

"What's this?" he asked.

"A name," she said. "One of my father's most trusted — well, no, most *knowledgeable* — associates."

"And?" said Rance, tucking the paper away.

"And perhaps you should call on him?" said Miss de Rohan. "It's a bit of a drive, but it will be worth it. He's frightfully bored in the country, so tell him I sent you. Ask him what he knows."

Rance tilted his head to one side. "And what does he know?"

"Oh, everything, more or less," said Miss de Rohan brightly. "And that which he does not know, he can winkle out of someone — or threaten it out, if he must."

Then she, too, kissed Anisha's cheek, and they were gone. Anisha stood in the open doorway until Geoff's carriage was rolling down the drive, the wind off the river damp in her face, and Rance's warmth at her back.

"Well, Nish," he murmured as she shut

the door, "this could have been worse, I suppose."

On a faintly hysterical laugh, Anisha turned. "Truly — ?" she said. "How?"

But Rance had not stepped back. Instead, he merely looked down at her from beneath a fringe of dark lashes. "Well, the beef was perfectly done," he said dryly. "The champagne was just the right temperature. Lucan had not *quite* deflowered the poor girl when we caught up with him. And you — well, you could have been going to Napier's mother's house for dinner, I suppose. That would be a bad sign."

"I beg your pardon?"

"Instead of the theater," he clarified, his eyes darkening. "You did promise to accompany him to the theater, I collect?"

She held up a warning finger. "Rance, do *not* start with me!"

His jaw was set in that rigid, all-too familiar line. "I am not starting," he said quietly. "I am finished, Nish. I don't know what else I can say."

"Nothing," she said, coming away from the door. "Look, do you want another whisky?"

He dragged a hand through his hair. "I ought to go, I suppose," he said. "Are you tired?"

"Tired of standing in the hall, yes," she said, starting down the passageway. "Beyond that, I scarcely know what I am. I feel as if I've been nailed shut in a barrel and rolled off a cliff."

Lazonby knew the feeling. Resisting his instinct to go, he followed her back into the parlor and retrieved his glass from the mantelpiece. As Anisha drew shut the pocket doors that opened onto the withdrawing room, he filled his glass, and one for her as well.

By the time she plopped back onto the sofa, he was pressing it into her hands. "I don't drink spirits," she said.

"Tonight you should," he said a little grimly. "Tonight we both need a drink."

He sat down beside her and watched as she took a little sip, her nose wrinkling most attractively. *"Hmm,"* she said. "That is an acquired taste, I believe."

He gave a bark of laughter and set his glass down.

"So," she said, edging forward on the sofa. "What did Miss de Rohan give you?"

Reminded of it, he extracted the note from his pocket and read it. "The address of some chap in Buckhurst Hill," he said, passing it to her. "George Kemble. Can't think as I know him."

"Nor do I," she murmured, studying it. "Not that that means much. Will you go?"

He thought about it for a moment. "It would seem ungrateful to spurn her suggestion," he finally said.

"When?" Lightly, she laid her hand over his. "And may I come with you?"

He looked down at their hands, hers so small and slender, the fingers lying coolly across his own, and resisted the urge to lift it to his lips. Lord, he was reluctant to further involve her. And just as reluctant to let go of whatever threads of her he dared cling to.

Perhaps he wanted to believe they were in this together.

They were not. This mess of his own making had nothing to do with her. And Miss de Rohan's offer aside, that faint spiraling of hope he'd felt in Ruthveyn's garden had been but a chimera; a fantasy bred of dreams and desperation. He was likely no closer to extricating himself from the tangle of deceit than the day the judge had banged his gavel and sent him to rot in the filth of Newgate.

But Anisha was looking at him expectantly with her wide-set, intelligent eyes; looking straight through to the heart of him, it often felt. And he, it seemed, was weak.

"I suppose we might go in a day or two if the weather holds," he finally answered. "But in a closed carriage this time, Nish. Our quiet friendship is one thing. But being too often on my arm in public? It won't do."

"I believe whom I'm seen with is my decision," she replied.

He found he could not look at her. "You must think of the boys, Nish, and of your future," he said quietly. "Besides, no one is going anywhere until I'm sure young Lucan has done his duty by Miss Rutledge."

"And if he does not?" she asked.

"I will be tempted, of course, to give him a good hiding with my riding crop," said Lazonby, his voice grim. "But, as someone so recently recommended, I am coming slowly to accept that I am not omnipotent. That I cannot force everyone to do my bidding — even when I know bloody well that I am right."

Anisha did not even remind him not to curse. Instead she lifted her hand away and sat quietly for a long moment, staring at her spurned glass as if the golden elixir might hold all the world's truths.

"You are taking this to heart, aren't you?" she said softly. "This business of looking after us?"

"You have known me a long while, Nish,"

he replied, "but known me, perhaps, at more of a distance than you realize."

She turned to him, her gaze quizzical. "I don't understand."

He tried to smile and failed. "You once said I was not what I pretended to be," he murmured. "I think perhaps you were right."

"I know I was," she said gently.

He stared into the cold, black depths of the hearth. "I try not to forget, Nish, the man my father brought me up to be," he said. "Some days, though, I must search pretty hard for him inside myself. But I am not so steeped in bitterness, so driven by revenge, that I've lost my course entirely. There is still a little of the gentleman in me, I suppose. Yes, I take this to heart. I swore to your brother that I would look after you for the year or so he's gone. And I will. Somehow."

Anisha drew a deep breath. "But this is just the theater, you know," she said, broaching the subject that hung like a dead weight between them. "It will be very public. And Luc is going with me."

"Oh, well then!" Lazonby threw his hands up. "I've nothing to worry about! After all, who could be more responsible than Luc?"

"Rance," she said, cutting him a chiding

glance. "Luc will do well enough for appearance's sake. But make no mistake — I am *responsible* for myself."

He drank for a moment in silence. The truth was, she was responsible for far more than herself. Her children. Her younger brother. The running of the house. More, even, than that in Ruthveyn's absence. Still, he wanted to rail at her, to tell her that *he* was responsible for her. That she was a fool for continuing to see Napier, and that he forbade it.

But that strategy had not thus far got him anywhere. And where did he wish it to get him, anyway? Anisha was not a fool. She was sensible and, for the most part, wise to the world. The problem — the *possessiveness* — was his.

And Napier, the arrogant coxcomb! Good God, Lazonby had wanted to throttle him tonight. Weeks ago, he had convinced himself that Geoff marrying Anisha was something he could have borne. Geoff was a good and worthy man. But he knew now that, even then, he had been lying to himself.

"Rance." Her soft voice severed his thoughts. "There is only one reason I continue to see Napier, and you know it. Now, may we change the subject? I wish to tell you about a garden party I've a notion to attend."

"A garden party?" He was instantly suspicious.

Anisha proceeded to lay out Lady Madeleine's plan to introduce her to Sir Wilfred Leeton.

He let his gaze drift over her face. "Nish, I'm not sure it's wise," he said. "And I don't recall hearing about Leeton's being knighted. Hannah must be proud enough to pop her stitches."

She turned a little toward him, her hand returning to lie lightly over his. "You know her?"

He lifted one shoulder. "Well, I remember her," he said. "She was a little outré in those days. A rich lady friend of Arthur's, actually."

"Ah, yes," said Anisha. "I heard a bit of gossip about Arthur and his so-called lady friends from Madeleine."

"Well, their romance — what little there was — didn't last long. They were just chums, I recollect." With an absent, natural gesture, Rance began to massage the palm of her hand with his thumb, wondering if she was tired. "Arthur introduced Hannah to Leeton. Brought her round quite a lot, actually, and the three of them fell into the same fast crowd — the demimonde, or dashed near it."

"And now she is respectable," Anisha murmured.

"Aye, well, money can do that, if you spread it around in the right places."

"How jaded that sounds — but alas, not untrue." Anisha lifted her hand away, leaving him suddenly cold and a little lost.

But why? It was just a touch. Merely her hand. And yet he found himself resisting the urge to seek it out again. To press and knead and work the day's stress from those small, capable fingers. And then to slip off her shoes and do the same.

But those, oddly, were amongst the most intimate of touches. And the very sort of intimacy he sought so desperately to avoid.

"Rance," she went on, "you might join us. You and Leeton get on, yes?"

"When I knew him, aye," said Rance. "But his garden party? I think not."

"Ah." She exhaled slowly. "Well, then."

He cast Anisha a sidelong glance to see that she'd reached up and begun to draw the elaborate feathers from her hair, her arms lifting her lush swell of cleavage. His gaze swept up, taking in her long, elegant neck, set to perfect advantage by her jeweled collar and long, dangling earrings; her full lips and her fine, faintly almond-shaped eyes, and knew that entire wars had been fought for women far less desirable than she.

It felt as if he was fighting one now.

Damn it, he needed to go home. To stay here in his current mood — and having been at Ruthveyn's whisky much of the night — was to court disaster.

He set the glass away again and rubbed at his eyes with his thumb and forefinger. "Nish, it's late," he said again as she tossed the last feather on the tea table. "You need your rest."

As always, it was as if she sensed his mood. Turning to face him, she tucked one leg beneath her and leaned near, setting a palm to his lapel. Her tiny slippers, he noticed, were bejeweled, as they so often were, and around one perfect, slender ankle dangled a charm on a gold chain.

Unable to resist, he reached out to lightly touch it. "I should go," he whispered.

"Is that really what you want, Rance?" she replied. "To *go?*"

Oh, there was a wealth of intimation in that small, simple question.

Something inside him went perfectly still. He dropped his hand and looked at her. Fleetingly he allowed himself the joy of drinking in that face, which was at once so beautiful and so familiar to him, and those huge brown eyes, like infinite pools of knowledge, so keen and so piercing when she pinned him that Lazonby knew he had few, if any, secrets from her.

"No," he said quietly. "No, I don't want to go. Does it make you any happier to have me say it?"

Her smile was muted. He picked up his whisky and drained it.

"You are angry with me," she said. "You don't want Napier to court me. But you have not asked me if I mean to court him in return."

"No," he said, putting the glass down with a heavy *clunk*. "I have counseled you against having anything to do with the man. But I have thus far resisted the urge to ask anything. It is not my place to do so — again, as you so recently pointed out."

But her gaze had hardened a little. "I want to take a lover, Rance," she pressed on. "I am a young woman still. I have grown weary of always sleeping alone."

Lazonby felt the knife of her words thrust deep and twist, goring at his heart. "Anisha, for God's sake, just don't —"

"No, hear me out," she interjected. "I want a lover, Rance, not necessarily a

335

husband. I want . . . *you.* Oh, I've tried not to. I've tried to want someone else — or something else — with no luck at all. And I can keep trying, I suppose, if that's the only choice left to me. I can go to the opera on the arm of a different man every night, and look about me for some temporary distraction. But who I truly want — alas, that will not change."

"Nish, *don't,*" he whispered, closing his eyes.

But her hand came up to stroke his face, her fingers warm against the flesh that ached for her touch. "So *if* you are interested in taking up that role, then yes," she went on. "Yes, you may have some say in what I do and with whom I do it. Yes, you may *ask* me not to see other gentlemen. You may *ask* me to stay away from Napier. As the man sharing my bed, you would have that right."

"And if I am not?" he rasped, looking at her.

She removed her hand, drew a little away, and set her cheek to the back of the sofa. "Then we will remain the dearest of friends," she whispered, gazing at him. "And I will listen to your advice always, because that's what friends are for. But in the end, I will do what I please, and you will have no right to be angry with me."

336

She was offering him a choice that was no sort of choice at all.

For a long time, he thought about what his response should be. His elbows propped on his knees, his hands dangling, he tried to form the right words — words about respect and selflessness and promises. But the words would not come — perhaps he, too, had grown weary of them — and when at last she leaned into him again, her warmth and exotic scent embracing him like a living thing, Lazonby felt himself shudder.

Her hand caught his shoulder and pushed him back against the sofa. "Close your eyes," she whispered, just before she set her lips to his throat.

And he did, God help him.

In a rattle of silk, he felt the sofa give under her weight as she came astraddle him. "Close your eyes," she said again, her mouth moving over him, setting his skin ashiver.

"Anisha," he whispered.

But he did not open his eyes, and instead let her hands and mouth roam over him. They were simple gestures; innocent, really. Her fingers stroking over his chest, along his waist, through his hair. Her lips on his eyes, his cheeks, under the turn of his jaw.

He stilled himself to it unflinchingly. And yet despite the simplicity, the powerful thread of desire began to run through him, to twist and to pull him like molten metal deeper into the heat of her.

She opened her mouth, warm against his cheek, then skimmed it down until the tip of her tongue stroked a ribbon of moisture along his bottom lip. She caught the swell of it between her teeth, nibbled and sucked, then moved on. Beneath the snug wool of his trousers, Lazonby's cock began to harden and throb, but it seemed an almost secondary thing; the sensations he felt were something deeper and more primal than mere lust.

He felt her mouth move along the bone of his eye socket, then his temple, until her lips hesitated, feather-light, upon his ear. "Take me upstairs to my bed, *meri jaan,*" she whispered. "Take me upstairs. Join your body to mine."

"Anisha —"

"No." The word was soft but sharp. "Don't speak. Just . . . for one night, *don't.*"

Her words falling away, Anisha shocked him by easing her hand down the fall of his trousers. With the tips of her fingers and the firmness of her palm, she rubbed back and forth along the ridge of his erection, causing him to suck air through his teeth.

She made a little sound of feminine satisfaction in the back of her throat. "Now *that*," she whispered, "is unmistakable desire."

"Did you have any doubt?" he rasped.

For an instant, she hesitated. "Not much, but one never likes to assume," she murmured, her mouth skimming round the turn of his throat. "Desire can be so . . . *complicated.*"

She was thinking, he suddenly realized, of Jack Coldwater. Of the compromising position in which she'd seen him — *must* have seen him — else she would never have wondered . . .

It had not been his proudest moment. And that recollection served only to further frustrate him, like lamp oil hurled onto a banked fire. He had nothing to prove, damn it.

And yet . . . and yet . . .

If was as if something inside him snapped. With one arm he lifted her, feather-light, from his lap, scooping beneath her knees with the other arm as he dragged her up. She gave a little cry of surprise, her arms lashing round his neck.

She did not want to talk, by God, he thought, striding from the parlor.

She did not want to take no for an answer.

Even having seen of him all that she had seen, and knowing all that Ruthveyn had likely told her, she was nonetheless bent on this — whatever *this* was going to be, in the end.

And tonight — just for tonight — he was weary of doing the right thing, for restraint had never been his strong suit. So he would give in and ruin her, he thought, going relentlessly up the stairs. He was going to give her — this one night — just what she was asking for, and damn the consequences.

It said something, he supposed, about his standing in this house and in this family that he knew to the very door which bedchamber was hers. He'd always known — but had he not, tonight's frantic search for Luc would have revealed it — for Anisha's very essence, her scent, her opulent colors, her tidy habits, all of it had been apparent in the room.

After shoving open the door and kicking it shut again with his heel, Lazonby strode in to deposit her onto the bed. By the light of the lamp turned low upon the night table, he watched her blink up at him, all beauty and innocence.

Then she held open her arms.

He waited long enough to strip off his coat. Hurling it to the floor, he followed her onto the bed, loosening the fall of his trousers as he went. Already his cock was hard as a constable's tipstaff, the blood thrumming through his loins and his brain in an urgent drumbeat.

"Anisha," he managed.

She clung to him and he settled against her, rucking up her skirts with his knee. His mouth found hers and he kissed her too roughly, thrusting deep into her mouth. Anisha did not hesitate but kissed him back, arching hard against him as her hands plunged into his hair.

On a groan, her head went back into the softness of the pillow. He thrust deep again, then more rhythmically, telling her plainly his intent. Half hoping, perhaps, she would push him away.

She did not. Instead, her fingers slid from his hair and went a little desperately to her skirts. She inched them up higher and he heard a stitch rip. She curled one leg hard about his waist.

He shifted his weight, settling himself fully between her thighs, his buttons already half undone. "Rance," she whispered, her eyes closed. "Oh, just . . . *please.*"

He found the silky fabric of her drawers and pressed his fingers deep into the wet softness between her legs.

"Yes," she said. "Now."

Oh, his body wanted *now.* But his heart

wanted slow.

She was Anisha, the beautiful, perfect thing he had desired from afar for so long he thought himself a little maddened by it. Whatever this was between them — this searing, just-once passion — he wanted it to be perfect; wanted to draw out her desire like a fine silk thread spun by the cleverest of hands upon the most delicate of wheels.

When she touched him again, however, easing her fingers between them, Lazonby realized that perfection was not what she asked. Not what she needed. She had been alone a long time, she said.

And he had been alone forever.

She kissed him again, her small nostrils delicately flaring. Her fingertips rubbed the hard ridge of him while her opposite hand threaded through his hair. Slipping loose the last of his buttons, he took himself in hand and pressed deep into her softness. Drawing up her knees, Anisha tilted her hips, crying out as he entered her.

Lazonby suppressed a jubilant sound from somewhere low in his throat and felt her warmth surround him, drawing him deeper. She was like the moon pulling the tide to shore. Unconditionally. Relentlessly.

Lifting himself a little, he rocked back and thrust again. Her breath seized, a soft, primal sound of feminine pleasure. He thrust and thrust again, then set a pace to match her need. Everything moved as if in a dream. He knew, vaguely, that this was a moment to be savored; that the physical act had never felt so exquisitely perfect to him, and never would be again. But the urgent madness was already upon him; an almost feral need to mate, to claim, to thrust.

Anisha's hair had tumbled down on one side, her beautiful gown tugged askew such that one breast was fully bared. The breath already sawing in and out of him, he took the swollen nipple into his mouth, teased it with his tongue, then bit until she cried out beneath him.

It was as if the sensation pushed her over the edge. She rose to him on an urgent cry, and he shifted his weight, instinctively intent on satisfying her. The sounds of her breath matched his thrusts, soft in the night, spiraling up as he rocked into her. As he drowned in the sensation of her tight, womanly flesh sliding over his.

When she rose to him at last for those perfect, final strokes, it was with a keening sound of pleasure, her nails digging into the silk of his waistcoat, her eyes shut tight as her head rolled back into the pillow. Lazonby went over the edge with her, felt his bollocks contract and his arms shudder with every thrust until he had filled her with the warmth of his seed.

He fell against her, conscious only of her scent and of a satisfaction so deep that for an instant, his mind was free, his life perfect. Lightly, he let his forehead rest on hers. Anisha opened her eyes and he stared into them, unwilling to blink; unwilling to shut her out in even the smallest of ways. They floated thus for a moment, utterly linked, utterly lost in one another. Perhaps they even slept. He was not certain, for it was as if time did not exist.

But life is never perfect for long. He came fully back to himself to the realization that someone was pecking lightly on the door, and that Anisha now lay beside him.

At the sound, she roused. "Go *away,* Janet," she managed, her eyes still closed. "Just go to bed. *Please.*"

A moment passed, followed by the sound of the footsteps retreating.

An awkward silence flooded in around them. As if to dispel it, Anisha kissed him again. He rolled to one side, his body leaving hers as he went, then pulled her hard against him.

"Will it be all right?" he murmured, stroking the hair back from her forehead.

"Janet?" she said drowsily. "Oh, she minds her own business."

He winced. "She knows, then."

She smiled softly. "Otherwise, she wouldn't have knocked."

He felt uneasy at the thought, but it was too late to fret over it now. It was not, however, too late to make his apology. "Anisha," he whispered, brushing his lips over her eyebrow, "you . . . madden me, I think. That was not my best."

Her eyes heavy and somnolent, she looked up at him. "I do hope you are not apologizing?"

On a small laugh, he rolled a little onto his back, taking her with him until she lay splayed over his chest. He kissed her again, then said, "The first time a man makes love to a woman, it should be sweetness and gentleness. Not rough impatience. Not madness."

"This wasn't my first time," she returned.

"Umm," he grunted, savoring the weight of her atop him. "That's not quite what I meant."

She rose up on her elbows, her fingers going to his waistcoat, long, loose tendrils of her hair tumbling over one shoulder. "That fire simmering between us, Rance, had to be put out," she whispered, slipping loose the buttons as she spoke. "The ancient texts — the *Kāmashastra* — teach us a hundred ways to delay gratification, any of which I would be pleased to share with you, should you wish it. But sometimes — sometimes, perhaps, when desire has been *too* long deferred — a conflagration explodes."

He looked at her a little curiously, but Anisha had shifted into a seated position beside him, her dress badly crushed. Her elegant, jewel-toned sari lay half off the bed, the other half having slithered onto the floor below.

"Don't leave," she ordered, rising. "Whatever must happen tomorrow, don't leave tonight, Rance. *That* is the one thing I could not forgive. Now keep my bed warm whilst I undress." With that, Anisha snatched up the sari, trailing one end of it over the carpet as she headed toward a second door.

It was then he remembered Janet. "Er, might I be of some help?" he said after her. "With your . . . ah, your corset?"

Anisha turned, her spine elegantly aligned, her breasts still beautifully high amidst the untidy tendrils of tumbled-down hair. "I do not own a corset," she said simply.

"Oh."

She smiled faintly. "I find them unhealthful," she added. "They restrict one's vital life forces — one's *prana* — and that hampers *citta* —"

"Ah," he said. "Which is . . . ?"

Anisha paused to think. "Well, awareness of life," she said. "Consciousness."

"So a woman can't think straight in a tight corset?"

Again came her odd little half-smile. "There are a lot of things a woman can't do in a tight corset," she said, pausing just long enough to toe off her dainty slippers before she vanished. He rolled back down into the softness of her bed, staring into the shimmering silk canopy above.

Good Lord. Anisha didn't wear a corset.

And they had made love with their shoes on.

The first was a little arousing. The second was simply lowering.

But he could scarcely be bothered. Instead, he simply lay, sated and lethargic, listening to the sound of water splashing, and imagined Anisha bathing. But eventually, thinking better of his lethargy, he rose, restored his clothing to some semblance of order, then locked the bedchamber door — as he should have done on his way in. Pushing off his shoes, he pondered what next to do.

He'd dragged Nish up here, all flash and

heat, in a mad rush to have her. Afraid to slow down long enough to give himself time to think it all through. He had believed, he supposed, that they would simply scratch the itch between them, and be done with it.

But he was assuredly not done with her — nor she, apparently, with him.

He closed his eyes and listened to a tap wrenching shut, but in the near dark, weighed down by the heavy silence, it was all too easy for the guilt to begin seeping in. He had accused Luc of treating Miss Rutledge like a ha'penny whore, then he'd turned round and made love to Anisha without so much as undressing, spilling himself inside her with nary a thought, nary a precaution.

That was what the flash and heat — the desire too long denied — had cost him.

Had cost *her.* Potentially.

A rope of creamy pearls trailed from a porcelain dish near the bed, and absently he picked them up. Incredibly long, they lay warm and heavy in his palm, oddly soothing to hold. Pondering his predicament, Rance let them run like a waterfall from hand to hand, bitterly acknowledging that nothing, really, had changed.

The world still believed him a cheat, a liar, and a cold-blooded killer. Anisha still moved on the tenuous edge of polite society, still had two impressionable children to raise. He still owed her brother his life.

And he'd just repaid that debt by doing the one thing Ruthveyn had asked him not to do — debauch his sister.

But Rance's good intentions, if he'd had any, flew from his head when Anisha reappeared, clad in an oddly familiar peignoir made of emerald silk heavily embroidered with gold — *zari,* she'd called it when he'd seen her stitching the shimmering banyan Ruthveyn so often wore.

As she approached through the gloom, however, he realized hers hung open, with no silk trousers — no *anything* — beneath. Her pile of luxurious hair had tumbled even further into disarray, and she still wore her magnificent jewels, as if she belonged in some exotic Mughal harem.

Pausing at the edge of the bed, she let her fingers trail temptingly over the muscles of his thigh. "I find myself," she said huskily, "in dire, desperate need —"

"Then I should be flogged for my failure," he whispered, catching her hand and drawing it to his mouth.

"— of a lady's maid," she finished, her face warming to a wicked smile, "despite my earlier refusal. Might you now oblige me?"

He sat up, his waistcoat still unbuttoned. "Gratefully," he said, holding her gaze, "provided you will put these pearls round your neck and come back to bed wearing absolutely nothing else."

She lifted those elegant, perfectly arched black eyebrows. "I would point out, my dear, that I am already naked, or almost. But you — ah, you still languish in your evening clothes."

Dropping the pearls onto the night table with a clatter, Rance pulled her between his legs and set his lips between her breasts. "I want to see you," he rasped, pushing the silk from her shoulders.

The robe slithered down her arms and off her back to pool about her feet on the carpet. On a moan of pleasure, Anisha speared her fingers into his hair, holding him to her. He turned and captured her areola in his mouth, slowly sucking. Then he focused his attention to the other breast, lightly rimming it with his tongue, watching in delight as her nipple peaked and hardened.

After a time, however, she stepped back, her breath already roughening. "Loosen my hair," she whispered. "Take off my choker.

This time, I want to be entirely naked with you. I want to enjoy you, Rance, as you were so obviously meant to be enjoyed."

"Madam's wish is my command," he murmured, and she turned around. When he pulled the last pin from her hair, he crooked his head and set his lips to the long curve of her neck, pushing away another needle of guilt.

Lifting her hair so that he might unclasp the jeweled collar, Anisha crooked her head to look back at him. "This is no one's business but our own," she said quietly, as if reading his mind. "The divine — in whatever form one imagines that celestial power — grants us the ability to take pleasure in one another. The means to move beyond ourselves and ascend into heaven here on earth, even if only fleetingly."

She was entirely serious. He laid the choker aside, and she turned in his arms.

"I wish to show you the divine, *meri jaan*," she whispered, cupping his face in her hands. "And I wish you to show me. The conflagration is over. Now the slow simmer should begin."

But Rance was already on simmer and edging near to boil. Still seated, he drew her back to him. "Good God, Anisha, you do know how to tempt a man," he whispered, setting his ear to her heart. It beat slow and strong, in tempo with his own, it seemed.

He pushed away the worry and savored her. Anisha was so small in his embrace, so perfectly formed, with round, high breasts, slightly flared hips, and a slight, ripe swell of a belly that made him think of lazy afternoons with his head resting just there.

After a moment had passed, however, his impatience got the better of him. Rance set her away and stood, his gaze holding hers as he began to strip off what had been, at the start of the evening, a remarkably elegant cravat.

"A thousand times, Nish," he whispered, "I have dreamt of this."

She caught her lip between her teeth and looked away. "I was never sure."

"Don't be foolish," he said too harshly. "No man could look at you and feel anything less. I have burned for you, Anisha, from the moment I bent down to pick that luscious scrap of green silk from the floor of your cabin and felt your scent swirl up like hot, sunlit flowers. And I think that I have burned for you every moment since."

"You remember it," she murmured, and this time she did push the waistcoat off. That done, her clever fingers began to tug up the hems of the shirt he had neatened just moments earlier. As if in surrender, he raised his arms and let her strip the garment from his body. It floated up, enveloping them in their mingled scents.

"But this *is* unwise," he said, looking down at her. "Tell me, Nish, to go away. Do you have the strength? I wish you did, for God knows I don't."

"Oh, I have the strength to do anything that must be done." But her gaze was drifting over his chest, her fingers already toying at his trouser buttons. "But send you away? No. If you wish to leave — if you care more for propriety than for *this* —then the door is that way."

"I don't give a damn about propriety," he rasped, catching her chin in his hand, forcing those hot-chocolate eyes to his own. "But I do care more for *you* than . . . well, than bears talking about. I care for Tom and Teddy. And I care for Ruthveyn's good opinion."

"I am responsible for myself," she said for the second time that night, "and for my children. I respect my brother, yes, and love him deeply. But I told you the day I arrived in London that I would not live under his thumb."

With each word, Anisha went on with her work, slipping free the buttons until his trousers bagged off his hips. He went on saying nothing, half afraid to break the spell. And when she looked up, there was a sultry certainty in her eyes, her face stripped free of impatience, of raw lust. It was a simmering look of promise, and no small amount of warning, as if they edged near an abyss of desire from which he might never extract himself.

With her, that had always been his deepest fear.

He had thought himself hard and jaded; believed that he had tasted all the world's indulgences until numbed by them. But he was beginning to think himself instead just unenlightened. That he was a man who had known only satiation but no passion. No pleasure. Never this sort of bone-deep yearning he felt for her.

She skimmed her hands low beneath the soft linen of his drawers, making his belly shiver with raw desire. *"Anisha."* He caught one hand, drew it up, and kissed the pulse of her wrist.

"Come," she said, stepping back from the vee of his legs and catching his fingers in hers. "Lie with me till dawn. There will be time enough later for your guilt, and for us to decide what must come next."

He shucked the rest of his clothes in a

heap as her eyes widened with what looked like feminine appreciation. Then he drew her into his embrace, bending her head back over his arm to plumb the sweet depths of her mouth in a kiss so decadent he felt her knees shaking.

When he'd finished, however, she turned the tables, leaning into him and brushing her lips down the curve of his throat then over his shoulder. There she lingered, drawing the pink tip of her tongue lightly down the pale, knotted scar that marred his upper arm.

"So beautiful, your many imperfections," she whispered. "A lover scorned, perhaps?"

He gave a soft laugh. "No, a steel *flissa* —a wicked blade wielded by a half-crazed Berber," he murmured. "But aye, many is the word, Nish, if it's imperfections you seek."

But already she had turned her attention, and her mouth, to the trace of blue-black stippling over the curve of his bicep, the remnants of an old powder burn. His battle-roughed spots seemed only to encourage her, and already he could feel the low stirring of desire in his loins.

She sensed it and let her hand slip between them, taking his length in her small, clever fingers to stroke him back to full erection.

When he gave a low moan, she broke the kiss, urging him toward the bed. "Sit back against the pillows for me," she whispered. "Tuck up your legs."

The mattress gave against his weight as he settled his back against the headboard, then folded his legs into one another in the way Ruthveyn did when relaxing in the privacy of his home. Anisha shocked him by climbing into his lap, facing him.

Wrapping one leg around his waist, her breasts wobbling enticingly as she settled in, she pressed the warm folds of her womanhood firmly against his cock, which had gone rock-hard against his belly.

He had barely grasped the raw sensuality of the position when, rising up, she came down on him, impaling herself on his length with a long, deep sigh.

"Good . . . *Lord,*" he managed to grunt.

Rance had never felt so intimately, so deeply, joined to a woman in his life. Buried deep inside Anisha, he touched her in every possible way; heart to heart, belly to belly. The weight of her hips on his thighs was like an exquisite pleasure.

He had somehow imagined himself in command here, but this was a different Anisha. A woman who understood her own sensuality. Rance found it wildly, tantalizingly erotic. She wrapped the other leg above his hip, across the small of his back, then twined one arm about his neck. Kissing him deeply, she let her other hand slip round his waist, leaving a trail of heat.

"This time," she said when she broke the kiss, "I think we should go slowly, *meri jaan.* Very slowly."

Then her hand slid to his buttock, right across the black tattoo of his Guardian's mark, urging him deeper inside her. He let his hand stroke along the turn of her waist, then around and down, scooping her up beneath her right buttock, instinctively lifting her to him as Anisha eased back and forth on his shaft with movements so slight as to be almost imperceptible.

"Umm," she said, but it was the barest of sounds; a mere vibration in her throat. And yet it carried with it exquisite feminine satisfaction. The position left her with much of the control but little room for maneuvering. And yet it hardly seemed to matter. It was the union, the warmth, and the feeling of his skin against hers that he seemed suddenly to ache for.

Rance had heard of such positions, of course. Across the brothels of France and the Maghreb, he'd learned a trick or two himself. But as Anisha stared deep into his eyes, scarcely moving, scarcely breathing, the intimacy of it began to feel like something just a notch beyond his ordinary experiences.

Ruthveyn often spoke in almost spiritual terms about the sex act, believing, apparently, that it was — or could be — a near-mystical thing. Rance had always suspected it had more to do with all the hashish they had smoked than anything nearing the divine.

Still, there was no disputing that intimacy was viewed differently in the Hindustan. One of Gauthier's lieutenants had often talked of having had a Bengali mistress for a time, and of her skill in what he had termed "the thousand ways of love." But the lady had died too young, and the lieutenant's passions had died with her — and the stories he had told afterward had seemed to Rance just a madman's erotic dreams. But now he was beginning to wonder . . .

Just then, Anisha rocked her hips back, then forward again, deepening the contact ever so slightly, and Rance decided she need know only one of those thousand ways — *this* one — because it was exquisite. His head swam with the rich scent of her, and it was as if his every nerve had come alive. And when she let her head fall back, exposing the creamy length of her throat, Rance bit his way down, then pressed butterfly kisses across her breasts.

To his surprise, Anisha suddenly reached out, scooping up the pearls he'd left lying loose on the night table. With a faintly wicked smile, she looped them around his neck, twisted them twice, then placed the opposite end around her own.

"I forgot," she said, her voice husky with desire, "that I'd promised to wear the pearls for you."

He laughed and looked down at the incongruity of it. The strand was long and made to be worn in three or four loops. In this fashion, however, even twined round the both of them, the pearls still trailed down her shoulders, just brushing between her breasts where they twisted, the contrast of the pale, shimmering ivory against her warm skin a wildly erotic vision.

Once again, it was as if Rance lost track of time as their bodies were perfectly joined in a slow, exquisite rhythm, their mouths and hands moving over one another as they shared their bodies. For what felt like hours he loved her, watching, bewitched, until she fell into a sensual, almost dreamlike trance, her smile soft, her gaze both far away and yet totally bound to his.

In time, it was as if she swept him away with her, washing him out to sea on a tide of sensual pleasure, setting him adrift in some otherworldly place where he became a part of her, and she a part of him; a place of utter physical harmony where their bodies and their breath were as one. The room, the faint creaking of the bed, even the flickering lamplight, became not a blur but a sort of sensual continuum, a part of their every touch and sigh.

Only his concern for her remained in the back of his mind, a tenuous and slender thread that bound him to reality even as his body was bound to hers. And eventually, a clock struck in the depths of the house, leaving him acutely aware his time with her, were it to last a hundred years, would always feel too short.

Anisha felt it, too, and seemed to bestir herself willingly back to awareness. These were stolen moments and they knew it, the both of them. A time out of place, and likely never destined to be repeated. And when eventually her gaze sharpened to his and she shifted onto her knees to begin to move on him in earnest, Rance thought he might go mad simply watching as the edge of her pleasure neared.

Eventually she unwrapped her arms from

his neck and seized hold of the headboard behind him. Again and again she rose, urging herself against the full length of his cock, which was hard as marble now. She threw back her head, the slender tendons of her throat tightening. The pearls slid back and forth in the dampness between her breasts and soon Anisha, too, was slick and hot against him, and Rance had to forcibly resist the urge to tumble her backward and take control by mounting her hard again.

Instead, he eased his hand between them and found the hard nub of her desire just above his shaft. He circled the pad of his thumb round and round, and Anisha cried out, then began to moan.

The beauty of her need as she rode him pushed Rance over the edge. He thrust inside her again and again until they came together in a meteoric shower of shuddering pleasure, his very life force surging inside Anisha. Exquisite, inexplicable sensations shot through him like molten lightning and left him gasping. Left him shaken to his very core.

They collapsed onto the mattress together, still shuddering, tangled in the pearls, Anisha coming to rest against his shoulder, weightless and perfect.

The breath still heaving from his chest,

Rance crooked his head to look down at her, still unable to get his mind wrapped around all that he'd experienced tonight. This was *Anisha*. The woman he admired more than any on earth. His friend and confidante.

His lover.

And yet through all the shuddering need, incredible pleasure, and shattering light, a new thought haunted Rance.

How was he ever to give this up?

Could he give it up? And if not, what did he have to offer her?

Very little, in truth.

Was that not the very reason he had avoided this thing for so long? The very reason he had held fast to their friendship even as he'd attempted to keep her at arm's length, both emotionally and physically?

But for once, he resolved not to think about what was *not*. As he grappled for sanity and for breath, Rance vowed that for tonight, he would think only of what was. He would savor the feel of this perfect woman's bare skin against his, and the weight of her head tucked on his shoulder.

Later, she had said, they would think about guilt. And hating himself now — in this sweet and perfect moment — would only dishonor her perfection.

The future . . . ah, now that was another thing altogether.

When his breathing calmed, he unwrapped the long strand from around his neck, then restored his end to her. "Lovely," he murmured, twisting his head around to nibble at her earlobe.

She laughed, the beads spilling from her hand as she clasped them to her breast. "I confess, I didn't choose them," she said. "But had I known you found them erotic, I would have worn them every day for the past year, merely to torment you."

He nuzzled her lightly on the cheek. "The last year has been torment enough, thank you," he said. "But why have I never seen them?"

Anisha fell back against his arm and stared up into the silk canopy above. After a few moments passed, she told him about the pearls, and how so often she put them on, only to take them off again, reminding Rance yet again of how precariously between two worlds she was caught.

"So you did that again tonight," he said softly, his gaze drifting over her face. "Put them on, and took them off? Then just tossed them in the dish?"

She rolled into him and smiled. "Careless, was it not?" she murmured. "And foolish, perhaps, to put on something so untraditional instead. Someday I'll send round to Garrard's and have the strand shortened, I suppose."

"But the jeweled collar and earrings were your mother's, weren't they?" he murmured, gazing at her. "And that charm round your ankle — that tiger's claw set in gold — I recognize it, you see, for Ruthveyn wears one round his neck. Those were hers, too. All of that is deeply traditional."

"Not *English* traditional," she said, looking away. "Not in the way people here expect. But it is very hard sometimes to —"

Her words jerked to a halt and he kissed her cheek again. "What?" he murmured. "Go on."

She cast him a chagrined glance. "It's just a strand of pearls."

"It's not *just* anything," he said. "It is a symbol. It is . . . your heritage."

"Yes. Exactly." For an instant, she caught her lip between her teeth in that way she so often did. "Sometimes, Rance, it's hard to be so many things at once," she eventually said. "To be a good English wife, as I once was, and a good mother, and . . . and to still be true to one's inner self. To keep the heart of one's self intact, and to acknowledge, even inwardly, one's differences. Yes, it is just a strand of pearls, and like my own essential *Britishness,* I try to wear it well. Yet so often . . . I fail."

Rance had no good answer to that; no simple platitude that would settle her inner conflict or undo the hurt he suspected her father and husband had slowly inflicted, or the doubt that they had inadvertently instilled in her heart.

Instead, he pulled her firmly against him, set his lips to her forehead, and spoke the truth of his own heart. "Nish, you have failed at nothing," he whispered against her skin. "Never. And you've earned the right to be yourself; earned it by being a dutiful daughter and an exemplary wife and mother."

In the dim stillness of the room, his answer seemed to please her, though he knew in the light of day she would likely have quarreled with it as too simplistic. But tonight she did not, and instead scooted tight against him, wrapping an arm round his waist and nestling her head in the crook of his arm. For long moments he lay there, simply listening to her breathe.

She could become so easily the keeper of his heart and his soul, he realized. Perhaps she already was. Perhaps he had entrusted his heart to her at almost first sight. He remembered the rage he'd felt upon seeing Jack Coldwater watching her; the cold, stark fear that the hate surrounding him might come to touch *her.*

Even now he could taste it like bile burning in the back of his throat. Rance forced his eyes shut and forced away the filth of his memories. Not even in his thoughts would he taint this perfect moment.

Eventually he felt her relax in his embrace, her body molded to his, and watched as the lamp's wick began to sputter, until at last Anisha slept. And though he lay beside her, soothed by the sound of her soft exhalations, he drowsed but little. His mind was caught up in the whirling machinations of those dreaded questions. The *how*s and the *why*s and the *if*s.

He looked down at the long tresses that spilled over his arm like a waterfall of raven silk, at the small, perfect breasts pressed to his ribs, and never had the answers seemed to matter more. And never had the truth seemed so illusory, so just beyond his reach.

He thought again of the slip of paper Anaïs de Rohan had given him, and he felt that fleeting sense of hope brush past again on wings so soft and ephemeral the hope mightn't have existed at all. The *Fraternitas*'s newest Guardian, he feared, still possessed the naïveté of girlhood. And this — a near decade and a half of fomented scandal — no, this would not be resolved by good intentions and a piece of paper, however well meant it all was.

But even had he been publicly exonerated and the real criminal caught — even if he understood his strange obsession with Jack Coldwater — he would still be who he was. A man hardened by years in prison and on the battlefield, and by too many days and nights passed with sybarites like Ruthveyn in a drug-induced haze of pleasure.

He was a mercenary and a libertine who had lived first by his skill at the gaming table, and later by his wits and his sword; no better, really, than Pinkie Ringgold and that tribe of bullyboys surrounding Quartermaine. And about the only thing he was innocent of was murdering Lord Percy Peveril.

And yet it was not this, entirely, which gave him pause. He was not ashamed of who he was. He had survived a life that would have done in many a man — hell, the despair alone would have broken most of them. But the cloud of guilt hanging over his head had blighted his entire family. It had killed both his parents; one quickly, the other slowly. It had driven his sister from

London and into the Highlands. It had pushed his so-called friends so deep into hiding that all that remained to back him up was the strength of the *Fraternitas.*

And nothing had changed. He could count on his fingers the members of the *ton* who believed him innocent of knifing Peveril.

As to Anisha, she was perilously placed as it was. Indians were fast becoming not England's allies but her subjects — slaves, practically, in some quarters. Anglo-Indian marriages, once marginally acceptable to society, were all but unheard of now. Prejudice and avarice were bleeding the heart out of the Hindustan. Anisha was right to fear for her children's future. A black pall was slowly falling over India, and even Lazonby could feel it.

For Ruthveyn, his wealth, his title, and his usefulness to the Queen had helped overcome much prejudice. But Anisha had not her brother's good fortune. Despite her elegance and beauty, Anisha had made few friends here. Time would tell whether tonight's dinner party had helped or hurt in that mission.

Rance's musings were cut suddenly short when he heard the clock downstairs strike four, the sounds doleful in the darkness.

Cutting a glance at the heavy draperies, already drawn for the night, he wondered how much longer he dared wait before slipping away.

The answer was *not long.*

On his next breath, a soft knock sounded at the door. Rance looked down, faintly uneasy, and jogged Anisha awake. Her eyes flared wide in the gloom, and she rolled up onto one elbow. "Umm?"

"Mamma — ?" came an urgent hiss through the keyhole. "Mamma, are you up?"

"Teddy!" Anisha came awake with alacrity. "Teddy, are you all right?"

Rance was already on his feet and snatching up his things. As Anisha leapt from the bed and jerked on her silk robe, he planted a swift kiss on her lips and vanished into the dressing room, pushing the door half shut on blessedly silent hinges.

"Mamma, I can't sleep," said the boy through the slab of wood. "Can I come in?"

Setting one shoulder to the doorframe and tilting an ear, Rance heard the lock snap and the bedchamber door creak open. "Teddy, love," she said softly, "big boys do not sleep with their mothers. You know that."

"I *know,*" he whined. "But I *can't* sleep. Not *anywhere.*"

He heard a rustle of silk, as if she'd knelt to hug him. "Come here, mouse," she said, her voice gentle. "Now, if this is about the broken vase — ?"

"No," said the boy.

"The trampled daffodils?"

"Not exactly."

"The snake in the scullery sink?"

"A little," he whined.

"For that, you've already been punished, love. There's nothing more to worry about."

"Well, I'd like to have him back," said the boy morosely. "But mostly I just want to talk."

Rance heard the moment's hesitation in her voice, but there was nothing else for it. "Of course," she said. "Come sit in bed for a moment and tell me why you can't sleep, *hmm?* Then I'll take you back to your own room and tuck you in."

"All right," he said.

Through the spill of moonlight that sliced through the cracked dressing room draperies, Rance began gingerly to dress, praying he had not left anything behind. A moment later he heard the soft creak of the bed as they settled in.

He wished, oddly, that he could have seen them together. How many times, he wondered, had he watched the boys, their fair heads bent to their mother's dark, elegant coiffure as they leaned together over a book or a task?

How many times had he heard the three of them laugh together? — a small, tight-knit family who had nonetheless welcomed him into their midst. But the boys mightn't be so quick to welcome him into their mother's bed.

Rance tried not to think of *that.*

"So what's the trouble, sweet?" he heard Anisha murmur. "Have you and Tommy quarreled again?"

There was a long silence. "No, but I think I just need bigger boys to play with, Mamma," Teddy finally said. "I think perhaps that's why I'm always getting into trouble."

"Oh?" she said evenly. "That's it, is it?"

"Well, Tom can't bat, and his legs are too short," said the boy as if that somehow explained it. "And Chatterjee is always busy with Uncle Luc now. So I have been thinking I want to go away to school. To Eton. Frankie Fitzwater says it's the only place for a boy of consequence."

"Hmm," said Anisha. "I am not sure that's much of a recommendation, Teddy. Perhaps Eton was the only school willing to take

371

Frankie Fitzwater? Did you ever think of that?"

The boy seemed to consider it. "Could be," he finally said. "Mr. Fitzwater *is* a little silly. But I want to go *somewhere.* All that droning on in the schoolroom puts me to sleep, and at Eton, there would be cricket. Wouldn't there?"

"Oh, yes, I daresay," Anisha softly answered. "Cricket, and other games, too."

In the heavy silence that followed, Rance froze, fearful of being heard.

Had he been able to speak, he would have told the lad that the bullies of Eton were nothing to the annoyances of a younger brother, and that his new instructors would be just as dull, but far better armed — with long hickory rods that, when switched briskly across one's palm, stung enough to keep the dead sitting up straight.

"But you know, Teddy," Anisha finally resumed, her voice withering, "those places — those English schools — they seem so cruel to me. And they always struck me as — well, as places for boys whose mothers will not miss them . . ."

He heard the bed creak again. "And would you miss me, Mamma?" he wheedled, clearly wanting it both ways.

"Oh, Teddy!" Her voice muffled, as if

she'd pulled him against her. "Teddy, you are my baby. Oh, yes, I should miss you so terribly!"

"But Mamma, you would still have Tom," he pointed out. "*He's* the baby. Besides, going to Eton is what proper English boys do. And isn't that why we came here? So that I could learn to be a proper English boy?"

"Yes, of course it is," she said, but Rance could hear the anguish in her voice. "Still, many English boys do have tutors, you know. And Tommy — well, then he will wish to go away, too, will he not? And right on your heels, I daresay."

"Probably," said Teddy glumly. "But that's all right, Mamma. I'll look after him. And you — well, you could just have some more babies. I mean — *couldn't* you? Then you'd not miss us at all."

For an instant, Rance couldn't breathe, his fingers stilling on his waistcoat buttons. The boy's words, flung so casually out, hung in the cool night air. And suddenly, it was as if Rance's whole life hung there, too — suspended by the thread of an awful question.

"Oh, Teddy, I should love that more than anything on earth!" said Anisha on a breathless rush. "Of *course* I want more babies. But one cannot simply —"

373

She halted, as if realizing what she'd just said.

"But what?" Teddy demanded.

Again, the long, awful pause.

Forcing himself to move, Rance shrugged into his coat, imagining Anisha's expression as she formed the words. As she walked back through her logic and realized the inevitable.

"It doesn't matter, Teddy," she finally managed, "because more children could never replace you and Tom. The two of you are irreplaceable. Whatever gave you such a mad notion?"

"Janet," he replied calmly. "And it isn't mad. She says it all the time. Just yesterday she said it."

"Yesterday?"

"When she was pressing out your dinner gown," the boy explained. "She said to Chatterjee that it was high time you had more babies, before it was too late."

"I beg your pardon?" returned Anisha sharply.

"I'm just saying what she *said*," Teddy reported. "That you were going to keep pining after what you couldn't have 'til everything you did have shriveled up and died. Whatever that means."

"Oh —" Anisha murmured. "Oh, dear God."

"You really ought not wait, Mamma, until it is too late," Teddy sagely advised. "It just sounded bad. What Janet said, I mean, about shriveling."

But the tenuous thread had snapped, dropping a chilling pall over Rance. It furled down and around him like a cold, dead thing, then drew deep into his chest to lay like a weight against his heart. Somehow he finished buttoning his waistcoat and felt, to his horror, the hot press of tears stinging at the backs of his eyes.

Never had he dreamt a small boy could blurt out a more innocent — or accurate — truth.

"Teddy," Anisha finally said, plainly changing the subject, "you really oughtn't have been belowstairs at all. What were you doing?"

"Shooting marbles down the passageway," he said, as if it had been obvious. "There's a big hump in the flagstone where it goes over the kitchen drain, and it makes 'em leap and jump all around."

Ever so silently, Rance turned and eased the door shut.

Already he felt like an interloper here. And Teddy — good God, could small children and servants see what Anisha could not? That life was moving on and passing her by. That she was waiting on something that was never going to happen. Waiting on *someone* —someone who had bollixed up his life so badly he was not worth waiting on.

Was that what Anisha had been doing for the last year? Waiting on him to get his mess of a life straightened out? With a deep sense of shame for what he'd just done — clouding the pristine waters of their friendship, painting false hope, risking pregnancy — he tossed his cravat round his neck in disgust.

Anisha did not want an *affaire.* She wanted *a life.* And she deserved it.

He could tell by the soft rumble of voices that mother and son had descended into argument — a lecture, most likely, on the dangers of shooting marbles where servants had to tread. The sweetness of the night now gone, Rance paced to the window and quietly pushed wide the draperies. Already he could see a hint of dawn limning the rooftops of Mayfair.

Later, he told himself that the approaching sunrise had been the urgency that had driven him as he'd quietly pushed up the sash and thrown one leg out the window. That, perhaps, and the pure masculine challenge of scaling down a drainpipe in the dark.

But even as his feet touched the gravel below and he strode out through Ruthveyn's rear gardens with his cravat hanging loose round his neck, he was never sure.

It was likely just pure cowardice.

That, and the awful dread of facing the truth he feared he might see in Anisha's eyes.

CHAPTER 9

So true a fool is *love* that in your will,
Though you do any thing, he thinks no ill.
William Shakespeare, Sonnet 57

Disappointments, the great William Penn had once written, are not always to be measured by the loss of the thing but by the overvaluation put upon it. Lady Anisha Stafford had believed herself inured to disappointment, having suffered more than a few. She had learned from an early age to temper her expectations, to value fairly what she had, and to cherish it while she had it, even as she remained ever mindful that joy, unlike disappointment, was often fleeting.

But Mr. Penn, Anisha darkly considered, had wed a sprightly chit of less than half his fifty-odd years who had proceeded to bear him eight children about as fast as other women tatted cushions. It did not seem to Anisha as if he had suffered too many disappointments in *that* regard.

On a sudden surge of bitterness, she tried to snap open her letter for the umpteenth time, but the paper had by now gone limp.

Behind her, Janet made a *tch-tch*ing sound. "Chin up, ma'am." Her voice was sharp, as if she spoke to a child. "I've got to get this mess of hair put up before the carriage comes round, or you'll be late."

Anisha jerked her eyes up from the letter. "I'm sorry?"

In the mirror, Janet held her gaze steadily, one of the hair combs poised high. "Lady Anisha," she said in mild exasperation. "You can keep readin' that thing 'till the chickens roost, and you know not a blessed word of it'll change."

Anisha's lips thinned. "I do hope, Janet, that you have not been reading my post."

Janet stabbed in the comb. "No need, ma'am," she said. "That's laid on your dressing table four days now, and I know Lazonby's hand, for it looks like wild monkeys trained him penmanship. And as to what's in it —" Here, she paused to twist one rope of hair elaborately around another, then softened her voice. "As to what's in it, my lady, well, I can guess as much, I daresay, from the look in your eyes."

Anisha folded the letter, drew it smooth

between her fingers, then gently laid it down. "That obvious, am I?"

"Well, I have known you, my lady, since coming out to India twenty-some years ago," said the maid, calmly drawing up the rest of Anisha's hair a long, even brushstroke. "Serene as pond water, you were, even as a wee girl."

"Was I?" Absently, Anisha fiddled with Janet's dish of hairpins. "I can't recall."

"Oh, I'll never forget." Janet began deftly twisting the length of Anisha's hair into an elegant coronet. "What a proper little Indian lady you looked in your bright silks, with that skinny spine straight as a stick and your manner so calm. Like an exotic duchess, you were. Even Captain Stafford, God rest him, and those two hellions upstairs couldn't throw you out. But Lazonby? Now *he* agitates you, ma'am, and always has. 'Tis a bad sign, that, when a man can knock a steadfast female all a'kilter."

Anisha made a pretense of poking about in the dish, biting hard at her lip so as not to cry. "Do not feel sorry for me, Janet," she warned when the urge had passed.

"Oh, Lord, I don't!" said the maid around the hairpins she'd just tucked between her lips. "You're a rich, beautiful widow with a family that loves you — even if they do take advantage of your good heart. And if Lazonby don't want you, ma'am, someone will."

"Janet, really — !"

But Janet ignored her disapprobation. "No, my lady, 'tis Lazonby I feel for, and no mistake," she continued. "Never saw a handsomer, more twisted-up sort of fellow. Oh, bless me — !" Stabbing a pin into place, Janet rammed a hand into her pocket and began rummaging. "Speaking of letters, Higgenthorpe gave me this. Then Tom chased that squirrel in through the conservatory, and Silk and Satin set off after it and I reckon my mind went skittering after 'em."

"The morning post?" Anisha caught Janet's gaze in the mirror as another letter was passed over her shoulder.

"No, that Mrs. Rutledge's footman brought it," said Janet. "T'will be good news, I pray."

Anisha prayed so, too.

She had confided Luc's indiscretion to Janet. Despite Anisha's halfhearted accusation about Rance's letter, she knew Janet was trustworthy to a fault. And Anisha had needed a second set of ears to guard against servants' gossip — of which there had been none, thank God.

Swiftly, she opened the letter and let her eyes sweep down it before placing it face-down on her dressing table, relief washing through her.

It was precisely what Frederica Rutledge had led Anisha to expect: a polite but carefully veiled refusal of Luc's offer, saying that the family feared he was too young and Lucy too headstrong to make a happy marriage, and expressing the Rutledges' warmest wish of seeing them both today.

It seemed Mrs. Rutledge had indeed been able to somehow smooth the matter over with her husband. Lucan had been saved, through no effort of his own, from an early marriage.

And Miss Rutledge had been saved from Lucan.

Despite her own personal despair, Anisha was grateful. "It is good news, Janet," she said quietly. "Lord Lucan has escaped the parson's grasp. He has been lucky indeed."

"Aye, and learnt a lesson, 'tis to be hoped," said Janet darkly. Suddenly, her expression brightened. "Oh! Speaking of lucky, my lady . . ."

"Yes?"

"I was just wondering." Janet colored a little as Anisha watched her in the mirror. "Might I trouble you again? About my stars and such?"

"Jyotish?" Anisha hardened her stare. "Janet, what are you up to?"

"The Plate, ma'am. 'Tis this Thursday." At Anisha's blank stare, she added, "At Epsom? The horse race?"

"Oh, Janet, for heaven's sake." Anisha looked at her askance. "You know I do not care for gambling."

But when Janet's face fell, Anisha relented and spun half around on her dressing stool. "Oh, very well," she said impatiently. "Just give me your hand."

With a soft smile, Janet presented it.

Anisha took it and spread her fingers wide, lightly tracing the lines as she struggled to remember the maid's particulars. "Such fine, long hands," she murmured, tracing Janet's heart line. "You are *Mithuna* ascendant, and so ruled by Mercury. Tell me about this race."

"Well, it's just the Grand Stand Plate, ma'am." At Anisha's blank look, she went on. " 'Tis run every year. My brother — the one who buttles for Lord Sherrell — says his lordship's to go, and he'll place one bet for the both of us. We've only to agree upon the horse."

"And who shall you choose?" Anisha asked, her attention fixed upon the palm.

383

"Jim — my brother — he says Idle Boy or Gardenia. But I thought perhaps Lord Chesterfield's Sampson, seeing as you once told me S was lucky for me."

"Usually, yes." Still Anisha did not look up at her. "But no, none of those. And remember, Janet, the stars are never static, just as our lives never are. We are all of us — always — in a state of constant and fluid change."

"Well . . ." said Janet pensively, "I wouldn't know about fluids. But there's always Lord Exeter's horse — or one o' them."

"What is the horse's name?" Anisha gently folded Janet's fingers in.

"Hmm, let me think which was the S one — oh, yes! 'Tis Swordplayer."

"Ah." Anisha gave Janet's fist a squeeze, and let it go. "Well. Have you the ruby chip pendant I gave you?"

"Yes, ma'am. In my room. But you told me not to wear it all the time."

"Indeed, but you must put it on now," said Anisha, "and wear it the rest of the week. Then tell Jim to place his bet on Swordplayer."

"Really, ma'am?" Janet sounded in alt. "And will we win, then?"

Anisha's smile was crooked. "Well, I believe life will fall into good order for you in the coming days," she said. "That is all I can tell you. Now, you must on no account let on to Luc we had this discussion, for he'll want me to —"

Just then, a knock sounded, and Luc himself dashed in, pinching a pair of waist-coats by their collars. Chatterjee stood behind him, his eyes catching Anisha's in a speaking glance.

Luc, it seemed, was being a problem this morning.

"Which, Nish?" he said a little nervously. "I can't decide. I don't know why."

Anisha turned her head so that Janet might insert the last comb. "You don't know why you can't decide?"

"Yes, precisely," said the young man, one guinea-gold curl bouncing down the center of his forehead. "Almost precisely. I mean, I can't decide whether to look dashing. Or dandyish. Or solemn. Or what." Here he thrust the waistcoats forward in turn. "Gold makes my eyes more vivid, but the charcoal looks more sedate. Sedate might be good, I daresay?"

"And you wish to please the Rutledges?" Anisha murmured. "You might have thought of that three days ago, and worried less about your waistcoats."

"Well, it's too late now, isn't it?" he said,

the old bitterness edging back into his voice. "Good God, do you mean to flog me over this forever, Nish?"

But the young man, Anisha realized, had no conception of what *forever* felt like.

Forever felt like a life lived waiting on your father's approval. A decade spent in a near-loveless marriage. A year wasted in wait of a kiss — or just a mere sidelong look of hopeless yearning.

Forever felt like her life.

Anisha felt the well of tears rush in again and was compelled to fight it down.

Something in her gaze must have softened Luc's tone. "Nish, I'm sorry," he said pleadingly, "for I know I've bollixed things up. But now I wish merely to make a good impression on Mr. Rutledge. Frankie Fitzwater said Rutledge was a sporting chap in his day, but not much of a blade — at least, not fashionwise . . ."

Anisha waved toward the charcoal. "Well, if he decides to run you through," she managed, "it will be easier for Chatterjee to get the bloodstains out of that one."

Luc groaned and flung himself onto her bed, sending Silk and Satin scattering. "Nish, good God!"

"Give me those," Chatterjee chided, nearly tripping over the cats to seize the garments. "Didn't I just press them? One cannot wallow about on good fabric like a pig."

Anisha turned around on her dressing stool and regarded the both of them steadily. "Chatterjee, we will find Lucan a new valet soon, I promise," she said. "One who will stay put this time."

"Oh, yes, yes," Chatterjee sang as he vanished, "and cows will leap over the moon!"

"As to you, Luc, you may relax," she dryly added, presenting the letter between two fingers. "Your suit of Lucy Rutledge has been politely refused."

Luc sat abruptly upright from the bed, blinking. *"Refused?"*

Anisha twitched the letter by way of proof.

But a red flush was creeping over Luc's face. "What, am I not good enough now?" he said, leaping up to snatch it. "What the devil does she want, then? A duke?"

"I cannot say," Anisha murmured. "Perhaps she does not want a husband at all. Is that so inconceivable?"

"Or perhaps she just doesn't want *me,*" said Luc indignantly.

Janet set the lid on the hairpins with a clatter. "No pleasing some folk," she muttered.

"Apparently not," said Anisha. "And the

fact is, Lucan, Lucy Rutledge is too young to know what she wants. As are you."

"Apparently," said Lucan a little bitterly, "age hasn't anything to do with it. Bessett seems to have had a devil of a time deciding what he wanted, and the man is all of thirty."

"Lucan, that is quite enough," she said warningly.

But the lad wasn't finished. "And you, Nish, do you know what you want?" he demanded. "And if you do, why aren't you fighting for it? Perhaps, had you done a little kissing and groping in the dark, you'd not be where you are now."

"Oh?" Anisha rose in a rustle of champagne-gold satin, her voice cold. "And where, precisely, am I, Lucan?"

"On your way to lifelong widowhood," he said sarcastically. "And to a wedding that could have been yours instead of Miss de Rohan's had you played your cards with a modicum of bravado."

Anisha felt herself trembling inside with a rage that was not entirely directed at her brother. "You, Lucan, do not know a bloody thing about me or what I want," she retorted, resisting the urge to slap him. "You know nothing of the life I've lived. Nothing of what it means to be a wife or mother or even a widow, come to that. You are just a cocksure little fool who hasn't the good sense to know the hell he just escaped. And now you dare to question the Rutledges' judgment? Or mine? Well, be damned to you."

Luc froze, his face instantly stricken.

They were likely the first curse words to pass Anisha's lips — certainly the first aimed at her brother. But now that she had spoken them, Anisha felt a little more free. A little more empowered. And very, very angry — at Luc. And at Rance.

Damn it, she was tired of presumptuous men.

But Lucan was still staring at her. "Nish, please forgive me. I . . . I am sorry."

Anisha snatched her shawl from the bed. "No, Luc, you are naïve, and without the sense to know it," she retorted. "Now go get into your coat. We've a wedding to attend."

Lord and Lady Bessett's wedding was a garden affair at a massive old house in Wellclose Square, a neighborhood far to the east of Mayfair. The bride, attired in a boldly colored gown of red and white silk, glowed with happiness.

For his part, Geoff looked inordinately pleased. He kissed Anaïs de Rohan lingeringly on the lips amidst a skirling shower of apple blossoms as the Reverend Mr. Sutherland, proudly beaming, pronounced them man and wife.

And as Anisha watched, smiling in all the right places, she thought about Lucan's accusation.

Had she been too passive? Had she not fought for what she wanted?

It felt to Anisha as if she'd been fighting the whole of her life. But fighting what? Her father? Her husband? Or just conformity, and the subservient role English society had cast her into?

Certainly she was not the bold and dashing Anaïs de Rohan. No, *"serene"* and *"proper"* had been Janet's words. And in hindsight, they sounded so frightfully dull.

Perhaps — just perhaps — there was something in between proper and dashing? Some middle ground the formerly serene might occupy while they looked about for what they truly wanted out of life? Or perhaps Lucan was right. Perhaps it was simply better to gird one's loins and *fight.* Today, somehow, that notion suited her.

Afterward, as the crowd melted from the gardens back into the house for a wedding breakfast, Geoff caught up with Anisha and companionably caught her arm in his.

"Thank you," he said. "Thank you for coming, Nish. This day would not have been as special without you here to celebrate with us."

"It was my great —" Her voice hitched as Rance passed by, his face expressionless.

Geoff stopped and turned to face her. "Nish?"

She forced a smile. "It was my great pleasure," she said, but the words came out a little husky. "Thank you for having us."

Geoff cut a dark look at Rance's back as he vanished into the shadows of the house. "Nish, what now?" he demanded. "Do I need to call the old boy out after all?"

She slid her hand around his arm. "Go on in, Geoff," she managed. "I'm fine. Truly. I need to keep an eye on Lucan and Miss Rutledge."

Geoff said nothing to that, but his eyes darkened. He was still watching her intently.

"You cannot read me, Geoff," she said, dropping her voice. "You can no more see into my world than I into yours. Is that not the one precious gift we shared? That drew us close? Go to your beautiful bride, and be happy."

He looked down at her through a sweep of dark lashes, his gaze suspicious. "But when do you get to be happy, Anisha?" he murmured. "Tell me that, and my happiness shall increase tenfold."

She managed to laugh. "Just this morning Janet reminded me somewhat testily that I am a rich, beautiful widow with a family that loves me," she said. "I have all the happiness I require. Go inside, and let us all toast your happiness, for we wish it so sincerely."

With a chary glance, he patted her hand, gave a curt nod, and slipped away. Anisha let out a sigh of relief. She lingered another moment, until Miss Rutledge went in on her father's arm, Luc following some twenty paces behind.

It was a wise distance, she judged. Mr. Rutledge was a handsome, athletic-looking man who carried himself with a sort of lethal grace and looked nothing like the rural squire he was purported to be. As with Rance, the gentleman appeared outwardly affable, but his smile was edged with something a little less benign than good humor if one looked closely.

Anisha wondered just what his wife had told him. A tempered version of the truth, perhaps. But it had been enough to put a steely glint in Lucy's father's eye.

When all the others had gone in, Mr. Sutherland gently took Anisha's hand and laid it on his arm. "Come, my girl," he said. "We are bringing up the rear, I'm afraid."

Anisha leaned near and lightly kissed his cheek. "I was waiting for you."

The Preost laughed, and together they went in. Anisha made her way around the room on his arm, grateful for his company. She had always been one of Sutherland's favorites, she knew, and until recently she'd spent a good deal of time in the St. James Society's reading rooms, which Sutherland oversaw.

In time, the health and happiness of the bride and groom was toasted, and a fine repast laid out in the dining room. Lucan filled Anisha's plate, then seated her at an empty table for six in the withdrawing room. Almost at once, Rance came in with Frederica Rutledge.

He looked at Anisha a little uncomfortably, then, left with no alternative, approached to put Mrs. Rutledge's plate down.

"Lady Anisha," he said, drawing out a chair for Mrs. Rutledge. "May we join you?"

"Why, nothing would please me more," she said.

He excused himself with a slight bow and returned to the dining room.

"Lord Lazonby is very kind, isn't he?" said

Mrs. Rutledge, watching him over her shoulder.

Anisha's gaze left the bull's-eye she had mentally painted between Rance's shoulder blades. "Quite, yes," she agreed.

"Lucy, however, was rather cowed by him," Mrs. Rutledge confessed, dropping her voice. "I trust you received my note this morning?"

"I did, thank you." Anisha cast a glance at Mr. Rutledge, who was seated with the bride's cousins. "But your husband has a rather strained look about his eyes. Is all well?"

"Not remotely." Her smile was wan. "Though he would never ruin Anaïs's special day, Bentley is wildly angry. Lucy has survived his wrath, but only just."

"I wonder he doesn't blame my brother," she remarked, her gaze falling to the linen napkin in her lap. "He would have every right to do so."

"Of course he does, a little," Mrs. Rutledge acknowledged. "But mostly he just blames himself."

"*Himself?*" Anisha jerked her chin up. "I cannot imagine why, particularly when he wasn't even present."

Mrs. Rutledge cast her husband a fond but faintly exasperated look. "I'm afraid my husband enjoyed a terribly misspent youth," she said. "His indiscretions were legendary, and his family nearly torn apart. He fears the twins take after him." Here, she stopped and heaved a sigh. "Which, honestly, they do. We've had years of nonstop roguery out of that pair."

Not for the first time, Anisha let her eyes drift over Frederica Rutledge's remarkably beautiful eyes and dark hair. "You must have married frightfully young."

"Yes." Mrs. Rutledge's cheeks turned faintly pink. "I'm afraid I was one of my husband's indiscretions. The *last* one."

Lightly, Anisha's fingertips touched her mouth. "I do beg your pardon," she said. "I am not usually so gauche. Your age — or your husband's past — is none of my business."

At that, Mrs. Rutledge laughed. "Well, let us just say I am a few years older than you."

"Not many," Anisha remarked in a low undertone.

"Not *too* many, perhaps." Mrs. Rutledge's eyes danced with good humor. "As to Lucy, I have left her father to deal with her indiscretion."

Anisha's heart sunk. "What will he do to her?"

"Nothing she does not deserve," said Mrs.

Rutledge grimly. "Lucy is going into service."

"Into *service* — ?" Anisha was appalled.

"In a manner of speaking," Mrs. Rutledge clarified. "She's to be a companion to a distant but dear cousin who is presently short of funds. She'll also serve as a sort of governess, too. Lucy will not be ill-treated for an instant. Isolated, yes. Underpaid, terribly. But it will all do her good, I daresay. If Lucy were to remain in Town — or even Gloucestershire — she would simply insist on kicking up her heels until she took a serious tumble."

"Oh," said Anisha, her face falling. "Oh, dear."

Mrs. Rutledge reached across the table and laid her hand over Anisha's. "Lucy needs a purpose in her life, and this will give her one," she said reassuringly. "Yes, Lady Anisha, I was married very young. Much younger than Lucy is, for this is her second Season and still she will not settle down. And yes, my marriage turned out brilliantly. But honestly, what were the chances, when circumstance, not choice, threw us together?"

"Not good," Anisha conceded.

"No, not good," the lady returned. "I will not try my luck again. And I *will not* have *my* family torn apart, either."

For the first time Anisha saw the grim, nearly ruthless determination in Frederica Rutledge's eyes. Here was a mother who guarded her cubs like a lioness, and the realization ratcheted the lady up about six notches in Anisha's estimation. And she realized, too, that Mr. Rutledge's reactions had likely been tempered by his wife's resolve. She might not have worn the trousers in the family, but Anisha rather doubted he would have dared gainsay her wishes.

Just then, Rance returned with a plate but half full and a wineglass filled with something a good deal darker than wine ought to be. Mr. Sutherland followed on his heels, smiling all around the table as he drew up his chair. As always, his calm presence softened the tension, and the four of them nibbled and talked politely of weather and politics until eventually Frederica Rutledge excused herself to attend the bride, who meant to change from her wedding gown.

Sutherland murmured something about having left his prayer book in the parlor and vanished on Mrs. Rutledge's heels. Anisha watched Rance from across the table, taking a perverse satisfaction in the bleak look about his eyes. The lines about his mouth, too, had deepened, and on the whole there was a worn, almost dissolute air about him today.

She had half expected him to make his excuses and follow the Preost out. But a scoundrel though he might have been, no one had ever called Rance a coward. He watched Sutherland go, then set his now-empty glass down with a determined thud.

"You received my letter?" he murmured without directly looking at her.

"How could I not when your footman brought it straight to my door?" she said in a grim undertone. "Brought it, mind you, before your scent was off my bedsheets. No, Rance, it did not get lost between the hall and my sitting room. Was that what you had hoped?"

He lifted his broad shoulders, as if his formal morning coat felt too tight, and for once he did indeed look to have been poured into it. "It was not, perhaps, the most diplomatic thing I'd ever written," he acknowledged.

"But was it heartfelt?" she asked bitterly. "That, you know, is the only thing that matters."

He looked across the table at her blankly.

She laid her fork down with a sharp *chink!* "In other words, when you used the phrase *'a terrible mistake,'* " she clarified, "was that indeed what you meant?"

"Anisha." He looked at her darkly. "That's precisely what it was. Yes. A mistake."

"And when you said I should *'look elsewhere in my romantic pursuits,'*" she whispered, "that was, indeed, what you wished?"

"I believe we have covered this ground before," Rance said, his voice dangerously soft. "In fact, we have nearly worn ruts in it."

"But that was before you took me to bed."

"Which was a mistake," he answered firmly.

"So we are back where we were a week ago, then," she murmured. "Is that it?"

He looked away, refusing to hold her gaze. "We cannot go back," he said quietly. "That's why it *was* such a devilish mistake. I have . . . tainted things between us, Nish. I have suggested something that was —"

Here, his words broke, and he shook his head.

"Suggested something that was never your intent?" she supplied a little tartly. "So there will be no marriage proposal forthcoming, then. Having lured you into my bed, I still can have no expectation of being the next Countess of Lazonby. Oh, dear. And I was already stitching the new monogram on my pillowslips."

The muscle in his jaw twitched danger-ously. "I need another whisky," he said, jerk-ing from his chair.

"No, you need to come out into the garden with me," she replied, tossing down her napkin. "What I have to say to you can-not be said in here."

"Why stop now?" he said grimly. "Half the room is watching us."

But he led the way through the house, almost slamming the back door open with the flat of his hand. With one last glance to ensure no one followed, Anisha matched his long, purposeful strides out into the bril-liant sunshine, into the depths of Miss de Rohan's garden, all the way back to the apple tree where only minutes earlier love had reigned and eternal vows had been spoken.

Rance set his back to the trunk and leaned against it, as if he expected to be a while. "Go on then," he said quietly, rolling his shoulders again. "You once said that I would do nothing but disappoint, Nish. And you were right. So have at it. But it won't change a thing."

They were the very words Janet had spoken, but Anisha heeded them no better now. Instead, she paced across the grass before him, trying to form her words, but temper and frustration had seized clarity from her mental grasp.

"Here is the problem," she finally said, stopping and turning to face him. "You do not have the right to patronize me, Rance. You do not have the right to decide how I live my life, what manner of risks I run with my name, or who I bed when —"

"No," he interjected coldly. "In that, you are regrettably correct. But I get to choose who *I* bed, Anisha."

Anisha felt herself suddenly trembling inside. "And you . . . and you do not choose me," she said. "Is that it?"

"I do not," he said tightly. "And I am not accountable to you, Anisha, for my choice. Not unless you find yourself with child."

Anisha stiffened her spine. "Oh?" she said, her voice arching. "And if I do, then what?"

"And then you know what," he said harshly. "And may God help us both. And may God help Tom and Teddy."

"Oh!" she said hotly. "Would it be so very terrible, Rance? To be married to me? To be a father to my boys?"

For an instant, his face froze. His expression went utterly blank.

"Would it?" she demanded. "Go on, Rance. Tell me you don't want me. I am not even asking you to marry me; indeed, you presume a vast deal to think I'd have you. But tell me you don't desire me. Say it straight to my face."

But the blank expression remained fixed upon his visage, as if he'd been carved of pale marble. Something inside him had shifted, and though he moved not a fraction, Anisha could all but feel the anger rolling through him like waves before a storm.

"Whoever marries you, Anisha, can account himself fortunate," he finally said. "But it will not be me. Would it be terrible? Not for some men. Myself, I have never contemplated marriage. The institution would suit me very ill."

To her shame, she almost lunged at him. "Oh, my God, you are *such* a liar!"

He caught her upper arms in his hands, his arms rigid. "Anisha," he rasped, giving her a little shake, "is there anything about me — anything you know, or anything you have seen — that would suggest to you that domestic life would suit me? Have I ever remained sober two days running? Or a whole week faithful to one woman? Ask yourself that, for God's sake, before you go spinning us some fantasy in your mind."

"So you have no wish to confine yourself to bedding just one woman," she said. "Is that it? Go on, say it!"

"Anisha, be silent."

"No, I won't be!" she cried, trying to jerk from his grasp. "I won't make this easier for you. And this isn't even *about* marriage. In that, yes, you flatter yourself. But go on, Rance. With a straight face, tell me you do not care for me —"

"Anisha, *hush!*"

"— or that your body doesn't ache for mine," she said, speaking over him. "Just try to say it. For you'll be a liar if you do. I've seen it in your eyes. Felt it in your touch. Even now lust shimmers off your skin like —"

"Oh, for God's sake, Nish, lust is just lust!" he interjected. "Men feel it for half the women that cross their paths."

"Lust is not just lust with us, Rance," she warned him. "The *Upanishads* teach us that all of a man's life is written. You and I, we are destined. And most days, I am as unhappy about it as you."

"Don't talk to me of your goddamned stars and Vedic nonsense," he growled. "I don't believe in any of it."

"Oh?" she challenged. "Then tell me you do not forget all others when I'm near. I *know* the truth of this, *meri jaan*. Sometimes I despair of it."

He cut her off with another shake, his

fingers digging into her arms, the skin around his mouth going white with rage. "Madam," he said tightly, "you try my restraint at your peril."

"And you, Rance, you try my sanity!" she cried. "I am sick to death of —"

His mouth was on hers in an instant.

Somehow it was her back that was set against the tree and Rance was kissing her with a roughness she could not have imagined. The force of his body held her tight to the tree as he dragged his mouth over hers, raking her skin with the stubble of his beard and driving her head back against the bark as he thrust inside her mouth.

This was desire, raw and unleashed. Dangerous in its heat. And all she could think of — strangely exult in — was the fact that *Rance burned for her.*

She thought again of Coldwater, and of her doubts. But having Rance in her bed — his kissing her now with no restraint — had utterly shattered them. Shattered her pretensions, too, and swept away the little scrap of herself she'd held back from him.

She was lost to him. Had been lost for a long time.

On and on the kiss went, desperate in its heat. He claimed her, possessed her, pressing his every inch to hers until her breath came in gasps and her knees shook. Rance's nostrils flared with lust and with rage, his brilliant blue eyes wide, as if daring her to look into them.

She did look. And realized at once she had pushed him too far.

Setting her hands to his shoulders, she shoved, but it was an impossibility. Something had shifted between them; the balance of power, perhaps, until he possessed it all and she held none. He shifted his thigh, urging it hard between her legs. She could feel the thick length of him swiftly hardening against her body.

At last she shoved him hard with the heels of her hands, then pounded at him. Rance tore his mouth from hers and finally stepped away, his breathing rough, his eyes still wild with something caught between lust and anger.

"Rance." She must have looked horrified, for the color drained from his face.

"God *damn* it, Anisha!" he said, half turning away from her. "Just damn it all to hell."

"Kindly stop cursing," she said, but her voice trembled. "Besides, I didn't do anything."

"No. No, *I* did." He dragged a hand through his curling, over-long hair. "For God's sake, Nish, can't you see? There was a . . . a line in the sand between us. And now it's gone. And I'm sorry. I never wanted this to happen."

"And I am sorry, too," she whispered, gathering herself. "I'm sorry your life is such an awful mess, and that you do not trust me to make the right decisions for myself."

"Nish, it isn't —"

"It *is*," she cried, coming away from the tree. "It is precisely that, Rance. You do not trust me to make even that most intimate and personal of choices — to choose a lover. To choose *you*. But here is the truth of it, my dear: beyond having you in my bed, I do not know what I want. Not from you. Not even from the rest of my life. The stars aside, I know only that I want what's best for my children."

"If you want what's best for them, Anisha," he replied, "then you know those boys need a father."

"My boys had a father!" she cried. "A father whom they scarcely knew, and who scarcely spared them a passing glance. But for good or ill, I've had to bury him, and now it's left to me to decide what my boys need — and thus far, I've done a more than adequate job of it."

To that he said nothing, but instead

shoved his hands into his pockets and started almost blindly into the depths of the garden.

"Rance, I know, even if you do not, that you would never bed me for sport," she said behind him. "On some level, you care for me, and it goes beyond the physical. But I'd sooner be boiled in oil than beg you for anything. You cannot keep playing this game, my dear."

"And what game is that?" he snapped.

"The one where you won't touch me, and you begrudge anyone else who might," she swiftly replied. "I am not some spun-glass ornament to be set upon a shelf, Rance. I am a flesh-and-blood woman."

"And I am not good enough for you — not as I am, caught in this godforsaken limbo," he muttered. "But I'm damned, Anisha, if I know anyone who is. I thought that Bessett —" Here, he threw his hand almost violently in the direction of the house. "I thought *he* might do, but now that's all come to naught. And God help me, Nish, if I am not glad. *I am glad.* So yes, I am guilty, perhaps, of just what you accuse me of."

"Oh, for God's sake, Rance!" she said impatiently. "I'm not some prize pig at the village fair. You cannot win my desire, nor even deserve it. It either is, or it isn't. And you must allow me my right to choose which things I do and don't worry about."

"And your children, Anisha?" he quietly reminded her. "The two things you love more than your own life? You gave up everything, Nish, to come here and make a better life for them. Would you now saddle them with me, and throw it all away?"

"Oh, without a moment's hesitation." Her voice was low and determined now. "And I would be throwing away nothing, for what my boys need, Rance, is a father who is strong enough to set a clear example of what a man should be. One who can teach them honor and fortitude in the face of adversity. One who can show them how to rise from defeat and injustice with their heads held high and know in their own hearts what they are. Do you know anyone better suited to do that, assuming, mind, I would even have you? For *that* is the big assumption, Rance, let me tell you. Not your suitability. You may be my destiny — and gifted beyond my wildest fantasies between the sheets. But none of that is enough for me."

At that remark, Rance cut a glace over his left shoulder, and at last his gaze met hers, rueful and chagrined. Some of the fight had gone out of him, and those cerulean eyes no longer glittered. An emotion which was perhaps vaguely akin to humor twitched at one corner of his mouth, and his shoulders finally gave, sagging with obvious fatigue.

"So you wish merely to use me," he murmured.

She stepped a little closer. "Two nights ago I wished to use you rather desperately," she admitted, dropping her voice suggestively. "As to future nights . . . well, I cannot say." She lifted her chin a little haughtily. "It will depend, I daresay, on whether you return to being my friend rather than some ogre set upon me by my arrogant brother."

A long moment passed as they stood there together on the grass. Above them, a gull wheeled as if in search of the sea, his cries a little mournful. The breeze rushed up from the river, so stiff it riffled across the grass like an unseen hand and stirred Anisha's skirts. She could see Rance mentally working through something, though she could not make out what.

At last he thrust out his hand.

She took it, oddly comforted by the hard, familiar feel of it.

"Pax, then," he said. "That's all I can say for now."

"Pax," she said, shaking then releasing it.

He rocked back on his heels and looked over his shoulder toward the house. "I will do what I can, Nish, to suit both our wishes," he said, narrowing his eyes against the sun. "I will try not to patronize you, or second-guess your choices. You will always have my friendship. I will always find you beautiful. Desirable." Here, his impossibly dark lashes swept down, his eyes closing for a mere instant. "But an open *affaire de coeur* — between us — oh, Nish. It will not do."

Feeling hollow and a little empty, Anisha shrugged. "Very well," she said. "You must suit yourself. But you will remember, I hope, what I have said."

He nodded. "I will remember."

"Fine, then," she said coolly. "Shall we go back inside?"

"Aye," he said quietly. "And now I desperately need that whisky — four or five, perhaps."

She went back through the gardens on his arm. They did not speak, but instead parted ways just inside the house, with Rance settling his hand over hers where it lay upon his arm. Then he patted it twice and left her to melt into the crowd.

And so they really were back where they had started.

Anisha watched him walk away, knowing

that nothing between them had really been settled; that she was still in love with Rance Welham and likely always would be. Worse, in two days' time, she was to attend the theater with Royden Napier.

And Rance, regrettably, had given her no reason not to go.

Chapter 10

A showing of a heavenly effect in an
earthly actor.
William Shakespeare,
All's Well That Ends Well

Applause rained down from the boxes and thundered up from the pit of the Royal Opera House as the Compt de Nevers swept Valentine from the stage, closing the third act of *Les Huguenots.* Anisha, awestruck, joined in, clapping breathlessly as the curtains swept shut.

Beside her, Royden Napier leaned back in his chair. Finally able to relax, she let her gaze roam about the theater, taking in the opulent décor, the giltwork, and the tier upon tier of fine boxes so elegantly draped, all of them centered around not just the impossibly deep stage but the extraordinary chandelier, which took one's breath at first sight.

But the beauty was offset now by the discordant sounds of scraping chairs and exuberant chatter as all around the grand perimeter, the theater patrons surged from their boxes in search of refreshment. She turned to smile at her companion.

"Did you like it?" Napier leaned so close she could smell his shaving soap. "I confess, I have seen Massol in better form."

Anisha was aware that her eyes were shining. "I thought he was *amazing*," she said. "Does that paint me an utter rustic?"

Napier's gaze flicked over her, showing little emotion. "If so, then a pleasant one," he said. "Would you care for something to drink?"

"Thank you, no."

Just then, however, Anisha felt the heat of someone's gaze upon them. She looked out across the theater. An elegantly dressed gentleman lingering in the box just to the right of the stage had raised a set of opera glasses to his eyes.

Anisha returned his stare, one eyebrow elevated.

The gentleman dropped the glasses and smoothly returned his attention to the man next to him, as if nothing had occurred.

And perhaps it had not. She had become fanciful, she feared. She smiled again at

Napier, who was rising. "I believe I shall stretch my legs," he said, "if you will be comfortable here without your brother?"

"By all means," she said.

Lucan, of course, had abandoned them between the first and second act to join a pack of young scoundrels milling about in the pit. It was as well, Anisha considered, for his raw mood had not abated since the wedding. Still, he had served his purpose in escorting her here and would eventually return to accompany her home again.

But there were two acts yet to play out. Rethinking the notion of refreshments, Anisha turned to call out to Napier. Before she could speak, however, the door to their box flew open, and a broad-shouldered gentleman with receding hair appeared at the door.

Napier's eyes widened. "Sir Wilfred," he said a little stiffly, stepping back. "What a surprise."

"Well, well, if it isn't Roughshod Roy Napier!" The man smiled jovially and came fully inside to thump Napier on the back. "By gad, I thought that was you! Laying claim to the family box, eh?"

With a thin smile, Napier introduced Anisha to Sir Wilfred Leeton. At first, the name was only vaguely familiar. Anisha gave a slight curtsey, and Sir Wilfred bowed elegantly over her hand.

"Lady Anisha," he repeated. "A pleasure."

"Likewise," she murmured, searching her memory even as she smiled at him. And suddenly, it came to her.

Mr. Leeton.

But his gaming salon, or whatever it had been, no longer existed. And he had become the wealthy Sir Wilfred. He was also a friend — or at least an acquaintance — of Napier's. How odd.

"You are in the theater business, Sir Wilfred, are you not?" Anisha managed.

Napier looked at her warily. "Have you two some prior acquaintance?"

Anisha felt her cheeks warm. "No, but we have a mutual friend," she said. "Lady Madeleine MacLachlan. I'm to accompany her to Lady Leeton's annual garden party."

Sir Wilfred was still smiling genially. "Any acquaintance of Lady Madeleine's would be most welcome," he declared. "And a pretty, charming lady added to our numbers could never go amiss."

"How kind you are," she said.

"This year, I am advised, there will be all manner of feminine fripperies for sale." He leaned in and dropped his voice conspiratorially. "Lace handkerchiefs and such — as well as our gypsy fortune-teller!"

Anisha tried not to laugh. "A fortune-teller?" she murmured. "How droll!"

"So, come to Covent Garden on reconnaissance, have you, Sir Wilfred?" said Napier, changing the subject. "I suppose one must steal a march on the competition by whatever means possible."

"Indeed, the theater business is a blood sport nowadays," said Sir Wilfred. "Meyerbeer's bringing his new opera from Paris in a few weeks' time, and I've come to discover if the die has been cast."

"I was unaware you had any interest in opera," said Napier, his voice cool.

"No, but I should be keenly interested in its profit margins," Sir Wilfred chuckled. "Ah, but I am being vulgar. My apologies, Lady Anisha. Napier, were you going out?"

"Briefly, yes."

Anisha got the oddest notion that Napier was not especially pleased to see Sir Wilfred. Perhaps he would have preferred their friendship to remain a secret — if indeed it was a friendship. Certainly the late Hanging Nick Napier had known the man. Sir Wilfred's name had appeared in Rance's murder file.

"Perhaps Sir Wilfred might bear me company until you return?" Anisha blurted, then wished at once she had not. "If, that is to say, Lady Leeton is not expecting you?"

Napier was looking at her a little oddly, his gaze dark and inscrutable.

"No, no, Hannah cannot abide the opera." Sir Wilfred shrugged. "She has her interests, and I have mine. Napier, be off and about your business. I rarely have the opportunity to sit beside a beauty and gossip about society."

With what looked like grave reluctance, Napier bowed to her again and departed. Anisha wondered vaguely what troubled him. Perhaps he was afraid of what she might learn.

But it would not do, Anisha realized, to launch into the questions she burned to ask of this man. Not yet. This was an unlooked-for opportunity to cultivate a friendship with Sir Wilfred.

They situated themselves in the seats nearest the balcony, and Sir Wilfred leaned back in the small chair, looking very much at ease. It was not, Anisha supposed, particularly surprising. The theater was his empire, the world of gaming having been left to men less burdened by their morals. Men like Ned Quartermaine.

Anisha snapped open her fan and began to ply it lazily, forcing a benign smile. She

417

had the distinct sense that Leeton was a fellow who would enjoy talking about himself. "You must tell me, Sir Wilfred, how you came to be in the theater business," she suggested, "and of your friendship with Lady Madeleine. I am somewhat new to London."

Sir Wilfred smiled wolfishly. "Oh, I came to it much as any good businessman does, I daresay."

"And how is that?"

"I saw an opportunity and I seized it."

Anisha laughed lightly.

"Actually," he said more soberly, "it was always my dream. I grew up around the stage, you see, for my mother, I'm not ashamed to say, once tread the boards. And then by some rare miracle, the Athenian in Soho came up for sale, and I was able to snatch it up."

"Oh, my!" she murmured. "The Athenian is known the world over. What a coup that must have been."

He chuckled. "It was, rather."

At Anisha's further urging, he spoke of his earliest acquisitions, and of how, following the easing of the theater laws, he'd engaged MacLachlan to begin building new ones across England. In total, he explained, he now owned a dozen. It took very little prodding to hear of how the Queen had knighted Sir Wilfred for his charitable works after he became involved in local government. There had even been, he ruefully admitted, talk of his being elevated to alderman or perhaps standing for the Commons.

All of this, however, Sir Wilfred brushed aside as poppycock. "But I'm just a businessman, Lady Anisha," he concluded genially. "And the talk — well, much of that, I fear, is Hannah's doing. She wants it, and is determined to have her way."

"Ah, but many a great man was pushed to his prominence by a woman," said Anisha on a laugh, ". . . usually his wife."

Still, it sounded as if Sir Wilfred Leeton was a veritable force of nature.

He remarked upon her background only once, when she mentioned her late husband's name. "Ah, yes, the Dorset Staffords," he said sympathetically. "I knew one or two of them as young men. A fine, old family."

"Yes," she agreed. "Though I confess I've not stayed in touch with them as well as I ought."

Indeed, save for sending word of her husband's death, Anisha had not stayed in touch with them at all. Captain Stafford's marriage to a mixed-blood Rajput had sent his father to an early grave, and Anisha's mother-in-law still wallowed in her bitterness.

No, they had no wish to hear from their daughter-in-law, nor even to lay eyes upon their grandchildren, despite their blonde curls and blue eyes. But she said none of this to Sir Wilfred, who, while a little pompous, seemed kind enough.

He gave her hand an avuncular pat. "Sobraon, you said," he murmured. "You have been widowed a while, then. And yet I've never seen you in Town, Lady Anisha. Come to the garden party and let me introduce you to a few suitable gentlemen."

"How kind you are." Anisha let her smile simmer as she sped up the fan. "But is Mr. Napier not suitable?"

Sir Wilfred's mouth opened, then shut again. "Why, eminently so," he finally said. "I beg your pardon. He's a sly one, old Royden. Are some sort of congratulations in order?"

At that, Anisha threw back her head and laughed, and thought of Rance as she did so. "No, indeed, Sir Wilfred," she said. "I am merely teasing you. By the way, you said that we might gossip."

Sir Wilfred collected himself. "Why, yes. Yes, of course."

She cut him a sly look. "Might I ask then how long you've known our mutual friend?"

"Who, Napier?" He puffed out his cheeks, then blew out the air. "I'm not perfectly sure. As I said, I'm involved in local government. I knew his father a bit, but he's long dead."

"I see," she murmured. "Mr. Napier seems a man of good character."

Sir Wilfred smiled and lifted one shoulder. "Oh, he's vain and stubborn, like most men," he acknowledged. "But he's a decent sort, yes."

He was not going to be led, Anisha realized. For whatever reason, he did not want to talk about Napier. It was just as well, for when she glanced down, Anisha saw that the audience was trickling back into the pit. Just then she heard a soft creak of their door opening, even as she caught the glint of glass to her right again.

She was tilting her head toward it when Napier eased silently back into his chair.

"Can you tell me, Sir Wilfred, whose box that is across the way?" she murmured, setting her hand lightly on his coat sleeve. "No, no, do not *quite* look, I beg you! A gentleman there keeps observing me through his opera glasses."

"Then he has good taste." Sir Wilfred cut

a surreptitious look past her shoulder, Napier following suit. "Heavens, that is the Duke of Gravenel's box."

"And Gravenel is the giant stooping to go out the door," Napier quietly added. "His size makes him unmistakable."

"And the elegant man with the opera glasses?" asked Anisha.

"The Duke's elder cousin," said Napier tightly. "You don't wish to know him, my dear."

"His *illegitimate* cousin, who is also his brother-in-law," Sir Wilfred added. "England's blue bloods do like to keep the money in the family, don't they, Royden? Indeed, they sometimes close ranks quite ruthlessly if an outsider is brought in."

But Napier did not answer that one. Instead, his jaw seemed to tighten, leaving Anisha the impression a tiny barb had been embedded in the remark. She wondered again at Napier's background, and his connection to the deceased Lord Hepplewood.

"And the tall, dapper gentleman seated beside the duke's cousin?" she pressed, keeping one eye on Napier. "With the silver hair? Is he respectable?"

Sir Wilfred shook his head, his brow furrowed. "He looks vaguely familiar."

"That is his particular friend," Napier

murmured. "And both of them dodgy despite all their elegance, if you want my opinion. But then Gravenel was never especially discerning in his choice of friends. Ah, look. The conductor has returned and the orchestra is drifting in."

At once, Sir Wilfred stood. "And that would be my cue."

After bowing again over Anisha's hand, he left the box as swiftly as he had come. When the door closed after him, Anisha cut a glance at Napier. "One might get the impression you did not enjoy that visit."

Napier flushed faintly. "I like Sir Wilfred well enough," he said. "But he still imagines himself a bit of a Lothario, despite the fact his corset creaks and his hair long ago exited the stage."

"I see." Anisha fell silent, considering her next words. "But Sir Wilfred has not always been Sir Wilfred, has he? And not always such a pattern of rectitude?"

Napier turned in his seat, his gaze sharpening. "To whom have you been speaking?"

"To Edward Quartermaine," she replied. "At the Quartermaine Club."

"Ned Quartermaine?" he said incredulously. "Surely you jest?"

"There is nothing to jest about," said Anisha. "I called on him to ask him legitimate questions after having read your files. Sir Wilfred featured rather prominently in those, you'll recall."

"I recall it," said Napier irritably. "Really, must we discuss Lazonby just now?"

Anisha looked at him in some surprise. "Heavens, I didn't bring him up," she said. "Indeed, I never mentioned his name, nor did I invite Sir Wilfred in."

Napier's posture relaxed, his mouth twitching again with some combination of irritation and humor. "So you didn't," he finally acknowledged. "I beg your pardon. That said, I should warn you —"

But his remarks were forestalled as the curtain rose with a dramatic flourish and Valentine reappeared on the stage.

In the King's Arms, Lazonby slumped at a beaten trestle table, his booted feet set wide as he nursed the last of a porter gone far too warm. He sucked down the dregs of it anyway, the taste like metal on his tongue as dusk settled beyond the wide window.

All around him, Hackney had gone still. Shops had shuttered and the rattle and clatter of carts and horses had faded away. This was not, after all, London, but a village of working folk. Even the chipper Min and her pretty blue eyes had deserted him; gone home to her mother, clutching her newly minted florin on a red silk cord.

Mrs. Ashton's laundress, as it happened, had not proven especially helpful; the servants in the white cottage were not a loquacious lot. Min had learned little, save for the facts that Mrs. Ashton spent much of her time volunteering at a charity school in Bethnal Green. As to Coldwater, he was rarely at home — and when he was, he never left his washing.

But she had managed to confirm that the pair hailed from Boston, where it was rumored the family had had some interest in a newspaper business. In Hackney, Mrs. Ashton was considered a handsome, well-bred woman who politely kept her distance and spurned all admirers — what few could be scared up in such a place, at any rate.

Down the lane in the deepening dusk Lazonby could still make out the arch of roses over the cottage's garden gate, now bursting into a cascade of small, white blossoms. On the ground floor, a candle burned in a front window, but above all was darkness. If Coldwater had lit a lamp upon entering the house, it had since been put out.

Likely he hadn't needed to. The sun had still been up when Lazonby had trailed him here — to what end, he could not now imagine. Perhaps because it was the only clue available to him, and he was growing increasingly desperate.

Or perhaps because if he had not come here, he would have remained at home, comforted only by *Madame la Fée* and his absinthe spoon, which, in the throws of the green hour, looked to be pierced with Satan's visage. The three of them — he, the fairy, and Old Scratch — would likely have partaken of one another's company until his eyes had rolled back in his head and the nightmares had come.

For to do nothing would have left him to think of Anisha.

On impulse, he jerked from his creaking chair, slapped a handful of coins on the bar, and strode toward the door, his riding boots ringing on the rough, planked floor as he went. Once he stood in the street, he looked it up and down, then set a course straight for the cottage, uncertain what he meant to do until he pushed open the front gate and knocked upon the door.

A quavering beam of candlelight cut across the flagstone. "Aye?" creaked a mob-capped servant.

"I wish to see Mr. Coldwater," Lazonby said, not unkindly. "Is he in?"

She blinked once, slowly, her eyes pale and rheumy in the gloom, and he realized that she was blind, or something near it.

"Mr. Coldwater's gone out," she said in a rote, weary voice. "D'ye wish to see the mistress?"

Lazonby took the old woman's measure, but she radiated neither suspicion nor ill will. "Thank you," he said, presenting her one of his old cards, which he sometimes found it prudent to carry.

The old woman rubbed the vellum uncertainly between her fingers.

"Welham," he said gently. "The name is Welham."

The old woman bobbed her head, offered a chair, which he declined, then shuffled through the small hall and vanished into the darkness, leaving her candle behind. In the depths of the house, Lazonby could hear the tinkling notes of a pianoforte. Listening with one ear, he looked about, still holding his hat, which the servant had failed to take.

The house appeared tidy and tastefully furnished. A drop-leaf table stood to one wall, flanked by a fine pair of Chippendale chairs, with a towering vase of ruby-throated gladioli upon it. No poverty here, then. Such flowers came hothouse-dear so early in the season.

This assumption was further borne out by a fine landscape hanging above the table; a painting of a child rolling a hoop through an expanse of green which a tiny brass plaque identified as Boston Common.

Suddenly, the notes of the sonata fell away. A few moments later a woman entered, her wide, flounced skirt barely swishing through the narrow doorway. As it had been when he'd espied her through the window, the lady's hair was a cascading mass of perfectly arranged chestnut curls. Her age was hard to judge; thirty, at most, and tonight her mouth was turned up in a quizzical half-smile.

"Mr. . . . Welham, is it?" Her voice was deep and oddly sultry. "How may I be of service?"

When she drew nearer, he realized how willowy she was. The resemblance between the lady and her brother was obvious, for she shared his keen, quick eyes.

"Actually, ma'am, I was looking for Mr. Coldwater." He returned her gaze just as steadily, attempting to judge her intent, but to no avail. "One of the ostlers at the King's Arms said he'd come this way an hour or two past."

"So he did." Her expression did not falter, and she exuded no emotion. "Then John took a bite of supper, collected a book he wanted, and went out again."

Lazonby doubted it. He'd been watching the door for two hours. "Ah," he said evenly. "I wonder how I missed him?"

"If you didn't see him pass by the Arms," she said coolly, "then he likely went out the back, toward Bethnal Green Road. He often does so, I believe, if he means to catch the omnibus."

"The omnibus?"

"A large, unwieldy wagon stuffed to the brim with passengers." One corner of her mouth lifted sardonically. "You do realize, Mr. Welham, that my brother does not live here?"

"I — no, I did not," he lied. "Someone at the *Chronicle* directed me here."

"I can't think why." She glanced again at his card. "Jack keeps rooms near Fleet Street."

"I beg your pardon," Lazonby interjected, thrusting out his hand. "We've not been properly introduced. I do not know your name."

Again, doubt sketched almost imperceptibly over her face. "Do you not?" she said lightly, taking his hand. "Well. I am Mrs. Ashton."

"A pleasure, I'm sure," he said, clinging

to her hand perhaps a moment longer than he ought. Yet even this close, the lady was like still, deep water to him. Perhaps, like her brother, she was what the *Fraternitas* called an Unknowable — one who, for reasons not well understood, was unintuitable.

Abruptly, she drew her hand from his grasp and swept past him, casting her gaze over her shoulder as she went, leaving Lazonby with the oddest sense that she was somehow taunting him.

"So, might I give my brother a message?" She began to make a pretense of rearranging the gladioli. "He generally comes round once or twice a week."

"Thank you, no." He followed her, picking up her clean, familiar scent; one that he couldn't quite put a name to. "I shall find Mr. Coldwater in Town."

Again, she cut an odd, almost heated glance at him over her shoulder, one hand holding a stem slightly aloft in the arrangement. "Yes," she said softly. "I daresay you will."

Her eyes were greenish-blue, and utterly remote now. And yet something seemed suddenly to thrum in the air around them — a sort of tension that was not quite sexual, but oddly evocative all the same.

And beneath it all lay a sense of challenge, like a hand of cards played so close to the vest one wondered if the next card would ever fall.

Or if there was even a game at all.

But there was. He could sense it. Never was he wrong about such things.

He took another swift step and caught her hand, stilling it as she lifted an impossibly long stem from the vase.

She did not startle but instead merely stared at their joined hands.

"These flowers are remarkably beautiful," he said quietly. "And costly."

"Some things are worth the price," she replied, looking up at him. "After all, they are so very lovely, with their pale, tender petals. And the throat, so deeply red. Like spilled blood, I often think. But tender things can be so fragile, can they not?"

He released her hand, something sick and uncertain running through him. "Have you a point, Mrs. Ashton?" he managed.

"Why, none whatever," she lightly returned. But that lightness, he now realized, was some sort of deception. But *what* sort?

He must have remained silent too long.

"I think, Mr. Welham," she quietly added, "that you had better go. My brother is not here, nor is he apt to return."

Dropping his hand, Lazonby stepped back and felt his usual detachment settle over him again. "Then I thank you for your time, ma'am," he said, turning toward the door to draw it open, "and bid you good evening."

But at the last instant, just as he stepped out into the cool of the night, Mrs. Ashton spoke again. "The flowers, Mr. Welham," she said abruptly. "The *Gladiolus undulates.* Do you know the common name?"

He lifted one eyebrow. "Just gladiolus, I think?"

"From the Latin *gladius,*" she said, twirling the stem between her fingers, "which means 'sword.' As in *gladiator.* And the flower — well, it is often called simply *the sword lily.*"

Somehow, he managed one of his flirtatious smiles. "Why, that sounds almost lethal, Mrs. Ashton."

"Yes." She did not return the smile. "It does, doesn't it?"

With one last bow of his head, Lazonby slapped his hat back on his head and left her standing in the elegant, candlelit hall. He walked away, his boot heels heavy upon the meandering flagstone. He did not shut the door behind him but instead left it for her to catch in midswing.

Mrs. Ashton, however, did not deign to trouble herself but instead simply stared after him. And from the low stoop of her threshold, all the way to the gate that shrieked on old, iron hinges, Lazonby could feel those cold eyes like icy daggers in his back.

He felt frustration and rage begin to swell up as the gate clattered behind him, but he ruthlessly damped them down. By God, the woman played a damned game, and he knew it. He wanted to throttle her just as he'd wished to throttle her brother. But all his anger had ever earned him was trouble heaped upon more trouble.

It was time, perhaps, to go home to his absinthe after all. But there was one last thing he meant to do.

At the Arms, he reclaimed his horse and returned to London by cutting through the heart of the City, then went on foot along a dark street that angled off Shoe Lane into the rabbit warren of shops and houses behind the *Chronicle*'s office. The building was familiar to him now, and the little flat on the second floor corner dark, as it almost always was.

Lazonby had reached the conclusion that Coldwater kept some sort of a mistress — or was himself kept by someone. One or

433

two wealthy, liberal-minded gentlemen of that persuasion came to mind. But wherever Coldwater hid out, Lazonby had seen him go in or out of the flat on just three occasions. Once he'd seen a woman depart with a wicker basket on her arm — the sword-wielding Mrs. Ashton, he now thought, though the night had been dark and her face obscured.

But no one was there tonight. That suited his purpose very well indeed.

Lazonby looked his chosen drainpipe up and down one last time, then gave it a solid jerk for good measure. Neither the metal nor its bracings gave.

Well. It was time, it seemed, to get intimately acquainted with his old friend Jack. Lazonby set his boot to the brickwork, seized the pipe well above his head, and hefted himself smoothly up.

CHAPTER 11

Vouchsafe, bright moon, and these thy
stars, to shine.
William Shakespeare, *Love's Labour's Lost*

Anisha rose the morning after her evening
with Royden Napier, seized with a newfound sense of urgency, a feeling she could
not ascribe to anything tangible. She responded with logic, spending an hour at her
Jyotish — specifically Rance's, methodically
working through the charts.

The feeling did not abate but instead
strengthened. Like all Guardians, Rance
was *Mesha Lagna,* or Aries ascendant, and
prone to haste and stubbornness, which
could bring with it extreme ill luck. And
now a great change was coming, and the
potential for something dire.

Driven by unease and a restlessness she
was increasingly unable to quell, Anisha
dressed in her old mourning clothes and

called for her brother's unmarked coach. It was time, she was quite certain, to take matters in hand.

"I'll not likely be back by dinner," she told Janet as she pinned on her hat, "so tell Lord Lucan to dine at White's. Oh, and I'll want my black traveling cloak."

"But my lady," said Janet, who was already shaking it out, "the weather bodes ill."

Anisha went to the window, rumbled up the sash, and craned her head out to better see the sky. "What nonsense," she said tartly. "There are a few fluffy clouds above. Nothing more."

"Aye, well, I feel a dampness in my bones," the maid warned, vanishing into the dressing room.

"That feeling is called *England,*" Anisha called after her, gingerly lowering the sash, "and there is nothing to be done about it."

"Hmph," said Janet, but the sound was muffled. And by the time Anisha finished putting on her jet earbobs and dashing a little power over her nose, the maid was standing by the door with a satchel in hand.

"Fresh linen," she said, thrusting it at Anisha. "Just in case."

Anisha tried to scowl, and failed. "Heavens, Janet, it's Buckhurst Hill, not the backside of Yorkshire," she said. "It cannot be much more than two hours away."

But at Janet's pursed lips, Anisha took the bag all the same and threw open the door.

And just in time, too, for Chatterjee teetered on the threshold, one fist poised to knock, and looking as if he might explode. "My lady! Janet! Oh, my God!" He burst in like a cyclone, rambling in a mad tangle of English and Bangla, little of which Anisha could make out.

"Chatterjee, what's happened?" Dropping her bag, Anisha tried to catch his elbow.

"Oh, my lady!" he shouted, rushing past her to the bed. "Janet! Look! The thing! The — the standing thing, 'tis done!"

"Lud, Chatt!" The maid snatched up the satchel. "Yer look fit ter have an apoplexy."

"Yes, yes, marvelous, is it not?" Wild-eyed, Chatterjee unfurled a newspaper atop the counterpane. "I have it all! Just here!"

"Awright, awright," said Janet. "Looks like the *Times* ter me."

"Yes!" he said, waving his hand over it with a flourish. "Yes, yes, yes! And so, Janet — *we are rich!*"

"Coo!" said Janet speciously. "I'll just be givin' me notice then, won't I?"

"Yes, yes, me, too, perhaps!" Chatterjee beamed around at the both of them. "And all because of your standing plate!"

"Wot?" Janet went perfectly still. "Chatt — *the Grand Stand Plate?* Is that what you mean — ?"

His face lit up even further. "Yes, that! Lord Exeter! It was Swordplayer by a-a" — he consulted the paper — "by a *length!* He won, Janet! *We* won!"

Janet dropped the satchel. It fell on its side, dumping Anisha's underclothes on the floor. But no one paid any heed, for Janet had seized the ordinarily dignified Chatterjee by the hands and was dancing him around the room.

"We won, m'lady!" she cried. "We won! We won! We're rich!"

"And now I must replace both my lady's maid *and* my right hand?" Anisha teased, picking up the paper to read. "Heavens, Janet! How much did your brother place on this horse?"

Janet stopped dancing and swallowed guiltily. "Well . . . all we had, really — and most of Chatt's."

"Janet!" Crushing the newspaper at her side, Anisha's eyes widened. "And you, Chatterjee! *You* know better! What were you thinking?"

Chatterjee bowed, some of his majesty returning. "I cannot perfectly put words to it, madam," he replied. "I just felt . . .

destined, I suppose. And Janet was wearing the ruby pendant. The stars, she said, were in perfect alignment."

"Oh, dear God." Anisha closed her eyes and quietly sent up a prayer.

The stars and prayers aside, they gradually returned to earth, the both of them. And after Anisha did a little arithmetic on the back of an old milliner's bill, it was collectively decided that neither Chatterjee nor Janet was *quite* rich after all.

"But you shall both be left quite comfortable," Anisha assured them.

"Ooh, right warm indeed," said Janet.

"Even toasty?" Chatterjee ventured.

"Toasty ain't a word, Chat," said Janet. "Not a cant word, at least."

And together they all had a laugh as Anisha at last let go of her fears. However much she might worry for them, and however foolish she felt for encouraging Janet in such a precarious venture, the truth was, all had turned out well. Better than well, actually.

She left them pondering the future of their employment and hoping they would not desert her, for she had come to depend upon them both quite desperately. Janet and Chatterjee had been with her forever. They had seen her safely into adulthood, stood by her in her marriage, and come along with her to this strange, new world. They had been more family than most of her blood kin.

But what was destined would come; this Anisha knew. And God knew the pair deserved a little good fortune. Shaking off her selfishness, Anisha pressed on with her plans.

After looking in on the boys in the schoolroom — and casting Mr. Jeffers, their tutor, a sympathetic glance — she sent up a prayer that *he* had not bet on Swordplayer, then went downstairs. There she rummaged through the parlor secretary for the notes she'd taken in Napier's office and stuffed them into Janet's satchel.

By half past ten, she was parked in Ebury Street. After folding down her veil of black bobbinet, she descended from the carriage and rang the bell. A drowsy-eyed footman with peach fuzz on his chin answered the door.

"I wish to see Lazonby," she announced, scooting past him.

At first he blinked, turning slowly, as if the command did not register. "I'm sorry, ma'am," he began, "but his lordship —"

"Emmit, is it not?" Anisha interjected, tugging off her gloves. "Emmit, don't bother to

440

say he isn't in, for I know perfectly well he's still abed, and ill as a bear in the bargain. I shall just show myself up."

And with that, she left him gape-mouthed, throwing up her veil as she went. There was no use insulting Rance's servants by pretending they were fools.

"But my lady!" the lad cried after her, following her up the stairs. "Wait! Please!"

"I'm afraid I cannot," she said matter-of-factly. "For if I do, he'll just tell you to tell me to go away, don't you imagine? And you'll have to do it. And I shan't go, of course. So you will have failed. Then we'll both be back where we started, if not worse. So would it not be best if I just saved you the trouble?"

"Indeed, ma'am," he said on her heels, sounding wretched, "but what will —"

"Oh, I'll just tell him I pushed past you, and trust me, he'll have no difficulty believing it." Anisha made a shooing motion over her shoulder and turned the next flight. "Now kindly hurry downstairs and fetch his lordship's bathwater. Pots of it, very hot. Trust me, he will thank you for it."

The young man hesitated on the landing. "But, ma'am, if you please," he cried up at her. "I don't think he will! Thank me, that is. Truly, you *must* wait —"

The strident echo of his voice in the hollow stairwell stopped her. Anisha turned on the step to look down at him. A chilling thought struck her, and it was as if her blood suddenly stilled. "What?" she managed. "Is he . . . not alone?"

The servant's face colored furiously. "No," he said. "I mean, *yes.* I think so. His lordship doesn't bring — that is to say, he would never —"

Anisha felt a foolish sort of relief rush through her. "Thank you, Emmit," she said, not unkindly. "I appreciate your concern. But I am used to Lazonby's temper — and his frightful language. Now kindly go and fetch that water. Oh, and send up his lordship's valet. Lazonby has a pressing appointment he has forgotten."

"Yes, ma'am." To her surprise, the lad turned and rushed back down the stairs, crying out, "Horsham! Horsham!" as he went.

Having pushed her way in, Anisha set about finding Rance's rooms. On the second floor, almost certainly. The house was not especially large, and the master's rooms would likely be situated on the street, since the house had no garden to speak of.

Her guess was right. She threw open the door at the end of the passageway to see a small gentleman's sitting room with a desk, a button-tufted leather settee, and a broad bookcase gone black with age. There was a second door giving off this — his bed-chamber, certainly, for even here, in this tidy bastion of masculinity, Rance's woody cologne and lime soap carried faintly in the air.

Ignoring the memories the scents re-kindled, Anisha tossed down her shawl and satchel, then unpinned the accursed hat and set it carefully on the desk. After rapping upon the inner door, she sang out to ask if he was decent. There was no answer, as she had expected.

Pushing open the door, she simply went it.

The room was steeped in gloom, but as her eyes adjusted Anisha was able to see a large bed in the center and three shadowy windows overlooking Ebury Street. Here, the scent went well beyond cologne and soap. Rance's masculine essence was redo-lent in the air; an almost sensual aroma, like the intimate scent of his hat being tossed aside, or of his coat being furled warmly about her shoulders — a realization which served only to remind her of how often Rance had done just that during her first months in England.

How many times, she wondered as she studied his shadowy, sleeping form, had he come striding through the house to find her curled up in the sunlit conservatory, her teeth chattering, her paisley shawl wrapped up to her neck? And always he would laugh at her, his blue eyes dancing, even as he stripped off his own coat and tucked it gently round her.

Once or twice he'd gone back to the hall for his hat and set it atop her head — and laughed all the harder at the sight. Then she would laugh with him. And suddenly, life in England hadn't seemed quite so bleak.

But more often he would simply nudge her into the small parlor and lay up a fire for her, though the house was full of servants who could have done the same. But Rance had known instinctively that she would not ask; that she was loath to be the outsider who could not grow accustomed to England's ways. Afterward they sometimes passed a little time with a hand of piquet and a glass of wine. Once they had pieced a jigsaw puzzle with the boys. Rance had always come and gone like a member of the family, for that was what Raju had wanted.

It was what *she* had wanted.

And it was in those bittersweet moments, she suspected, that she had begun to fall in love with him. Or perhaps it had begun that day on the drive home from the Docklands. Perhaps it had been love at first sight.

Still staring hard into the gloom, she felt her own eyes begin to sting.

Oh, what nonsense!

Why think of these things now, as she stared into the depths of his bedchamber, the urgency of their journey needling at her? Was she such a ninnyhammer that the mere scent of a man could addle her senses? Irritated, Anisha strode to the windows and began to hurl back the heavy draperies, the rings skating shrilly over the rods. However evocative Rance's scent might be, it was a sure sign the room had been too long shut up and — as she recalled from living with her brothers — a likely indication of a long, hard night at the bottle. There was nothing starry-eyed in *that.*

Turning from the window, she looked about to see a room in utter disarray. Clothes were tossed hither and yon, a tin of tobacco had tumbled off the writing table, and his cravat had been slung over his cheval glass and left trailing down the center.

She shifted, and a shaft of morning sun cut across Rance's bed. He grunted and rolled away from the light, taking the sheet with him.

Well, in a manner of speaking. The sheet was actually snarled about his waist. The rest of him — so far as she could see — was bare. One long, well-muscled leg was uncovered, revealing the dusting of dark hair over a calf that could have been carved of Carrara marble. As to the hair on his head, however, now *that* looked as if rats had nested in it.

She approached the bed gingerly, if impatiently. Two empty bottles sat upon the night table, along with a flute containing the dregs of something that looked vile and sticky. Anisha picked it up and inhaled deeply. Her nose, honed by her practice of ayurveda, easily detected anise and fennel. And something else. Something she knew but could not bring to mind.

She set the flute down with a *clunk* and picked up the bottle.

Absinthe.

The rare spirit was distilled from a form of artemisia similar to *nagadamni,* an ayurvedic herb with magical properties. To Europeans, the plant was known as wormwood and believed poisonous. And its victim looked as if that might indeed be the case.

"Rance?" she whispered, setting a hand

446

on his bare shoulder.

He tossed almost feverishly, muttering something she couldn't make out. Lightly, she tapped him, softly calling his name. He thrashed again, this time turning toward her. Anisha could see his eyes were slightly open, but glassy and distant, and his face contorted as if with pain. She set her hand to his cheek, stubbled with black, unshaven beard. He felt not feverish but instead cold as death.

"No, no," he replied, jerking against her touch, then muttering something in French.

"What's that?" She gave his face a gentle pat. "Come, can you wake up?"

"Non." Suddenly, his eyes flared wide but remained unfocused, his pupils like ha'pennies. He seized her arm violently. *"C'est toi!"* he rasped accusingly. *"La sirène —"*

"Rance, it's Anish—"

"All *fucking* night —" With one jerk, he yanked her across the solid width of his chest with such force that her feet left the floor. "Damn you, *stop!* Stop! Do you hear me?"

She tried to lift herself away, but her arm was wrenched awkwardly. "Rance, wake up," she commanded.

He merely tightened his grip, dragging her

up his chest with inhuman strength. Anisha's heart sped up, something akin to fear chasing through her. They were face-to-face, her breasts flattened hard to his chest, so close his breath stirred her hair.

"Rance, wake up," she said sternly. "You've had too much to drink."

In response, he forced her head down and kissed her, his empty hand spearing almost brutally into her hair. Anisha gasped and tried to roll away. It was out of the question. No mere caress, this was a kiss of passion unfettered; a raw, rough claiming that left no choice but surrender. Opening his mouth over hers, he invaded, pushing his tongue deep with long, sinuous strokes that left her shivering.

On a swallowed cry, she set her hands to his shoulders as if to push away. And yet she did not. Rance's arm came fully around her, bunching up her skirts as his hand massaged her left hip, urging her to him. He withdrew from her mouth for an instant, then thrust again, each stroke more sensual than the last, the stubble of his beard raking her face.

Dimly Anisha remembered the servants. They would be coming. She tried to twist away, to lift herself up. It was no use. His arm was like iron, his strength that of a madman. He shifted, and in an instant she was thrown flat on her back, Rance coming half atop her.

Snaring both her wrists, he forced them into the softness of the bolster, pinning her with the weight of his body. The evidence of his arousal was hard and unmistakable now. Fleetingly, their gazes locked. His eyes were wild. *"La sirène,"* he growled, gasping. *"You will torment me no more!"*

Anisha struggled for breath. "There's *no siren!*" she shouted, pounding at his shoulders. "There's no *torment!* Wake up, for heaven's sake!"

Suddenly footfalls sounded, pounding into the room. "Good God, man!" a deep voice barked. "Release that woman! Emmit, seize him!"

There was the heavy clank of a bucket, and in a trice the weight was yanked away. Rance was dragged back by a broad-shouldered gentleman in a dark suit, the ashen-faced footman aiding him.

"Criminy, Horsham!" the lad croaked. " 'E's gone mad."

But the man called Horsham was undeterred. "Sir, you must wake up!" he shouted, dragging him to the bolster. "This won't do."

"No, damn you." Rance fell back onto the

bed, eyes closing, the heels of his hands going to his temples. With a practiced snap, Horsham threw up the sheets, covering him to the chest.

"He's having some sort of nightmare." Anisha had jerked upright to untwist her skirts. "Perhaps he's been drugged?"

"Done it himself, more like." Horsham jostled Rance hard. "Sir, come now! Open your eyes."

Anisha clambered backward off the bed. Emmit leapt deferentially back, almost tripping over the brass cans he'd carried up. Horsham shot a grim look across the mattress.

"I beg your pardon, ma'am," he said, "but this is no fit place for a lady. If you might wait just inside the study? Emmit, help me get him up."

Anisha realized she was being chided. "Lazonby has an appointment to keep, and I knew he would refuse," she said a little defensively. "Is he ill? Must we call a doctor? He seems quite out of his head."

No . . . damned . . . doctors," said a thready whisper.

Anisha looked down to see Rance's eyes fluttering.

"He is quite all right, ma'am, or will be," said Horsham tightly. "He's had a bad

450

night. He often does. Now if you would be so good as to withdraw, we'll heft him into his bath and pour a little water over his head. That, and some strong coffee, will usually revive him."

Her face suffusing with heat, Anisha went into the study without closing the door. Horsham did not spare her another glance.

Between the two servants, Rance was more or less hauled up, grumbling as he went. *"Devil fly . . . fly away wiff . . ."* he muttered, but the rest of his imprecation trailed away.

At least he was rousing.

Exhaling on a sigh of relief, she collapsed onto the leather settee. The young footman returned to seize the brass cans, his entire face turning pink. An instant later, there came a loud clattering of brass upon porcelain and the unmistakable sound of a good dowsing.

"Bloody hell!" Rance began to cough amidst the splashing. "Damn you to blazes!"

"You may damn the absinthe, sir," Horsham firmly replied, "and it's entirely your own fault. Emmit, go help with the rest of the bathwater."

"Horsham, you're sacked," Rance bellowed, sounding more himself. "Why the hell did I just hire you anyway? God almighty, someone's hammered a railway spike through my skull."

"Done by your own hand, sir, I'm afraid," the servant calmly replied. "And you really oughtn't dismiss me."

There came an unintelligible response.

"Because being a military man, I'm most adept with firearms." This declaration was followed by another great cascading of water. "And since you have . . . *manhandled* Lady Anisha Stafford, I daresay her brother will be calling you out."

A long moment of silence followed.

"What?" Lazonby finally rasped.

A great deal of low conversation ensued. Anisha leaned forward, attempting to hear.

"Dear God," she heard Rance muttering. "Where?"

"In your study, my lord." The words were clipped. "She wishes to see you. But not, I collect, in your altogether — which seemed to be the aspect you were intent on presenting her."

Rance groaned, but whether from shame or pain, Anisha could not have said.

Just then another footman came in with coffee. The next twenty minutes passed in relative peace. Rance stopped swearing. Horsham kept murmuring. The door onto the passageway flew open again, and a rotation of servants bearing steaming cans of water commenced trundling past.

Through it all, Anisha sat, twiddling her thumbs and cursing her own impatience. A few minutes ago, Rance had clearly not been awake — or himself. And though she had not been *too* terribly frightened, she had certainly given his servants a turn, a circumstance she deeply regretted.

And she had made them question her good sense. Perhaps even her decency. Yes, she was an old friend, and a widow of some years. But English society was far more rigid than she might wish. She should not have come here; not like this. But it was too late now, and she was as certain as ever that they had no time to spare.

She sat thus in her impatience until eventually she heard Rance again snap at the much put-upon Horsham, this time declaring amidst a streak of blue that he could bloody well shave himself.

Shortly after that, Horsham was again damned, sacked, and ordered out. This time he went, casting her one last censorious glance as he crossed the study, then slamming the door behind him. Five minutes later, Rance appeared on the threshold, bare from the waist up, one long arm resting high upon the doorframe, the other clutching the folds of a white towel that hid almost nothing. He appeared haggard, his expression grim. Still, the stippling of harsh beard was gone, and he looked more or less awake.

She regarded him calmly, wondering what a well-bred lady said to a man who'd just mauled her. But Rance spoke first. "Well, Nish," he croaked, "it would seem I owe you a monstrous apology."

"You had a difficult night, I collect?"

Eyes rueful, he dropped his arm and dragged his hand through his damp curls. "Aye."

"Are you . . . feeling yourself now?" she asked. "May we move on to something more pressing?"

His gaze locked to hers. "More pressing than the fact that I apparently tried to . . . to what? Force myself on you?"

"You kissed me." She remained perfectly still on the leather settee. "Rather determinedly, yes. But I'm fine."

A bitter smile curved his mouth. "Aye, well, if ever a chap kisses *you* any other way, then he's not a man worthy of the name."

"Thank you, I suppose." She dipped her gaze. "But you didn't know who you were kissing. You were . . . hallucinating, I think."

"Aye, perhaps. I remember some of it, too . . . I dreamt the whole night. Awful, tormenting stuff. Some of it was —" His words falling away, Rance shook his head in disbelief. His thick, dark curls were starting to spring softly to life as they dried.

"Well, I'm perfectly fine," she said. "And Horsham is right. You should give up the absinthe. I'm told it's a vile habit. Now, may we drop this discussion?"

He let his arm drop. "For now, aye," he said wearily. "But let us press on to a related topic. You've caused a stir, Nish, coming here. But you just don't care, do you? You are too bloody stubborn to see the risk in —"

"Thank you," she stiffly interjected, "but I have already been thoroughly lectured by your valet."

He set his shoulder to the door and regarded her through heavy, bloodshot eyes. "You would drag us right out into the open, wouldn't you?" he said.

"Is there an *us?"* she asked sharply.

He just shook his head. "Despite what I said to you in the garden the other day, you are going to . . . to *push* this to the point of doing yourself irreparable harm. And I — well, I'm just a man, Nish, with a man's desires. I'm half afraid I'll let you."

"You said you would not declare any affection for me openly." She willed her voice to calm, breathed deep, and folded her hands together. "And that is your choice. I cannot compel you to do anything. I cannot force you to declare your feelings for me. Perhaps" — to her shame, her voice quavered — "perhaps you have none."

"Nish!" He strode across the room to go down onto one knee, his free hand cupping round the turn of her cheek. "Oh, Anisha, love. *Unfair.*"

"Is it?" She managed a light shrug. "In any case, I cannot compel you. But I'm done trying to fit myself into a conventional box, Rance. And you cannot compel me to alter how I feel, or too behave as you think I ought."

"No," he said dryly, rising. "Apparently not."

"We are lovers — or were," she said, lifting her chin to look up at him. "Because you wanted it, Rance. You won't put this off on me entirely."

He dragged in his breath. "Aye, you're right," he said quietly.

Smoothly, Anisha rose, sliding her hands down her skirts to tidy them. "Do I still have your friendship, then?" she asked softly. "Do you still find me beautiful? Desirable? For those are the things you promised me in the garden that day. And those are the only things I can — or would even attempt — to hold you to."

He shocked her then by catching her chin between his thumb and forefinger, and lowering his lips to hers. She did not tremble or step away, for it was a kiss of exquisite gentleness. For a seemingly infinite moment, his lips lingered, molded warmly over hers, until Anisha had to close her eyes and almost bite her tongue — all to keep from begging him for something more.

"God, Anisha," he whispered a long while later. "Yes. You are all those things to me. And more, in ways I dare not think of."

"But . . . ?"

"But you have taken it upon yourself to unilaterally declare us to be intimate." His eyes hardened a little. "To take whatever it is we have and drag it out into the open. My servants are by no means loose-lipped. But to come by my house alone, in the middle of the day, love, is to court ruin —"

"Stop." She laid a finger to his lips. "I came in a closed, unmarked coach with a veil down. I wore a hat, for God's sake — all to appease you, not me. Do not make worse of this than it is."

He held her gaze for a long while, his face etched with weariness and concern. "Aye, then," he said. "Well, why are you here? Going somewhere, am I?"

"Yes," she said firmly. "To a village called Buckhurst Hill."

His eyes widened. "Whatever for, pray?"

"To see the gentleman whose name Miss de Rohan — excuse me, Lady Bessett — gave you. And I'm going, too. I've brought Raju's traveling coach, since you insisted on something closed. Now hurry and dress."

His gaze shifted to deep reluctance. "I'm not going anywhere in that lumbering old contraption," he said. "Besides, my valet has deserted me."

Anisha rolled her eyes heavenward, seized him by the arm, and propelled him back into the lion's den. "Whoa!" he declared.

"No, here's how it is, Rance," she said, less gently. "We're pressed for time, and you are getting dressed. And you don't need Horsham to help."

"Do I not?" His mouth twitched. "And you know this how?"

She cast him a humorless glance. "You're a soldier," she said, "not some mincing dandy who cares how his cravat gets knotted. Don't start pretending you give a tuppence how you look."

"Ouch!" A grin tugged at his mouth. "Aiming for the heart, are you?"

"Oh, just give me the towel," she said

briskly. "Where do you keep your shirts and drawers?"

"Really, Nish?" He lifted both eyebrows. "You think this is appropriate?"

"I'm long past caring," she said, snatching the towel away.

Somehow, she managed not to ogle his lean, tautly muscled form, or the fine shaft of manhood that lay half-hardened in the nest of curls above his thighs. Instead, she waltzed past him to toss the damp towel into the bathroom, where it landed in a heap by the tub. Then, going to a tallboy by the windows, she yanked open a drawer and began to dig through it.

"Now, I shall find what you need if you're so pampered you —"

"Nish." His big hand settled over her smaller, darker one, stilling it on a pile of his handkerchiefs. "Stop all this. There's no reason to rush off and —"

Something inside her snapped then, and she whirled on him. "But there is *every* reason!" she cried, throwing her hands up. "Rance, can't you see? This . . . this black *thing* hangs over you, blighting your life. I'm tired of it. We must do something. And this man, Anaïs thinks he might be able to —"

"Oh, yes, the all-knowing Anaïs and the ever-popular *'might'!*" Rance cut in, throwing up his hands. "Half my life, Anisha, has been built upon *might*. I grow *mightily* tired of it, too. No one outside the *Fraternitas* family is going to help me, and you know it. So the only choice left to me is to beat the truth of this business out of Jack Coldwater."

"You don't know that!" she cried, catching his arm. "Just stop saying it! It is getting you nowhere. And leave Jack Coldwater alone, do you hear me? He cannot help you. And your obsession with him is . . . is simply *unnatural*."

Rance froze. *"Unnatural?"* His voice had dropped to a whisper. "Perhaps, Anisha, you'd like to clarify that?"

She did not answer but instead yanked a pair of drawers from the chest. "Just put those on," she said, hurling them at him.

"No." He snatched them in midair, stalking toward her. "No, Anisha, I don't think I will. Not until we settle this business. You are referring, I take it, to that afternoon at the St. James Society? When you found Jack with me in the bookroom?"

"Yes." Her voice falling to a whisper, Anisha realized tears had sprung to her eyes. "Yes, that's precisely it."

"And what, *precisely,* did you think was going on?" he rasped.

She looked at him accusingly. "You were — the two of you were —" She stopped and shook her head. "I don't know what you were. But ever since that day, Rance, your obsession with him has worsened, and it needs to stop. Not for *me.* For *you.*"

Rance snapped out the drawers. "I will not stand here stark-arsed whilst we bicker like fishwives," he said, yanking them on almost savagely. "Pull the bloody bell, since you're so very much at home here. Tell Emmit to bring round my curricle."

"So now we don't need a closed carriage?" Anisha retorted.

"What we need is to make haste and get back before dark," he answered, throwing open a massive mahogany armoire. "The day is getting on."

"And whose fault is that?"

"Mine," he shouted, yanking out a fresh shirt and hurling it onto the bed. "There, Nish, are you pleased? Every damned bit of this is my fault. Hell, all the world's ills are likely my fault."

"How like you to exaggerate!" she snapped. "It's no more than half, at best."

An hour later, his jaw gritted hard, Rance watched as the edges of greater London went flying past his carriage. Anisha sat

461

stiffly on the seat beside him, her shoulders rigid as rafters, her bobbinet veil down and her parasol up. No one could possibly have identified her — not, he reminded himself, that there was any problem with a respectable widow spending the afternoon alone with a gentleman, enjoying the countryside.

Not if the gentleman himself were respectable.

But they had spent a great deal of time together of late. Too much. Rance forced away the thought and tried to ignore the dull ache still lingering across the base of his skull. At least his head was clear now. The day, however, had turned hazy, the air dangerously still. Rance cast a glance heavenward and did not like what he saw.

"It is going to rain."

"What of it?" she said.

"Perhaps we should have kept Ruthveyn's carriage," he muttered.

With an impatient gesture, Anisha reached up and snapped her parasol shut. "You wanted to make better time," she said tartly. "Drive on. I'll run the risk of returning to London in a downpour."

"Out of the question," he snapped. "You might take ill."

She turned to him with a mockingly sweet expression. "Must we have an argument before its time?" she asked. "There are so many more pertinent quarrels to be had. Shall I choose one?"

"If I'm such vexing company, I wonder you insist on coming along," he grumbled.

"Oh, I am not *coming along,*" she answered. "I am making you go. Trust me, Rance, there is a world of difference."

He cut her a dark, sidelong glance but felt his lips twitch tellingly. "The dictionary according to Anisha, eh?" he said, wishing to the devil he could stay angry with her.

Had he been able to, perhaps he could have shut out the sense of impending doom that had begun to haunt him. That awful black feeling that trailed him like a bloodhound and nudged him from his sleep. That grim realization that needled him in the middle of dinner, stilled his hand upon his whisky glass, and fluttered vaguely about in the back of his mind through his every waking moment.

Not his impending doom. *Hers.*

Anisha was going to end up with him if he was not very, very careful.

She and Tom and Teddy were going to be saddled with him and his vile reputation for the rest of their natural lives. And regardless of what she said, it *did* matter. It mattered greatly. The blight upon his name would become a blight upon her family. She would have sacrificed her home, her country, and her life in order to make a better one for her boys, only to toss it all away again — and for what? For *him?*

It was madness.

Dismayed, he looked about and realized they had entered Hackney; there was no shorter way to Buckhurst Hill. They were going to drive straight past Coldwater's house. As traffic had fallen away now, he clicked up his horses. But he could not make the place invisible.

As the King's Arms flew past, he tilted his head toward the large white cottage beyond. "Coldwater's house," he said. "Or his sister's, I should say. I tracked him up here a time or two."

Anisha turned to look at it. "How lovely," she said neutrally. "The family must be prosperous."

"Aye, American newspaper money," he said. "They hail from Boston."

"Oh."

The silence felt heavy. "I went there last night," he finally said. "The sister — I met her. I just knocked on the door and claimed I was looking for Jack. I don't know, really, what I hoped to learn."

"What was she like?"

"She was . . . strange." Rance tried to put it into words. "Taunting — like Jack, but more subtle. Whatever he's up to, she's part and parcel to it."

He didn't know what else to say; the woman *was* like Jack. She muddled his ordinarily acute senses in a way he couldn't quite grasp.

"And that was the end of it?" Anisha pressed. "You just . . . left?"

"Not exactly." He cut her a sheepish look. "I broke into Coldwater's flat and had a poke around. But there was nothing. The place looked scarcely lived in."

Her eyes flashed disapprovingly. *"Hmm."*

Silence fell over them again, and soon Hackney was vanishing in the distance. After a time they came to a stretch punctuated by nothing but the occasional farmhouse, with empty green fields rolling out to either side and no traffic in either direction.

Rance considered his next words carefully. "You wanted to know about Jack," he finally said. "About that day in the bookroom."

"No." Anisha did not look at him. "I didn't."

He resisted the urge to snap his whip over his horses' heads, since none of this was their fault. "Let me rephrase that," he said tightly. "You are suffering under a misconception — one from which I insist upon disabusing you."

Her face having lost much of its color, Anisha's gaze focused straight down the lane. "I should rather you kept your thoughts of Mr. Coldwater private."

"No," he said. "I will not. That is what the word *insist* means, you see. You *insist* upon accompanying me to Essex. In turn, I *insist* upon your listening to me — since you are, by your own choice, my captive audience."

Anisha colored furiously and tightened her grip on the seat. "So you have a strange obsession with Coldwater," she said. "I do not judge. Even the ancient scriptures are vague on this subject. Indeed, the *Kāamashastra* says that men may —"

"Anisha, *do* hush," he cut in sharply.

She did, shooting him a dark, sidelong glance.

And then, to his horror, Rance did not know what to say.

"Nish, I do not —" Here, he seized the excuse of cutting his horses round an especially deep rut. But the rut was not deep enough to long save him.

"I do not sexually desire Jack Coldwater," he finally added. "I loathe the little bastard. I've tried to beat him senseless on numerous occasions, but someone always stops me."

"Yes, but what you describe is passion," said Anisha coolly.

"*Passion?* Are you mad — ?"

She lifted one slender shoulder beneath the black bombazine of her gown. "Passion is an emotion that takes many forms. Passion is deceptive; it can transform itself into something else altogether before one is fully aware."

He turned to glare at her. "Aye, and right now the passion I feel for you is transforming itself into a burning desire to turn you over my knee."

She flashed a crooked smile. "And thus is my point proven."

Rance returned his gaze to the road and felt his teeth grind. "I was trying to throttle Coldwater, and that's all," he barked. "He said something about Geoff — about how I'd conned a once-decent man into falling in with my lies, and now he meant to ruin us both. He said he knew Geoff had a secret. Something he meant to expose — and you can guess what it was."

"Oh!" Anisha's hand went to her heart. *"No."*

Rance winced, though the sun wasn't in his eyes. "It had begun to feel, Nish, as if everyone I loved was going to pay for my sins," he rasped. "My mother and father both dead. Sutherland's living gone. Old Sir Greville lost half his business filing my pleas, and Ruthveyn called in every diplomatic chit he ever had with the Queen merely to —"

"Raju *wanted* to," she interjected. "It was his duty."

"Still, to then see Geoff hurt — well, I just snapped. I went for Jack across the sofa, I guess, and that bloody porcelain thing — Aristotle, or whoever the chap was — I knocked him over and he shattered into a hundred pieces, and all I could think was that now Ruthveyn was going to kill me. That I'd broken his blasted sculpture and he would be furious and it was all Jack's fault — which gave me two reasons to throttle him — and then I got hold of him and . . . and . . . and . . ."

Anisha laid a hand on his arm. *"Breathe,"* she said. "Deeply."

"Breathing, Nish, is not the solution to every damned thing!" he snapped. "I'm just trying to tell you how it was. I got him forced up against the wall, and got my hands round his throat, and then you and Ruthveyn burst in. And that's *all it was.*"

Anisha cut him an odd glance. "Raju

468

thought you were forcing him into something rather more intimate," she said calmly. "As did I, frankly. That's . . . that's what it looked like. Like a man taking the spoils of war. Jack was terrified. He ran past me in a blind panic."

"A wise choice," gritted Rance.

She hesitated a heartbeat. "But Rance, Coldwater had never been afraid of you before," she quietly pointed out. "He never ran away before — not even when he should have done."

Rance just shook his head and pressed his lips into a thin line. Her words left him vaguely ill, for there was some truth in what she said.

He had been a soldier for nearly a third of his life; he had seen violence heaped upon violence; seen men rape and pillage without restraint. But never had he done so, nor even felt the temptation. And yet what he had felt that day in the study had frightened him. He had wanted, fleetingly, to teach Jack Coldwater a lesson; a lesson that had had little to do with Jack's insults, and everything to do with raw dominance and power.

He had wanted Jack to pay the ultimate price.

But why *that* price?

Why not just kill him? That, he could have got away with. Murder done under the roof of the St. James Society, surrounded by the brotherhood — hell, they could have buried the bastard in their secret, underground chapel and none the wiser.

It was chilling to realize how near the truth Anisha was.

But never would he admit it. "You're asking me to explain Jack Coldwater's motivations," he answered, evading the subject like another rut in the road, "something I've never been able to do. Isn't that the very reason we're going to Essex?"

Anisha cut a quick, assessing glance at him. "No, we're going to see this Mr. Kemble who once had connections to the underworld," she said. "We are going to see if he can tell us what Ned Quartermaine could not — the name of the person who so desperately wanted you hanged all those years ago. And that person was most assuredly *not* Coldwater. He can't be a day over twenty-five."

The home of Mr. George Jacob Kemble was an elegant Georgian manor house well northwest of the village, tucked into a crook of forestland that swept around it like a verdant embrace. It was the prettiest house

Anisha had ever seen — once they actually found it, for the house stood at the end of a half-mile carriage lane and required them to ask further directions at an inn, a public house, and a cow byre, where a laconic farmer merely leaned on his pitchfork and pointed at a gap in the hedgerow.

After that, everything was a little *too* easy. At the end of the drive, a footman hastened down the front steps to take Rance's horses well before they had drawn up. At the top of the staircase, a second man, a sort of butler, took their cards and swept out an arm, motioning down the polished marble passageway that bisected the opulent home from front to back.

"Theez way, *s'il vous plaît*," he said. "Monsieur Kemble eez een hez rose garden."

Anisha hesitated. "You will not wish to enquire of him first?"

"Eet eez not needed, *madame*." The butler smiled almost patronizingly. "Monsieur Kemble has been expecting you."

Rance and Anisha exchanged curious glances, then followed the man to a set of six French windows that opened onto a terrace. Here, a second flight of steps some thirty feet wide descended into a lush, formal garden. At the back, along the rear wall, Anisha could see a man in a dark coat atop a narrow ladder, snipping away at a climbing rose that was almost over the wall. A taller, silver-haired man was gingerly picking up the cuttings and dropping them into a wicker basket.

"Monsieur Kemble eez up there, madame," he said, pointing at the ladder.

But the man had already noted their approach and descended, whereupon the tall gentleman spun him around to brush off his coat with short, impatient motions.

". . . never spare a thought, George, for the effort that goes . . ." Tart snippets carried on the breeze. "Five hundred stitches . . . just in that sleeve!"

But the dark man pushed past him, looking fixedly at Anisha as he stepped from the greenery and onto the stone path. She caught his gaze, and he smiled almost predatorily.

"Good Lord!" she murmured. "The man from the theater?"

Rance glanced down. "What man?"

But it was too late. Mr. Kemble had floated like a wraith across the last parterre. "Lady Anisha Stafford!" he murmured, bowing gracefully over her hand. "What an unlooked-for pleasure!"

"B-But your butler," Anisha uttered, "—

he said you were expecting us."

"Lazonby," Rance interjected, along with his hand. "At your service, sir."

Mr. Kemble looked him up and down, his lips quirking a little. "Well, at last we meet," he murmured. "Or perhaps I should say, at last we are introduced?"

Rance's brow furrowed. "Have we met, sir?"

Kemble waved dismissively. "Oh, I used to see you round Town," he said, "back before they hanged you."

Just then the taller man cleared his throat. "George, *really.*"

Mr. Kemble urged him forward and introduced him as his friend, Maurice Giroux. Anisha recognized him as the second man seated in the Duke of Gravenel's box at the Royal Opera House.

Giroux bowed over her hand. "I should put the kettle on," he said with perhaps a hint of a Continental accent. "George, take them into the orangery. It's private."

"A lovely notion," Kemble murmured, motioning them along the garden wall.

Anisha followed, taking his measure. He was a lithe, slender man — and a wealthy one, apparently, for his attire looked expensive and classically *à la mode.* Moving with a silky, catlike grace, he led them through the garden, politely remarking upon various features of the garden, casting breezy gestures this way and that.

Hyacinth. Hellebore. Hawthorne. A trio of rare Asian lilies whose name Anisha couldn't pronounce. All of it was lush and lovely, but rather than focus upon it, Anisha found herself wondering at Mr. Kemble's *udaya lagna.* He was a water sign, almost certainly. *Karkata* — Cancer — most probably, for unless she missed her guess, Mr. Kemble had exquisite taste and a flair for the dramatic.

He was also many decades past his youth, for, though his skin bore few wrinkles, his temples were generously touched with silver, and there was an air of *ennui* about him.

A few yards along, the garden wall cornered left and became a sunny fruit wall espaliered with pear and plum. In the center a glass house jutted out, connected to the manor house by a long, vine-covered pergola. Here, their host threw open the door to a room filled with potted citrus trees and flowering shrubs, in the center of which sat a gurgling fountain, surrounded by an assortment of rattan furniture arranged upon a flagstone circle.

With the heavy weight of Rance's hand at the small of her back, Anisha waded into the lush greenery, feeling instantly at home in the moist, delicious heat. "How lovely," she murmured.

Mr. Kemble offered them the small wicker sofa. As soon as they were settled, he sat and turned the whole of his attention to her.

"So now you must tell me, Lady Anisha," he said with an airy gesture, "how did you find *Les Huguenots?* Was it all you had hoped for?"

"I thought it marvelous. And you?"

Mr. Kemble sniffed. "Well, I'd seen the premier in Paris a dozen years ago, but Maurice is a great friend of Madame Dorus-Gras" — he dropped his voice — "who, frankly, has no business still playing Marguerite. My God, poor Julie's *forty* if she's a day — and working on a second chin!"

"Oh," said Anisha. "I don't think I could see that from my seat."

"For my part," Kemble continued, lifting one eyebrow, "I was more interested in dropping by *your* box."

"You knew who I was?"

"My dear girl, I know who everyone is." He paused to pluck a small, green thorn from his coat sleeve. "Besides, Anaïs had suggested the two of you might be by — which left me *most* intrigued, a thing sadly rare nowadays. But just as I began to contemplate the pleasure of your company, cheered as I was by the imminent departure of he-who-we-probably-oughtn't-mention" — here, he shot her a saucy wink — "that buffoon Sir Wilfred turned up."

"Sir *Wilfred?*" Rance interjected. "Sir Wilfred Leeton?"

"Oh, the very same, my lord," said Kemble, rather too cheerfully. "I believe you have a passing acquaintance with the gentleman?"

But Rance was not looking at Kemble. He had turned to glower at Anisha. "I don't like the sound of this," he said grimly. "What, exactly, have you been up to?"

Anisha lifted both hands, palms out. "I just went to the theater."

"With he-who-we-probably-oughtn't-mention," Kemble added, leaning in conspiratorially.

Rance's glower expanded. "I am aware, sir, in whose company she went to the theater," he snapped. "What I don't understand is how Leeton came to be involved in it. And I'll say again: I do not like the sound of it."

"Heavens, my lord!" Mr. Kemble set his fingertips together. "Sir Wilfred is a pillar of our community. Surely you do not doubt his good character?"

476

After a heartbeat, Rance eased back against the sofa, his wide shoulders relaxing. "I've no quarrel with the fellow," he answered. "But I know *exactly* what he is."

At that, Kemble laughed, and Anisha wasn't sure why. Moreover, Rance's expression had not entirely relented.

"What, pray, was *I* to do?" She set a hand on his sleeve and felt his muscle flex beneath. "Send him away? The man seemed well-acquainted with Napier and —"

"Oops!" chirped Kemble. "There's that unmentionable name!"

Rance shot Kemble a nasty look. "What, sir, is your point?"

Kemble looked positively waggish now. "Why, nothing at all!" Then his voice fell to a more serious tone. "But the two of you have not come all this way merely to gossip, I think?"

The room fell silent. "You understand, then, why we are here?" Rance finally said, his voice edged with reluctance.

"Oh, yes." Kemble opened his hands expansively. "And I am but a happy tool of the Home Office."

"And just why is that?" said Rance suspiciously.

Kemble made a vague motion. "Well, if I must confess, I've grown a little fond of de

Vendenheim over the years," he said. "Besides, when it comes to my business affairs, the Home Office has been looking the other way so long their necks are cricked."

"Royden Napier works for the Home Office," Rance pointed out.

"Not your half," Kemble countered.

"I don't have so much as a sliver," Rance grumbled, "let alone half."

Kemble laughed. "Oh, surely *I* need not explain the breadth of *Fraternitas* influence to *you,*" he chortled. "You've as good as got Napier's . . . er . . . leash in hand now."

Anisha's eyes widened. The *Fraternitas?* Beyond the brotherhood, she'd never heard the name tossed casually out. Rance, however, didn't flinch.

"Because Lady Bessett's father is the Vicomte de Vendenheim?"

"Yes, Lord Lazonby," said Mr. Kemble sardonically. "It is called *politics* — the game of kings — and one at which I, too, am most adept. So, shall we play?"

Anisha leaned intently forward. "We just need information —"

"Of which I am a veritable font," said Kemble, expanding his hands.

"Fine, then," said Rance grimly. "Tell us what your role was in London's underworld."

Kemble drew back, fingertips pressed to his chest. "But *underworld* is such a vile word," he said. "It makes one think of . . . why, trolls. Or earthworms. I should rather refer to it as a sort of tertiary economic system — political bribery, of course, being second."

"Fine," said Rance tightly. "And your roll?"

Mr. Kemble admired his own manicure for a moment. "Well, I used to make quite a nice living in — well, let us call it brokering life's fineries," he finally said. "Art, jewels, antiquities. That sort of thing."

"You kept a shop?"

"Sometimes," he said coyly.

"You were a thief?"

"Lazonby!" Anisha chided.

"Oh, heavens no!" Mr. Kemble set a hand over his heart. "Nothing so tawdry! I was a fence."

"A *fence?*" Anisha turned to Rance.

"A receiver," he said quietly. "Of stolen property."

"Not all of it was stolen," Kemble advised. "Some was willingly surrendered. Desperate young gentlemen were my stock-in-trade."

"By desperate you mean gamesters?" said Rance quietly.

"Well, I was on speaking terms with the managers of every hell in Town, and a few of the better clubs," he said. "Players who'd beggared themselves came to me, and oftentimes, I went to them. You see, it was occasionally — well, let us call it *prudent* — for an astute businessman to call in his debt whilst the player in question was still within his establishment, particularly if fellow in question wasn't *quite* a gentleman and hadn't a name to protect."

"You mean he'd run too high a loss and they were afraid his IOU would be hard to collect," said Rance.

"I see you perfectly understand." Kemble beamed as if he'd discovered a prodigy.

"Desperate men, indeed," said Rance. "And desperate men can be dangerous."

Kemble's smile turned faintly malicious. "Oh, I never worried overmuch," he said. "I have a finely honed grasp of how to — oh, let us call it *motivate* people. So a hell might summon me to help relieve the fellow of his emerald cravat pin or his watch chain or his gold-chased snuffbox. In the height of such emotion, it was best to call upon someone impartial."

Rance looked at him flatly. "And that would be you."

"Well, I'm nothing if not honest," said

Kemble.

As if sent by God, a horrific crack of lightning rent the air, followed by an ominous roll of thunder. "Damnation!" Rance muttered, casting his gaze up.

"Oh, good!" Kemble clapped his hands. "It's going to rain on my roses. And look! Here's the tea."

Monsieur Giroux did not reappear but had sent a servant with the tray. Kemble dismissed him at once and began to pour himself, which Anisha thought a little odd.

"This is *Shui Xian,* Lady Anisha, from the Wuyi Mountains," said Kemble, tipping out a bloodred stream. It swirled cleverly round the inside of an Imari tea bowl so thin one could see his fingers. "And of the very best grade," he continued, "for it's been roasted, then aged ten years. You'll find it rather different from your assams and darjeelings."

"Ten *years?*" she said as he passed her the dainty bowl.

"Yes, and I counsel you strongly against the English habit of tainting it," he said, waving his hand over the milk and sugar, "but there, if you must! I shall simply turn my head from the carnage."

"Why, I wouldn't think of it," she murmured.

As he continued to pour, Anisha glanced

up to see the sky darkening ominously. There was a chill settling over the glass house now, and with it a vague sense of unease. Worse, she could feel the press of time — and the heat of Rance's thigh along hers. Both were disconcerting. Janet had been right; if they lingered much longer, or if the storm broke, she and Rance would not make it home tonight.

She tried to steer the conversation forward. "Mr. Kemble, it certainly sounds as if you had intimate knowledge of the gaming salons," she said. "And because of those salons, Lord Lazonby was falsely accused of a heinous crime, so —"

"— so coming right to the point, you wish to know who shivved old Percy?" he said, putting the pot down with a *clunk.*

Anisha and Rance exchanged glances. "Heavens, have you some idea?" she asked.

Kemble relaxed into his chair. "My dear child, everything in the world is motivated by one of two things," he said, fanning out his fingers, much like a magician about to pull a scarf from his coat sleeve. "One has only to winkle out *which* in order to know *who.*"

Anisha gave a little shake of her head, attempting to clear it. "And those things would be . . . ?"

"Firstly, money, which equates to power," he said, "and secondly, that age-old delight, sexual intercourse."

"Good God, man!" Rance cut a protective glance at Anisha. "Gentlemen don't speak of —"

"Money, yes, I know." Kemble had the audacity to wink again. "But it's been suggested I'm only half a gentleman. The other half being . . . well, *French*."

Anisha set a restraining hand to Rance's sleeve. "But this murder," she said stridently, "and Lazonby's false conviction — it cannot have been done without collusion. Can it?"

"Well, dead men tell no tales," said Kemble, taking up his tea with an elegantly crooked finger, "but I wonder if anyone ever looked closely at Hanging Nick Napier? Now there was a fellow who lived well — a little *too* well, if you ask me."

"At last, something we can agree on," Rance growled.

Anisha ignored him. "I got the impression there was some money in the family," she mused, remembering Napier's theater box and Sir Wilfred Leeton's odd comments.

"None old Nick got a taste of," said Kemble. "He was disowned for marrying down. *Napier* was his wife's name."

"But Englishmen sometimes take their wives' names," Anisha countered.

"Only for money, my dear!" Kemble sagely advised. "And the late Mrs. Napier was descended from nothing more than a long line of government toadies. Yet Mr. Napier managed very well indeed — in Eaton Square, no less, in a house acquired just after Royden's birth."

"Aye," said Rance pensively, "and he didn't buy that on a government salary, did he?"

"Oh, I fancy not." Kemble sipped delicately at his tea. "And we now realize Royden maintains a friendship with Sir Wilfred Leeton, the sort of man who should have been the bane of his father's existence."

"But Leeton is upstanding now," said Rance. "And the Crown forced him to testify at my trial — not that he had much to say."

"No, I'll just bet he didn't," said Kemble. "By the time Leeton was finished tweaking his tale, the judge likely believed he was running a charity hospital out of that house in Berwick Street and simply found you and poor Peveril hiding in his pantry with a pack of cards in hand."

"Well, it wasn't even a gaming hell, was it?" Anisha glanced at Rance.

"Oh, heavens no!" trilled Kemble. "It was ever so genteel. Gentlemen dropped cards on a silver salver as if they were calling on the Duchess of Devonshire. And Leeton never touched money; if one owed the house, one was 'invited' to leave it in a little dish on the sideboard or some such nonsense. Quite honestly, the veteran hell owners laughed at him."

"Oh, my," Anisha murmured.

"Nonetheless, one did need nerves of steel to play at Leeton's," Kemble added almost admiringly. "Cards only, and play was devilish deep. But despite Leeton's façade of gentility, every gaming salon in Town paid off *someone,* even if it was just a couple of shillings to the local constable."

"Aye, you're right about that," Rance grudgingly admitted.

"So we are back to the sex and the money," Kemble continued, "for I can assure you they drive mankind's every breath, though they may wear the guise of something else — revenge and jealousy, most often."

"Fine, then," Rance snapped. "Which applied to Lord Percy Peveril?"

"Oh, heavens, money!" said Kemble, shuddering. "No one wanted to sleep with

485

Percy. Did you ever look closely at the fellow?"

"Not in that precise light," Rance returned.

"Well, he had a curious gap between his teeth, Percy," said Kemble airily. "Worse, he laughed through his nose. Why, I once saw him spew a vintage *eau de vie* halfway across a roulette table."

"Never noticed any of it," said Rance dismissively. "What about Sir Arthur Colburne turning up his toes?"

Here, Mr. Kemble hesitated. "Incidental, I'd guess," he finally answered. "Indeed, prior to poor Percy's coming up to scratch over Miss Colburne — a matter in which you were *used,* Lord Lazonby, in case you were unaware — it was widely rumored Arthur would either try to marry money himself or flee his creditors by going to France, or perhaps his sister in Canada."

"Canada?" said Anisha.

"Well, it might have been Connecticut." Kemble made a dismissive gesture. "In any case, Miss Colburne was horrified, and old Percy fast became the lesser of three evils — the first being a stepmamma, the second being a life of grinding poverty in Pawcatuck or Manitoba or some equally unpronounceable backwater. But at worst, some-

486

one wanted him gone, not dead. He may have been vain, gutless, and venal, but Artie was harmless and everyone knew it."

Anisha leaned into the conversation. "So, who made money, Mr. Kemble, by having Rance accused of murder?"

Kemble reached out and gave her hand an avuncular pat. "The better question, dear girl, is, *who stopped losing money?* And the answer is, every gaming salon and hell-hole from Westminster to Wapping. Your boon companion here was bleeding them like a jar of leeches. Slowly — but deadly if it goes on long enough."

"But I've looked closely at each of those men," Rance protested, setting his tea down with a clatter. "Most have died, aye, or vanished. But I'm not a fool, Mr. Kemble."

Kemble just shrugged. "Looked at *each* of them, eh? But have you looked at *all* of them?"

Eyes widening, Anisha seized her satchel and dug out her sheaf of papers. On top were the folded gaming vowels. "I stole those," she said, "from Royden Napier."

"Oh, bravo!" Kemble brightened hopefully. "What have we here?"

"Perhaps Sir Wilfred Leeton didn't want to pay his debt to Rance?" she suggested as Kemble's eyes swept over the notes. "Perhaps he killed Peveril?"

"Over this sum?" Kemble murmured. "I doubt it. Old Will could have raised twice that by selling out his stables."

Anisha had not thought the sum so paltry. "Lady Madeleine MacLachlan is taking me to the Leetons' garden party on Monday," she murmured. "Do you think he would know anything?"

"You might do better to ask the wife," Kemble said, his finger stroking lightly round the penciled circle. "*She's* a frightful gossip."

"I saw that notation, too," she said a little breathlessly. "What would you guess it means?"

Kemble tucked the papers back and pushed the file away. "Oh, I need not guess, child!" he said. "That is a reference to the Black Horse syndicate. Hanging Nick was wondering, you see, if Leeton was a member. And assuming he made the proper inquiries, he would have learnt that, no, he was not. He was far too junior, and while his house was pernicious as an adder's den, it was as much about Leeton rubbing elbows with the nobs as making money. And in the world of serious gaming, that sentiment held no sway."

"The Black Horse syndicate?" Rance

straightened in his chair. "What the devil is that?"

Kemble made an airy gesture with his hand. "Oh, think of it as a sort of London guild," he said. "Rather like the Worshipful Company of Fishmongers, but for gaming establishments — only the old pros, mind. It was quite something to aspire to. They dined twice a month in a private room over the Black Horse in Cripplegate. It was a shady crew, but I knew a few of them."

"What did they do, exactly?" Anisha asked.

Kemble shrugged. "Oh, guarded one another's backs, hired out bullyboys, kept a running list of counters and sharpers that wanted watching — and on rare occasion, they covered one another's losses from a mutual aid fund."

"Good God, like . . . *fire insurance?*" said Rance. "I never heard of it."

"Oddly enough, they did not advertise," said Kemble snidely. "Certainly not to you. More likely yours was the first name on their list."

"But I —" Anisha bit back her words.

Both men turned to look at her. "Yes?" Kemble murmured. "What is it, my dear?"

Anisha shot Rance a sidelong look. "It's just that I showed those to Edward Quartermaine," she said quietly. "He runs one of the most profitable hells in London. But he said he thought the words had no significance."

"Quartermaine — ?" Rance turned to glower at her again.

Kemble merely chortled with laughter. "Oh, I'll just bet he did! Young Ned was ever a sly one. But he's right, in a manner of speaking. A den of thieves soon turns on itself, and the Black Horse gang died out, some fleeing to the Continent as rascals will do, and others going on to that great faro board in the sky. Well, all save for the chap who thought it up to begin with."

"And who was that?" said Rance.

"Oh, that would be one Mr. Alfred Hedge, who is presently hacking up his lungs in the salubrious sea air of Brighton after a lifetime of London dissipation," said Mr. Kemble. "You might call him the original Prime Warden of that merry guild. But Ned Quartermaine? I think he just calls him *Papa*."

Chapter 12

They are greater storms and tempests
than almanacs can report.
William Shakespeare,
Antony and Cleopatra

Half an hour later, both the sky and the mood had only grown blacker. "Good God," said Rance grimly as they bore down upon Mr. Kemble's gateposts. "Remember what you once said about being nailed shut in a barrel?"

"Feeling it, old thing?" Through her black veil, Anisha cut a curious glance at him. "I believe Quartermaine has led us a merry dance."

Rance shook his head. "I know the fellow's short on Christian charity, but I wouldn't have believed him a liar," he said, cutting his horses onto the main road. Then his jaw hardened, and he shot her a censorious glance. "Nor would I have believed you fool enough to go back there alone."

Anisha bit back her temper as the horses dug in hard to pull them over a set of deep ruts in the turn — just the sort of soft, bare earth, she knew, that could turn to mud in an instant, caking one's wheels. She took a fierce grip on the side of the calash as they clattered over the rough, Rance having put the cover up before setting off again. But it would not be enough to shield them if the storm broke.

Rance was still waiting for her to say something. "I did not go alone," she finally answered. "There, are you satisfied?"

He shut his eyes an instant as the cow byre flew past. "Please, Nish. Not with Napier."

"Do you really think me such a fool?" she snapped. "I had Mr. Ringgold send Quartermaine across the street to the bookroom, though he was none too pleased about it. I offered him tea, showed him the notes, then simply sat there whilst he lied to my face, then lectured me like a child — a tendency the two of you share, I might mention."

Rance snapped his whip high, and the horses sped up. "I'm sorry, Nish," he said after a quarter mile had passed. "I'm sorry I fret. I'm sorry I dragged you out here. You mean only to help, I know, and I'm not sure I deserve it. And now, blast it all, we're in for a drenching."

There was indeed little hope now the storm would go around them. "Perhaps we should have stayed with Mr. Kemble and Monsieur Giroux?" she said. "They did offer."

"Perhaps," he admitted. "But it seemed . . . unwise. He helped us, aye. But I know his sort. He may provide information to the Home Office — or to us — as it suits him, but his loyalty lies with himself."

Anisha set one hand on her hat against a sudden, whipping wind. "Did you sense anything of him?" she asked quietly.

Rance gave a tight nod. "That chap reads like an open book," he answered. "Beneath all that persnickity charm, he's utterly ruthless. He seems almost . . . fey at times. But he's not. He's *dangerous* — and amoral as an alley cat."

"But was he dishonest?"

"No." Rance turned his gaze from the road, acknowledgement in his eyes. "Not today, at any rate, and that's a fair point, Nish. Everything he said was the truth as he knew it. I'm sure of that. Still, he didn't tell us everything he could have."

"Well, I wouldn't want him as an enemy," said Anisha, just as lightning flashed in the distance. The low sound of thunder followed soon after, rolling around them like some monstrous barrel in the sky. But the horses carried on at a brisk clip, the hedgerows flying past. They fell into an uncomfortable silence, Anisha mulling over everything Mr. Kemble had told them.

Interestingly, the man had never once questioned Rance's innocence. Instead, without prompting, he'd proposed Anisha's theory — that there had been a conspiracy against Rance. Still, it seemed odd under such circumstances to frame a man for murder. Anisha wished for an instant to return to the manor house and ask Kemble why such a thing made sense.

London had hundreds of dark alleys and a deep, deadly river running through the middle of it. If a gang of hooligans wanted rid of someone, why not simply crack him across the sconce and pitch him off Waterloo Bridge? Why take that extra step of killing someone else, then fixing the blame?

She was inexplicably frustrated with Edward Quartermaine, too, though why it should be so, Anisha could not have said. The man had never represented himself as anything *but* a scoundrel. And eventually Rance would have his revenge. Next time they met, he might just plant the fellow a facer, for Rance hadn't the patience to simply call a man out as a gentleman should.

But that mightn't be soon. At his first opportunity, Rance would be off to Brighton, and he wouldn't return until he'd wrung every drop of information to be had from Quartermaine's father.

Just now, however, he was fretting more about her than either Quartermaine or his sire. Her peevishness giving way to affection, she eased her hand beneath his elbow and curled it round his sleeve.

After an instant's hesitation, he tucked his arm closer, pressing her hand to his ribs. "Blast," he said. "Do you see that black sky to the south? That's London under a torrent — with more black coming behind it."

"Go back to that inn," she said in a firm voice. "The one with all those apple trees where we asked directions."

"Nish —" he began.

"Rance, I'm not riding twenty miles in a downpour to salvage what you imagine is my reputation," she said just as the rain began to drum down on the calash. "You may do as you please. But you will set me down in the inn yard. Now, how far is it?"

"Three miles," he grumbled. "I hope you won't miss me."

But even Anisha could see that she had won.

And she knew, even if he did not, that Rance would never abandon her.

By the time they reached the old coaching inn, the rain was hammering hard. His breeches soaked through at the knees, Rance maneuvered his horses through the carriage gate, drawing up beneath the inn's upper story. The din upon the calash ceased, but the splatter beyond was still deafening, the rain so heavy he could barely make out the yard's fringe of gnarled fruit trees that had earlier been apparent.

A young ostler sprang from the lee of the stables, massive boots splashing through the puddles as he came — though *puddle* did not quite define it; the yard was now a shallow pond that was washing beneath the gate.

Rain streaming off his hat, Rance leapt down and tossed the lad two shillings as they passed. "Grab your satchel, Nish," he shouted over the din, "and throw your arms round my neck."

Anisha gave a little shriek when he scooped her up beneath the knees and hefted her out of the curricle, but her shoes and hems, he knew, were no match for the water. Holding her slight form to his chest and damning himself for dragging her out in such a mess, Rance slogged his way round to the side door beneath the carriage gate.

After shouldering his way through, he found himself in an empty tavern room that smelled of damp dogs and soured ale, where a fire crackled in the hearth in some vain attempt to ward off mold. He looked about the place and decided it would have to do.

"Go sit by the fire," he murmured, setting her gently onto her feet, "and keep your veil down."

Along a short passageway, a pair of bow windows gave onto what passed for the village high street. A balding, bespectacled man looked up from his counter and closed his baize ledger.

"Have you a pair of rooms?" Rance asked, shaking the damp from his hat. "I'm just on my way back to London, but my wife has taken ill. And now the roads —"

"Oh, frightful," he said, cutting a curious glance at Anisha and her veil.

"A migraine," said Rance, setting a finger to his lips. "A dark, quiet room might be best."

The man's face pinched with sympathy. "My late mother was the very same, bless her," he murmured. "Best put you in the back."

Moments later, Rance ushered Anisha into a small sitting room which, the innkeeper proudly informed him, connected the two bedchambers. His best intentions already thwarted, Rance sighed, then ordered hot water, two buckets of coal, and an early dinner. Nodding, the innkeeper went out again.

"Oh, thank God!" Anisha was already pulling the pins from her hat. She set it aside, then drew her black traveling cloak snug again. She was freezing, Rance knew, and it took all his restraint not to go to her and fold her in his arms.

Instead, he went to the window and feigned an interest in the stables below. "Have you something dry in that satchel?" he asked hopefully.

"Enough, I expect. Janet is remarkably efficient."

He set a hand high on the deep window frame and stared into the murk. "Put it on, then, after the hot water comes," he said, watching raindrops race down the glass, "and hang your wet things up in here. I'll have a good fire for you shortly."

Half an hour later, the hearth was glowing and a cold supper was laid out on a small gate-legged table he and the innkeeper dragged near the hearth, situating it between an old oak settle gone black with age and the only chair.

A few minutes after the door closed, Anisha peeped out. "All bathed and dry," she declared. "Ooh, what's that smell?"

Rance had returned to the window, as if keeping his distance might help. "Roast capon stuffed with onions, I'm told," he said, smiling. "Still a bit warm from lunch."

At that, she came all the way into the room. To his disquiet, however, she wore the green silk peignoir he was so achingly familiar with, and under it a similarly embroidered nightdress. To make matters worse, her heavy black hair was down, shimmering like satin as she moved.

She paused by the fire and stretched. "*Umm,* you always build the best fires," she said, closing her eyes for an instant.

One hip hitched high on the deep box of the windowsill, Rance went utterly still inside.

So often with her it was like this. So often came those quiet, unexpected moments when he would find himself simply awestruck by the turn of her face, or the way she lifted her arms. Moments against which he had to steel himself, or be swamped by the yearning. And just now — when she looked so small and beautiful, her face aglow with reflected firelight, the green silk and black hair shimmering with a warmth that came from inside as well as out — he knew, with crystal clarity, what the outcome of all this would be.

He could sit in the window till hell froze over, but in the end he would make love to Anisha.

There was no point deceiving himself or telling himself his intentions were good. They weren't. Whether it stemmed from some newfound sense of hope, or whether the old hopelessness had simply driven him mad, Rance knew what he was going to do, and it wouldn't have much mattered had the innkeeper locked her in the attics and him in the cellars. Spending the night under the same roof was far too much temptation — especially for a man who'd never been good at denying his own appetites.

And good God, did he hunger for her.

When she at last left the hearth and closed the distance between them, Rance caught her round the waist and watched her eyes flare with surprise as he drew her between his legs.

"There's no use pretending I'm going to do the right thing here, is there?" he murmured, cupping her face in his hand. "And you won't say no, will you, Nish? You won't slap my face as I deserve."

She leaned into him, her hair sliding over her shoulder in a silky curtain. "But what *is* the right thing?" she whispered. "You tell me."

She stood motionless between his thighs, forcing him to make the first move.

He made it. Catching the curtain of her hair, he roped it twice round his hand, slowly pulling her face to his. When their lips met, he kissed her lingeringly at first, molding his mouth over hers, then gently tasting her, plumbing her spicy-sweet depths with his tongue until she surrendered, pressing herself closer, urging the softness of her belly between the vee of his thighs.

On a soft moan, he let his hand slide down to lightly palm the swell of her derriere, then deepened the kiss. He felt her need ratchet up and lifted her fully against his hardening erection. Anisha answered by setting one knee to the windowsill beside his hip, hitching up the green silk and climbing astraddle him. Relaxing against the cool of the glass, he let her follow him back into the well of the window, kissing her until she was breathless.

Her silks bunched across her thighs, she pressed her feminine heat to him in open invitation. The scent of soap and warmth and woman flooded his senses. Temptation got the better of him. With motions as awkward as they were desperate, he worked his hand between them and began to unhitch his trouser buttons. She pushed the wool away with impatient shoves until his shaft was straining at the lawn of his drawers, pressing against the soft curls between her legs.

On a soft sound of need, Anisha caught the thin fabric with her thumb and urged it awkwardly down. It was this, perhaps, that finally sliced through the haze of lust. He caught her hand and pulled it gently away. *"Wait,"* he whispered.

"No," she murmured against his lips.

But situated in the window as they were, the deepening dusk would soon provide a rather shocking silhouette to anyone below. He kissed his way back from the edge of madness, brushing his lips over her eyes, along the turn of her cheek, and finally down her throat.

With a sound of frustration, Anisha scooted off, landing on her feet.

He looked down at her through teasing eyes. "And *that,* old thing, is a taste of your own medicine," he said.

"Mine — ?" She looked at him incredulously.

His smile was rueful. "Aye, you can torment me by simply strolling into a room."

In the graying light, her cheeks flushed. "You hide it rather well."

"As a gentleman should." His trousers still bagging loose, Rance turned to draw out the shutters.

"A gentleman might finish what he started," she said tartly.

He flattened the shutters against the glass and latched them shut, deepening the gloom. "Aye, well, just sit down and eat something," he said, turning back to her. "There will be time enough later to ruin your life."

She sighed, then surprised him by kneeling down. "Then give me your boot," she said. "They are sodden."

"I can get them off myself," he said, "I think."

"Give me the dashed boot," she said, snapping her fingers. "There, are you pleased? You've reduced me to bad language. Still, I don't fancy being bedded by a lout in wet boots."

"But an ordinary lout in his dry altogether will do?"

She cut him a wry glance. "We shall see,"

she answered. "I'll put him through his paces and see if he can please me."

"Witch," he said, yanking her up from the floor and kissing her again, this time with no hint of restraint. And when he'd finished, there was no laughter in Anisha; just a look of dazed desire in her eyes and a slight tremble in her knees.

"Now go sit down near the fire," he said more gently, turning her in his arms to face the table. "Fill our plates and pour the wine. I'll see to the boots."

Casting a dark glance over her shoulder as she went, Anisha did as he ordered, going to the little table and uncovering the dishes. Rance managed to drag off his wet boots and set them by the hearth. His waistcoat followed, and then his trousers and stockings, which he hung from a pair of hooks that had been hammered into the thick wooden mantel, likely for just such a purpose.

Down to his shirt and drawers, he sat opposite her on the settle.

"So my lout is going to dine in his small-clothes," Anisha teased, sliding a thick slice of bread onto his plate. "Hmm."

"I'm afraid Horsham hadn't Janet's foresight," he said, taking up his glass in mock salute. "Or perhaps he harbored a secret hope I'd take pneumonia and die quietly in some roadside ditch."

"Alas, here's to poor Horsham." Anisha touched the brim of her glass to his with a sharp, ringing sound. "For he's about to find himself sadly disillusioned. If your years in the French Foreign Legion and being twice tossed in prison didn't kill you, I rather doubt the Essex damp will do it."

He laughed and began to eat, quietly watching her.

As usual, Anisha picked at her food. The hour being early, a proper dinner was not ready, but they managed well enough with the warm chicken and a surprisingly good wine. The aftereffects of his absinthe having passed, Rance was hungry enough — and still soldier enough — that it scarcely mattered, but throughout their near-silent meal, he wondered if he should order something special for her.

"All jests about poor Horsham aside, however," she finally said, severing his musings, "you do give the impression of being invincible."

He finished chewing. "Invincible, eh?"

She propped her chin on her hands and studied him. "Not that I don't worry for you, mind," she mused. "I do, Rance, all the time. But out of all of them, it is you

who has always seemed so solid and inde-
structible."

"Ah, Nish," he said. "No one is."

But she was speaking, he knew, of the *Fraternitas* — primarily of Geoff and her elder
brother. They had been nearly inseparable,
the three of them, for a great many years
now.

And yet Anisha very nearly had separated
him from Geoff, for they'd all but come to
blows. She likely *would* separate him from
Ruthveyn, before all was said and done,
though none of it was her doing. Still, her
brother would likely return from India
knowing the truth; that his best friend had
gone back on what was practically a blood
oath. He would have tolerated the union,
perhaps, had Rance's name been cleared —
but it had not.

Geoff, at least, was happy now.

Rance set his glass down. "I goaded him,
you know," he said, staring hard at the
scarred tabletop. "Like some green stripling,
I just . . . *pushed* him."

Anisha looked up from a forkful of peas.
"I beg your pardon?"

"Geoff." He looked up but found himself
unable to hold her gaze. "That night in the
temple — the night we were supposed to
initiate Miss de Rohan — I goaded him into

courting you. He said if I didn't have the guts to do it, he did. Does that sound . . . *invincible?* Because I *was* gutless. I told him —" He hesitated.

"What?" she softly urged.

He shook his head. "I told him, Nish, you were like a sister to me," he said after a moment had passed. "And that's not true. It never has been. I just thought . . . I thought, Nish, that Geoff would look after you and the boys as you deserve. That he would be more of a gentleman than I could ever be, and that Ruthveyn would be happy. But you didn't deserve to be saddled with Geoff. Because you were right. He hadn't any passion for you."

She stared at him across the table for a time. "And do you, Rance?" she finally asked. "Do *you* have a passion for me?"

"Oh, aye," he whispered, his voice oddly breaking.

Passion a thousand times over.

The sort of passion, he was increasingly certain, that never died.

But he made no move toward her, nor did she seem to expect it. Only the storm raging beyond the windows broke the silence.

"Well," she finally said, "I have a feeling we shall come to a point on that one soon enough."

"Aye?" Grimly, he studied her. "How so?"

Anisha picked up her glass and swirled her wine about in the bowl. "I feel as if Mr. Kemble has pointed us to water after a long walk in the desert," she finally answered, her voice pensive. "You won't believe me, of course, but I see a sort of — oh, call it *closure* — drawing near."

"Closure?"

Her gaze had turned inward. "Your stars," she said. "A great change is coming. And with it no small amount of danger."

"Anisha," he said warningly.

She shrugged and set her glass down. "Now is a time of grave risk and great opportunity," she said more certainly. "*Jyotish* shows us the path, Rance, and in this, the stars are clear. You must not move with your usual haste. Promise me —" Here, her voice caught, belying her calm. "*Promise me, Rance,* that you will set every foot with care along this path. That you will not let your temper or your impatience get the better of you as you finish these things Mr. Kemble has set in motion."

He could sense her disquiet. "Anisha, love," he said, holding out his arms. "Come here."

She rose and circled the old table. Rance turned sideways on the settle, leaning back against what passed for an arm. Anisha sat down, and against his better judgment, he pulled her to his chest.

"I promise," he said, planting a kiss atop her head, "that I will set every foot with care."

She settled her head on his shoulder. "Thank you," she said softly.

He pressed his lips to her hair again and laid his hand over her heart, as he had done the night they'd made love. Holding her felt so disconcertingly right; it brought him a kind of quiet joy that tugged at him in a way he couldn't quite put words to. And it was that yearning — that half seeking a pure and perfect whole — which had drawn him, solitary and stoic, into her orbit, beginning with the day he'd burst into that tiny cabin to flirt and to tease and to carry her home to her brother.

But that had been before he'd fully comprehended the risk. Before the realization had come to him, sharp as a newly forged blade: There were some women with whom a man dared not flirt.

Or in his case, *one* woman.

He drew a deep breath and let it out again. "Tell me, Anisha," he said quietly, "about . . . that thing — that Hindu notion you and Ruthveyn sometimes argue about.

Karma, is it?"

She lifted her head and looked up at him for an instant, as if to see if he was serious. Thunder rumbled again in the distance, and rain suddenly clattered across the windows like a fistful of birdshot. Disdaining the temptation her bare legs might present, Anisha sat up, absently crossing and tucking them beneath her.

"*Karma* is a common enough concept," she finally answered. "You would find similarities to the passage in Galatians which says —"

"Aye, '*Be not deceived, for God is not mocked*'?" he quoted. "I remember you flinging that at your brother once in the heat of some argument."

"Yes, for it goes on to explain that, '*For whatsoever a man soweth, that shall he also reap,*'" she continued. " '*For he that soweth to his flesh shall of the flesh reap corruption; but he that soweth to the Spirit shall of the Spirit reap life everlasting.*' The *Upanishads* — the ancient Vedic scriptures — contain a very similar passage."

"So *karma* is the way to everlasting life?" he murmured. "I thought it was something about evil deeds following you around forever."

"It's both, in a way." For a moment, it was as if she struggled to find the words. "In my mother's world, *karma* is the belief that one's deeds determine who we can become in the next life. One should strive to do good — to *be* good — not just in one's acts but in one's thoughts as well. And in this way, from one life to the next, one moves to a higher and higher plane of existence — *samsara* — until one reaches *moksha,* a oneness with God, and the end of the cycle of rebirth."

Rance gave a grunt of understanding. "So I'll be trapped on this mortal coil for all eternity."

She reached out to set a hand over his. "It's not like that," she said. "No one is trapped, save by his own choice or his own recalcitrance. Even the most evil person can change, can strive for *dharma* — the path of righteousness — and can find grace through devotion. And Rance, you are so far from evil . . ." She stopped, and shook her head. "Why are we even having this odd discussion? Does it have something to do with what Mr. Kemble said about Sir Arthur and Lord Percy?"

Rance shrugged, his shoulder scrubbing the back of the settle. "I guess I can't escape the sense that I did, in a twisted way, cause

511

Percy's death."

"And because Percy is dead, you deserve no happiness?" she suggested. "That's rubbish, all of it."

"But he wasn't a bad sort." His eyes held hers grimly. "And admit it, Anisha — I was a cheat. Sutherland has always said — and quite rightly — that I had no business at a gaming table. I had an advantage over those fellows, many of them. Because I could so often sense their emotions; their fear, their elation, even their propensity for taking risks —"

"Which is not the same as seeing their cards, Rance."

"Pretty damned close," he said, "especially after you play with a fellow for a while, as I had with Percy. But I was so . . . *afraid.*"

"Afraid how?"

"Afraid of becoming like my mother, I think," he quietly admitted. "Afraid of madness."

Anisha's gaze turned inward. "When Raju was young, I remember Papa once warning Mamma that, absent a strong will, a strong Gift could madden a person," she said. "I think that's why Papa was so hard on him — to toughen his will. To *protect* him."

"But when you're young, how do you know if you're strong enough? Or if fate will bring you to your knees?" He opened one hand plaintively. "To me, it seemed best not to think of it. To just deny whatever gifts I possessed — even to myself."

"And you were so young," Anisha murmured.

He nodded. "But what I did not realize then was that whatever skill I had — call it the Gift, or just instinct — it was nothing like hers, nor was it ever going to be," he whispered. "Hers slowly consumed her with grief. But my going to prison — ah, *that* was the grief that ended her."

"Yes, Raju said —" Sympathy flashing across her face, Anisha reached out to tuck a curl behind his ear. "He said Lady Lazonby died by her own hand."

Rance felt his fist clench involuntarily. "It's not commonly known," he said. "But aye, she was in a dark place, and I was the last straw. As to me . . . well, I cheated those men. I cheated *Percy.* I didn't kill him — but why can't I escape the feeling that I did, and that what I'm reaping now is karma?"

Anisha didn't answer but instead sat pensively for a time, one hand resting over his own, the warmth oddly comforting. After a few moments, she unfolded herself languidly and rose to pour more wine. Pressing a glass into his hands, she drifted to the narrow casement window overlooking the orchard.

Outside, water still rattled in the gutters and poured down the glass. The storm was vicious now, lightning splintering the sky as it crept ever closer. He watched Anisha quietly as she stood there, lithe and beautiful in the firelight, and wondered what she was thinking.

Most probably she was wishing she hadn't come on this dreadful journey; that she could have been spared the ordeal of listening to him whine. Damn it, he *never* whined. Always, he had borne his sins and his grief in silence. And yet there had always been something about Anisha that tempted him to loosen his tongue — and his heart.

He should have seen it coming, he supposed. One could not maintain so close a friendship as they had without being ultimately drawn into that deepest of the intimacies; intimacies which had little to do with the bedchamber and everything to do with the soul.

It was easy to fall into bed with a woman. It was hard to confess the nagging uncertainties and harsh truths that haunted a man in the wee hours of the night when sleep would not come and circumstance compelled him to look back at what he'd made of his life.

Except with Anisha, it was not hard.

And that, he supposed, was the most telling truth of all.

She finished her wine slowly, her gaze still scanning the heavens, as if she saw past the raging storm. Perhaps she did. He had learned not to doubt her. The glass empty, Anisha set it on the windowsill. Suddenly, there came at once a frightful, splintering *ka-crack! ka-boom!* Loud as cannon fire, it lit the room, washing her in a ghostly glow that illuminated even the orchard far beyond.

"Come away from the glass, love," he said, holding out his hand.

But it was as if she did not hear him. Instead, Anisha set her hand lightly to one of the leaded diamonds, as though she might reach through the pane for something far beyond.

"Nish?" he said. "What's wrong?"

For a moment, he thought she mightn't answer.

"I was thinking of Mamma," she finally answered, her voice oddly flat. "It was her favorite thing, a purifying storm at nightfall. She always said it was the earth purging itself to breath free again."

He smiled. "Von Althausen says it's just

releasing ozone," he said, "whatever that is."

"Oh, your brother Savant will not explain this one with his beakers and his books," said Anisha certainly. "This has to do with the movement of the heavens. The timing of it, the lucidity the storm brings, the formations of the stars that precipitate it — and all of it taken together has meaning for you, Rance. The clarity you seek draws near. I am increasingly sure of it."

As if he'd willed it, every hair on his neck prickled. "And what good will clarity do me if you're struck dead?" he said, already exploding off the settle.

He was across the room in three strides, yanking Anisha from the glass and hurling her to the floor. Lightning split the heavens like the hand of God; an awful, cracking noise that reverberated to the rafters. From just beyond the window came the loud splintering of a tree cleaved apart. Thunder rolled overhead, seemingly into infinity, until at last quiet settled in again, broken only by the spatter of rain on the glass.

"Good God!" Pinned over her on the floor, he couldn't move for a moment. "Bloody hell, that was close," he said, rolling away. "Nish, you all right?"

"Y-Yes." Anisha levered up onto one elbow. "Did it hit?"

"Aye, too bloody close for me," he said. "I think the downspout carried it off — into that near apple tree, by the sound of it."

"*Thank* you," she said.

He cupped her face with one hand, but despite the fright, he could see she had that vague look in her eyes; the one he so often saw in Ruthveyn when his defenses were down and fatigue had begun to wear away his control. A part of her was still in the heavens, pondering what was to come. It was nothing to do with the Gift — not as Rance knew it. It was the mystic in them; that part of their mother they so rarely gave words to.

He rolled onto his feet, still shaken, and helped her from the floor. "I didn't hurt you, did I?"

"No, no," she said. "But I had my hand on the leaded window, didn't I? The metal — how foolish! — but I was thinking of Mamma. Of what she might advise, were she here."

Rance was still shaken. The strike had been far too close for his comfort. He did not say so but instead lightly kissed her nose, then drew her back to the settle. Anisha, however, did not sit.

Instead she began to pace back and forth by the table.

"Here is the thing, Rance, my mother would advise," she finally said. "If you truly think you have wronged Percy, then you have. The heart knows the mind's will, no matter how subtle, or almost unintentional, it may be. And so you must begin to seek *dharma*. You must negate your bad deeds with good ones."

She was speaking, he thought, of something specific. He followed her to the hearth. "I can try," he answered. "Go on."

She stopped and set one hand on the mantel. "I think you must avenge his death to make this right," she said. "You must find the man who killed him — not just for yourself but for everyone whose life this evil has touched. But you must seek *justice*. Not a blood vengeance."

He looked at her incredulously. "So I should . . . what, Nish?" he asked. "Resist the urge to throttle the fellow and instead haul him off to the magistrate for a fair trial? That's a damned sight more than I ever got."

"But that's what *dharma* is, you see," she said. "The path of righteous living is not the easy path, or even the path according to some moldering religious tome. It is the path according to the universal laws — sometimes even the laws of man — the

518

things that bring happiness and peace to the mortal world."

He reached out and slicked a hand down her hair. "Nish," he said quietly, "I have lived so hard for so long, I wouldn't know a righteous path if it jumped up and bit me in the arse."

"Yes. You would." With a muted smile, Anisha set her cheek to his shoulder and set a hand over his heart. "You would know it here. You are going to learn something important when you go to Brighton. That is the first leg of your path."

He laughed. "Packing me off to Brighton, are you?"

"We both know you've been planning to go ever since we left Mr. Kemble." But there was no accusation in her voice. "And now fate is with you. When you go, you will find this man, this Mr. Hedge. You will learn the truth, or something near it. And then you will do the honorable thing. I am sure of it."

"You've an awful lot of faith in me," he said hesitantly.

She lifted her head, stood on her tiptoes, and kissed him. Her eyes were more somnolent than distant now, and she seemed to have come entirely back to herself.

"I do have faith," she said quietly. "You

will go, and you will do the right thing."
Then she pulled a little away from him, her
gaze softening almost seductively. "But you
did, as I recall, claim that tonight you were
going to do the *wrong* thing. I hope you
don't mean to renege on that promise?"

He laughed, remembering his words to
her. Though little more than an hour had
passed, the moment seemed a lifetime ago.
But suddenly — with Anisha's warmth
pressed so sweetly against him and his heart
perhaps a little unburdened — it didn't
seem nearly as wrong. It made, in fact, a
disconcerting amount of sense.

He managed to grin down at her. "Aye,
well, enough of this redemption business,"
he said. "A sinner I might be, but ne'er a
liar."

With little effort, he scooped Anisha up
again, just as he had lifted her from the carriage, this time to carry her around the
table. She laughed and threw her hands
round his neck.

The door to her tiny bedchamber was half
open to allow the fire's warmth to perme-
ate. A lamp burned low by the bed, which
was already turned back. Elbowing his way
through, Rance perched her on the edge of
the impossibly high mattress. For a moment, Anisha's earnest brown eyes held his,

and she looked, he thought, as happy as ever he'd seen her.

And he had done that.

He, somehow, had put that light in her eyes.

So he'd bloody well manage to keep it there. Kissing the tip of her nose, he stepped back a pace. "Well, Nish, here's to doing the wrong thing," he said, turning his shirt inside out as he dragged it over his head.

She made a faint sound of appreciation, her eyes warming in the lamplight as they drifted down him; all the way down to the drawers which now hung loosely off his hips, and just a little lower still, for his hardening cock was unmistakable now.

"Do you not begin to wonder, Rance," she murmured, her gaze focused there, "if doing the right thing isn't vastly overrated?"

He gave a sharp bark of laughter. "Aye, well, just remember, love — if one day old Ruthveyn yanks that wicked jezail of his off his wall and shoots me dead for it, the *wrong thing* was still worth it to me."

But Anisha's gaze did not rise. "Seriously, you are *magnificent*," she said huskily. "I remember wondering all those many months ago . . . well, let us just say, *meri jaan,* that nothing about you falls short of a lady's fantasies. And you are beautiful in the bargain."

He tossed the shirt aside, certain her eyes were clouded by something — just feminine lust, perhaps. As a lad, yes, he had been handsome. When he'd first come down to London at scarcely eighteen, alone and looking for mischief, *it* had found *him* — and in myriad forms. At first the ladies of the *ton* had simply winked at one another behind their fans. But eventually, more than one had brazenly tipped a finger beneath his chin and called him *pretty* in a voice that had been pure invitation.

And Rance had said *yes.* To a lot of them.

But he was no longer a pretty boy. Now he was just a hard man with a bad name who had lived an ugly life and been scarred by it, inside and out, then boiled down, he often thought, to the pure essence of what a man was: sinew and bone. Muscle and grim determination. There was nothing more to him than that.

But it was what Anisha wanted, it seemed. She scooted back off the bed, her eyes glowing with a warmth even the most practiced of courtesans could not have feigned. And when she crooked her finger, the last little scrap of what might have been a good intention vanished.

He stepped close, and her small, clever

fingers went at once to the tie of his drawers, tugging free the knot. In an instant, they breezed down his legs to pool on the old planks. Then, catching her hand, he drew her up and unfastened the gold-embroidered ties of her peignoir. Sliding his hands over her slender shoulders, he pushed it off. It slithered down her back to join his shirt and drawers on the floor.

Rance kissed her again, hot and hard, fisting up her nightgown as he thrust and circled her tongue. He broke the kiss just long enough to drag the green silk over her head. At the sight and scent of her, his cock stirred, brushing the soft flesh of her belly.

He set her a little away and tried to drink his fill as she stood a little shyly before him. But he knew it would never be so; that with Anisha, he would never be sated. In the last hellish year, his had become a well of need that flowed over all boundaries, eternally replenishing.

Good God, she was so small and perfect — like a little jewel, exquisite in her dark beauty. His eyes drifted down over her face, past her small, round breasts, catching on the sweet flare of her hip bones and the soft place his cock had just teased. Unable to stop himself, Rance let his hand slide down to cover her there, his broad fingers splaying over her womb, and thought of the miracles that had been.

Of the miracles that could still be.

More than anything on earth, Anisha had told Teddy, *she yearned for more children.*

The thought sent a wave of protectiveness and desire surging. And the guilt that usually followed his desire for her was . . . well, still there.

But the desire and the dream had muted it; the yearning he felt for her was beginning to set free inside him a rush of possibilities — the sense that certain things were meant to be, and that it fell to him to make them happen. To endure whatever had to be endured, and to make certain she suffered no regret.

He drew her to him and held her there, burying his face against her neck. "I love you, Nish," he whispered. "I have always loved you. Tell me you know that."

"I know," she said simply. "I have just been waiting for *you* to know."

He gave a harsh laugh and pressed his lips to the warm pulse point beneath her ear. "I have always known," he said. "Almost from the moment I saw you on that ship, so small and lost and yet so full of courage —"

She cut him off with a gentle poke in the ribs.

"Ow!" he said, nipping at her throat. *"What?"*

"You make me sound like a stray cat," she declared.

He laughed and pushed her onto the bed, following her down. "Oh, you are no stray," he said, crawling predatorily over her. "I'm much afraid you're mine — at least for tonight. And after that, well, heaven help you."

Propped back on her elbows, Anisha looked up at him through a shock of silky, disordered hair. *"Hmm,"* she said. But she was not, he thought, displeased.

Bracing himself above her, he brushed the hair from her face, then bent his head and kissed her, this time slowly. With his eyes open, literally and figuratively, he circled her tongue with his, then stroked sinuously back and forth. He wanted her to *know.* He was laying claim — as near as he dared — and he yearned for Anisha to ache with the wanting as he did.

He thrust again, one hand weighing her breast in the warmth of his palm, his thumb plucking and teasing her nipple to a hard, sweet bud of desire, until at last she arched beneath him on a soft cry. His blood surged, hot and urgent, and Rance knew he hadn't the strength to turn back, even had he possessed the inclination.

And he didn't. He was done with doing the right thing.

Ever so lightly, he pinched the pink bud between his fingers, and a tremble ran through her. Kissing his way along her cheek, Rance paused long enough to whisper sweetly in her ear — just enough to tease — then let his mouth take her breast, soothing the nipple with his tongue.

He suckled her slowly, drawing out her need like the gold thread of her *zari,* reveling in her sighs and gasps. She arched her hips again and whispered his name, her fingers spearing into the hair at his temples. In response, Rance kissed his way down her belly, all the way to her navel, then drew his tongue lightly over the swell of her womb and lower still, to tease at the thatch of dark curls between her thighs.

Anisha's head tipped back into the pillows. "Oh!" she said softly.

He drew in her scent and felt raw lust shiver beneath his skin. She was enough to madden the sanest of men. Desire surged through him now, throbbing with the beat of his blood. Sliding one hand beneath to cradle her hip, he touched her again, this time more intimately. Her answering cry was a sweet, thready sound. Beneath his relentlessly delving tongue, she began to tremble. Her hand fisted in his hair, and one dainty foot slid restlessly up the sheet, the tiger's claw charm on her ankle brushing coolly along his skin.

Again and again Rance drew his tongue deep through her silken flesh, until he heard her nails rake the sheets. *"Ah —"* she cried.

Gently he eased one finger, and then another, into the velvet heat. One hand twisting at the bed linen, Anisha begged him, vowed it was too much. Too intense. But already her gasps were soft and tellingly rhythmic. He stroked again, lightly coaxing her sweet, erect nub with tiny flicks of his tongue as she whimpered.

At last she cried out beneath him, shuddering with her release, beautiful beyond words.

Kissing her lightly on her soft inner thigh, Rance eventually shifted his weight to rest his head on her belly, curling himself protectively about her.

Anisha's hand was threading limply through his hair. *"Oh — !"* she said on a long, breathy sigh. "That was . . . oh — utterly *enslaving.*"

"Ah." Rance rimmed her navel with the tip of his tongue, then curled one arm round her hips. "Are you my slave now, love?"

She swallowed hard. "Perhaps," she said. "Could you do it again? So that I might be perfectly sure?"

He did laugh then, brushing his lips over her belly. "It was something new?" he murmured.

Her voice hitched. "Not entirely," she said. "I've only seen it."

"*Seen* it?"

"In drawings and carvings," she said a little defensively. "And the *Kāmashastra* teaches it as a permissible way to experience bliss with one's lover."

He laughed softly and nuzzled her belly. "And bliss it was," he conceded. "But Nish, you . . . you were married —"

"Yes, for a long while," she softly interjected, "to an Englishman with no imagination, and even less wish to please me. But that is over. You and I, however" — her hand fisted a little roughly in his hair — "we are not over, *meri jaan.* I did warn you, did I not, that I meant to put you through your paces?"

His cock was already throbbing, and hard as the old oak bedpost. He lifted his head to look at her, and Anisha rolled up onto one elbow, her firm breasts wobbling enticingly. "Shall I show you another, slightly *im-*permissible pleasure of the *Kāmashastra?*" she suggested, her voice pitched seductively low.

He let his gaze drift over her nakedness. "I find myself your eager pupil."

Her face flushing sweetly pink, Anisha urged him off and onto his back, then crawled atop his legs, her knees set to either side of his. *"Umm,"* she said, running her hands up the muscles of his thighs. "Like solid marble — ah, *everywhere,* I see."

Watching, he laughed a little uneasily. "Nish, you're up to mischief."

To his shock, her hand eased artfully — and firmly — round the base of his rigid shaft. "Yes, something wicked," she agreed. "Something a lady ought not do — or so the teachings say."

"Then *don't,*" he advised, crooking his finger to draw her up.

A naughty, sideways smile tilted one corner of her mouth. "Does it not strike you, *meri jaan,* that the rules of bed-sport are written by men who wish to imagine their lady wives boringly perfect? — which might explain their propensity to take mistresses, now I think on it."

"No real man," he said firmly, "could ever want more than you."

Nonetheless, she fisted her hand round his shaft and eased it up and down. He could not suppress a groan of pleasure, and when her other hand worked lower, to caress him in that most erotic of ways, he felt his bollocks seize with pleasure in her palm.

"Nish . . ." he said warningly.

But he was not a saint, and she — well, she was just quietly stubborn. However gently a burn might flow amongst the braes, it was still, like Anisha, a force of nature. And so he surrendered; actually closed his eyes, when he felt the softness of her hair tease across his belly as she bent over him. Lightly, her tongue stroked up his shaft.

"Oh, *minx* — *!*" he groaned.

She laughed her light, musical laugh again. "This is called *auparishtaka,*" she said, just before her tongue flicked over his swollen head.

"Oh, that's not" — he gasped through his teeth at the next long stroke — "what I'd call it."

"The *Kama Sutra* teaches that this is a skill best practiced by eunuchs," she said, her voice light and teasing, "or prostitutes."

"Nish — !" he grunted.

But it was too late. Her hand tightening at the base, Anisha swallowed him deep into her warmth. Rance felt every muscle in his belly go taut as the sensitive head of his cock slicked across the roof of her mouth. And then he could only moan.

Her actions now were a little artless, perhaps even clumsy, but it scarcely mattered. For long moments he lost himself in a kaleidoscope of pleasure — her womanly warmth spread across his knees, her nipples teasing his thighs as she bent, the silken slide of his swollen flesh through her lips, and the heat of her palm massaging the pooling weight of his seed — until the pleasure nearly crested and he knew it had to end.

Eyes flying open, he stilled her hand with his. "Anisha," he rasped, "— *stop.*"

At last she listened, sitting obediently up and rocking back onto his knees. He came bolt upright and folded his arms around her. "Nish," he murmured, burying his face in the turn of her neck. "Oh, love. This is dangerous deep — and I don't mean literally. You know that, yes?"

She speared her fingers into his hair. "Yes," she said. "But it always has been. And you know that."

"Aye, I know it," he whispered. And then he kissed her again, his hands cupping both sides of her face, her silken hair falling over his hands and spilling over her shoulders.

"Lie down," he rasped when the kiss was broken.

Anisha did so, stretching her slight form across the sheets and settling her head on the thin bolster. Dragging his body over her, Rance urged her legs wide with one knee, fighting the urge to enter swiftly. Lingeringly he kissed her, their comingled scents teasing at his nostrils, his fingers buried in the inky silk of hair, his cock throbbing against Anisha's nest of curls.

He tasted her thoroughly, thrusting into her mouth and curling his tongue around hers. Anisha returned the intimacy in full measure, her body already restless and rising beneath his, her nails curling into the flesh of his buttocks.

By the time he pulled away, her breath was coming fast, her eyes glassy with need. Sitting back on his heels, Rance allowed himself the pleasure of letting his gaze drift down her small yet womanly body.

"Rance," she whispered. *"Now."*

Her small breasts rose and fell with her breath, her areolas a dusky dark rose against her honey-colored skin, her nipples peaking into sweet, tempting nubs. He could feel the heat rolling off her in waves and marveled it was he who possessed such power over such a fey and wondrous creature.

And still he did not enter her. Fleetingly he closed his eyes, willing fortitude. He wished to hold time suspended; to treasure this moment of pure longing as if it was his last — for tomorrow, he knew, Anisha might well come to her senses.

"Rance." His eyes flew wide to see her hands moving restlessly over her breasts. *"Please."*

In response he bent over her and set his mouth to her areola, drawing the pink tip between his teeth. She gasped at the slight nip, her nails raking lightly down his back. Over and over he suckled her, moving between her breasts, kissing feather-light across her breastbone, and less gently where it mattered.

Her breath seized and her hips tried to buck. *"Now,"* she said.

He lifted his head to see her left hand curled into the bedcovers, her head tilted backward into the softness of the bolster, as if ecstasy already neared.

"Anisha," he whispered. "So beautiful."

Anisha began to fear she was losing her mind. *Did he mean to torment her all night?* At last she felt the warmth of his hand cup her face.

"Do you want me inside, love?" Rance's

voice was thick and abrupt. "Are you willing to risk it?"

"*Yes,*" she whispered. "Anything. Just —"

A dam of restraint seemed to burst inside him then. A little roughly, he pushed her legs wider, entering her on one deep, triumphant stroke, the width and length of him stretching her impossibly wide.

"Oh!" he grunted. "*Nish.* Good . . . Lord."

She looked up to see his face turned, straining, to one side, and his black curls spilling down his neck, realizing vaguely that his hair had grown too long. But the thought left as swiftly as it came, her hips rising to his involuntarily.

He drew back, his throat corded with tendons, and thrust again. And again. Over and over he slid deep, forcing himself into her in a way that should have been impossible. *Taking* her, in every carnal sense of the word. Joining his body to hers in a raw, unrestrained rhythm that left her shuddering under his weight and aching for more.

His strength unflagging, Rance set one big hand to the mattress just above her shoulder and slid the other beneath her hips, cupping the swell of her buttock as he lifted her to take him. The sound of their warm, slightly slick bodies was almost primitively erotic against the backdrop of falling rain as flesh rose to meet flesh, and blind need drew them deeper into that sensuous abyss that only lovers know.

Rance's breath was rough now. "Anisha, love," he murmured. "Oh, *witch! Ma sirène.*"

His thrusts came powerfully and deeply now. Anisha felt breath and his need — his pure, sensual essence — swirling around her. Calling to her. Clutching his thick shoulders, she strained to rise to him, to take him deep inside herself. To become one with him. To bind herself unassailably to him.

Suddenly his hands captured hers, pinning them to the bed as his weight bore her down into the softness of the bed. Anisha lifted her legs, twining them round his waist. She was faintly sobbing now; her need for him like a physical ache, her blood thrumming in time with his.

And in that perfect moment, with her desire drawn taut as a sitar's string, they came together in a blinding rush that outshone the lightning and forged them, ever so fleetingly, into one soul.

CHAPTER 13

Th' hast spoken right, 'tis true.
The wheel is come full circle, I am here.
William Shakespeare, *King Lear*

Rance awoke not once but twice the next morning, the second time to a shaft of brilliant sunshine streaming through Anisha's bedchamber window. Cupped around her, he rolled a little away and lifted an arm to block the light, his head falling back onto the bolster near hers.

Beside him, Anisha made a sweet, breathy sound, tucking her derriere back against his hip bone, and a strange, warm feeling began to steal over him, beginning at his toes and sweeping pleasantly upward, then spreading and surging, like an unfurling flower.

It was a long moment before he knew the feeling for what it was.

Happiness.

The pure, unadulterated kind, not the

false, fleeting cheer that could be bought with brandy or worse. Here, at the beginning of a new day, with the storm settled and Anisha's warmth beside him, he felt happy, and wonderfully ordinary. Almost at peace, the ax hanging over his head briefly forgotten.

Only the unpleasant tasks before him blighted the serenity of his new morning. But for perhaps half an hour, he managed to hold perfectly still and savor it, unwilling to break the spell even as the stable yard began to stir with activity and the old inn's stairs began to creak beneath the tread of servants' feet.

But how long, really, could one remain locked in a fantasy?

This wasn't real life, this rustic little inn in the middle of nearly nowhere. He might prefer not to think of it, but soon enough they would be back in London; back to the tasks that lay before him, one of which was a doubtless unpleasant trip down to Brighton. Back to his old life — with Jack Coldwater dogging his every step; reminding him at every turn of the promises he'd broken and the damage rumor might do.

And back to Tom and Teddy, who needed their mother — and a good father, too.

Was that him? Was he good enough?

It would have to be. *He* would have to be. He rolled back to fold Anisha to his chest, certain now he could never let her go to another. Not now. Not after this. In all likelihood, he never could have.

He was lucky, he suddenly realized, that Geoff had refused her and saved him the awful task of dragging two dear friendships asunder instead of just the one. For that, he now realized, he might well have done. Because, in the end, he would have had no choice. Because she was Anisha, and they were fated. Because he was increasingly, perhaps selfishly, certain he could not live without her.

He buried his face in her hair, breathed her rare scent deep into his lungs, and wondered if ever he would have enough of her. How long could a need like his last?

Forever. He knew that was the answer. Forever he would feel like a part of him had been torn away were he never to make love to her again.

She was awake now, turning in his arms to smile at him. *"Umm,"* she said, stretching her length like a bestirred housecat. "You look like a wicked pirate, *meri jaan,* with your harsh beard and your too-long curls. And yet you are more handsome in the morning than in the night."

Returning her dreamy smile, Rance set his lips to her temple. "What does it mean, Nish?" he asked softly. *"Meri jaan?"*

She looked languidly into his eyes. "Literally? It means *my life,*" she said, threading her fingers through his hair. "As in *you are my life.* My love. That's what it means, really. My love."

He drew himself up in the bed and levered onto his elbow to look at her. "And is that what it means, Nish, when you say it?" he asked, lightly stroking his thumb over her cheek. "Are you sure?"

She held his gaze unblinkingly. "You know I am," she said. "As you have always loved me, I have always loved you. You are *meri jaan,* Rance. You are my life. You always have been."

"And my life . . . it's still rather a mess," he admitted. "What if I never get it sorted?"

She shrugged one slender shoulder against the pillow. "Then I'll stand by you," she said. "But you will, Rance. You'll go to Brighton tomorrow, won't you?"

"Aye," he said. "We've a *Fraternitas* contact there. I penned a message to Belkadi whilst you slept and carried it out to the stables. They were to send it at daybreak with a fast rider. Belkadi will go smoke this Hedge fellow out."

She widened her eyes. "You think time is of the essence?"

"It could be." Rance spread his hand across her womb again. "We cannot know for certain. And you are the thing that matters most to me in all the world, Nish. I almost wish it was not so. I almost wish —"

She cut him off with a chiding sound, setting a finger to his lips. "Not now," she commanded. "Not today, when we have beautiful sunshine and a few hours yet to be together."

"Aye, you're right." He dragged a hand through his hair. "But I'm going to have to write to Ruthveyn soon. I'm going to have to tell your brother . . . *something*."

"Tell him that you love me, and that you will take care of me, for that is all he needs to hear," she said, curling her arm round his waist and setting her head on his thigh. "But not today. Today — or part of it — belongs to us. And I think we should use our time wisely. I think, *meri jaan,* that you should make love to me again."

He laughed, and felt the happiness slowly well up again — this time a little lower than his heart. And so he rolled her onto her back and mounted her slowly as his mouth took hers. This time it was a loving of exquisite gentleness, with no rush or raw need between them, but merely the joining of two bodies and two souls. Anisha rose to him as naturally as the wind, and again he drew to her like the tide. And this time, when they found bliss, it was in a quiet, shuddering moment of joy, tinged with the hope of something more to come.

But hope and happiness are tenuous things when a man's life is fraught with uncertainty and perfection lies just beyond his grasp. They drove away from the inn yard just as two stable hands came striding out with broad-headed axes in hand, their newly honed blades glistening in the sun as they headed toward the ruined apple tree, much of which now leaned precariously against the inn's wall.

Anisha turned halfway round as they clattered under the carriage gate. "They cannot save it," she said sadly. "It has been splintered and cleaved apart."

With a snap of his whip, Rance turned his horses onto the village road, afraid to look back. Afraid, really, that the ax and the tree were metaphors for the truth of his life.

That it had been splintered and cleaved apart; unsalvageable.

And that the ax was still destined to fall.

Anisha arrived home alone in the early

afternoon, having insisted that Rance set her down in the drive and hasten on. Tomorrow he had a train to catch — and they, she was increasingly hopeful, just might have a life to get on with.

Even before she had extracted her key, however, she was greeted by a great hue and cry that seemed to rise up from the rear of the house. Slipping inside, she flung aside her hat and shawl. The sound was echoing from the conservatory.

Hastening through the house, she went out to find Lucan stretched supine on her chaise, the cats piled atop him and Milo perched along the curved rattan back. It looked a peaceful scene, until the bird saw Anisha.

"Pawk!" said the giant parakeet, rising up on great, green wings. *"Pretty, pretty! Pretty pretty!"*

"Good God, could someone *please* pluck that imp and roast him?" Lucan rolled limply up on one elbow, clutching to his forehead what Anisha recognized as ice Chatterjee had bagged up in gutta-percha.

"Ah, well! No rest for the wicked," said Anisha as Milo sailed onto her shoulder with a soft *whuff!* But Silk and Satin, disturbed from their languor, had bounded down onto the flagstone with disdainful backward glances.

Luc's gaze narrowed. "Where've you been, anyway?"

"Never mind that." Anisha strolled nearer, regarding Luc with disapprobation. "Got the morning-head again, I see. You'll pardon me if I feel little sympathy."

"Pawk!" said Milo, now toddling across her shoulder to pluck at her dangling earbobs. *"Pretty, pretty!"*

"Ungh," said Luc, collapsing back onto the chaise.

But a second scream sent Milo flapping and Anisha bolting for the garden. "Oh, heavens, has Tom broken another bone?"

"No, you've a visitor," Luc managed. "They're having a romp, I collect."

But the clamor came again, this time peals of laughter. Anisha froze, one hand on the garden door. "A caller?"

"That hoyden of Bessett's," he muttered, eyes closed now. "Chatterjee let her in."

"Lady Bessett?" Anisha turned slowly around. "But it sounded like bloody murder when I came in."

"Could be." He rolled to one side with another grunt of pain. "Last I looked, she was playing King Edward, and the lads were Mortimer's minions, locking her up in Berkeley Castle."

"Ooh," said Anisha, wincing. "That did not end well."

"Nor will this, I daresay." Luc waved a limp hand in the general direction of the door. "Best go and save her, eh? And be warned — the lads have swords."

Exiting through the door set in the conservatory's glass wall, Anisha waded out into the brilliant green of the garden. Situated in the rear, now cast in deep shade, the arbor had been roped around some five or six times, the ends now hanging slack, forgotten.

Tom and Teddy stood with their backs to her, arms akimbo, gazing up at the sky.

"Go! Go!" she heard Tom shout. "*Do* it!"

"Now!" chimed Teddy.

Anisha's gaze followed theirs up. "Good heavens!" she cried, propelled into action. "Miss de Rohan, really! You *mustn't!*"

But her legs didn't carry her fast enough. Perched atop the arbor, Lady Bessett lifted her arms — or something that passed for arms — and came sailing off the arbor in a billow of blue muslin and petticoats, landing with a splintering sound in a patch of daffodils beyond.

"Huzzah!" Tom and Teddy were cheering and jumping, arms waving madly about.

"Thirty feet, at least!" cried Teddy.

Anisha ran past them to kneel into the daffodils beside her. "My dear girl!" she cried. "Oh, *say* something!"

Lady Bessett levered herself awkwardly up onto her elbows, which Anisha now realized were strapped into some sort of basketry. "Did I make it?" she asked, looking at Teddy through a shock of black hair.

"Oh, yes!" the boy exclaimed. "A proper flight, that was!"

Anisha collapsed onto her derriere in the flowers. "Dear Lord, you three scared the life out of me!" she cried. "What in God's name? Lady Bessett, what *are* those frightful things on your arms?"

"Trugs," Tom proudly interjected. "Teddy and me found 'em. In the box room over the mews. Brogden said we might have 'em."

"T-Teddy *and I*," said Anisha reflexively, her heart slowing. "And what, pray, are trugs?"

"Grain baskets," piped Tom. "Made of willow."

"And chestnut," Teddy added. "We sawed part of the frames off 'em. We thought we might fly."

"You thought you might *fly?*" Anisha felt suddenly queasy. "And you . . . you used a *saw?*"

"And some old harnesses," Tom cheerfully added.

Anisha forced herself to breathe deep and exhale slowly. Sometimes she was not entirely sure her *prana* was up to the challenge of motherhood.

Arms bound oddly outward, Lady Bessett staggered to her feet. "Here, Teddy, unstrap me," she said, giving an unladylike shimmy to shake down her skirts. "I need a word with your mother."

Anisha was still glowering at Teddy, though it was awkward, given that Lady Bessett was involved. "Well, we are all lucky someone didn't lose a finger or worse," she said, managing to her feet. "And our guest might have been killed."

Lady Bessett cast a sheepish glance at Anisha. "They were bound and determined to try it," she said aside. "I thought better me than them, you know?"

"Yes, well . . . I daresay," Anisha managed. "But Lady Bessett, you are a *married* woman now."

Lady Bessett grinned. "Oh, Bessett knows how I am," she said.

Anisha widened her eyes quite deliberately and set a hand over her own womb. "That is not what I meant!" she said more hotly. "You are *married* — *?*"

Lady Bessett's color drained as the last willow contraption fell away. "Oh," she murmured weakly. "Oh, heavens. I take your point." She turned to beam down at the boys. "Well, that was quite a lark, wasn't it, lads? But best take those back to Brogden, eh? For safekeeping?"

After picking up their wooden swords, the boys went glumly through the back gate in the direction of the mews. The ladies set off down the garden path arm in arm. Despite the fright, Anisha was very glad to see her new friend.

Inside the conservatory, Luc was still wallowing in misery.

"Out!" said Anisha as he staggered to his feet. "Go upstairs to bed."

After bowing and scraping and kissing Lady Bessett's hand, Luc went, his gutta-percha bag tucked behind his back. At least he had the good grace to be ashamed of his condition.

Anisha rang for tea, and they settled into the deep rattan chairs amidst the ferns and palms. The setting reminded Anisha of her odd visit to Mr. Kemble's, and once more hope stirred. She opened her mouth to tell Lady Bessett all about it, but her guest spoke first.

"I'm so sorry we frightened you," she said

just as Milo sailed back onto Anisha's shoulder and took up his battle with the earbobs again. "Good heavens! *That* is a big parrot!"

"Actually, he's just a parakeet," said Anisha. "I found him in my garden along the Hooghly River. He was no bigger than a teacup."

Lady Bessett drew back an inch. "Does he . . . talk?"

"Pretty, pretty!" Milo declared. *"Help, help! British prisoner! Let-me-out!"*

"Oh, my!" Lady Bessett set her fingers to her mouth, her eyes dancing. "Do the cats trouble him?"

"Oh, not anymore," declared Anisha. "But let's talk about you. How do you find married life, my dear?"

Lady Bessett grinned shamelessly. "Ooh, I find it very nice indeed," she said in a low undertone. "In fact, I think it vastly *under-rated*, if you know what I mean."

"I daresay I do," said Anisha on a spurt of laughter. "Congratulations, then. You have chosen well."

Her smile deepening, Lady Bessett leaned conspiratorially nearer. "And what of yourself?" she asked. "Have you brought the dashing Lord Lazonby to heel yet?"

For an instant, Anisha grappled for words.

"I am not sure such a thing is possible," she finally answered. "I fear he is not much amenable to a leash."

At that, Lady Bessett laughed — and in a most unladylike fashion, too. For an instant, Anisha wondered how she got on with Lady Madeleine MacLachlan, who was grace and elegance personified. But she had not long to wonder. All was well, it seemed.

"Mamma asked me to go with the two of you to Lady Leeton's party on Monday," Lady Bessett said when the tea had been brought. "But I wish to spend some time with my parents before they leave again."

"So she has asked you to call her Mamma," said Anisha, who had never been invited to address her mother-in-law as anything — not even Mrs. Stafford. "You must account yourself fortunate to have such a welcome."

"Oh, I do!" said Lady Bessett earnestly. "Bessett has some hope, I believe, that she will prove a civilizing influence on me. And I begin to hope so, too, quite honestly." She paused to catch her lip in her teeth. "Your little gesture in the garden just now — oh, *that* swiftly brought me to the realization that my life has altered."

"Indeed, it has," Anisha agreed, passing her a cup of tea. "I'm sorry you can't go with us to the party."

"I did get to meet Hannah Leeton," Lady Bessett confided. "Mamma and I went with her yesterday to Regent Street to choose the bunting colors for the bandstand." Then her shoulders fell a little. "The color theme is yellow and white. I tried to pretend I cared, but I haven't many feminine virtues, I fear."

Anisha set down her tea and reached out to pat the younger woman's hand. "You have all the feminine virtues your husband requires," she said, "or he would not have married you so swiftly. He is an excellent judge of character."

Lady Bessett looked up a little dewy-eyed. "And he thinks so highly of you, too!" she cried. "And you have been so terribly kind to me . . ."

Suddenly Anisha got the dreadful sense that the young lady was at last going to apologize for stealing her fiancé. "Well, enough of that," she said hastily. "May I buy you anything in the stalls Monday? I mean to purchase a new lace fichu and some other fripperies for Janet. She may be leaving me soon for a new life."

"Oh!" Lady Bessett set her cup abruptly down. "That's *precisely* why I came by!"

Anisha felt her brow furrow. "About Janet — ?"

"No, no, about the Leetons' maid. The girl's mother fell ill and they sent her off to Chester on the mail coach yesterday." At Anisha's blank look, she added, "The maid who is the gypsy fortune-teller."

"Oh, yes! To raise funds for the charity."

"Indeed, she's done it for years — Hannah had a little red tent made for her and everything. People have come to quite count on it." Lady Bessett rang her hands a little. "Hannah was almost in tears. And then Madeleine said —"

"Yes?" Anisha's odd feeling shifted.

Again, Lady Bessett snared her lip. "You mightn't like this," she went on, "but Madeleine — I mean *Mamma* — told her that perhaps you might be persuaded to do it . . . with palms, I mean. Not the crystal ball."

"Good heavens!" Anisha set her teacup down with a discordant clatter. "Surely not?"

Lady Bessett winced. "Geoff must have told her you study palmistry," she answered. "I think, honestly, that even after all these years of struggling to raise him, she does not quite understand the Gift. She knows, of course, that it is not a parlor trick, but she cannot quite grasp —"

Anisha threw up a hand. "I don't have any sort of *Gift,*" she swiftly interjected. "My mother was skilled in certain arts, and yes, she and my aunt taught me much. But *hasta samudrika shastra* is based on science, and ideally used in concert with *Jyotish.* Neither is a trivial thing. And done properly, they take hours."

"I *know* — *!*" Lady Bessett wailed. "But Hannah's face just lit up! And I couldn't think what to tell Mamma. So I thought, you see, I'd best come round myself so she didn't spring it on you tomorrow." She stopped and sighed deeply. "You might just say you've the headache," she advised. "Or perhaps you could just pretend to read palms?"

Anisha sighed. "I'm not sure that would be ethical," she said, almost to herself.

Still, it *was* for a worthy cause. Moreover, there were always a few basic things one could honestly tell a person without a great deal of analysis. Just a little something — the sort of thing she'd done in the garden that afternoon for Lady Bessett.

But the thought left her a little breathless. The awful truth was, Anisha had studied no one's hand seriously since that frightful day so many months ago when she had looked at Grace's. Grace had not been Anisha's sister-in-law then but rather Tom and Teddy's governess — and, Anisha had correctly guessed, Raju's lover. But Grace had also been Anisha's dear friend. And she had been in terrible trouble.

With Grace, Anisha had been most thorough, beginning by charting her stars in detail. Then one day she had come upon Grace in the schoolroom as Luc had been taking the boys out for cricket. Anisha had rung for tea and had all but forced Grace to submit her hands.

Grace, ever good-natured, had done so.

It had begun innocently enough. Anisha had been curious about the prospects for marriage and children; she had hoped for both between Grace and her brother. But despite her benign intentions, a strange and horrible thing had happened. Anisha had had a vision; an almost out-of-body experience. It was as if the blood had drained from her extremities and her mind had gone to another place. With horrific, bone-chilling clarity, she had seen the danger Grace had faced.

And yet, as so often was the case, it had been a symbolic sort of clarity; one she had struggled mightily to interpret.

Her mother would not have struggled. Her mother had had no fear of trances or deep meditation, or even of visions. She had known their value, their interpretations, and how to use them all as the tools they'd been, with great skill and calm.

Anisha had not been calm. She had been terrified. And when she had come out of it — whatever *it* had been — it had been to find she'd still held Grace's hands across the schoolroom table. It had seemed like mere moments, but it had been . . . only God knew how long. But the tea had gone stone-cold, and neither she nor Grace had felt the time pass.

And then Anisha had done the worst thing of all. By misinterpreting the signs, she had very nearly sent Grace to her death.

Afterward — after Raju and Mr. Napier had saved Grace and put everything to rights again — it had quickly dawned on Anisha that she would never be what her mother had been, a gifted *rishika*. Her mother was gone and Anisha was here, left like some inadequate chef-in-training, with too many sharp knives in her kitchen block and not nearly enough real knowledge. She had studied just long enough to be danger-ous.

"You aren't going to do it, are you?" Lady Bessett's voice cut into her thoughts.

Anisha lifted her eyes to her guest's earnest gaze, and thought of all that Geoff's mother had done for her — and all that she had been willing to do. To accept her warmly into the MacLachlan family as Geoff's bride. To help her make her way in polite society. And the latter she was doing anyway, despite the fact that her son had married elsewhere.

Anisha lowered her hands into her lap, crushing her skirts. "How could I disappoint Lady Madeleine?" she finally said. "Giving a little advice would do no harm, I daresay. But I cannot draw any real conclusions. They mightn't be accurate."

But the warning was muffled, for Lady Bessett had already leapt up and rushed across the room to hug her.

"Oh, Anisha, *thank* you!" she cried.

"You're welcome," said Anisha into a crush of blue muslin.

As the terminus of the London, Brighton & South Coast Railway, Brighton Station was a wide and soaring temple of modernity, with every imaginable convenience within. At an hour fast approaching nightfall, the gaslight had been fired, casting the capacious space in a ghostly glow as the last train from London Bridge came clattering in amidst a shriek of metal and a haze of smoke.

Rance stepped down onto the platform as

passengers and porters surged round the cast-iron columns like froth, washed past him, then branched into streams and rivulets as they trickled toward exits, vendors, and ticket windows. Portmanteau in hand, Rance moved with more deliberation, his eyes scanning the crowd ahead.

As he strode past, a locomotive on the opposite platform sounded a shrill whistle, blasting smoke into the air. In response, a few black-suited businessmen began to toss aside newspapers and drift toward the platform, intent on boarding the last train back to London. Ahead, toddling toward the exit, a gaggle of children followed their nanny, the latter waving for a porter to bear their trunks away, most probably down the hill to one of the many guesthouses that lined the seashore.

Seeing no one familiar, Rance wove his way toward a wide portal marked Trafalgar Street. After passing beneath an elegant colonnade, he emerged into a broad, carriage-filled lane bounded on one side by a massive wall, passing between a pair of hawking newsboys as he did so.

" *'Earld!* Get yer *'Earld* 'ere!" bellowed the first.

The second, more resourceful, drowned him out with, "Clipper sinks off Ivory

Coast! *Brighton Gazette!* Survivors speak!"

Just then, a gig with a gray horse set off from the curb in a clatter, and beyond the first lad's shoulder, Rance saw Samir Belkadi uncross his arms and come away from a sputtering lamppost. His stride long and sure, the young man dashed between drays and carriages to meet him on the pavement, pressing a slip of paper into Rance's palm as he did so.

"You found Blevins?" Rance kept his voice low.

"*Oui,* at home," said Belkadi. "The good doctor knew all the hotels — and, more importantly, all the lodging houses. It required us but one day's searching to find your Mr. Hedge."

Rance unfolded the paper. It was an address in George Street.

"A lodging house catering to invalids," said Belkadi. "Retired sea captains and the like. Run by a woman named Ford. The street is just past the Royal York, not far from here. I booked you a suite of rooms and bespoke dinner."

Rance shook his head. "I've no appetite," he said. "I should rather go straight to this fellow."

"*Non.*" Belkadi set a restraining hand on his sleeve. "Blevins knows the proprietor and made inquiries. Hedge is old, frail, and requires much laudanum to sleep at night. He will be of no use to you until morning — if then."

After tugging out his pocket watch for one last, hopeful glance, Rance sighed. "Aye, you're right, Sam," he said. "Look, hurry on now. That's the last train."

"You do not need me?"

Rance managed a weak grin. "To manage a laudanum-addled old man?" he said. "God, I hope not."

With a flash of his brilliant white teeth, Belkadi gave a curt bow and vanished into the terminal's yawning entrance.

After finding the hotel with little difficulty, Rance ordered himself a rare beefsteak and a bottle of their best wine, then went promptly to bed in the hope of speeding the day's arrival. Perhaps it was just the exquisite night spent in Anisha's arms, or his newfound sense of hope propelling him forward ever faster, but he could not escape the sense that time was of the essence. And now this Hedge fellow was on his deathbed.

He rose at dawn having slept little, and spent the early morning strolling the long promenade that stretched between the King's Road and the seafront. The air coming off the Channel was sharp, the skies a reflection of the watery gray-blue below, and filled with the cry of wheeling gulls. Rance drew the sea air deep into his lungs — the smell of freedom, it still seemed to him, for the sea was something an Englishman sorely missed when trapped in the gloom of a prison, or the grit and heat of the desert.

Attired as he was in a dark suit of finest worsted, along with his tall beaver hat and brass-knobbed walking stick, he apparently looked the part of a rich and respectable aristocrat taking the air, for here — unlike much of London — most of the gentlemen tipped their hats and bid him good morning, while a few of the ladies cut him lingering, sidelong looks as they promenaded past.

But none of it was sufficient to distract him from the press of time, and impatience had begun to bite at him when Rance tugged out his pocket watch for perhaps the third time in as many hours, only to hear the bells at St. Nicholas toll ten o'clock. It was as close to a respectable hour as he could manage. Turning on his heel, he retraced his steps past his hotel and into the maze of streets that lay east of it.

The address was easily found, the lodging house large and fronted with bow windows around which the paint had begun to peel; perhaps from proximity to the sea, or more likely from neglect. The steps, too, were unswept.

He rang the bell and was shown in by a gray-garbed maid who seemed not to care who he was. "Visitors from twelve 'til three only, sir," said the girl. "Come back then, and we'll have all the lodgers dressed and down."

Gritting his teeth against the impatience, Rance nodded curtly and went back down the steps. The delay was understandable, he supposed. The house was obviously a place of business; one of those vile, pathetic lodgings just one step from the workhouse, and reserved for the last days of the reduced and dying; those with no family who would take them, but just enough money to get by. He envied neither them, nor Mrs. Ford, truth to tell.

At one o'clock, the girl was back, this time with a smut on her nose and an enquiring look on her face.

"Mr. Alfred Hedge?" he prompted.

"Ooh, right! 'E's been put in the garden for the afternoon," she said. "But another gent was here to see him before you. If you might just wait in the back parlor?"

Rance reluctantly agreed and handed the girl his stick.

He passed through the house to see something less than a dozen elderly men dotting the front reception rooms, most drowsing in chairs, but there were two fellows sitting at a chess board, and another being fussed over by a rotund lady in black; the proprietress, no doubt.

The back parlor was a shabby room dripping in chintz and overlooking a large, unkempt garden. Through the cloud of dust motes that danced in the morning sun, Rance could see a pale, hook-nosed man slumped in a sort of Bath chair, a blanket laid over his knees. On a stone bench beside him sat a white-haired fellow in a cleric's collar and black coat. The latter was leaning forward, a black book clutched loosely between his hands.

Though Rance was too far from either to sense any sort of intent, the aim of the priest was clear. Their conversation became increasingly heated, if gestures could be depended upon — until at last the old man lifted his fist in the air and shook it in obvious threat.

The priest jerked at once to his feet and came striding up the garden path, letting himself in and slamming the door behind. Rance waited a full minute before deciding the maid did not mean to reappear, then went round the corner and let himself into the garden. The skies, he noticed, had suddenly darkened — portentously, perhaps.

The man ignored, or perhaps could not hear, his approach.

"Alfred Hedge?" Rance said, standing over him.

The old man crooked his head to look up. His profile was harsh, his eyes small and sharp like a crow's, but one could still see shades of blonde in his hair and handsomeness in his face — the source of Ned Quartermaine's golden good looks, perhaps.

"Are you Alfred Hedge?" Rance demanded.

"Who wants to know?" Hedge said disdainfully. "If you're another prosy, do-good moralizer, you can just take yourself off with the last."

"I believe I can safely attest those are adjectives never once applied to me," said Rance. "But you might ask your son. I'm an acquaintance of Quartermaine's."

At that, the old man wheezed with laughter. "Little Ned, eh?" he chortled. "Surprised the bastard remembered where to find his dear old papa."

"Oh, he remembered," Rance bluffed. "And, with the right motivation, he was eager to tell me."

For an instant, the old man hitched. "Well,

give the lad my best, won't you?" he croaked. "My best wishes, I mean to say, that he rots in hell. It must cost him all of — what, two shillings a quarter? — to keep me in such rarified luxury."

Rance cut another glance at the sky, then sat down uninvited. "I daresay I can return his same kind regards to you," he said, tossing aside his hat. "My name, you see, is Welham. I suspect that will ring a bell or two."

At last there came a solid reaction, the old man flinching as if struck. But like any hardened gamester, he swiftly recovered himself. "Rance Welham, eh?" he sneered. "Still alive, then, you card-sharping upstart?"

"Oh, still very much alive." Rance stretched one arm along the back of the bench. "And very much wishing to taste revenge, since, I'm reliably informed, it's best when served up cold — and mine will be frigid indeed."

The old man cackled, then dragged a hand beneath his nose. "Well, if that's what you're after, you've come to the wrong place," he said. "I can do nothing for you, Welham. And should you choose to put a bullet through me for it, I might say you'd done me a favor."

Rance regarded him with unassailable

563

calm; he had waited for this moment nearly half his life. "Killing would be far too merciful, sir," he said coolly. "Besides, I am entirely unarmed — and quite deliberately, for I came here certain in the knowledge you would sorely tempt me."

This time Hedge did not laugh. "Get out," he snapped. "I'm an old man. I've nothing to say to you."

"Have you not?" Rance regarded him calmly. "Perhaps you think, Hedge, that I will feel some sympathy for you — old, ill, and diminished as you are. But I can assure you that is not the case. I am quite as cruel and callous as I have been painted."

"You ever were a cold-handed son of a bitch," the old man retorted, settling back into his chair. "Go on, then. Rail to your heart's content. I don't give a damn for your censure."

"I won't waste my breath," said Rance. "Tell me about the Black Horse syndicate."

Hedge narrowed one eye, but his breath was roughening. "A fantasy, that," he wheezed. "Who told you such a tale?"

"The Duke of Gravenel's cousin," said Rance, "George Kemble. I believe you may once have done business with him."

"Hmph!" But Rance could see a shiver of fear go through him. "And why should I

564

care what that vicious, light-footed little Lucifer has to say, eh? What's he going to do to me now?"

Rance turned his hat round and round by its brim, carefully weighing his next words and hoping his assessment of Kemble had been accurate. "I couldn't say; he seems a nasty piece of work," he said lightly. "I heard he once ripped out a chap's fingernails with a pair of rusty pliers."

The old man shrugged. "Not this decade, for Kemble's gone honest," he said. "Had to, didn't he, once his sister married up?"

"And what about little Ned?" asked Rance, forcing a bitter smile. "Is he capable of ripping out fingernails? Or turning his dear papa off entirely?"

"I'm not afraid of Ned," the old man blustered. "But what's it to me? I can tell you what you want to know, I reckon. It's no skin off my nose. Nothing can be proven. Not now."

"Excellent." Rance relaxed against the bench and prepared to play his greatest bluff ever. "Begin at the beginning, won't you? The syndicate. I want names."

Hedge seemed to stiffen with pride. "There were eleven of us, and bloody enterprising chaps we were, too," he said. "But all gone or dead now. And it wasn't just gaming; we had nunneries, doss-houses — Billy Boyton once had a promise of some fine Herati opium. Wonder what the lads of London would have thought of that, eh?" Suddenly, his face fell. "Sank though, the whole bloody ship."

"A leveling blow indeed," said Rance dryly. "Now which of those eleven ordered me framed for killing Peveril? Or was it the lot of you?"

Here, the old man began to pick almost absently at the lint on his blanket.

"I think, sir, you waste your time," said Rance. "You might better concern yourself with what Ned might do if you lie to me."

"Ned hasn't the bollocks to do a damned thing." The old man curled his lip. "The better part of that boy ran down my leg when I fucked his mother."

"He seems to have managed well enough." Rance lifted a hand and waved it at the house and garden. "And you, sir, are insolvent — or something near it, else you would not be living on your son's charity."

Lamely, Hedge shrugged. "And so?"

"And so what if he should cast you off?" Rance threatened. "I'll tell you what: eventually, if you live long enough, you'll end up on the parish dole —"

The old man made a strained, choking sound.

"— assuming, of course, you don't end your days in Coldbath Fields, picking oakum from your fine" — Rance paused to wave a hand at the Bath chair — *"wheeled conveyance."*

Here, Hedge began to wheeze in earnest. With a spotted, tremulous hand, he withdrew a blood-spattered handkerchief and began to cough violently into it. "Go bugger yourself, Welham," he rasped.

Ignoring the remark, Rance leaned into Hedge's face and propped his elbows on his knees. "Now I am, as you might recall, a dangerously fine card player," he said very quietly. "And your son owns a gaming salon. The twain have met, as it happens, and Mr. Quartermaine has come away owing me — well, let's just call it a near-tragic amount of money."

"Fine." Breath rasping now, Hedge stuffed away his handkerchief. "I hope he pays you."

"Oh, we have struck a most equitable bargain," said Rance. "Because we're friends of a fashion, he has offered to trade me what I seek — revenge, in the form of some documents he retained upon leaving your employ. Mr. Kemble has explained to me, you see, just where Ned learned his incredible

567

skill with numbers. And Ned — well, he wrote *everything* down . . ."

The old man's hands clenched on the arms of the chair. "You're a lying cheat," he wheezed. "Ned set a fire and robbed me blind. The whole place burned."

Rance pulled a sympathetic face. "I fear that last is not *quite* true," he murmured. "Your son had the remarkable foresight to keep a few things — just on the off chance he might someday have need of them."

The old man played a gambler's game — bluster aplenty but no hand at all, the stench of fear rising from him like carrion beneath a hot sun. "I made him earn his keep, aye," he said. "No law against it."

"But there are laws against gaming," said Rance. "And extortion. And prostitution. And murder. And framing innocent men for murder —"

"Oh, no, *that* was none of my doing!" Hedge exploded, but the words seemed to strangle him. "Had my wishes — wishes been — heeded — you would — w-would . . ."

"Would what?" Rance snarled.

"Would — would ha' been — *shivved.*" He choked out the words, his skin gone gray now. "Left in an alley — t-to-die — in your own bl-blood."

"Thank you," said Rance amidst the coughing, "for your candor. Nonetheless, Ned assures me there's enough to convict you of *something.* He's willing to sell you out to keep his club running, if he must — so I daresay you taught him something after all."

But Hedge's eyes seemed to bulge from their sockets. He was looking decidedly unwell.

Unsympathetically, Rance set a hand on Hedge's arm and leaned nearer still. "And if I can't loosen your tongue, Hedge, prison surely will," he continued. "I've only to bide my time. Hanging Nick Napier is in his grave, and no one at the Metropolitan Police is going to help you now. Besides, you haven't the money to bribe them. Now *who* came after me — ?"

Hedge was wheezing badly now, his eyes darting about the garden a little madly, as if the ghosts of his past were creeping out to haunt him. Then his face began to twist, like a man sinking in on himself, and he gave a small, almost mewling cry.

The skies were deepening with darkness now, the wind whipping up with a squall. Rance tightened his grip on the old man's arm, and suddenly a strange chill washed over him. He felt the brush of evil like a tangible thing; a rush of ice down his spine and a fight-or-flight surge in his gut.

But it wasn't Hedge. It was something far more dire. He felt his forehead break out in a sweat and thought, strangely, of Anisha.

Anisha, whom he loved more than life itself.

Anisha, who might already carry his child.

The man's eyes were fading now, the bright, birdlike light gone. Rance came to his feet and seized the chair arm, jerking it hard just as the wind blew open the garden gate on shrieking hinges. "Damn it, you're halfway to St. Peter already, Hedge," he said, leaning over him. "Who came after me? Who set me up?"

Hedge was scrabbling for the handkerchief again, and even Rance could see he was done. "Came to us — said he needed — money," he said, his words gargling in the back of his throat. "Kill . . . kill two birds. One . . . *st-stone.*"

"Who — ?" Rance seized hold of his collar. "Speak up, damn you!"

"Needed money . . . to finance . . ." But pink froth was foaming at the corner of his mouth now, and his head was lolling to one side. "Cold," he muttered. "I'm . . . cold."

Behind him, Rance heard the back door slam. "Mr. Hedge?" came a sharp, matronly voice. "Come along, lovie, there's a squall blowing in."

Suddenly, the feeling swept over Rance again, like a ghost walking over his grave. And this time it was a sick, all-encompassing sensation, as if ice water surged in his veins.

With a jerk, he released Hedge's arm, but the sensation did not fully relent.

Two birds with one stone.

And suddenly, he knew.

CHAPTER 14

Nay, if an oily palm be not a fruitful
prognostication, I cannot scratch mine
ear.
William Shakespeare,
Antony and Cleopatra

The wind lifted lightly, flapping at Anisha's tent door, which had been folded back and secured with gaudy yellow ribbons now threatening to come undone. Red and yellow, according to Hannah Leeton, were the colors of choice for Gypsy fortune-tellers, and even the tablecloth on which Anisha worked was striped in the same brilliant shades.

Glancing up at her most recent customer, Anisha smiled, gently closed the young lady's fist, and gave it one last, reassuring squeeze. "It was a pleasure to meet you, Jane," she said. "And yes, my dear. I think you shall find love soon. Very soon indeed."

A titter ran through the gaggle of girls standing behind Jane's chair. "But will it be *this* Season?" pleaded a petite, beribboned blonde. "Really, ma'am, it *must* be! Else Frederick will be off on his grand tour of Italy!"

"Or perhaps a grand honeymoon instead?" chimed another, nudging the first.

"Fate knows no *must,*" Anisha warned. "It cannot be altered to suit anyone's convenience."

"See, Maud?" Jane, the last of the gaggle to be read, cast a doe-eyed glance over her shoulder. "Don't jinx me! Besides, you only wish me married so that Mamma will let you be next."

Just then, their hostess, Hannah Leeton, appeared silhouetted in the tent opening, motioning for Anisha.

Anisha caught her gaze then returned to the girls. "Well, my dears, it was an honor for the Great and Mysterious Karishma to study your palms." Rising, she set her hands together and bowed. *"Namaste."*

"Lud, a Hindu fortune-teller this year!" she heard the blonde whisper as they passed back through the tent flaps. "How can she do it without the crystal ball?"

Hannah Leeton stepped into the tent, casting an indulgent look after them. "O

Great and Mysterious Karishma, you deserve a glass of lemonade," she declared. "Come, your queue is finally gone and the refreshment tent beckons."

Anisha laughed. "Thank you, I'm perishing of thirst."

Swiftly she unfurled the brilliantly hued sari she'd wrapped herself in, and lifted off her jeweled and feathered turban, neither of which was remotely realistic. Still, it was best to play her role to the hilt, she had decided. And Lady Leeton had chortled with glee at the sight of her.

Outside in the bright sunshine, the good lady linked her arm in Anisha's, then scowled up at the sky. "There's rain coming in off the Channel," she declared. "I hope it will not ruin the rest of my afternoon."

"It would not dare," Anisha assured her as they set off across the massive lawn. "Not for such a worthy cause."

As they passed between the now-empty booths that had constituted the bazaar, the fiddlers began a merry tune in the bandstand at the opposite end. Picnicking and dancing had already begun and the crowd was slowly shifting that way.

Lady Leeton cut Anisha a warm smile. "I am deeply in your debt, Lady Anisha, for saving my party," she said. "I realize, of course, that you must think this fortune-telling business both foolish and clichéd — which serves only to emphasize your kindness. Particularly when we've just met."

"It's my pleasure," said Anisha, her skirts catching lightly on the close-cropped grass as they strolled. "And I do know Sir Wilfred. Indeed, he has been most kind."

"Has he?" Lady Leeton's voice held a curious edge. "Well, my dear, if there is ever anything we might do to repay the favor, you've only to let us know."

Anisha considered it, slowing her gait a little. She really had saved the day, to a degree. Oh, the bazaar and the music had amused the crowd, yes. But for the whole of the afternoon, the queue outside Anisha's tent had been unflagging, requiring Lady Leeton's footmen to move two of the stalls and empty the donation jar three times.

Lady Leeton crooked her head. She was a lush, dark woman who had obviously been a beauty in her day. "Tell me, my dear, why are you not remarried?" she said speculatively. "Now that her eldest is fixed, perhaps Madeleine ought to turn her attention to you?"

Anisha's gaze was focused on the distant refreshments tent. "Oh, some days I rather like my widowhood," she said vaguely.

At that Hannah Leeton laughed. "As did I," she said. "In fact, I enjoyed it rather *too* much — not, mind you, that I did not miss my husband. I did. He was a kind man who adored me and left me rich. Sometimes now, when I look back, I think . . . ah, but never mind that. Old stories are very dull."

Anisha stopped abruptly on the grass and laid a hand over hers. "I disagree," she said. "I should like to hear your story. Widow-hood can be so difficult, yet in an odd way, liberating, too."

Hannah looked vaguely embarrassed. "And you have likely heard I was rather outré during mine," she said. "You have been wiser than I, my dear. I ran with a fast crowd of scoundrels, and looking back I wonder if grief — and a little outrage — didn't drive me to it."

"Outrage?" Anisha murmured.

For a moment, Hannah Leeton pursed her lips. "I married my first husband for his money," she finally said, "and that was no secret to anyone — not even him. He was much older, and a rich, respected business-man, and I was just an apothecary's daugh-ter from Cheapside. More than a few thought I'd got above myself. After Isaac died, well, I kicked up my heels a bit — one might charitably call it youthful rebellion, for I was just twenty-five."

Gently, Anisha turned the subject. "I had heard, Lady Leeton, that in those days you and Sir Wilfred were acquainted with my brother's best friend," Anisha lightly suggested. "Mr. Welham, who is now Lord Lazonby. Do you remember him?"

Hannah Leeton's eyes lit up. "Heavens, Rance Welham!" she said. "Indeed, we had a passing acquaintance. I felt sorry for him when that scandal broke. He often played cards with my beau at the time — devilish gamesters, the both of them."

"Your beau?" Anisha enquired.

Again, the lady blushed. "Sir Arthur Colburne," she said. "Oh, you would not think it to look at me now, my dear, but in those days I was much sought after — as was he."

"I'm sure you were a beauty," said Anisha. "You still are."

At that, Lady Leeton laughed. "You needn't be charitable," she said, not unkindly.

Anisha carefully considered her next words. "Lady Leeton, I find myself in an awkward position," she said. "You asked if there was something you might do for me. And there is. You might help me better understand what happened all those years ago."

"Indeed?" Her hostess lifted both eyebrows. "May I ask why?"

Anisha felt herself color. "If I may speak in perfect confidence?"

"To be sure." But she still looked suspicious.

Anisha plunged in. "I have reason to believe Lazonby might ask for my hand," she said. "Though I could be wrong. Still, Madeleine speaks highly of your judgment, and I should very much like to know if you think . . ."

"Yes?" Intrigue was written on Lady Leeton's face.

"Well, is it true that —" Anisha stopped and bit her lip.

"Oh, go on, my dear!" she said on a laugh. "It probably *was* true, if it's a rumor to do with our scandalous lot."

"I know that their deaths were tragic," said Anisha, "but I just keep wondering if it was true that Lord Percy Peveril was a fool, and Sir Arthur a fortune hunter?"

"Oh, poor Percy was an idiot." Suddenly the lady's eyes saddened. "And Arthur had gaping holes where his pockets should have been. Still, one couldn't help but fall in love with the rogue. Not even when one knew perfectly well what he was after. He was, after all, so very . . . well, let us call it *charming*."

"I had heard that," said Anisha, remembering Madeleine's polite euphemism. "And so you were quite fond of him?"

Again the lady laughed, but it was a laugh edged with something darker. "Dear me! Arthur and I have not been the subject of gossip for a long, long while," she said. "But he was a good sort, Arthur. Just weak, Lady Anisha. Most men are, you know. But not, I think, the resolute Lord Lazonby? He turned out to be made of sterner stuff than any of us might have guessed."

"I believe you are right," said Anisha, casting a rueful glance at her hostess. "Lady Leeton, might I ask you a horrid question?"

This time, she hesitated. "You may," she agreed, "but I mightn't answer it."

Anisha drew up her courage. "Could Sir Arthur have killed Percy in a quarrel?" she suggested, "then killed himself out of remorse? Perhaps Percy wished to . . . I don't know, call off the betrothal to Arthur's daughter?"

The lady shook her head. "I don't think Arthur had it in him, my dear," she said. "But you might ask Wilfred. He and Arthur were close. Heavens, Arthur introduced us! No, I think Arthur couldn't have done that to his girls."

"His girls?"

"Elinor and Elizabeth," said Lady Leeton. "Arthur was a handsome rogue, but he never gainsaid his girls. Trust me, I know *that* better than anyone."

Anisha could not miss the bitterness in her voice. "You sound as if you do," she murmured.

Lady Leeton cast her another odd glance. "The truth is, Lady Anisha, I was willing to drag Arthur out of the River Tick myself," she said. "In a somewhat sentimental moment, I hinted we might marry — yes, even knowing he was just a handsome scoundrel with nothing but skill in the — well, never mind that. I was a little besotted, even if I hid it well."

"I see," Anisha murmured. "I had heard, you know, that Sir Arthur meant to save himself from financial ruin by fleeing to France. Or to America, perhaps?"

"Yes, but that would have broken my heart," she said, "and the girls, frankly, refused to go. So I proposed to Arthur. It seemed a good solution. But his daughters were even more horrified by that prospect."

"Horrified? Why?"

Lady Leeton's odd smile twisted. "Oh, I was not of their dear, sainted mother's class," she replied. "Worse, my late husband was a Jew. His money and his kindness were meaningless to them. And yes, such high-handed ingratitude left me more than a little outraged. Still, I ought not have been surprised."

"But . . . but that is monstrous," said Anisha, suddenly wondering if Lady Leeton was as angry as she looked.

"I think you know, my dear, that is how the world works," she replied. "A gentleman will look the other way if the woman is lovely enough or rich enough, and I was both. But to those haughty daughters — especially to Elinor — it did not matter. They were having none of it. So Elinor made her choice — a hard one — and teased Percy until the poor dolt was fairly salivating. And Arthur killed himself, I daresay, for no reason save that he was drunk and mired in despair."

"But that is tragic!" said Anisha. "How sad for you — and for his foolish daughters, too."

Lady Leeton shrugged. "I was already inured to grief and prejudice," she said simply. "And I had Wilfred's shoulder to cry on. By then we were old chums, and we both loved Arthur. But those girls — oh, they suffered."

"Dear me," Anisha murmured. "What became of them?"

"They got what they deserved," said Lady Leeton simply. "They were packed off to America anyway, poor as a pair of church mice. Then Elinor died of a fever."

"And the other girl?" asked Anisha. "Was she younger?"

"Too young to be out," said Lady Leeton. "But it little mattered, for even Arthur said she'd never be a bankable beauty like the elder. I met her just once. Gangly, with the most unfortunate hair — bright red curls — and an obdurateness about her which I could not abide."

"What became of her?"

Again, Lady Leeton shrugged. "I have no notion," she said. "Oh, look! There is Wilfred with Lady Madeleine. Perhaps he can tell us?"

Anisha rather wished she had not brought up the subject, but Sir Wilfred had turned his attention from Madeleine and was looking at them expectantly. "Tell you what, my dear?" he asked as they drew up.

"Lady Anisha and I are gossiping," she lightly confessed. "Indeed, I've just discovered Lord Ruthveyn is a great friend of that young man we once knew — Rance Welham, who got into all that trouble?"

"Indeed?" Sir Wilfred smiled indulgently.

"Oh, Rance is a dear friend of my son's," Lady Madeleine chimed. "I like him very well, myself."

"Yes, I always thought him a capital fellow," said Sir Wilfred, wagging his brows. "But a dangerous man to sit down with, if you know what I mean."

"Indeed, but that's not what we were talking about," said his wife. "The whole thing led me to mention Arthur's girls. And I was just wondering, Wilfred — what became of her, that youngest? The one with the stubborn lip?"

Sir Wilfred's gaze drew distant. "*Hmm,* well," he said. "I exchanged letters with Arthur's sister a time or two — they took her in. After that, I didn't keep up. I should have done, I suppose."

Just then a woman in black approached, a set of brass keys dangling from a chatelaine at her waist. She was followed by three pretty ladies in clothing nearly as colorless as her own, all of whom Anisha had seen drifting about the garden party. Two of them, in fact, had been in her tent to have their palms read. The third, however — by far the youngest — had not.

"If you please, ma'am, you're wanted on the platform in a quarter hour," said the woman in black. "We'll be awarding the prizes for Best Girl and such."

"Oh, yes! Our charity school presentations." Setting her hands rather proudly together, Lady Leeton smiled round at all of them. "Lady Madeleine, Lady Anisha, permit me the honor of introducing our school's matron, Mrs. Day, and our wonderful volunteers. This is Mrs. Drummond, who helps with deportment. And Mrs. Howe, who oversees needlework. And lastly, Mrs. Ashton, who helps with grammar. I cannot *think* what we would do without them."

Each of the ladies curtseyed in turn as Lady Madeleine made a gracious fuss over them. Anisha held back, one eye upon Sir Wilfred, for she had a sudden notion.

At last the four ladies drifted away.

"Well, if you will excuse me," said Lady Leeton. "Oh, and Wilfred — I shall wish you to manage the striking of the stalls once afternoon tea has commenced. Everything goes on the carts back to the stables. Now mind you watch Potter and the footmen, and do not let them dawdle."

Sir Wilfred tugged his forelock subserviently. "Yes, ma'am!" he said speciously. "I am your servant. At least donations have nearly doubled last year's, most of it from the fortune-teller's tent."

Lady Leeton's gaze fell upon Anisha, and she darted impulsively forward, giving her a little hug. "Oh, my dear, how ever can I thank you!" she declared. "You have quite amazed everyone. What a flair for the dramatic you have."

"Thank you," Anisha murmured.

"Oh, Anisha has a great many talents." Lady Madeleine caught Anisha's arm through her own almost protectively. "I never cease to be amazed. Why, she understands the movements of the heavens better than half the Royal Astronomical Society, and she's an expert in herbs and botanic medicine."

"Are you?" exclaimed Lady Leeton. "Do you know, Lady Anisha, the subject of herbals utterly fascinated my father. As an apothecary, he amassed a famous collection of . . . oh, dear, what are they called, Wilfred?"

Leeton smiled wearily. "*Pharmacopoeia, my dear.*"

"Yes, that!" she said brightly. "Papa had some dating back to the fifteenth century. You must come inside and see the moldering old things. Perhaps you can make something of them, for heaven knows I cannot —" Abruptly, her gaze shifted. "Oh, look!

There is Mr. Hundley, who has not yet made a donation this year. Pardon me, ladies."

Leeton watched her go with a vague smile. "Hannah is nothing if not ruthless," he said musingly. "Poor Hundley will be walking back to Mayfair in his drawers by the time she's finished."

But Madeleine had turned to a lady in a green dress who was enquiring after one of the lace fichus she had purchased. Anisha seized her chance.

"I wonder, Sir Wilfred, if we might take a turn about the bandstand?" she asked quietly. "There was something . . . well, something a little awkward I wished your advice on."

Leeton pulled a sympathetic face and offered his arm. "I have thought all day, my dear, that something troubled you."

"Yes, though I have been loath to discuss it with anyone," she said. "But I remember your kind advice at the Royal Opera House. The matter concerns two gentlemen, you see, whose characters you know."

"Well, my discerning judgment has been often remarked by my friends," he said a little pompously. "How may I help?"

Anisha feigned embarrassment and they set off, her arm resting lightly upon his. "I think, Sir Wilfred, that I am being courted," she confessed when they had drawn away from the crowd.

"Oh, heavens!" He grinned down at her. "*That* troubles you?"

"No, it is just that I cannot decide whose suit I ought to favor," she said. "The first gentleman, as you might guess, is our mutual friend."

"Ah ha!" Leeton patted her hand. "I knew old Royden was smitten!"

"But the second gentleman —" Here, she lowered her lashes and snared her lip for an instant. "The second you know as well. It is my brother's friend, the Earl of Lazonby."

She felt the faintest hitch in Leeton's gait. "Ah," he answered. "Lazonby, eh? Well, well. A handsome fellow, to be sure. And rich as Croesus now."

Anisha cast a glance over her shoulder as if watchful. "But his *character,* sir," she said, dropping her voice. "I have been told, if you will forgive my saying, that you once knew him well?"

It was Leeton's turn to color faintly. "Ordinarily Hannah does not like me to speak of the past," he grumbled. "But she started it, didn't she? Before we married, you see, I settled down and ceased my . . . my less salubrious activities."

"How good of you."

"Well, that vile business with Sir Percy drew too much police attention, and by then I'd seen my way into the theater business." He shrugged. "In fact, I'd already contracted to purchase the Athenian. But in my wilder days, yes, I knew Lazonby. A dashing young rogue, by gad."

"Oh, he can be most charming," Anisha agreed. "And I have to tell you, fond as I am of Mr. Napier, I think I am leaning toward Lazonby. But perhaps I'm naïve? Do you imagine, Sir Wilfred, that he did anything wicked? There have been the most frightful stories in the *Chronicle* this past year."

"Oh, stuff and nonsense, I expect," said Sir Wilfred. "There's a young fellow on their staff with some sort of liberal ax to grind. Tried once or twice to barge in on me. But I put a cinder in his ear and sent him off again, I can tell you."

"So Lazonby didn't murder anyone?"

Here, Sir Wilfred hesitated. "I thought not at the time," he answered, "and I told what little I knew on the witness stand. Still, I was shocked it came to a trial. Figured he'd make a run for it — off to the hells of Paris, or such, after he got my message."

"Your message?"

"Indeed," said Sir Wilfred. "As soon as the police called on me, I saw which way the wind was blowing."

"Because of his quarrel with Lord Percy?"

"It was more of a harangue," he answered, "for it takes two to quarrel. Lazonby was a hardened gamester, there's no disputing. And, despite his tender years, dashed good at it. But I never saw him lose his temper at the table. If anything, he took life too lightly."

"But Lord Percy called him a cheat."

"So he did, in a fit of pique," Sir Wilfred agreed. "But Percy was jealous of Lazonby. There'd been a little trouble with a female who had eyes for Lazonby — ah, but I oughtn't speak of such things to you."

"Oh, I know Lord Lazonby was a bit of a womanizer," she assured him. "My brother warned me. I won't have him if I can't bring him to heel."

"Well, best of luck with that," said Sir Wilfred doubtfully. "In any case, it wasn't the first time someone had called Rance Welham a cheat. If he'd killed them all, we could have laid the corpses end to end round Trafalgar Square."

Anisha stopped on the grass some distance from the bandstand. "Sir Wilfred, you much reassure me," she said. "And I was wondering, too . . ."

"Yes?" he said solicitously.

Anisha weighed her words, wondering how far to press him. Wondering, too, if she'd had the whole of the truth from Lady Leeton.

"What is it, my dear?" said Sir Wilfred gently. "You are still worried?"

"A little." Anisha averted her eyes for an instant. "I was wondering, Sir Wilfred, if ever you had heard of a thing called the Black Horse syndicate?"

For a moment, he was dead silent. "Well," he finally said, "if I had, I would not admit it, my dear. Do you understand me? And I must ask you where *you* heard tell of such a thing."

Anisha bit her lip. "Lady Bessett gave me the name of a fellow — a police contact of her father's. He's retired now, but he once was involved, I collect, in the criminal underworld."

Sir Wilfred frowned down at her. "You ladies called on such a fellow?" he said disapprovingly. "Really, my dear. I fear the two of you are involving yourselves in ugly — possibly even dangerous — matters. I do wish you would not."

"Oh, Lady Bessett did not accompany me," Anisha insisted. "But I did have some papers to show him."

"What sort of papers?" Sir Wilfred was still scowling.

On impulse, Anisha withdrew the gaming vowels from her reticule. "I found these tucked in a book in Lazonby's withdrawing room when my brother and I were there for dinner," she said, not knowing how else to explain their possession. "I was curious, you see, about these pencil markings."

Sir Wilfred took them, and an odd smile passed over his face. "Heavens," he said. "I thought the police still had those. It all seems a lifetime ago. So I still owe Lazonby nine hundred pounds, eh?"

Anisha laughed. "I'm quite sure he's forgotten," she said. "But I did think, perhaps, that the markings might mean something. So I showed them to Mr. Kemble."

"Mr. *Kemble* — ?" said Sir Wilfred. "He was watching you at the theater."

"And now we know why." Anisha shrugged. "But it little matters, for Mr. Kemble said the notes were worthless. But he did mention this thing — the Black Horse syndicate — though he wasn't sure who was in it."

"Memories do fade," said Sir Wilfred sympathetically. "Ah, well. I really should settle my debt with Lazonby."

"I'm sure it's not necessary." Then, to stick with her lie, she abruptly added, "—because I shouldn't wish him to know we discussed it, or that I took these."

"Indeed, no good can come of needling old wounds, my dear," he agreed. "In fact, it would be best if you let me destroy them now."

Anisha gave a long sigh. "Oh, I had better tuck them back where I got them next time I get the chance," she said, putting them away. "Women will insist upon being the most trouble-making creatures on earth, will they not?"

At that, Leeton laughed and resumed their sedate stroll. "Oh, I am a happily married man for a reason, my dear," he said. "I shall say nothing to incriminate myself!"

They had turned the entire circle around the bandstand. Madeleine was still with the lady in green, and Lady Bessett had joined them. All eyes were turned to the platform, where Lady Leeton was calling for everyone's attention.

The next minutes were spent in awarding various end-of-term prizes to the students of the charity school. No less than a score of fresh-faced young misses trod across the platform to curtsey before Hannah Leeton, who was clearly in her element playing Lady Bountiful as she handed out awards for stitchery, arithmetic, deportment, penmanship, and a host of other subjects.

When it was over and the girls thoroughly applauded, Anisha turned to her companions, dismayed to realize she'd never got her lemonade. "Well, the Mysterious Karishma must return to her duties," she declared.

"That would be the *Great* and Mysterious Karishma," Lady Madeleine advised. "Never sell yourself short. Wait, you never took any refreshment. Shall I send you something?"

"Oh, thank you!" Anisha declared. "Anything wet."

Back in Lady Leeton's gaudy tent, she had scarcely wrapped her sari when a shadow appeared at the opening.

"Lady Anisha?" One of the school volunteers poked her head into the tent. "I was coming this way, and Lady Madeleine wished you to have a lemonade."

"Oh, thank you!" Anisha smiled, and motioned her in. "Mrs. Drummond, isn't it? You are quite as kind as your palm suggested."

"Heavens, it's nothing." The lady came in with a smile and set the glass down, but the other two volunteers remained outside.

Anisha nodded toward the tent flaps. "I see the Great and Mysterious Karishma has one victim remaining amongst you," she said drolly. "Would she not like to come in and have her palm read?"

Mrs. Drummond grinned mischievously. "Oh, Mrs. Ashton!" she sang over her shoulder. "You've been spotted. You must come in and pay your shilling to the Great and Mysterious Karishma, or she may cast a curse upon you."

On a laugh, the third lady — Mrs. Howe — dragged Mrs. Ashton into the tent. "Come along now, my dear," she declared. "Miriam and I have already done it. You must have your palm read."

The younger lady hesitated. "I should be happy, of course, to donate," she demurred.

"Oh, we shan't be satisfied with that!" Mrs. Howe teased. "Out with your hand!"

Mrs. Drummond, too, continued the cajoling, and soon Mrs. Ashton was seated opposite Anisha, but her posture was stiff. Anisha felt most unhappy, and more than a little responsible for the lady's discomfort.

Mrs. Ashton was a lithe, pretty woman, but not quite an elegant one, for she slumped her shoulders as if in compensation for her height — a troubling habit, since it limited one's *pranayama* and brought on illness, Anisha firmly believed. Fully framed by massive ringlets of thick chestnut hair, her face, too, was vaguely familiar — someone from church, perhaps, Anisha thought. But her eyes; oh, they were the green of frozen pond water, and just about as welcoming.

Anisha left aside her silly turban, suddenly disquieted. "*Namaste,* Mrs. Ashton," she said, bowing. "Do you wish an audience? Or shall this be a private reading?"

Mrs. Ashton surprised her. "Private," she said, her voice oddly clipped.

Their faces falling with disappointment, the older ladies nodded and swept from the tent.

Anisha joined her in sitting down, but Mrs. Ashton still looked decidedly uncomfortable. For a long moment, Anisha studied her across the table, finding herself inexplicably troubled. She was not going to like what she saw; she knew this without so much as unfurling the woman's fingers.

Mrs. Ashton, she suspected, knew it, too.

Anisha sighed. "We do not need to do this, you know," she said quietly. "We may simply sit here quietly until your friends are convinced you have surrendered with grace."

Some dark, fleeting emotion sketched

across the woman's face, and she flung out her right hand, palm up. "No sensible person is afraid of nonsense," she said haughtily. "Go ahead, mysterious Karishma. What do you see there? Six children and a brilliant marriage? Or riches beyond my wildest dreams?"

Anisha surrendered to the inevitable. "Either, I daresay, is possible," she said, drawing the hand nearer.

And yet she knew that, for this woman, neither was likely.

For a time she delayed the truth, merely tracing the life and heart lines, along with their many obstructions, then methodically working her thumb over the hard Venus, the coarse Moon, the over-large Sun, all the while wondering at the sadness of it all.

After a time she shook her head. "This is not your dominant hand."

The woman faltered. "What do you mean?"

"The hand you use most," said Anisha. "Which is it?"

"I . . . it is both," said the woman. "I'm ambidextrous. What of it?"

"Can you write with both hands?" Anisha prodded. "Sew with both hands? When you step, which foot goes first? One part of our nature, you see, must always lead the other."

Mrs. Ashton simply blinked at her. "I step with the foot that is best positioned," she said. "Yes, I can write and sew with both hands. A little better, perhaps, with the left."

Anisha accepted this by nodding. "Give me the left as well, then, if you please."

She had expected the woman would refuse, but she did not. "By all means," said Mrs. Ashton, throwing open the left hand beside the right. "I have nothing to hide."

But Anisha was very much afraid she might. Again, she inspected the open hand carefully. Never had she seen such a conflicting array of mounds and lines; such emotional inconsistencies and such a duality of nature.

At last she sat back on her stool. "You are Gemini born, are you not?" she said quietly. "In early June?"

Mrs. Ashton gave a swift intake of breath. "Yes."

Anisha nodded. "And like many of your kind, you are of two natures," she continued. "Natures which are often in conflict. You are torn in half, your better self being dominated by your lesser self. Indeed, ma'am, I fear you could be driven to destruction if you do not have a care."

Mrs. Ashton sneered and drew back her hands. "What utter drivel."

"I think you know it is not," Anisha gently pressed. "Indeed, I think it is the very reason you sent your friends away. Though you hide it exceedingly well, in much of life you are confused and filled with doubt. But you refuse to acknowledge this uncertainty, even to your inner self. I sense you are a deeply unhappy woman, Mrs. Ashton, for all your kindnesses and volunteer work."

The woman surprised her by throwing out both hands again. "Show me how you decide such nonsense," she challenged.

Anisha did so, tracing over the lines and pointing out the ones that were stunted, the mounds which were more or less than was optimal, and the signs of conflict etched so deeply into both hands. "And perhaps most importantly," she explained, "here your Sun mound is disproportionately large. It reveals your devotion — your *passion,* if you will."

"And devotion has become a bad thing?" said Mrs. Ashton snidely.

"When you are devoted to something which is destructive, yes," said Anisha. "You have the courage of your convictions, Mrs. Ashton — and they are eating you alive. And this — *ketu* — it is overdeveloped. This is called in English something like 'tail of the dragon,' and in *Mithuna rashi* — in Gemini rising — developed as yours is, it is most unhealthy."

The woman gave a sharp laugh. "Unhealthy in what way?"

"You have no freedom of spirit," said Anisha. "You have also a remarkable ability to deny yourself pleasure. Moreover, your mind has been at times unwell, and you know this."

"How dare you!" The woman recoiled. "You suggest that I am *mad?*"

"No, no." Anisha let her shoulders sag; it was as she had expected. Too hard to explain. Too hard, even, for her to fully comprehend. How did someone become so tormented and unhappy?

"You are not mad," she finally said. "Far from it. But you have let your anger and your determination and your denial of joy push you past rational thought. And if you continue on as you are, Mrs. Ashton, you could lose your moral compass entirely. Is this what you wish?"

"I think *you* are mad." The woman trembled with rage now.

Anisha sat calmly. "Everyone can change, Mrs. Ashton," she said quietly. "Shall I tell you how? For you, it can be done by focusing on your heart line and —"

"No, I should sooner tell *you* something," she interjected, sweeping to her feet in a rustle of muslin and petticoats. *"Go. To. Hell."*

Anisha felt a cold sense of fatalism now. "In my experience, we often make our own hell on this earth," she replied. "Here is what it comes down to, Mrs. Ashton. You must choose a hand. Right? Or left? You must choose a side. Darkness? Or light? You cannot continue in pain as you are, half of you yearning for the goodness of your better self, and half of you caught in your own bitterness. I warn you out of genuine concern, and nothing more."

"The only thing I'm *choosing* is to walk out of here." Mrs. Ashton had already thrown back the tent flaps. "I know quite well what I'm about. As to grim warnings, let me share one with you — a good, Christian adage, too, not some half-baked Hindu balderdash dreamt up in a cloud of smoke and herbs."

"Pray go ahead," said Anisha evenly. "I try to keep an open mind."

"Fine, then," she said over her shoulder as she pushed past her startled friends. *"Lie down with dogs, get up with fleas!* Now put that in your hookah and smoke it, *Lady* Anisha Stafford."

Mouth agape, Mrs. Drummond stepped back inside the flaps. Mrs. Howe had

600

clapped a hand over her mouth. For a long moment, they simply stared after their coworker, who was marching away, ramrod stiff, hands fisted, her skirts swishing over the grass at a rapidly increasing pace.

"My heavens!" Mrs. Howe finally said. "What's got into Mrs. Ashton?"

Anisha lifted her gaze to meet Mrs. Howe's. "I collect," she said quietly, "that the lady did not wish her fortune told after all."

Rance sat slumped on the well-cushioned banquette of his first-class compartment, holding the unread newspaper he'd purchased while anxiously pacing Brighton Station. His gaze was focused instead on the rolling green Surrey countryside beyond the spitting rain, but his mind — at least half of it — was still in Mrs. Ford's overgrown garden.

At the thought, his right hand curled involuntarily into the lush upholstery, as if it might, even now, choke the truth out of Alfred Hedge. But he had got as much as he ever would, he knew, out of that venal son of a bitch. And Hedge was going on to his great reward still clutching his secrets — if not today, then very soon indeed. There would be no vengeance on this earth, and in that, Rance could not help but feel cheated.

Nonetheless, he'd promised Anisha he would seek justice, not vengeance, and it was she who lay at the forefront of his mind. Anisha, and the strange sensations — the strange *certainty* — which even now seemed to connect him to her. Even as he hastened back to London, having departed in such haste that he'd not stopped to collect his belongings, he could not put away the sense of urgency — the near panic — that was driving him back to her.

Just then, however, the train lurched, the *clackity-clack-clack* slowing abruptly in a shriek of brakes. Thrown nearly off his seat, Rance seized hold of the door until the lugging of the train halted. Panic rising, he stood and craned his neck to look down the tracks.

The high brick arch of the Merstham tunnel stared back at him from its chalky outcropping, but Rance could not quite see the black entrance below that swallowed up the tracks.

From somewhere in the depths of the carriage behind him, he heard a door creak open, and in a moment a porter came trudging past in the mist, his footsteps crunching in the loose gravel below.

A moment later he came back again, shoulders slumping.

Rance flung open his door and looked down at the fellow. "What the devil is holding us up?" he demanded.

The porter blinked up at him through the mist. "Cows," he said.

"Cows?" said Rance. "How the devil did cows get up this narrow passage?"

"Only the devil would know," said the porter somewhat impertinently. "But cows there be, and they must be coaxed back down the line, for they cannot very well go through now, can they?"

"Well, for God's sake, man!" Rance said. "Go and coax! We cannot simply sit here."

"Well, I've got to get me boots on, don't I?" said the fellow.

"Oh, a fashion plate for a porter!" said Rance, flinging the door wider. "God save us. I'll see to the bloody cows myself."

"Oh, sir," said the fellow, flinging up a hand. "I wouldn't!"

But it was too late. Rance had leapt down onto the gravel, and squarely into a pile of warm manure, splattering it high. "Bloody hell!" he gritted.

The porter squawked and leapt back — but not quickly enough. "Damn and blast," said the fellow, fumbling in his massive pocket. "Another accursed Monday!"

Rance looked up from his fouled boots to see the poor chap wiping manure off his cheek. "Monday?"

His gaze caught Rance's, accusing. "It's always a Monday something goes arse over teakettle!" he grumbled, wiping down his coat sleeve. "Loose track last month. Falling rocks a fortnight past. Why, Monday last, a woman nearly gave birth rolling into Brighton Station! And if you think manure is a mess — well, at any rate, seems I oughtn't trouble myself to get out of bed a' Monday."

But Rance stood frozen, stock-still on the track's graveled verge.

The fellow was right. In all the haze of thwarted hope and long-denied passion, Rance had lost track of days. But this was *Monday.*

And suddenly the impetus behind his awful sense of urgency came clear. Dear God. It was Monday. He had to get back to London. And he had to do it *now.*

"Come along," he gritted, hitching the fellow by the arm. "We are moving those cows — and by God, we're doing it this instant, never mind the damned boots."

Anisha was inordinately relieved when, at

long last, Lady Leeton's footmen came to strike down the gaudy tent and haul the furnishings away. Along the grassy promenade, the stalls were being disassembled, too, and what remained of the Leetons' guests had again shifted to the refreshment tent for afternoon tea.

"Here's the last of it," Sir Wilfred declared, gathering up the poles.

Anisha turned to the young servant who was loading. "Thank you," she said as he piled the chairs onto a barrow. "Is the whole of your stables filled with tents and lumber?"

"Just the east block," said Sir Wilfred grimly. "Even the bandstand comes apart. Hannah sold half my stable to make room for the lot."

Anisha smiled. "As you say, she is determined."

He laughed and, as the servant pushed the barrow away, Anisha raised a hand to her eyes, for unlike the graying south, the northerly sky was still bright with sunshine. Far across the lawns, she could see Lady Leeton walking toward the stables alongside her butler, and gesturing instructively at various tents and stalls, as if to say which should be taken down first.

"Pardon me," said Leeton grimly, "but I'd best catch up with Hannah and do my part."

Anisha felt suddenly grateful for a few moments of quiet. Glancing over her shoulder, she weighed returning to Madeleine and Lady Bessett in the refreshment tent, but the efficient Mrs. Day was presiding over tea, and Anisha had no wish to face Mrs. Ashton again.

She had not long to consider it, for Sir Wilfred nodded to his wife, turned, and started coming swiftly back along the path toward her, puffing, and red in the face.

"Hannah wishes to take you down to her stillroom to see her father's collection of herbals," he said when he drew up beside her. "Will you give her ten minutes, then meet her at the house? I must help Potter direct the unloading."

"Yes, of course," said Anisha. "How kind."

Leeton glanced over his shoulder at the house. "Best go round back to the kitchen garden," he said. "The house is locked up, and all the staff out here."

After gathering up her reticule, Anisha ambled her way along a shady path that meandered by the garden wall, hoping no one would see her. The long afternoon spent in the warmth of the tent, crowded in by too many people and surrounded by too much clamor, had left her drained.

In time, it was an easy matter to make her

way through the formal parterres that flanked the house, and under the stone archway that gave onto the rear. Here the walled gardens continued, lower now, with one section given over to root crops, just beginning to flourish, the next to vegetables, and the final and smallest, to herbs.

Against the herb wall someone had left a pile of mud-caked garden tools, but Anisha was distracted from this minor nuisance by the long double row of fruit trees leading away from the house, at the end of which lay a sunken stone structure that appeared almost embraced by the earth and topped with a cupola — the dairy, perhaps, or a large icehouse. This bucolic prospect was made complete by a chaffinch perched in the nearest tree chortling *peep-peep-chirrup!* as if happy to have a visitor.

Shutting away the vision of Mrs. Ashton and her outrage, Anisha went perfectly still, drawing her breath slow and deep for a time, and willing away the day's frustrations. For a few moments, she lost track of time, aware only of the soft grass beneath her feet, of the birdsong pouring over her, and of the scents of rich, fresh-turned soil. Aware only of God's perfect and eternal strength that spurred such green, growing sweetness from the earth.

But thoughts of eternal strength brought her mind round to Rance again; to the utter happiness that seemed almost within her grasp. In moments such as this, it was a quiet joy to stop and remember the night of passion they had spent together, and the promise not yet fulfilled.

He loved her. *He had always loved her.* And she had known it; known it in that way which only two bound and fated souls could know. Moreover, they were at long last on the verge of accepting that fate. She almost resented having to come here. How much sweeter it would have been to have lingered, alone with her memories, in the serenity of her own garden.

After a time, however, feeling a little more at peace, she exhaled slowly, opened her eyes, and turned into the herb garden. Methodically, she began to examine Lady Leeton's choices, going row by row. Like those of most English gardens, they were not especially exciting, or even useful. Nor were they as kempt as the Leetons' showy public gardens, Anisha decided, bending to flick a beetle from a leaf of sweet marjoram.

Just then, the chaffinch went eerily still.

Anisha froze, her hand hovering. There came an odd breeze — the merest of sounds, as if the bird had flown too near her temple. A white, splintering light shot through her head, then vanished, ephemeral as the sound. She threw out a hand against the blackness and felt the soft earth rise up to meet her.

Anisha came awake to find herself floating. Floating flat atop a slab of ice that lay cold beneath her body, with the trickling sound of water echoing all around her.

A cave? A cold cave. Ice-cold pain had bored into her very marrow.

Fragments of memory rose up, whirling about her like a flock of startled finches. Mentally, she reached for one. It fluttered off again and was lost. She groaned, her consciousness melting into the ice.

When next she woke, it was to the sound of wood scraping over stone. There was a deathly chill beneath her cheek and her palms, and the tang of blood in her mouth.

She cracked one eye and saw a blur of sticks.

No, not sticks. Wooden legs. A dozen, it seemed. But the vision sharpened, then became three. *A stool.* And with it, two large, well-shod feet. Anisha opened the other eye and ran her tongue round her teeth, tasting blood.

"Tsk, tsk," said a soft voice from above.

"Coming round, are we?"

She tried to speak but couldn't. The awful clank of metal striking stone rang out. A garden spade clattered in front of her face, the back smeared with blood.

"It would have been easier for us both, perhaps," the voice went on, "had you never woken."

She struggled to lift herself up and failed. Reality was returning, and with it a sick, terrible fear. She had been struck. The gentle voice was not gentle. Vaguely she knew she must run, and yet her limbs would not move.

Better to feign a stupor and gather her wits.

She let her lashes flutter shut and squinted through them. She lay not upon ice, she realized, but upon a white tiled floor. Recognition stirred. *The little dairy beyond the trees.* It had to be. There was the dank, soured scent of old milk in the air. And the gurgle of water. A spring, perhaps.

"Lazonby just couldn't let sleeping dogs lie, could he?" The melancholy words echoed through the stone enclosure. "Good God, he had his freedom. What the devil does he want?"

Me, she thought vaguely. *He wants me.*

He'd wanted to be good enough; wanted

his family's honor back. Surely such devotion had not come to this? Anisha drew in a slow, ragged breath and vowed she would not let it.

Somehow, she rolled slightly onto her side and looked up into the bleak, blue eyes of Sir Wilfred Leeton. *"You . . . you killed"* — she whispered — *"Lord Percy."*

He sat upon a three-legged milking stool, elbows on his knees and hands dangling as he leaned plaintively over her body. Only the bloody spade at his feet betrayed his vicious nature.

"I didn't want to," he said, whining a little through his nose. "But I needed rid of Arthur. I couldn't quite kill him — we were mates of a fashion — but Arthur had to go. What choice did I have?"

"Arthur?" Anisha struggled to make sense of it. *"Wh— Wh . . . ?"*

Sir Wilfred sighed, dragging both hands through what was left of his hair. "Oh, she'd never have spared me a glance otherwise," he said. "All that coin, ripe for the picking — and Arthur's chits stubbed up over blood! You, of all people, will appreciate how foolish *that* is. Jewish gold, nabob gold — it all jingles the same in a chap's pocket, eh? Though it does wear on a fellow, playing the doting husband to a fishwife."

Somehow, she levered up onto one elbow. "You . . . you hated him," she whispered.

Sir Wilfred's blue eyes widened innocently. "Arthur? No! I just wanted him to run off to France. He said he planned to — *promised* it, really."

"No, R— R—" Anisha surrendered, and let her head fall back onto the floor.

"Ah, Lazonby? No, no." Suddenly, his voice turned inward. "Oh, it could gall a chap to see the ladies pant over him like bitches in heat," he said. "And true, at that particular moment I could ill afford the nine hundred pounds I owed him. But it was the Black Horse boys that wanted rid of Lazonby."

Vaguely, Anisha knew she had to keep him talking. "Why . . . ?" she managed, spittling blood.

Leeton lifted one shoulder. "They'd pegged him for some sort of sharper but couldn't make out what," he replied. "Had 'em worried. So they offered me what I direly needed — financing for the Athenian. And in return, I'd ensure Lazonby troubled them no more."

Anisha tried to summon her strength, and set both hands flat to the icy floor. *"For that . . . you would kill?"* she rasped.

"Only Percy!" he countered, as if it had

somehow been logical. "I mean, who knew Arthur would turn coward? And who'd have dreamt Lazonby would stand and fight? I even warned him — I told him to run, the damned fool." Sir Wilfred looked down almost pitifully and shook his head. "And now I am going to have to let you go, Lady Anisha, much as it pains me."

At first, she thought remorse had overcome him. But then he lifted his hand, gesturing with clear distaste at something beyond her view, toward the sound of the gurgling water.

Then he licked his lips uncertainly. "Everyone will question, of course, why you wandered out here alone, but no one will question the tragedy of it," he said, his words falling faster and faster. "A wet floor. A foot misplaced — and all too near the springbox. Admittedly not my best plan, but you've given me so little time, my dear. Those papers — good God — if I allow you to keep them . . . should Lazonby ever find them . . . there'll be an avalanche of suspicion. And that damned George Kemble — oh, that wicked, meddling fellow will unravel my little clew quick as I draw breath . . . or tell Lazonby how to do it."

It is too late, she wanted to say. *You are undone, you craven dog.*

Perhaps that would save her. "They . . . have seen," she murmured, fighting the wish to close her eyes and sleep. "They know."

"No, they don't know." His voice had taken on a strange edge. "They can't — not yet — or you wouldn't be here."

Anisha shut her eyes and fought to remember who knew what. But she saw only a vision of Durga, the many-armed warrior-goddess, bearing her swords, her thunder, and her powerful retribution. *Leeton had killed for money. Left Rance to hang for it like a common criminal.* She imagined Durga lifting her thunderbolt and aiming it straight at Leeton's visage. The image brought her courage — and a terrible thirst for vengeance.

The spade. The handle of the spade, she realized, was within her grasp, had she the strength to wield it. She slowly drew in her breath and tried to block the pain.

"A person can drown, Lady Anisha, in a quart of water," Sir Wilfred murmured, "when incapacitated. Or held under. Did you know that?"

"Yes . . ." she whispered, rolling ever so slightly nearer.

And an infidel can die a thousand deaths.

"Do you see why I wish you had never woken? I've nothing against you — or even

your race! Good Lord, I can see why
Lazonby lusts after you. Even now, I must
say, you're a tempting little morsel." He
smacked his lips, then drew a hand down
his face. "But I'm not, of course, *depraved.*
Still, why did you have to dredge up those
old notes of hand, my dear? And ask such
vile questions?"

Anisha writhed as if in pain, curling her
hand nearer the spade. *"How — How —
could you?"* she choked. "Your . . . *friends."*

"But just handsome scoundrels, the both
of them!" His voice was pleading — almost
wheedling — now. "I said to myself, 'Will,
old boy, play it out right and you'll kill two
birds with one stone! Arthur will run — and
Lazonby right after him. The syndicate will
be happy. And Arthur's sniveling brats can
just choke on their bloody pride.' "

And it was in that moment that everything
changed. As if timed by God, Anisha seized
the spade, and at once the door came crashing open.

Leeton leapt from his stool, half tripping
over the spade handle. In a billow of gray
muslin, Mrs. Ashton leapt down the short
flight of steps, her face a mask of wild rage.

"You bastard!" she hissed.

On a hideous shriek, Leeton recoiled.

Anisha realized the woman held a pocket

pistol clutched in both hands.

"You! All along, it was *you!*" Mrs. Ashton shook almost uncontrollably, but her elbows were locked solid, her finger on the trigger. "And you — !" she spat, cutting a glance down at Anisha. "Get out. This no longer concerns you."

Still holding the shovel, Anisha tried to leap up, but balance failed her. She staggered awkwardly, wrenching her ankle. Somehow, she dragged herself backward, to the edge of the cement trough.

Mrs. Ashton jerked her head toward Leeton. "Get *down,*" she commanded. "Get down on your knees, Wilfred Leeton, and pray to God if you've got one, for I'm about to give you the coward's death you deserve."

Leeton's eyes were like saucers. "Who — ?" he hooted, drawing back against the wall. "Who *are* you?"

She marched two steps toward him. Anisha didn't doubt the woman's intent for an instant. Her eyes had gone bloody with rage. Panicked, Anisha looked about. The room was utterly made of stone. The floors. The walls. The steps. The Portland cement springbox. A marble counter spanning one wall. A shot could ricochet wild. Any one of them could die — Mrs. Ashton included.

Fleetingly, she tried to rise. The ankle

gave. The spade fell with a frightful clatter. Mrs. Ashton snapped around. "Get *out* or get *down*," she warned, gun shaking. "Or so help me God, I'll shoot you, too. Now you, Leeton, on your knees!"

Anisha drew back against the wall. Just then, a shadow passed by the door. A movement so faint, she might have imagined it.

"What do you want?" Leeton had stumbled to his knees and begun to burble. "*What,* for God's sake? I don't even know you."

Mrs. Ashton leveled the gun squarely at the top of Leeton's bald spot. "Oh, we met once," she said in a voice hollow as death. "I was walking in the park, holding my father's hand."

"I . . . I don't remember," he sniveled. "I'm sorry. Do you want money? I've a cashbox in the house."

"Yes, it all comes down to money to you," she sneered. "No, Leeton, you won't buy your way out of here. I'm Elizabeth Colburne — and all I want is your blood spilt across this floor. And I won't be leaving till I've seen every drop drain from your corpse."

The shadow returned, this time filling the door.

Elizabeth Colburne cut the merest glance

up the steps, then panic shot across her face.

Calmly, Rance squatted and reached down his hand, his face serene, his every movement smooth. "Give me the pistol, Miss Colburne," he said quietly. "You do not want this."

Anger blazed in her eyes. "Get out, Lazonby," she spat. "This doesn't concern you now."

Rance had one hand resting almost casually on the doorframe, his other still outstretched as he squatted there in his tall, black boots. "It does concern me," he said. "It has always concerned me. And even had it not, I was nonetheless dragged into it. But Wilfred here killed Percy, I'm now guessing?"

"And a pity you couldn't have guessed a little sooner," Mrs. Ashton snapped. She still had a bead on Leeton's bald spot, but her whole body was shaking now.

"Give me the gun, Miss Colburne," Rance said again, his voice smooth as silk. "Trust me, there is no greater, more slow-grinding hell than Newgate Prison. And Leeton will rot in it."

"No," she growled. "Oh, no. Leeton's going to bleed like a slaughtered hog on his own bloody flagstone — *exsanguination,* the doctors called it, when Papa died. It sounds

better, I suppose, than saying *murdered* by his so-called friend."

"No, no! I didn't!" Leeton, still on his knees, waved his hands in surrender. "I didn't touch Arthur. I *just stabbed Percy!* And, yes, I bribed Hanging Nick and that porter chap. And fixed the blame, I suppose, on Lazonby here. But that's it! I liked Arthur. I *did.* I — why, after I persuaded Hannah to marry me, I meant us to visit him. In France. Or wherever."

His lip curling into a sneer, Rance let his arm fall. "Do you know what I think, Miss Colburne?"

"No," she snarled, "and I don't give a damn."

"I think," Rance softly continued, "that perhaps you *should* shoot him."

"Lazonby!" cried Leeton. "Good God, man! Are you mad?"

"In fact," Rance went on, his voice rich as cream now, "I think I'll *let* you shoot him. But Miss Colburne, you have hounded me and haunted me — and quite likely delayed my uncovering Leeton's perfidy. In short, you've made my life hell."

"And what of it?" she snapped. "I've bigger fish to fry than you now."

"Here's what of it," he said. "You *owe* me, Miss Colburne. And make no mistake — I am *letting* you hold that weapon. I'm fast — far faster than you, my dear — and you know it. Only my fear of a wild shot makes me hesitate."

"I will shoot!" she declared. "I *will.*"

"Oh, I don't doubt it for an instant," said Rance smoothly. "I know exactly who you are now. Would you like to lift off that mass of chestnut curls? No, I thought not. So here is what I ask, in small recompense for being hounded half to the grave: You will let me step inside and carry Lady Anisha out to safety — because, when that gun goes off, unless your aim is true, that bullet will fly wild. And if you kill *her* — if you harm so much as a hair on her head — then you will know what a true hell is."

She flicked a guilty gaze toward the door. "V-Very well," she said, shuffling back a step to make way. "Get down here. But be quick about it."

His gaze locked to Anisha's, Rance rose and came slowly down the stairs. Anisha realized she, too, was shaking now, her teeth literally chattering. Carefully and unhesitatingly, Rance passed through the line of fire, paced across the flagstone, then knelt to scoop her up. She was ashamed to hear herself burst into tears.

"Shush, love, I have you," he said, pulling

her to him.

But it was in that split second — just as Anisha threw her arms round Rance's neck — that Leeton sprang. He launched himself at Mrs. Ashton, taking her over backward. She hitched up hard against the marble counter. The roar of gunpowder exploded. On instinct, Rance hurled himself over Anisha, attempting to cover her with his body. Deafened by the reverberation, she saw rather than heard Mrs. Ashton's keening wail.

"Bloody hell!" Flicking a glance over his shoulder, Rance snatched Anisha up and spun on his boot heel. Wilfred Leeton lay dead at Mrs. Ashton's feet, eyes staring into the rafters, a massive black hole square in the middle of his forehead.

"Oh!" Mrs. Ashton held up her shaking hands as if they'd been foreign, the gun clattering to the flagstones. "Oh, *God* — *!*"

Suddenly, Samir Belkadi swung in through the narrow door, landing below like a cat. *"Mon dieu! Qu'est-ce qui s'est passé?"*

Mrs. Ashton clasped her hands to her mouth.

"Coldwater shot the bastard," said Rance matter-of-factly. "Here, take Anisha. She's badly hurt."

"Coldwater?" But Belkadi seized Anisha

621

and carried her up the three steps.

"Stop," she ordered, dashing away her tears. "Set me down."

"Non, madame," he said firmly. "You are bleeding. We are going to the tent."

"Belkadi!" Somehow, she pounded at his shoulders. "Set me down. We must settle this."

He crooked one dark brow, then set her down gently on an old millstone that lay near the door, surrounded by wildflowers. She gave a hysterical laugh at the contrast.

Beyond the house, a hue and cry had arisen. Rance looked shaken now, his gaze darting continually to hers as if to reassure himself she was well.

Elizabeth Colburne, however, was pacing the floor. "I've killed him!" she cried, clawing at her hair as if she was mad. "I've *killed* him."

Rance reached out and caught her arm. She jerked, knocking the chestnut wig askew to reveal the red curls beneath. "Don't touch me!" she cried. Then her face crumpled. "Oh, God, I did it! I *shot* him."

Sympathy sketched across Rance's face. He tightened his grip and drew her back. "No, Jack Coldwater killed him," he said. "Leeton lunged. Jack fired. It was self-defense."

Her eyes were wild. "But I meant to kill him!" she shrieked. "I *did.* Not then. Not at that second. But I wanted him to die. *Don't you see?*"

This time Rance jerked her so hard her neck snapped. "Miss Colburne, get hold of yourself," he ordered. "Do you hear that crowd coming? Now listen to me. Jack Coldwater — your brother — killed Leeton. There was a quarrel. Lady Anisha tried to intervene and was struck on the head. Jack shot Leeton and fled."

"B-But I don't have a brother!" she cried.

Anisha saw his fingers dig into her arm, watched his mind work feverishly for an instant. "Your mysterious *illegitimate* brother," he said. "*Jack Coldwater.* He shot Leeton, having discovered the truth, and now he has fled — never to be seen again. Do you understand me?"

"I . . . yes," she whispered. "But . . . why?"

"Why what?" said Rance tersely.

"Why do this?" Her eyes were pleading now. "— and for *me?*"

Rance cut one lingering glance at Anisha. "Because someone once told me it was better to have justice than vengeance," he said quietly, "and this bloody well looks like justice to me."

"A-All right." Miss Colburne smoothed

623

her hands down her skirts as if to calm herself. "I understand what . . . what to say."

Rance looked round at Anisha and Belkadi. "Sam, do you understand?" he demanded.

"Oh, *oui,* perfectly!" said Belkadi smoothly. "All is obvious!"

"But I . . . I don't understand anything," said Anisha, whose temple still throbbed.

"Because you have taken a terrible blow to the head," said Rance gently, "and will never remember a thing; you are not to be further involved. Samir has already sent for Napier, who will see to the rest of this business. He will *make it go away.*"

"Ah, you think so?" asked Belkadi snidely.

Rance shrugged. "Or he can open an investigation," he said, "and explain his father's duplicity. That's the choice I mean to give him. And you, Nish — you remember *nothing.* You will say not one word."

"Oh," said Anisha wanly. "Oh, that much I can manage . . . !"

But Rance had come to the door and reached through. His face twisted a little with grief as he set his hand to the turn of her cheek, now matted with hair and blood.

His eyes said he would never forgive himself.

But Anisha's heart said she would ensure
he did.

Epilogue

I'll set thee in a shower of gold, and hail
Rich pearls upon thee.
> William Shakespeare,
> *Antony and Cleopatra*

Ten days after Jack Coldwater vanished from that mortal coil called London, Lord Lazonby prepared to shut up his house in Ebury Street and send all his servants on holiday. Well, all save Horsham and young Emmit. It little mattered anyway; he'd moved at once into Ruthveyn's guest suite and had no intention of moving out anytime soon. Not until he judged Tom and Teddy ready to move on to a new life, and Lord Lucan safe to be left unsupervised.

He imagined it would be a while.

And so it was that Lazonby was sitting at his desk during one of his brief visits home, counting out the quarter-day salaries a whole fortnight early, when Horsham came in to complain about it all.

"I don't understand," said the valet bitterly, "why we are not to go on holiday, too."

Rance flipped open his bankbook and looked up with a scowl. "Because you are being punished," he said, snatching up his pen, "for letting Lady Anisha Stafford in my house."

"For letting *her* in *your* house?" said Horsham indignantly. "But my lord, you've been *living* in hers! Indeed, you've not slept a night in your own bed in nearly two weeks!"

Rance cocked one eyebrow in warning. "Nor have I been sleeping in hers," he said tightly. "She is a lady, I would beg you to recall. A lady with small children. And a brother to guard her virtue."

Horsham sniffed, and flicked a piece of lint off the desk. "Much good *that one* will do!"

"He'll do well enough for my purposes," said Rance, pushing away to yank open his top drawer. His eyes scanned over the contents. "Damn it, Horsham, where's that case?"

"Case?" said the valet. "What case?"

"The case I sent you off to Garrard's with," Rance snapped. "And the same one you brought back again yesterday."

Horsham sniffed again, came round to the

other side, and drew open the bottom drawer, which held Lazonby's massive cash-box. "I locked it up," he returned. "I can't think you want something like that just lying about."

"Aye, you're right. Thank you." Lazonby unlocked the box just as the valet turned to go. "And Horsham?"

"What?"

Rance sighed and lifted out the padded velvet case. "You're being kept because I need you. There are plans afoot."

The valet drew himself up. "So I am indispensable?"

"Aye, and arrogant," said Lazonby. "Don't push your luck. I need you in Upper Grosvenor Street. And once there, you are going to make a valet out of young Emmit. Chatterjee, Lord Lucan's man, has quit in a snit, taken himself a cottage, and bought himself a broodmare."

"Good God!" said Horsham.

"Don't get any ideas," said Lazonby. "Now have my cabriolet brought round."

Half an hour later, he found Anisha in her bedchamber, curled up against a pile of pillows with a thick book, Tom and Teddy nestled to either side of her. After a soft knock on the open door, he strolled in, grinning down at the three of them.

"Ah!" he said, "what is the subject today?"

Anisha smiled and straightened up. "Astronomy," she said, softly closing the book. "One of the few things I'm actually qualified to teach."

Rance smiled into her eyes, the case held discreetly behind his back. "Oh, I don't know about that, old thing," he said with perfect solemnity. "You've taught me a vast deal."

Anisha laughed and handed Tom the book. "All right, boys, back upstairs with you," she said. "It is time for Mr. Jeffers and Latin."

"Oh, *veni, vidi, vici!*" said Teddy, collapsing onto the mattress with a huff. "That's Latin, Lazonby, for *I'm so bored, I could just die!*"

"Oh, I think you shall survive it." Rance offered down a hand to heft the boy back up. "God knows I did. Now come along, lads. Do as your mother says, and no wheedling."

But Teddy just scowled up at him and let his arms flop back into the softness of the bed. "You aren't really supposed to be in here, you know," he complained, but there was no true rancor in his tone. "Not unless you are *married.*"

Rance pulled a long face. "Well, I thought perhaps I might get away with it? If I just left the door open?"

Teddy shook his head, his blonde curls scrubbing the counterpane.

Rance sighed and patted his pocket. "All right, then," he said. "You are demanding I do the honorable thing, I collect?"

"I guess so," said Teddy, blinking innocently up at him.

"Well, you leave me no choice," he said, extracting a slip of paper. "Here you go, Teddy. A special license, and the ink scarcely dry."

Teddy grinned and bounced up to look it. "Like a license to get married?"

"It seems I cannot keep visiting your mother's bedchamber otherwise," said Rance.

Tom laid the book down and looked solemnly up at him. "Are you going to be our father?" he asked.

Rance ruffled his gold curls, his gaze catching Anisha's, which had gone soft. "I am going to be your mother's husband," he replied, "if she'll have me. And I should very much like to be your father. But you must choose, for you've already had one. You mightn't want a replacement."

Tom looked uncharacteristically shy. "I don't really remember him," he said. "I think I should quite like to have a new father."

But Teddy remained recalcitrant. "For my part," he complained, "I should like a father who won't make me study Latin."

"Aye, mayhap, but that's not the kind you get," said Rance grimly. "Sorry about that, my boy."

Teddy stuck his lip out, then suddenly brightened again. "Are you any good at cricket?"

Rance smiled down into Anisha's eyes again, deeper and deeper. Straight to her heart, he prayed. "Lethally good," he said. "Really, really good. I can play cricket, my boy, till your lungs want to burst and your legs want to collapse and your brain wishes to sleep for a se'night — all of which would serve you well, frankly, and keep you out of a vast deal of trouble, too, I daresay."

"Well, *hmm*." Teddy finally took Rance's hand and clambered off the tall bed. "I shall go upstairs and think on it."

"Excellent," said Rance. "I trust we may come to some mutual agreement about your mother's future. Now off you go, and right this minute. Today's the day I'm going to get down on bended knee and beg her to become Lady Lazonby, and no man wants a witness to such mortifying prostration."

"What's prostration?"

"Oh, someday you will meet the perfect woman, Teddy," said Rance, "and then you will surely know. Until then, go, and remain blithe in your ignorance."

"My, is it really such a misery to be in love?" asked Anisha, grinning up at him when the boys were gone.

Rance set one knee to the bed and leaned over. "Humbling," he said, lightly kissing her. "Utterly lowering." He kissed the turn of her throat. "I am your slave, my dear, and entirely without will. Please say that you will have me, and put me out of my misery?"

Anisha ran a hand through his mane of unruly curls. "Very well, I shall have you," she said lightly, "*if* you will get a haircut."

"My God, you are *so* easy!" he said, settling lightly onto the bed beside her. "Fine, then. A haircut. Here, my girl, I've brought you something."

He laid the green velvet case in her lap, and she gasped with pleasure. "A betrothal gift!" she cried.

He shook his head. "No, actually it was already yours," he said. "Janet helped me steal it — and I'm glad she isn't leaving, by the way."

"Well, I had to double her salary," said

Anisha, "and Chatterjee's, too, more or less. He's going to work half days — but at least he's back."

Rance grinned. "Just like what's in this case, my dear," he said, tapping it with one finger. "Gone but briefly, now home again."

Her perfectly arched brows snapped together. "How very odd," she said. "And am I to open it?"

Propped up on one elbow, he lifted his other hand, palm up. "As I say, my dear, it is yours."

Anisha flicked open the brass clasp, lifted the lid, and gasped. Her mother's wide kundan choker blinked up at her, newly polished — and just a little different.

"Oh, my heavens!" she cried, gently lifting it out. "It's . . . altered somehow."

"Lift up the next layer," Rance suggested.

"Really?" Setting the choker back in, Anisha lifted the top compartment fully out. A long strand of pearls lay nestled in the bottom of the box. "More pearls?" she said, mystified. "No, wait — that ruby clasp — why, these are Grandmamma Forsythe's pearls!"

"Yes," said Rance, "but different. Much shorter, in fact."

Anisha returned her gaze to the brilliantly hued choker, which now dangled with fat, creamy pearls. Three pearls per strand, all suspended from the last row of gemstones, positioned such that they caught the deep colors of the jewels and reflected them up again in a rich rainbow of sapphire, emerald, and ruby.

At last, recognition dawned. "Oh, my God!" she cried. "You . . . you hung *Grandmamma Forsythe's* pearls on *Mother's* choker?"

Rance reached out and lightly brushed one with the tip of his finger, setting it ashimmer in the morning light. "I thought Saraswati might approve," he said softly, "because you are not, my girl, a simple thing. You are deeply complex — like fine jewelry, a precious amalgam of more than one thing. And I love and embrace all that you are. I just . . . well, I guess I just wanted you to be utterly sure of that."

"Oh, Rance — !" she whispered, eyes aglow. "How perfectly brilliant this is!"

"So now, Nish, your jewelry matches you," he said. "For you're perfectly brilliant just as you are — all blended together — and all the more beautiful for it."

At that, she practically hurled the jewels aside and kissed him long and hard. "Oh!" she whispered a long moment later. "Oh, Rance! When you asked me to marry you, did I remember to say *yes?*"

"Yes." He kissed her again, this time cradling her face in his hands. "Yes. You said *yes* — which is a good thing, since Sutherland is coming in the morning."

She laughed, and kissed him again.

"However," he managed to say between kisses, "*if* I were any sort of gentleman at all, I would write to your brother, plead my case, ask his permission — and his forgiveness — then wait respectfully for his answer."

Anisha looked up, her eyes dancing — yet glinting a little dangerously, too.

"Rance Welham," she said firmly, "you haven't behaved respectfully in the whole of your life. And if you start now — if you postpone for one more day giving me what I want out of some misplaced sense of honor — then *I* shall respectfully wrap what is left of Grandmamma Forsythe's pearls round your throat *and throttle you with them!*"